Praise for Bianca D'Arc's
Grady's Awakening

"I absolutely loved all the characters in this novel, both primary and secondary. ...Oh, and talk about catchy hooks for a sequel, wait till you read the epilogue! Ms. D'Arc has left me waiting with bated breath for book five in this absolutely tremendous series."

~ *Merrylee, Fallen Angel Reviews*

"Grady's Awakening consumed me from page one with its vibrant characters and their intense emotional and physical connections. Ms. D'Arc has written a heartwarming book with a compelling storyline and a sizzling ménage that's so sensual in nature it sent shivers down my spine. Reading Grady's Awakening was like being granted a slice of heaven. Ms. D'Arc creates a riveting, compassionate story that had me enthralled from beginning to end and begging from more as I read the last page. I didn't want it to end. I wanted to know what happened next, by God. I needed more, craved more, and can't wait for the next book in the Resonance Mates series. ... Not only would I recommend this book and series to my friends, I'd buy it for them as the perfect Christmas gift. Bravo Ms. D'Arc...Bravo!"

~ *Jasmine, Whipped Cream Reviews*

Look for these titles by
Bianca D'Arc

Now Available:

Wings of Change
Forever Valentine
Sweeter than Wine

Dragon Knights Series
Maiden Flight (Book 1)
Border Lair (Book 2)
Ladies of the Lair—Dragon Knights 1 & 2 (print)
The Ice Dragon (Book 3)
Prince of Spies (Book 4)
FireDrake (Book 5)

Tales of the Were Series
Lords of the Were (Book 1)
Inferno (Book 2)

Resonance Mates Series
Hara's Legacy (Book 1) Jane & Caleb, Mic\e, Justin
Davin's Quest (Book 2) Callie & Davin,
Jaci's Experiment (Book 3) Jaci 1928 mikey David
Grady's Awakening (Book 4) Gina & Grady, Jim

Brotherhood of Blood Series
One and Only (Book 1)
Rare Vintage (Book 2)
Phantom Desires (Book 3)

Print Anthologies
I Dream of Dragons Vol 1
Caught By Cupid

Grady's Awakening

Bianca D'Arc

A Samhain Publishing, Ltd. publication.

Samhain Publishing, Ltd.
577 Mulberry Street, Suite 1520
Macon, GA 31201
www.samhainpublishing.com

Editing by Bethany Morgan
Cover by Anne Cain

First Samhain Publishing, Ltd. electronic publication: August 2009
First Samhain Publishing, Ltd. print publication: June 2010

Dedication

I'd like to thank the lovely ladies on my chat group. They're always there when I need to vent or discuss things. Thank you all for the love and support. You really keep me going!

Thanks also to Bethany, my super editor.

And as always, my love and thanks to my family who support my work and my dreams.

Prologue

Gina took the bar of soap from the tiled dispenser and worked up a lather while steam wafted around her shoulders. A moment later, the soap was taken from her hands as the steam thickened and a hard, male body filled the space next to her in the decadently large shower enclosure.

One of his hands roamed down her shoulder, onto her back, massaging, caressing. The other cupped her sensitive breasts, tweaking the nipples with slippery, soapy fingers as her breath caught.

A second presence loomed out of the steam. Another man, larger than the first, stood on her other side. He grasped her hips, massaging downward with enticing thoroughness. The fingers of one hand roamed forward as his other hand moved aft, meeting in the juncture between her thighs with explosive results.

Gina gasped as the first man turned her head, sealing his lips to hers, his tongue sweeping inside her mouth, while the other man thrust one long finger into her core. The kiss drugged her even as the other's touch electrified her increasingly desperate body. The rush of sensations curled her toes.

This was the most delicious dream she'd ever had.

Yet...something told her this was more than a dream. She'd had prophetic dreams before. Not often and never quite so erotic, but she knew the flavor of such portents. These men—shockingly, two of them—would be in her life soon.

She'd never been good at guiding her dreams. She wanted more than anything to see their faces. She wanted to be able to recognize them when she saw them, but the steam was thick and the things they were doing sidetracked her.

The second man's fingers brought her to the precipice as the first man's kiss and enticing caresses took her over the top. She came with a gasping cry even as she jolted to full wakefulness. Only a few final impressions were left in her hazy mind.

The first man had had dark hair and the hands of a warrior. His muscles had been sleek, like a panther coiled to strike. He had felt deadly and dangerously attractive.

The second man had been more of a puzzle. Pale hair had gleamed in the uncertain light and she had the impression of flashing blue eyes that crinkled at the corners when he smiled. She'd felt deep and true emotion from him, a shuddering need that made his calloused hands shake.

"Did you have the dream again, Gina?" a soft voice asked from the darkness of the dormitory-style room she shared with a roommate.

Gina sighed heavily. "It was...more...this time. I saw them more clearly."

Her roommate had a much stronger gift of foresight, and they had discussed Gina's dreams before. A variation on the shower dream had been plaguing her the last several nights, but tonight's dream had been the most vivid by far.

"So, spill. Who are they?"

"I don't know. One has brown hair, tanned skin, sleek muscles like a fighter. He was tall and though I couldn't see his face clearly in the steam, I know he was handsome. Sharp cheekbones and deep-set eyes was the impression I got."

"Hubba, hubba. So he's human. He's not one of the Brotherhood or you probably would have recognized him. Intriguing." She paused. "Maybe he's a new recruit. Could be you'll meet him right here one day soon. Or you might run across him when they send you out on a mission. How about the other one? Were they a set? Like twins?"

"No." Gina thought back to the hazy dream images. "The second one was even taller than the first and bigger all the way around. He was deeply muscled, yet he moved with a warrior's grace."

"Oh, I like the sound of that. What else?"

"He was shaking with emotion too long denied. At least that was the impression I was left with."

"Another human then." She spoke with finality in the darkness. Her words made Gina pause.

She'd cupped his head in her hand as she broke from the dream and felt...the slender point of his ear.

That stark realization made her sit bolt upright on her small bed. The second man in her dream had been Alvian.

Chapter One

"Why wasn't I made aware of this before?" Grady Prime demanded of the Governing Council as they met in a secret session. One by one, the Councilors stared him down. Even Primes were not permitted to behave with disrespect toward the Council. Grady Prime was treading a thin line. Of course, he'd been walking on eggshells for the past few weeks—ever since he'd taken the drug that was awakening emotions he'd never felt before.

"Your current demobilized status and superior skill set make you the most logical operative to send on this mission," Councilor Gildereth, representing the military, said blandly. "It is unlikely you will ever return to your former duties and status among the regular army, given your participation in Mara 12's experiment. You had to have known that when you volunteered to let her tamper with your DNA. However, you are too valuable an asset to retire. We can use your skills and perhaps your new understanding of the consequences of Mara 12's experiment to discover the truth of the disturbing rumors we've heard."

"There are rumors about a winged man?" Grady asked sharply. Perhaps too sharply. He'd have to watch his tone with these stone-faced, emotionless politicians. "Which populations have been talking? Is it localized to one city or region? That would give me a place to start."

"The rumors of which we speak were not heard from our people," Councilor Beyan, the crystallographer, cut in, her expression almost embarrassed—though being Alvian, she could not feel such things, of course. "The winged man is spoken of by Breed captives. Monitoring stations in every Breed enclosure have recorded and flagged references to what they call an *angel*. We have tracked the word to various religious mythologies that existed before the crystal seeding. We find this problematic when paired with the fact that we know at least one of our winged experimental squad is unaccounted for."

Problematic, she'd said. Grady Prime had to bite back a laugh. He fought the urge to scoff at the Councilor's poor grasp of what the appearance of a creature out of human mythology could mean to the captives. Especially a creature with mytho-religious origins.

"Perhaps it would be beneficial for me to know more about this experimental squad. I assume there are more of these winged men?"

Councilor Gildereth looked at him with a considering gaze, then relented. "Grady Prime, please remember that anything you hear in secret session is protected information at the highest level. You are not to divulge this information." The Councilor waited until Grady nodded acknowledgment. "I believe it would be prudent for you to talk to some of the squadron members. The new Prime would probably be of greatest assistance as you begin your search for the one who escaped."

"Escaped?" Grady Prime could have bitten his tongue. His curiosity was getting the better of him—something that had rarely happened before he'd been dosed with the DNA-altering agent. The experimental agent was starting to manifest emotions in him that had been bred out of the rest of his people.

"You'll recall the attempt made on Chief Engineer Davin's life. That was an assassination attempt authorized by a rogue element of this Council who has since been replaced." Councilor Orin, representing artisans, nodded over at the newest member of the group and Grady recalled the scene that had played out with the Councilor who used to sit in that seat and the Chief Engineer. Davin had publicly exposed Councilor Troyan's role in ordering Davin's assassination without knowledge or approval of the rest of the Council. The Council had responded by turning their backs on Troyan, effectively dismissing him from the Council. Another had been chosen to take his place representing the clerical trades and now sat in the seat.

"The assassin was captured and held briefly," Councilor Gildereth said. "He managed to escape in the tumult. I believe there are too many Breeds in Davin's facility given too much freedom. The throwback demands it be that way. The security there is lax in my opinion." The Councilor sniffed, elegantly expressing his mild disdain for the way things had been handled.

"Do recall the assassin was our best. The man was a Prime with superior skills. I, for one, would have been disappointed if he had not escaped," Councilor Orin added. Grady Prime's curiosity rose another notch, though he wisely kept silent.

A Prime had been the secret assassin? A *winged* assassin? Grady Prime thought he knew all the Primes. There were comparatively few of that elite rank. One headed each genetic line. Only one Prime had died in the past few years, and he'd been of warrior stock.

"Sinclair Prime Past had wings?" Grady Prime wasn't reprimanded for speaking out of turn. Rather, most of the Councilors seemed pleased he'd pieced together the obvious clues to arrive at his conclusion.

Grady Prime had known the former Sinclair Prime, designated Sinclair Prime *Past* now that he was no longer the current Prime. They'd trained together on a few memorable occasions, though Sinclair Prime's posted territory lay far to the west. Still, they'd run joint exercises from time to time. Grady Prime had never suspected Sinclair Prime of being anything other than a remarkably talented example of the Alvian warrior class.

"Indeed. Sinclair Prime Past and also the new Sinclair Prime and the entire squad he commands are winged. They are hybrids, created from a base of Alvian warrior DNA of several different genetic lines, plus traits taken from preserved Avarel genetic samples. Specifically, we chose the traits that would enable a man to fly." The Councilor who spoke was of the science branch, a woman of the Ardarin genetic line.

Grady Prime was stunned to learn they'd created a whole squadron of soldiers who could fly under their own power. He was also amazed they'd been able to keep such an experiment secret from everyone—including him—though he prided himself on knowing things that were hidden from others.

"I should start by talking to the current Sinclair Prime and some of Prime Past's men. I'll need insight into the individual before I can begin to assess where he might be hiding. I thought I knew Sinclair Prime Past well, having worked with him on several occasions. I see now I did not. I had no idea he, or any of his men, had wings. If he could keep that secret, he probably had many other secrets it would be helpful to know before I set out on his trail."

"You also need to know that he was the first test subject in Mara 12's experiment—even before the current batch, of which you are part. He was nearing retirement, and we allowed Mara 12 to proceed with one test case before approving her larger experiment. Sinclair Prime Past volunteered and was dosed with the gene-altering agent approximately one week before the rogue Council member activated him to assassinate Chief Engineer Davin. Mara 12 was disappointed with his disappearance of course. Since he had survived the initial dosage, we allowed her to continue her experiment." Councilor Ardarin filled him in on the details. "More troubling was his failure to comply with a Councilor's orders after the treatment, though we are satisfied with the result, since the rest of us did not authorize Chief Engineer Davin's death."

So tidy, Grady Prime thought. They spoke of people's lives like tokens on a game board. They were *troubled* by the fact that their pet assassin hadn't followed orders to kill an innocent man. They were *disappointed* that they'd lost their test subject—a man who was one of the most important in Alvian society as a Prime. To them he was only a game piece. Grady Prime's eyes were opened to the callousness of the Council. He'd never felt warmly toward any of them, but now, with new emotions flooding his confused brain, he detested them. Truly loathed each and every one of them.

He dared not let it show. He'd come this far by pretending to be as cool and calm as he'd always been. He wouldn't mess it up now. Not after spending the past weeks under intense scrutiny by Mara 12 and her team of ghouls.

All the test subjects were being monitored every waking moment it seemed. They were watched in their quarters and guarded even in their sleep. There were only a few people in this first—or make that second—group of Alvians to be given the gene-altering agent, and each was reacting somewhat differently. Most were calm fortunately. Those that spent time with Caleb O'Hara were doing the best. They were learning about emotion from a Breed they respected due to the predominance of Hara DNA in Caleb's genealogy.

Also, Caleb was a strong presence. A leader of men. He'd led his family through the adversity of the crystal seeding—what the humans called the cataclysm—and the lawless times after. He'd forged a path that kept his family safe and he knew how to inspire confidence, trust and even hope.

When Grady Prime had first sought Caleb's company shortly after taking the drug, he knew Mara 12 had followed his every move. Every word of his initial conversation with Caleb and his nephew Harry had been recorded, analyzed and dissected. After their second discussion, Grady Prime had taken it upon himself to suggest to Mara 12 that introducing the other test subjects to Caleb or Harry would be helpful. She'd thought about his idea for a day or two, then arranged a group meeting at which both Caleb and Harry were the guests of honor.

Those group meetings had become a way for the test subjects to learn about integrating emotion from beings who already understood emotions. They were also a way for the test subjects to get to know each other. There were five in total. One had been a high-level bookkeeper who was retired and tasked to teach the younger generation. His name was Galin 4 and as the eldest of the group, he took on a patriarchal role toward the other three, who were all female and of subordinate personalities.

There was Linley 17, the eldest of the women, who'd been in charge of one of the largest crèche facilities where young were raised until the age of thirteen. Soft spoken and strong, she had been nearing retirement as well and had divulged her desire to understand the odd nurturing instincts she felt when dealing with her young charges.

Fian 34 had been a merchant arbiter who orchestrated trades of indigenous goods and supplies among the cities and sometimes for elite clients. She'd put her prosperous business on hold while taking part in the experiment and had hoped to be able to pick up her work as soon as Mara 12 was done with her. Fian 34 had an engaging personality and a quick wit. Grady Prime understood why she'd worked so well with people, sorting out differences of opinion and value of goods and services. He didn't completely understand her motives in volunteering for this experiment, but he liked her as a person.

And the youngest of the group was a quiet lab tech called Jaci 647. Though she claimed to have volunteered, Grady Prime suspected the low-level tech had been ordered to participate by Mara 12. The girl was shy and very unsure of herself. She was nothing like the other Jaci lab tech Grady Prime had hunted for all those weeks. This Jaci was convinced of her inferiority and barely spoke. A few times, Grady Prime had walked in to a planned session with Caleb to find Jaci 647 there early, sobbing in the arms of Caleb O'Hara. The young girl was taking her new emotions hard. She cried a lot and spent the rest of the time jumping at every sound. If any of them were going to lose their minds because of this experiment, Grady Prime had to sadly admit, it would be her.

Grady Prime had managed to escape the constant monitoring only because the Council had summoned him to a secret session. He knew there was an escort waiting for him outside the door and the personal monitors would reactivate the moment the Council turned off their dampening fields. He didn't like living under a microscope.

The more his emotions manifested, the more he realized he'd done the right thing in volunteering for the experiment. He liked feeling. He liked having an opinion based not only on dry facts, but also on emotion. He liked being—almost—human. And the effects would only deepen the longer the DNA-altering agent worked through his system, changing him forever on a molecular level.

"We are troubled by the Breed rumors of an angel. The idea that a winged man is out there somewhere seems to inspire unrest in the Breeds. We prefer them to be calm as we continue our studies." Grady Prime realized how little Councilor Ardarin understood emotion and the Breeds her scientists studied. The *unrest*, as she described it, was probably a manifestation of hope.

Hope was something Alvians no longer comprehended. They also had no understanding of the finer emotions, the most important of which was love. Grady Prime had experienced fondness and something he suspected was love when he thought of the O'Hara children and the open way they'd always greeted him when he visited their ranch in the wilds of the Waste. He wasn't sure. The emotion those memories stirred was powerful and touching, inspiring his protective instincts. He hadn't had a chance to really talk about it with Caleb, but he thought what he felt in those moments was something like a paternal instinct to care for and protect the young.

"Are you certain these rumors refer to the missing Prime Past? It is possible—however unlikely—that members of the secret winged squadron have been observed."

"True," Councilor Gildereth admitted. "That is why you will begin your inquiries with his squadron."

"We know you are under monitoring by Mara 12, and we have made allowances for the monitoring to continue on a limited basis," Councilor Ardarin continued. "However, we believe at the current rate of DNA assimilation, you will be ready for the next phase of Mara 12's study by next week. Phase Two of the study involves observing the test subject under conditions similar to their normal working conditions. The other four test subjects will be monitored in the city as they go about their tasks. Your work will have to be monitored from afar as you conduct your investigation. I will personally filter the feeds from your data collection unit and pass on relevant data to Mara 12. Even she is unaware of the Avarel hybridization experiment. That honor was given to Mara Prime alone. It is with him you will work upon reaching the squadron's secret base of operations. You are not to discuss this case with anyone other than Mara Prime or this Council. You may question the winged squadron at your discretion. They will be instructed to cooperate fully with your investigation."

"I will most likely need to spend time in the terrain, searching the area around the squadron's base for signs of trespass. I may also need to track Sinclair Prime Past in remote areas, depending on what I find."

"We have thought of that and will trust in your discretion. This investigation is of great importance to the Council. You are uniquely qualified—both by your past demonstration of skill and your current status and understanding of what the Past Prime may be experiencing as a test subject. We want you on this mission. We will work with Mara 12. If necessary, we will make allowances for gaps in monitoring while you are in areas that are too remote for reliable signal relay." The head of the Council had just eased Grady Prime's mind, but he tried hard not to let it show. He might have a few days free of the constant monitoring. It was a blessing in disguise for a man who had always valued his privacy.

"Mara 12 has four other subjects in the current batch," Councilor Ardarin said. "If necessary, we can authorize her to select another warrior to test since she wanted a broad range of work specialties represented. One more soldier, more or less, should not be that much of a problem."

Grady Prime bit his lip to keep from expressing his disgust at such a cavalier attitude. Each and every one of his men was a special being. They were his brothers in arms, his only family. They dedicated their lives to protecting all Alvians, at the Council's direction. To hear them discussed in such disrespectful terms was both abhorrent and eye opening.

"You have authorization to travel to the winged squadron's base as soon as Mara 12 clears you. We expect that to be early next week. Please have your gear in order and be ready to leave at any moment. We will have a ship sent from the base to conduct you there, as its location is a closely guarded secret." Councilor Hearn spoke in a monotonous tone, as if reciting a list. "Fare well on your mission and report directly to the Council as soon as you have any news. Any questions?"

"Just one." Grady Prime stood strong before the Council, his gaze assessing each and every one of them. "What do you want me to do with Sinclair Past Prime if and when I find him?"

Councilor Gildereth turned to look at him, his expression blank. "I thought that was obvious. You are authorized to kill him."

A few days later, Grady Prime sat for yet another of the invasive medical examinations Mara 12's techs and doctors treated the test subjects to on a regular basis. They collected all kinds of samples from him, running a multitude of tests on every imaginable bodily system.

"You're at eighty-five percent conversion," the doctor stated as he stared at the instrumentation panel on his diagnostic unit. "We've hypothesized that the last few percentages take longer to assimilate. The rapid integration of the new DNA sequences have slowed and will continue to decelerate as propagation nears completion."

"Then I'll have less mood swings now that the conversion is almost complete?"

"Most likely, though of course we need more data from yourself and your fellow subjects before we can make any conclusions. But that is the working theory."

"Excellent."

"We have notice from the Council that you are to be released from sequestered study when integration reached this level." The doctor squinted, a faint echo of annoyance. "It would be better to have you here for study until the new DNA sequences are fully integrated. Of course, Council orders come first. Thank you for your cooperation over these past weeks. It has been agreeable to work with you, Grady Prime. I wish you well."

That was more than Grady Prime had expected from the austere doctor. He stood from the examination table and gave the other man a short bow as he left.

When Grady Prime returned to his quarters, he found a communication from the Council waiting for him. A ship was already on its way to retrieve him for the mission he'd been assigned last week. Word of his status had traveled fast, he thought, as he packed a few small personal items in the bag he'd had ready for days.

He'd thought his days of traveling light and fast had ended when he volunteered for Mara 12's experiment. He had gladly traded the enjoyable aspects of his job for the chance to finally understand the faint echoes of emotion he'd been subject to over the years. Now he was to have both. He had been given a chance not only to do the job he loved—and he realized now that he truly *loved* his occupation as a protector and defender of innocent people—but to do it, experiencing the new emotions that had been making his life fuller and more robust over the past weeks.

He felt a sense of hopeful anticipation that made his abdomen bubble with excitement. His blood sang for adventure, and his muscles quivered to be off. Adrenaline rushed through his system even though there was no immediately perceived threat. The only times he'd experienced an adrenaline rush before, he'd been in mortal danger. He'd lived for those times when he felt...something.

Now he was discovering he could feel that same rush of energy without the life or death circumstances. He could feel the same determination to survive—multiplied tenfold—without doing anything but *thinking* of what was to come. It was a fantastic thing. Something he wanted to explore further. Unfortunately, that would have to wait. A second communication to his personal unit directed him to meet a specific scout ship at the landing area.

A brisk walk down a maze of corridors and he was in the sunshine. The yellow sun of Earth was a beautiful sight to a man who'd spent decades on a space ship preparing to land and who-knows-how-many years before that in stasis on the same ship, preserved by the ship's computers for the long journey here.

Grady Prime loved everything about their new home. The wild places called to him and he thought back fondly on the times he'd camped out in the forests and deserts, doing his job. He wondered where the hidden base would be. Would it be in a forest, surrounded by towering trees? Or would it be on the rocky slopes of the highest mountains, covered in snow? Would he be going to a desert? Or would it be a secluded tropical island? He was eager to explore all those possibilities.

There was a spring in his step as he entered the landing area and located the ship. It was a small, nondescript transport, with nothing to differentiate it from any of the others sitting nearby. Grady Prime recognized the pilot leaning against the fuselage, waiting for him. The man had been Sinclair 2 until the disappearance of the Past Prime. Grady Prime supposed he was Sinclair Prime now, though in rare instances rankings didn't always follow predictable patterns.

"Grady Prime, it is good to see you again." The other soldier held out his hand for a greeting of equals, signaling his new status in a subtle yet undeniable way. Grady Prime returned the gesture.

"Congratulations on your ascension to Prime."

"Thank you, though it was not something I had anticipated or needed." A dark look passed over the new Prime's face as they both turned toward the open ship. "But we will talk of that as we travel. I've been instructed to speak to you as if to one of my men, which is something unexpected, yet welcome."

Grady Prime waited to speak until the hatch was closed behind them. "I assume the ship is secure?"

"It is. And I assume you were also granted leave to be candid with me about the reason for your new assignment?"

"To a certain extent," Grady Prime allowed. This new Prime had earned his respect as a young officer when their respective squadrons had trained together. This man, in particular, had saved the lives of several of his men when a malfunction had caused the young soldiers to become trapped in a burning ship. He had darker coloring than most Alvians, with a burnished gold light in his longer-than-regulation hair and a healthy, golden tan to his skin.

"As second in command, I was aware of the genetic modifications for which my former Prime volunteered. I was even tasked by Mara Prime to observe Prime Past after he took the treatment. I know you've become part of the follow-up study."

"Are you observing me as well?" Grady raised one eyebrow as they settled into their seats, and Sinclair Prime started the engine.

The new Prime laughed. "No. I'm through spying on my friends. I hope I can call you that, Grady Prime. I have had great respect for your abilities and your style of leadership for many years."

"And I have admired your courage since the training mishap," Grady Prime allowed.

As they rose above the city, Sinclair Prime turned to him. "We are completely unmonitored in this ship. Now that I'm Prime, I find myself in a unique position. I never expected Prime Past to abandon me or the squad. He was our leader and I always thought that if and when he stepped down from that role, he'd still be around to guide me as I took over. I've had to fly blind more than I ever anticipated, and I'm afraid the squad has suffered for it."

Most startling to Grady Prime was the real echo of fear and uncertainty he could hear in the young Prime's voice. "The Council told me you were created from a combination of Alvian and Avarel DNA. I know from personal experience that soldier stock is more aggressive and has more remnants of feeling than our less combative Alvian brethren. You have an added element in your DNA. I've been wondering since I found out about it, what that entails for your emotions."

Respect showed on the young Prime's face. "We feel more. It's not something we encourage and not something we talk about, but it's been documented. We don't have real emotions. We feel stronger echoes than even the most aggressive of warrior lines. It's what made Prime Past volunteer for the first experiment. He told me so himself."

Grady Prime was silent as he thought through that revelation. He'd liked this young officer for a long time and liked even more the honesty with which he seemed to want to start their closer working relationship. Here was an ally.

"That's the very reason I chose to participate in the experiment. All my life I felt these echoes of...something. And then as I observed the Breeds interacting, I wanted to understand them. I wanted to *feel*. Just once, before I die."

"Are you that certain it will kill you? Prime Past seemed to think it would free him, not kill him."

"I'm fairly certain it will drive me mad in the end. I've made a study of our history and that is the fate of most unmated males. I have little hope I will find a Resonance Mate to keep the madness at bay. Our women have no understanding of emotion and rarely resonate with anyone. I had some small hope about the three women in the study with me, but I've touched them all and there was not a single Hum to be heard."

"What about a human woman?" Sinclair Prime shot him a questioning look and it was not lost on Grady Prime that he used the word the Breeds called themselves. Somehow this soldier had contact with the Breeds and had come to be familiar with their language.

"There are so few. It hardly seems fair to seek among them. After what our people have done to them, it's unlikely any of them will accept an Alvian—much less a warrior Prime—as her mate. I had some small hope of it before emotion began to manifest. I understand the impossibility of it now. Most of them will never forgive us for what we've done to their planet and to them."

"The Chief Engineer has a human mate."

"Callie was the exception to the rule, as was Davin. He was a throwback to begin with. He always had emotions. And Callie is an empath. She understands him in a way few people can."

"You know them?"

"I've known Callie since she was a baby. She is a beautiful woman, inside and out. As is her mother."

"I didn't realize you had such close contact with them."

"I visited the family often as part of Mara 12's guard. Then in later years, I would go out to drop off supplies and pick up data collected by Mick O'Hara. Sometimes I shared meals with the family. They are a boisterous group with many young who are curious enough to ask impertinent questions." A smile curved his lips as Grady Prime thought of the O'Hara clan.

"You like them," Sinclair Prime accused with a smile.

"Yes," Grady acknowledged. "I feel great affection for them all." Now there was a statement. Grady Prime still marveled at the fact that he actually could *feel* things. "They were kind to me when I couldn't appreciate it and have continued to be so. Caleb O'Hara is helping counsel those of us in Mara 12's experiment and he has been of great help."

"You are fortunate to have an ally to aid you in this trial. I was briefed on the experiment before Prime Past took part in the initial experiment. Part of my duty was to observe him, since my normal duties involve routine observation of highly placed Alvian citizens."

"Then you're—"

"*Zxerah*. The whole squad is. We are part of the ghost squadron, and you are among the very few to know that for certain outside the Council."

Grady Prime was shocked. "I was going to guess ghost squadron. I'll admit you've taken me by surprise with talk of the *Zxerah* Brotherhood. I thought they were only a myth from ancient times."

"I can assure you, we are very real. All of us with wings are *Zxerah*. No winged soldiers exist beyond the Brotherhood, but there are more *Zxerah* who are unable to fly. The Patriarch authorized me to speak freely to you. For some reason, he believes you may hold the key to our future plans."

"I've heard rumors of a ghost squadron. I discounted most of the wilder claims about them. Even the worst of the conspiracy theories never mentioned the Brotherhood. All *Zxerah* were supposed to have been lost before the migration."

"Not all," Sinclair Prime said. "A few survived to pass down the skills. It was the Patriarch who first put forward the idea of adding Avarel DNA to our line. A previous Patriarch had approached Mara Prime Past with the idea two generations ago. He was refused. The current Patriarch reissued the request once we awakened on the ship and the current Mara Prime agreed to try, with approval of the High Council. My squadron and I are the result. Other *Zxerah* were not given wings to act as a control group. They continue to live in a secret enclave."

Grady Prime knew the history. The *Zxerah* were a warrior clan that had lived in a remote mountain region of the home world. They had not had contact with the outside world, but had allowed pilgrims to join their ranks if they proved worthy. They had lived ascetic lives, studying fighting and concealment arts day and night. They had been accredited with feats of skill, strength, endurance, stealth and bravery that were so fantastic as to be unbelievable. Most Alvians thought they had died off before the mass exodus from the home system.

Perhaps not. That there was a *Zxerah* Patriarch still living was incredible. All modern Alvians were separated by genetic lines, each holding a rank within their genetic line based on age, skill, accomplishments and other factors. Primes were the best of the best of their line. No line had a Patriarch. Such designations had died out as the geneticists took control of the vast majority of Alvian reproduction.

The *Zxerah* had always been different. If any group could retain their ancient identity, even with the changes wrought to all Alvian DNA, it would be them. Grady Prime also supposed that the Council liked having the *Zxerah* to use as a secret, deadly and highly skilled weapon. No wonder they let them keep their anonymity.

"I'm impressed and astonished," Grady Prime admitted. "I thought the *Zxerah* were only a legend. But if any Alvian sought the power to fly, it would be the fabled *Zxerah.* I should not have been so quick to credit the scientists for coming up with the idea."

"The *Zxerah* had the Avarel genetic samples. Avarel kept in contact with the *Zxerah* long after they'd cut off communications with the rest of our race. It is said the Avarel respected our ability to control our aggressive tendencies and our desire to seek enlightenment. The *Zxerah* embraced the genetic changes the geneticists proposed many generations ago, always looking for ways to improve themselves. The Patriarch told me he had begun to believe we'd gone too far. Control of destructive emotion is a good thing, so the ancient teachings say, but complete lack of emotion is not. The Patriarch had hoped the addition of Avarel DNA would return what was lost in addition to giving us the ability to fly. It worked to a very limited degree. As I said, we feel more than other soldier lines. It's still not much. We don't really understand humans at all, though we try."

"Your revelations astound me." Grady Prime wasn't sure why he was being trusted with such sensitive information and was wary of it.

"I tell you this now, so you will understand what you see when you meet my men. We are all winged, and we are all *Zxerah.*" Sinclair Prime faced him in the small cockpit. "Mara Prime is our keeper, our observer. We also observe him, and many other top Alvians as part of our duty to both the Council and the *Zxerah* Patriarch. Our allegiance is to the Alvian race, not necessarily the Council. Too often of late, they have asked things of us, which make us uncomfortable. Capturing humans is one example."

Grady Prime sighed with regret. "I have done my share of capture at their direction. My only defense is that I didn't understand the implications of my actions. It is no excuse, and I will spend the rest of my days regretting what I've done to certain people."

"I hoped you would say that. I must ask that if you do find Prime Past, you take that into consideration. It is my belief that he failed to kill his assigned target specifically for that reason. He was not a man who *could* miss a target. If he did, it was deliberate, and he had to have had a good reason for it."

"You feel strongly about this," Grady Prime observed.

"I do. Though the irony of your wording is not lost on me. It is because Prime Past was starting to manifest feelings that I believe he acted in such a way. I've had many months to think about this, and

25

it's the only conclusion that makes sense."

"You understand I've been tasked to hunt him?"

Sinclair Prime nodded, turning back to the controls. "I do. I want you to find him, and will assist in that endeavor. What happens after that is up to you. I hope you will find pity among your new emotions. Prime Past deserves whatever happiness he can find in his new life. I miss him and his counsel. We all do. His departure brought echoes of sorrow to all *Zxerah* and especially to those of us with wings. He was the best of us and whatever his path now, I know he will live with honor. He is a great man."

"Then why do you want me to find him? I'm ordered to kill him." Grady Prime was blunt on purpose. He wanted to see how the new Prime would react.

"Several reasons. First, I want him to know what I've told you. He deserves to know that the Brotherhood, at least, has not abandoned him. Second, I'd like him to know that others have followed his path and taken the treatment that changed him so radically. It is my hope that you will find some common ground. Perhaps you could help each other."

"You want us to become friends? Do you suppose sharing the burden of emotions will draw us together?" Grady Prime injected sarcasm into his words, trying to provoke the other man.

"I hope for that. Yes." Sinclair Prime agreed, surprising him. "If your test group does well, more Alvians will undergo the treatment. It is what the Patriarch wants. My duty is to help Mara 12's experiment succeed. I believe if you can discuss your condition with Prime Past, you may gain insight about how to move forward."

The young man had nerve. Grady Prime would give him that.

"I can make no promises. When I find Prime Past, I'll keep your words in mind, but will have to make my decision when the time comes."

"I know you to be a fair and honorable man," Sinclair Prime said after a moment. "I'll trust your judgment when the time comes. Do not underestimate Prime Past. You may be the Prime of your own talented line, but Prime Past is that and *Zxerah* too. He has skills beyond your comprehension."

"Perhaps after this is all over, I could learn some of those skills," Grady Prime offered, only half joking. He was a soldier who enjoyed learning new methods. If there were truly *Zxerah* left in the universe, he would be a fool not to seek them out for training.

Sinclair Prime looked at him consideringly. "Perhaps."

Chapter Two

Deep inside a mountain in what had once been called Colorado, sweat dripped down a man's face as he spun into a high roundhouse kick. His opponent ducked, blocking the main force of the blow as he delivered a counterstrike. They'd been sparring for hours, but neither one would call a halt. Too many people depended on them and the other members of their elite group. Too many needed them to be in top form at all times—ready for anything.

"She's coming!"

The scream was repeated down the cavernous hall outside the training area, echoing off cemented rock walls.

By silent agreement, both men stopped, ending their sparring session. One of their people needed them.

A moment later, a ragged woman ran into view. Her hair flew wildly around her ravaged face, her eyes wide with fear and not quite sane.

The leader reached out to her, folding the trembling woman in his arms as he'd done many times before, offering comfort.

"It's okay, Tory. Everything will be all right."

He soothed her as his lieutenant watched in sympathy. A flick of his head toward the hall sent Pierre after some of the others who would help settle Tory after the storm had passed. Sometimes it must really suck to be a seer, he thought. Tory suffered from the gift, and at times it drove her back into the madness from which she was only just beginning to emerge.

He murmured nonsense to her, hoping to ease her quaking shudders, but she remained agitated. She kept repeating that someone was coming. At times, he'd learned it was best to help her work through a vision rather than try to stop it. Perhaps this was one of those times.

"Who's coming, Tory? A friend?"

Her wild gaze turned to him, and he had to stifle the urge to sigh. Tory had made good progress in the past year, but she still hovered on the edge of madness too much of the time.

"A friend?" She paused, seeming to think it over. "She could be, to us. She will also be friend to the angels. She will bring the angels to us."

"Angels?" He didn't like the sound of that. "Like the angel of death? Will she bring death to us, Tory?"

"Perhaps." Tory's eyes began to dim just slightly, giving him hope this episode was near an end. "The angels aren't good or bad. They just are. They kill. They also protect. They'll protect us, if we let them, and she'll bring them. She'll bring them. She'll bring them." Those three words kept repeating as she quieted, her words fading to a whisper as he tucked her close, stroking her back, offering the comfort of his touch—of his protection.

Poor, fractured Tory was under his protection, as were many other souls in this complex. He wouldn't let anyone or anything hurt them. Angels, devils, Alvians or otherwise. He would defend his people to his last breath.

Hopefully it wouldn't come to that. Not yet at least.

Their destination was beyond anything Grady Prime had dreamed. Towering red trees made the people and buildings below look like miniatures. Sinclair Prime wove through the massive trunks of the behemoths with a skill and ease that Grady Prime respected and even envied.

"Are these trees real?" he asked in a hushed tone as he looked at one of the most glorious sites he'd ever beheld.

"Magnificent, aren't they? The humans call them giant sequoia or redwoods. Some of them are thousands of years old. This area was hard hit by the tsunamis and was unstable for a long time, which is why the Council let us settle here. The trees are massive enough to hide our base and provide cover for our flight—though flying under the canopy is quite an obstacle course. Good for training too."

Even as they made final approach to a very small landing area,

Grady saw a winged man swoop down out of the branches to fly alongside the ship. He turned his head and looked right into the cockpit, raising one hand in salute as Sinclair Prime returned the gesture.

The man's tawny wingspan was impressive, and the fact that he could keep up with a ship—even one slowing for landing—was shocking. Grady Prime's eyes sought the place on his shoulders where the man's wings joined his back. He realized that while the man's musculature was brawny, the wings themselves were of light construction. Then he realized the man sitting at the controls next to him probably had wings just like this, hidden somewhere under his uniform. Grady Prime took a second look, but found it difficult to discern anything odd about the fit of Sinclair Prime's uniform, though it was somewhat baggier than the norm.

"Hiding our wings is one of the first things we learn if we ever hope to see other people." Sinclair Prime sent him a small grin. "The bones of the wings are light and resilient, and our wingspan is shorter than the ancient Avarel. It's enough to get us aloft and we are good sprinters, but we cannot fly for prolonged periods as true Avarel could. We are only hybrids. Echoes of what they were."

"Still, those wings are amazing."

"Thank you. You're one of the few who know our secret."

"Frankly, I'm surprised the Council would allow me to know such things, especially considering my involvement in Mara 12's experiment. Of course, I'll bet that's also the reason they allowed me to investigate this matter."

"Participation in the experiment probably ended your career anyway you mean?" Sinclair Prime's eyebrow rose in Grady's direction. The man was quick witted, which Grady Prime appreciated.

"I expected to be put out to pasture and welcomed it if it meant I could discover what it was like to feel. Now that I'm back in the field again, I find that I missed being busy these past weeks. I missed working and interacting with other soldiers. I missed my men. Civilians are not the same."

Sinclair Prime laughed aloud. "You will not get an argument from me on that point, my friend. I do not understand civilians at all. I do better with soldiers, but among the *Zxerah* is where I truly belong—even more so if they are winged. The unwinged members of the

Brotherhood do not always understand the challenges I and my winged brethren face."

"I can only imagine," Grady Prime commiserated. "And yet, I confess I am feeling envy of your ability to fly. What I have just seen of your wings is a thing of great beauty, Sinclair Prime."

Sinclair looked at him with a kind smile. "It means a great deal to me for you to say that, Grady Prime. I've often wondered how the rest of the Alvian population would react if they learned of our existence. Would they think of us as freaks and demand our destruction? Or would they accept us—even admire us?"

"I would bet on admiration and if they could feel it, envy such as I am experiencing. It is a novel feeling." Grady Prime examined the sensations he was experiencing as Sinclair landed the small ship. "It is envy but not in a bad sense. It's more wonder and wishing that somehow I could experience the marvel of self-propelled flight."

"It sounds like you've become adept at analyzing the emotions you've been facing. To be honest, I was concerned when I realized you'd undergone the treatment so recently. The first weeks for Prime Past were confusing at best, I think. You seem to be making very good progress at integrating emotions into your life. You seem more stable than he was in those first days." Sinclair Prime attended to the shutdown procedures and unstrapped his safety harness while Grady did the same.

"I'll confess, I was very confused at first. It was overwhelming at times. The O'Haras were of great help. I believe their assistance made my group of test subjects more successful than we otherwise would have been."

"Do you think they will proceed with further testing?"

"It's hard to tell, but if my group's success is any indication, they should. None of my fellow test subjects have gone mad or had other truly adverse reactions to this point. Most seem to be dealing well with their new status. I think the human influence and advice had a lot to do with our stability."

They exited the ship, and Grady Prime breathed the clean, fresh scent of the damp forest. He took a look around and marveled at the giant trees that sheltered them as if in some wondrous cathedral of nature.

"Beautiful, isn't it?" Sinclair Prime asked, undoubtedly noting

Grady's fascinated survey of the huge trees.

"I have rarely seen anything to rival this. You are a lucky man to live and work in such a place."

"I have long thought so," a new voice added from over Grady Prime's left shoulder. Caught off guard, he spun on his heel to see who had managed to sneak up on him, and came face to face with an unknown Alvian.

The man was almost un-Alvian looking, with his shoulder-length brown hair and hazel eyes. He had the darkest hair color Grady Prime had ever seen on an Alvian, yet he was undoubtedly a member of his race. For one thing, he had the pointy ears, though that was not always a foolproof method of identification. He also had the cold feel to him that Grady Prime had recently begun to associate with Alvians.

Now that Grady Prime could feel, he could more easily recognize those who could not. Sinclair Prime, for all that he claimed to feel more than the average Alvian, was still noticeably *cold* to Grady Prime's new emotion-enhanced senses. This man was colder still.

"Patriarch, you honor us with your presence."

Grady Prime was clued in by Sinclair Prime's respectful tone. This man was most likely the *Zxerah* Patriarch. A fabled being of immense power and ability. Grady Prime looked him over, surprised the Patriarch was such a young-looking man. He was only an inch shorter than Grady Prime and appeared to be more slender, but Grady knew as well as any soldier that appearances could be deceiving.

"Grady Prime, it is a pleasure to finally meet you." The Patriarch held out his hand in the way of soldiers. "I am Ronin Prime, Patriarch of the *Zxerah* Brotherhood."

Grady Prime took the man's hand and his measure, as he was measured in return. Power flowed from the Patriarch, tangible yet banked. Like a glowing ember that could be fanned to flame at any moment.

"It is an honor to meet you," Grady Prime replied politely, holding the man's gaze as they ended the friendly handclasp.

"Mara Prime is going to want to meet you, of course. I hope you'll both join me for dinner after." The Patriarch included Sinclair Prime in his invitation with a nod of his head.

"Of course, Patriarch," Sinclair Prime answered quickly as the man turned to go.

Grady Prime didn't get a chance to say much of anything. Ronin Prime moved like the wind. One minute he was there, the next he was gone like a puff of smoke.

"Doesn't let any grass grow under his feet, does he?" Grady asked with some humor as they resumed walking up the path that led from the landing area.

"The Patriarch marches to the beat of his own drum."

Grady Prime laughed. "It seems we both have been consorting with humans too long if we have adopted their race's sayings as our own. As they would say, *touché*, my friend."

Sinclair Prime joined in his laughter and as they rounded a final curve in the narrow path, they came face to face with an old Alvian male with hair gone white with age. Grady Prime knew this one. This was Mara Prime, the top geneticist for their race. Grady had dealt with the quiet old man from time to time as he worked with Mara 12 and the O'Haras in the early days, but he hadn't seen him in many years.

"It is good to see you again, Mara Prime. I hope you are well." Grady gave the elder a traditional sign of respect. He would have offered his hand, but that was a greeting reserved mostly for soldiers and not one Mara Prime had ever responded well to in the past. He was very reserved, even among Alvians.

"Well enough, thank you, Grady Prime. I would like a report on your progress before you continue with your duties. Follow me."

The old man turned without another word, clearly expecting to be obeyed. Grady Prime followed behind, knowing he had to get this over with if he was going to be allowed to get on with his work. So different, this greeting of Prime to Prime than the meeting with the *Zxerah* Patriarch. Grady Prime had liked the Patriarch right off—respected his power and the aura of authority around him—even on such short acquaintance. Grady Prime didn't much care for Mara Prime's cold ways and never had.

After a thorough debriefing in Mara Prime's sparsely decorated office, Grady Prime was finally free to resume his duties. Sinclair Prime met him outside the small building where Mara Prime's offices and laboratory were located.

"There is little sun left today, especially here under the canopy of trees. Dinner is not far off," Sinclair Prime explained. "I thought perhaps I could show you a little of the base on our way to meet the

Patriarch for dinner."

Grady thought it an excellent plan and followed eagerly after Sinclair Prime. He'd changed his uniform top for one that had openings in back for his wings. Grady Prime was shocked at first to see the tawny golden feathers of his wings folded along the curves of Sinclair Prime's back. Although it was probably rude, Grady found he couldn't stop himself from stealing glances at them.

Finally, Sinclair Prime stopped, a huge grin on his face as he turned to face Grady and very deliberately spread his wings.

"Does this help?" He cocked one eyebrow and grinned. Grady Prime laughed in answer.

"I apologize. I am simply fascinated by your wings."

Sinclair Prime stood still, his wings outstretched while Grady Prime got a good long look. The tawny color was not uniform. The long feathered shafts had patterns on them of gold, brown, white and rust. The pattern had elements in common with that of other birds of prey Grady Prime had seen both on this planet and on his homeworld of Alvia Prime. Yet somehow, it was different. Chevrons of color danced down each extra-long shaft, interspersed with smaller feathers here and there.

"Your wings are truly amazing," Grady said after a long moment. "What happens when you lose feathers? I assume as a soldier you've run into injuries from time to time."

Sinclair Prime folded his right wing along his back, bringing his left wing forward so he could touch the feathers with his hands.

"Look at this one," he pointed to a particularly thick shaft. "This one broke off a week ago, and I glued it back on as a temporary measure until the new shaft grows into place. It's not ideal, but it works. Sometimes you can't save the broken shaft and you just have to fly with a gap until the new plumage grows in. And we molt every once in a while. When we're young, the new feathers come in every year until we reach adolescence. Then the process slows. We're out of commission flying-wise every decade for a complete molt. Otherwise we only lose feathers occasionally, never grounded unless we receive very serious injury such as a broken bone."

"Fascinating," Grady Prime said, inspecting the broken feather at the other man's invitation. The whole idea had him captivated.

Sinclair Prime tucked his wing back behind him and resumed the tour. He showed Grady Prime the barracks and the guest room he'd been assigned, where his pack had already been stowed. Sinclair also showed him the mess hall, break room and other facilities, introducing him to a few others as they went through the various public areas. All of the winged soldiers seemed surprised to see non-winged Grady Prime in their sanctuary, but they were welcoming for the most part.

Not all were of the Sinclair bloodline. Grady Prime met a few Hanlons, a Shaugness, a Lear and some Malens as well. Each had wings in varying shades of blond and brown with otherworldly markings along the long shafts of improbable feathers. The men were soldiers, well built and long of limb with varying lengths of wing that would support them in the air. Grady Prime also noted patrols flying or resting in the trees, watching over the compound below.

"You run an impressive operation here, Sinclair Prime," Grady complimented the other Prime with genuine admiration as they neared a structure set apart from the others.

"We do all right, though we sometimes miss the company of females. None were created with wings. The Patriarch brings some of the non-winged brethren to visit us here once in a while. Some among them are female and do not object to our altered bodies. And of course Mara Prime has his lab techs who see to us on a regular schedule."

Grady Prime didn't comment on the new, chilly feelings he got when he remembered his own encounters with lab techs and the few women who didn't mind servicing soldier stock. Every encounter except that last one with Jaci 192 was tainted in his memory. But Jaci 192 had given him something none of the others had ever shown him. She'd given him a glimpse into what sex could be like between beings with feelings. She'd been under the influence of the gene-altering agent at the time, though nobody had known then about the laboratory accident that had exposed her. She'd begun to feel. She had shown him true responses of a woman who enjoyed what her partner demanded of her and participated fully in both the physical and emotional side of lovemaking.

Later, when he'd found her frolicking with her true Resonance Mates, she'd given him hope. He despaired of ever finding a woman who could resonate with him on such an intimate level, but now that he had emotions, he found he couldn't kill the small kernel of hope that insisted on living in his previously cold heart.

The one-story square structure they entered was different from the others. Grady Prime felt the echoes of something...strange...in this new building as he entered. There was a small outer room that led to a large, bare, rectangular hall that had a very high ceiling and no fixtures to speak of. One long wall was covered with mirrors and the opposite wall was made up of floor-to-ceiling doors that were open to a fenced-in courtyard beyond.

Sinclair Prime led him around the edge of the large open space to the outer wall and into the courtyard that was sparsely populated with long, cylindrical plants reaching for the heavens only on the perimeter of the walled area. In the center of the outdoor space, a long table had been set up with several chairs and laden with covered platters, plates and place settings. It looked like a feast had been prepared.

"Welcome, Grady Prime. We dine well this night, in your honor. I have long admired your work."

The Patriarch had snuck up on him again and Grady didn't like it. Of course, if anyone were going to sneak up on him, it wasn't too distressing that the fabled *Zxerah* Patriarch would be the one able to do it.

"Thank you for your invitation, Patriarch," Grady Prime said politely. Behind the Patriarch, two more winged soldiers filed in, followed by two without wings and most shockingly, a small human woman.

Grady Prime tried not to stare. Something about the woman set off all kinds of internal alarms in his mind.

"Please be seated in the place of honor, Grady Prime." The Patriarch indicated the place opposite as he sat at one end of the long table.

Grady Prime moved to the other end of the table, as requested. He waited to be seated until everyone else had found their places, as good manners demanded of the lower ranked. Then they all sat at once. He was pleased to find the woman seated on his right and Sinclair Prime on his left. The others ranged down the table, toward the Patriarch.

All eyes turned to the Patriarch as he signaled to them to join hands for the ancient prayer. It was unusual, but some Alvians still practiced the old ways and Grady Prime had witnessed such ceremonies before. He took Sinclair Prime's hand with only slight hesitation. He was eager to touch the pretty human female's skin. The eagerness alone was something to savor—a precious emotion he'd only just learned to appreciate.

It shouldn't have come as such a shock then, that when he took her hand, a delicate, musical Hum reverberated through the air. Grady Prime's heart stopped as his eyes widened. He looked at the beautiful woman, then to the Patriarch who recited the ancient prayer, speaking of the forefathers and the blessed home crystal of Alvia Prime. A slight nod from the Patriarch was the only indication Grady had that the other man had heard the miraculous Hum. It was obvious the human woman heard nothing—the tone was most likely too far out of her natural range of hearing. But the other Alvians all had varying degrees of interest on their faces as Grady Prime looked down the table and started to breathe again.

The prayer ended and he, regrettably, had to let her go. Immediately the Hum ceased.

"You are no doubt surprised to find a human among our number, are you not, Grady Prime?" The Patriarch didn't mention the Hum as the covers were removed from the serving dishes. They all began to hand the platters around the table, serving themselves.

"I am, Patriarch." Grady Prime took his cue from his host. If the Patriarch didn't mention the Hum, neither would he. "Of course, until today I had no idea the *Zxerah* Brotherhood still existed. This seems to be a day of discovery for me."

He couldn't keep his gaze from the lovely creature sitting on his right. She had dark hair and eyes, her features angular and fine, her bone structure neither symmetrical nor ordinary. Instead, she was extraordinary in almost every way. Her petite frame was lithe and sleek from what he could tell under her plain dark clothing. He wondered what her skin would look and feel like without the concealment of cloth and felt himself grow unaccountably warm.

"Well said, Grady Prime. Allow me to introduce Gina, the first human I encountered on this planet. She was the first of their number to be inducted into the Brotherhood, but hardly the last."

The woman turned to look at him fully, and Grady Prime's mouth went dry as their eyes met. She spoke, and her voice sent shivers down his spine. He'd never reacted so strongly to any female—but then he'd never Hummed with any female. Ever.

The Hum was the first of the resonance tests. If a couple Hummed, they could then proceed to the next tests to see if they were in fact, Resonance Mates. While a male might Hum with more than one woman, few would pass the second test—the Kiss. And it was said only one woman for each male would receive the Embrace with a positive result, confirming that they were indeed, true Resonance Mates.

Grady wanted to try the next test with this human woman, and he wanted to try it now. It was so unbelievable that he should find any woman to Hum with him, that he wanted desperately to see if she could make the crystals glow like the sun, confirming their resonance. That could hardly be done at the dinner table, especially on such short acquaintance. He'd have to find a way. Soon. Or go mad.

The Patriarch introduced the rest of the people at the table, but Grady Prime heard little. His attention was focused almost entirely on the woman and thankfully, the Patriarch and the others left him mostly to his thoughts while they ate. The others talked among themselves, occasionally directing questions to Grady, which he answered gladly. Otherwise, he did his best to engage the woman—Gina—in conversation.

She wasn't shy, but she wasn't forward either. He found her utterly charming and her conversation interesting. They talked on many general subjects and laughed a great deal before she looked at him with curious eyes.

"You're not like other Alvians." Suspicion sounded in her low, melodic voice. "Are you a throwback?"

Grady Prime put down his fork and turned to face her. This was too important. He wanted to see her reaction to the news of his altered status.

"I was not born a throwback, but due to some recent changes, I now have emotions. Sharp of you to notice, Gina. If I may ask, what gave me away?"

She tilted her head to one side in a way he was coming to love. In fact, he was charmed by everything about her. Her laugh, her smile, her sparkling eyes and her quick wit were very attractive.

"You smile more than any of them, even the winged ones. And you seem to have a better understanding of humans than most Alvians."

"I have been around humans many times in my duties even before I gained emotion. I did not truly understand them until recently."

"You captured humans?" Her tone was accusing and sent a shaft of shame and regret through his heart, but he couldn't lie to her.

"I did. I have superior tracking skills. I was only sent after the hard cases. Others did the bulk of capture detail. I will admit that even before I could feel as I do now, I never enjoyed what came after the chase ended. I liked pitting my skills against a worthy opponent and coming out the victor. In those days, the echoes of exhilaration, satisfaction and even a small amount of triumph were the closest I could come to true emotion."

"So you'd be the kind of fisherman to go after a shark, land him, then throw him back to fight again another day." Her lips curled in amusement, and he was sidetracked by the sight until he got himself in hand. It wouldn't do to make a fool of himself with the first attractive female to actually Hum with him.

"I have never fished for shark, only small fish to eat while camping, but I think I understand what you mean."

"Do you like camping? I never did as a child, but the great outdoors has grown on me since living with the *Zxerah*."

"I love sleeping under the stars, or the tree canopy as it sighs overhead. I even like the patter of rain in manageable quantities when I have suitable gear with me." His small attempt at humor met with success as her lips lifted in that lovely smile once again. "Tell me, do you like your life among the *Zxerah*? Would you not rather be among humans?"

Suddenly her answer took on great importance to him. Would she prefer the company of her own kind or could she be happy among Alvians? He had to know.

"I didn't do too well with the other humans I encountered during my first few weeks in the wilderness. Then I ran into the Patriarch and all in all, I celebrate the day we found each other in the woods. The more I think about it, the more I believe God must have led me to that place and played a role in our meeting. Few women were trained as I was, and I don't think someone with lesser skills could have impressed the Patriarch enough to take a second look at us humans."

"Of what skills do you speak?" Grady Prime was pleased by her answer. He wanted to know everything he could possibly learn about this beautiful creature.

"She has a mean right hook and her flying roundhouse kicks are a guaranteed concussion if you don't duck fast enough," Sinclair Prime put in from across the table. The man chuckled and Gina followed suit, sharing a glance with the winged warrior that made Grady Prime feel an altogether new emotion—jealousy. He didn't like the feeling.

"You are a warrior?" he asked, regaining her attention. Frankly, she was so petite in comparison to a typical Alvian that he doubted the claim. Perhaps Sinclair Prime was teasing her.

"In the old world we had a sports contest every four years called the Olympics. The best athletes in many different sports would gather together from every nation and compete for two weeks to see who was the best in the world. I led the Olympic team into the arena and brought home first place gold medals for martial arts, as my father had, many years before me. He trained me from the time I was a little girl, along with my brothers and many others in his world-famous *dojo.*" Her eyes grew sad and Grady Prime reached out to touch her hand, offering comfort. When the Hum started up, he felt the eyes of everyone at the table turn to them, but he refused to release her. She was so sad. It hurt his heart.

"You miss your family." He spoke in what he hoped was a comforting tone. Offering comfort was new to him.

"I do. They were the best, and I never was able to find out what happened to them. I was traveling on this coast when the bombardment started. My home and family were on the other side of the continent."

"I'm sorry, Gina."

She looked up at him with a searching expression before a small smile lit her eyes. "You know, I actually believe you. Of all the Alvians I've met, I think you're the only one who has ever uttered those words with real sincerity." She placed her other hand over his on the table, pressing lightly as his breath caught. "Thank you, Grady."

"What is that noise?" Sinclair Prime asked from across the table. He had his fork halfway to his mouth and a puzzled look on his face.

Grady didn't know what to say since Gina clearly couldn't hear it. The Patriarch answered, his words simple and devastating at the same time.

"They Hum." All eyes turned to the Patriarch at the head of the table. "It is something I have heard only rarely and never among Alvians, I'm sorry to say. A few of the mated human pairs in our enclave Hum. Of course the tone is outside of their range of hearing."

"What's this about humming? I don't hear anything." Gina looked around, suspicious.

"Precisely, my dear." The Patriarch smiled at her. "When you touch Grady Prime, you resonate on a level that is outside of human hearing. We can hear the Hum, just below the surface. It is a pleasant sound, actually, and reassures me that there is hope for our people. If we can form Resonance Matings among ourselves and humans, there is some hope for the entire planet—Alvians and humans alike."

"I don't understand." Gina retracted her hands from Grady's. He was sorry to see her move away and the Hum stopped, but his attention was caught by the Patriarch's words.

"I know of several true Resonance Matings between humans and Alvians, Patriarch. I have heard the Hum and seen the crystals glow for two Alvians already. I had no hope I could be so lucky. You see—" he turned to speak directly to Gina, "—I have never Hummed with any female. Meeting you brings me hope." He loved watching the emotions flit across her expressive face.

"Tell me of the Resonance Mates you have observed, Grady Prime," the Patriarch invited. "I assume you speak of Chief Engineer Davin and his mate, but who is the other?"

Grady Prime considered his options. Nearly overwhelmed by the incredible Hum when he'd least expected it, he wasn't so far gone that he would potentially put others in danger. Especially not Callie or Jaci. Both women were special to him in different ways and he did not want to see either of them come to harm.

He had to make a decision. Could he truly trust the Patriarch and the people around this table? Could he trust the fabled *Zxerah* sense of honor? Having little hard data, he had to go with his instincts, his gut. It was something he'd relied on even before he had emotions. The ability had only grown stronger since he'd taken the gene-altering agent. With feelings came an enhanced ability to read people and situations.

Grady's gut was telling him that these *Zxerah*—these people out of legend—were exactly what they claimed to be. Grady Prime instinctively trusted the Patriarch. He didn't understand why he was so certain of the mysterious man's disposition, or for that matter, the rest of them. His instincts were pushing him harder than ever before to take the calculated risk and speak of some matters that he'd previously kept only to himself.

He wouldn't go so far as to reveal all he knew, but he would trust them—to a point.

"I am not at liberty to divulge the identity or circumstances of the second pairing. I can tell you that it is a true Resonance Mating between an Alvian female who was exposed to the same gene-altering agent that I took, and two human males. As for the Chief Engineer, I have known his mate, Callie, since she was an infant. What is not commonly known is that there is a second male in their household—a human male—who is also a true Resonance Mate to Callie."

"I thought there was only supposed to be one true mate for every person," Sinclair Prime stated. "Why are they mating in multiples?"

"The working theory is that because of the shortage of females on this planet, nature—or God, if you prefer—" he looked directly at Gina, since she seemed to believe in the deity of the humans strongly, "—intervened to allow more than one male to be true mate to one female. There is evidence in the ancient records of multiple matings in situations where the ratio of females to males was severely deficient. I discussed this with Callie and Davin when I was trying to decide whether or not to participate in the experiment. I wanted to know more about resonance and I knew that if anyone had studied the topic it would be the Chief Engineer. He'd compiled data from ancient records—particularly in reference to multi-partner matings. He even documented such among his human charges in the Southern Engineering Facility and Callie O'Hara's parents have such a mating. I have witnessed all three O'Hara brothers Humming with their wife Jane. They are all human, but they also fulfill the tests of resonance."

"This is interesting news. I will endeavor to learn more of the Chief Engineer's studies." The Patriarch looked pensive.

"Davin is a good man," Grady Prime felt the need to add. "He will talk to you if you approach him directly. If you wish, I could introduce you as a friend. Callie is a very strong empath. She will discern your intent. If she senses you are truly interested and have no malice in your heart, she will more than likely tell Davin and he will speak freely."

"An empath?" The Patriarch sat back and regarded Grady Prime, but he got the impression the other man was seeing well beyond him as his eyes focused on some goal only he could see.

"As is her mother, Jane O'Hara. The psychic talents in that family are very potent and nearly infallible. Caleb, the eldest O'Hara brother, can see the future."

"I am familiar with foresight," the Patriarch said, refocusing on Grady Prime. "I didn't know how closely these people were interconnected or that you were so well acquainted with them all."

"I traveled to their home many times in the course of my duties and had a chance to watch their children—Callie and Harry in particular—grow from infant to young adult. It was an enriching experience and one that helped me decide to follow my present course. Even before I could feel, I enjoyed observing the youngsters as they thrived in a caring environment. It gave me a glimpse into what life must have been like on this planet and even on Alvia Prime, before the geneticists began to change our people."

Grady Prime noted that everyone around the table was looking at him. He'd captured all their attention with his unguarded words and observations. He had one further revelation—if they didn't know it already. From everything he'd seen so far, it was entirely possible they didn't know.

"It's been conclusively proven that all three O'Hara brothers and all their children are descendants of a common Alvian ancestor." This, more than anything, would guarantee the safety of his human friends from all but the most cutthroat of his Alvian brethren.

"I was aware that Mara 12 was working on a theory that our ancestors may have intermixed with the native population. I did not know they could trace their ancestry."

Grady Prime sat back in his chair, regarding the Patriarch with a measuring gaze. Best he could tell, the powerful *Zxerah* leader truly didn't know. This could get interesting.

"Her so-called theory was proven many years ago though it has been kept secret in the scientific community until recently. It is true that our most revered ancestors settled on this planet long ago. Caleb, Justin, Mick and all of the O'Hara clan carry a large amount of Hara DNA." The shocked silence was deafening. Hara had been the greatest of them, the most revered, the savior of their people when all hope had been lost. That alone would guarantee the O'Hara clan's safety and status, but there was more. "Mara 12 confirmed her discovery by personally breeding with Justin O'Hara nearly twenty years ago. The resulting child is called simply Hara by the scientific team. He is known as Harry to his human family."

"She had a baby with a human man?" Gina seemed scandalized.

"She did. Harry spends most of his time these days in the Northern City where his uncle, Caleb O'Hara, is currently being confined for study. I have long suspected that Harry acts as a conduit between his imprisoned uncle and the rest of the family. They have strong bonds—emotional bonds that Mara 12 does not understand. I did not understand it myself until just recently. Caleb and Harry have been of great help to me and the other test subjects as we progressed through the emotional changes and upheavals of those first few weeks. Without their help, I don't know how successful our test group would have been."

The Patriarch sat back and steepled his fingers, deep in thought as his gaze drifted around the table, finally settling back on Grady Prime. Everyone else was silent, each contemplating his revelations in their own way, and waiting to see what their leader would have to say.

Finally, he lowered his hands and leaned forward, his gaze intense. "This is excellent news. Astounding news."

Chapter Three

The Patriarch was as animated as Gina had ever seen him. If she didn't know better, she would think he was having an emotional reaction to Grady's words. But she'd been around him long enough to know that was impossible. He was better than most Alvians, but he didn't truly feel anything. Nothing worth mentioning, anyway. She'd watched him struggle with faint echoes from time to time over the years, and her heart had gone out to him.

Compassion was the emotion that came most often when she was in his presence. He wanted to understand, yet he could not. She believed he wanted only what was best for his people, yet he was convinced they had been on the wrong path for many centuries. He worked hard to change all of that, but was hampered by the need for secrecy.

"I thank you again, Grady Prime, for all that you have revealed to us tonight. I sense this could not have been an easy decision for you. After all, you have only just met us. By contrast, we have followed your career from afar for many years. You have always been a credit to our race, and I now believe you may be a conduit to a better future." The Patriarch sat forward, his energy palpable to everyone around him. "Hara DNA on Earth! Proven and tested. Do you know what this means?"

"It means we can move forward with our plans," Sinclair Prime said in a low, almost excited tone.

"We can, indeed," the Patriarch replied before turning back to Grady Prime. "What is he like, this young man called Hara?"

Although Gina had no idea what this particular strain of DNA meant to her Alvian friends, she could tell by looking at the faces of all those around her that this was something very significant to them. She wondered what the child of an Alvian scientist and a human male would be like. Would he take after his emotionless mother? Or would he be more human? Would he have psychic gifts? The idea was tantalizing.

"Harry was raised for the most part by his human family. Mara 12 was ill equipped to handle the demands of an infant, and brought him to the O'Haras soon after his birth. As I recall from their discussions at the time, the child was already a strong telepath. He communicated his needs in images to Mara 12 even before he could speak."

"He could communicate telepathically with his mother when she had no psychic ability?" one of the others asked, incredulous.

Grady Prime nodded. "He sent very specific images to her. After some confusion on Mara 12's part, she finally comprehended what he wanted. As a result, she allowed him to stay with his human family as he requested. That's why I spent so much time at their home. I provided security for Mara 12 when she visited him for study purposes."

"Is he still such a strong telepath or was that something unique due to his close relationship with his mother?" Sinclair Prime wanted to know.

"I am unsure exactly how the humans measure such things. From what I understand, his abilities rival and even exceed those of his father and uncles. From all accounts, the three O'Hara brothers have superior psychic abilities. Caleb is a seer with a near perfect record of accuracy, documented by Mara 12 and her staff over the past few years. Justin is primarily telekinetic, and Mick is a powerful telepath."

"Hara manifested his uncle's power of telepathy very young," the Patriarch mused. "Does he share his father's telekinetic gift as well?"

"I believe so, but I don't think he's told his mother everything he can do. Harry is a cagey young man, who I suspect has his own agenda. He feels. He identifies with his human family. He seems to respect his mother, but Mara 12 has never really had an active role in his life other than as a scientist monitoring his progress. Jane O'Hara is the one who mothered him in the fullest sense of the word. He calls her Mama Jane and has always exhibited high levels of care, compassion and protectiveness toward her."

"I want to meet him," the Patriarch said suddenly. "This changes things and yet... Things could not be more perfect. Gina," he snapped out, clearly thinking fast and plotting his next moves. "I want you to prepare for departure. You'll be leaving the day after tomorrow, as will I. Sinclair Prime, I'll need you and your squad to run interference when we go in order to avoid Mara Prime. The less he knows of our movements, the better."

Gina was disconcerted to know that their carefully laid plans had just been accelerated to a considerable degree, but she was ready. She'd spent a lot of time in preparation for her mission since the Patriarch had first approached her with the idea. She wanted to do this. At the same time she felt conflicted. The emotion was a new one that had arrived on the scene at exactly the same moment she first saw Grady Prime.

She recognized him. Or thought she did. She could almost swear he was one of the men from her dreams. She'd never seen his face clearly. She'd felt his emotion and recognized him as Alvian. She'd felt his body, knew his height and size. All those things matched with what she now saw in Grady Prime.

She'd nearly stopped short when she walked into the courtyard and saw him for the first time. An instant of recognition, followed by an hour of careful watching, measuring and digging back into her memory for clues about her dream lover. Even if she hadn't dreamed of him, this warrior would have intrigued her. He bedeviled her. With a single glance, he piqued her interest. And he was just plain hot.

A more gorgeous specimen of Alvian manhood she had never seen. A golden god with that extra spark of life in his gorgeous blue eyes— that quintessential something that was missing from every other Alvian she'd ever met. He could feel.

Emotions were new to him. There was little doubt he had some trouble interpreting the impulses that must have been so confusing to him at first. Gina admired the fact that he'd taken such a dangerous chance and joined the experiment. Not only that, but he'd overcome what had to be poor odds to succeed in his quest to understand and experience emotion firsthand. She gave him credit for that.

Most warriors she knew—most men of either race, for that matter—didn't spend a lot of time pondering their existence. To have undertaken such a drastic step, she knew Grady Prime had searched his own soul, long and hard. It was an attractive thought.

Almost as attractive as she found him. The attraction grew with each breath, each word from his mouth, each moment in his presence.

Now she was being sent away.

The mission was one she had eagerly accepted and had looked forward to implementing for some time, but things had changed in the space of mere minutes. Why she found Grady Prime so compelling, she had no idea. She wished things could be different and that she could have just a little more time to discover the answer.

But it was not meant to be. Sooner than she'd expected, she would leave here—leave him—and move on to the next part of her mission, the next part of her life. If she was successful, it would be some time before she could return to the protective fold of the *Zxerah* Brotherhood. Even then, there was no guarantee she would ever cross paths with Grady Prime again. These few minutes were probably all they would ever have.

Gina felt a pang for what could never be. She knew her duty was not only to the Patriarch, but to her own race. If things went well, all life on this planet could change for the better. It was the goal she had dedicated her life to, and the only thing that should really matter. The only thing she could let matter.

"I'll start with the Chief Engineer," the Patriarch continued his fast-paced decision-making. "Grady Prime, would you be kind enough to record an introductory message I could deliver to Davin and his mate? I would take you with me to perform the introductions in person, but your mission here is too high profile in certain quarters and I cannot interfere with it to that extent. Under no circumstances do I want the Council aware of my movements at this critical time."

Grady Prime answered in the affirmative and Gina's eyes were drawn once again to his firm jaw, his sparkling eyes and the sheer strength of the man. He was appealing on a visceral level that was hard to resist.

The Patriarch went on with his plans. Gina didn't really listen. The others were all talking now as he stirred them up. Only Grady Prime and she sat in relative silence and watched. He watched everyone, and she watched him. At least, she thought he'd been watching everyone, but after a while, she realized he was covertly scrutinizing her.

And then he wasn't being so covert.

They stared into each other's eyes as the conversation and

planning went on around them, each unblinking, unsure what the rapt attention of the other signified. Gina felt it. Her empathic abilities were low key, but Grady Prime was close enough for her to read and he wasn't adept at hiding his emotions yet. They were still too new.

After a while, the conversation died and the dinner was over. Some of the men had already been dispatched to get the ball rolling on the Patriarch's plans. The rest followed quickly after. Only Sinclair Prime and the Patriarch remained as she and Grady walked with them toward the exit.

The Patriarch thanked Grady once more before leaving the group just outside the building. Sinclair Prime gave them a speculative glance before saying goodnight himself and leaping into the air to fly away.

"May I walk you to your accommodations?" Grady Prime asked politely.

"That would be nice. Thank you."

They walked together down the dark pathway toward the main area of the compound. Neither of them seemed to want to move very quickly. Instead, they set a leisurely pace to maximize the amount of time they could spend together.

"I confess..." Gina spoke hesitantly, trying to make conversation. "I'm intrigued by this guy Harry you talked about at dinner. You sure got the Patriarch hopping, though I don't understand exactly why."

"Harry's DNA is important to our people. You may have noticed the significance of bloodlines to us. Well, Hara—the progenitor of Harry's line—was one of our greatest explorers and leaders. He was believed lost to us, as was the rest of his exploration party. Finding residual evidence of them here on Earth is an amazing discovery that will affect every Alvian."

"This young man is really that important?"

"Not him per se, but his genetic code could spell great changes for Alvians and humans alike. The Alvian population would no longer be able to believe themselves superior genetically if the native humans were proven to share not only Alvian DNA but that from one of the most highly respected of our ancestors. It would change things—most likely for the better for humans."

"Which is probably why your Council has hidden this for so long. What you did tonight, by telling the Patriarch the truth, was a good thing, Grady."

She tried to see him in the darkness, but her night vision wasn't up to Alvian standards. Instead, she reached for his hand, gratified when he seemed startled for just a moment, then interlaced his fingers with hers. She squeezed his hand, hoping to convey the very real admiration she had for him. It was a simple gesture, but she knew how rare it was for Alvians to touch, even in friendship.

She suspected that since gaining emotions, Grady needed to be touched. Like an infant, he needed reassurance from other feeling beings and she liked that he'd taken her hand and seemed unlikely and unwilling to let it go.

"Harry is a good man," he said with genuine warmth in his tone. "I read a human book once called *The Once and Future King* by T.S. Elliot. Mick O'Hara loaned it to me when I asked why they referred to Harry as the second coming of Merlin."

"You mean Merlin like in Camelot and King Arthur?"

"The very one." She could hear the approving smile in his voice. "Apparently Harry's gifts were so many and so strong even his gifted family thought he was a magician of some kind."

"That's cool."

His warm chuckle sent a river of warm lava down her spine. "It also indicates to me—although I am no expert on the genetic intricacies—that the mixture of human and Alvian DNA might very well produce more beings like Harry. The humans we've encountered are many generations removed from their original Alvian progenitors. It could be that a fresh infusion of Alvian DNA into the human race, or human DNA into Alvians, would produce the next evolution of both races. Psychically gifted beings that can be stronger than either one of our races are alone."

"I bet your Council would consider your words as treason. Aren't you concerned by their reaction should your candor with us be discovered?"

"At this point there's very little they can do to me. I gave up my occupation and most of what had been important to me in order to participate in Mara 12's study. I wouldn't change it for the world, but it's put me in a unique position. I can take risks now that I wouldn't have before."

She turned to him on the darkened path. A shaft of moonlight filtered through the trees, lighting his face enough for her to read his expression. She found her own desire mirrored there, and her breath caught.

"You're a dangerous man, Grady Prime."

His head lowered, and she knew he was going to kiss her. She didn't pull away. She wanted to feel his kiss more than anything. She stood on tiptoe to meet his descending lips.

His mouth was warm and tasted like spiced wine, heady and exciting. Gina hadn't experienced such feelings in far too long— perhaps not ever. Grady Prime was an excellent kisser.

She reached up to twine one arm around his neck, drawing him downward as she rose up to press closer to his muscular body. He lifted her other hand, fingers still entwined with his, to his chest, pressing close but not releasing her fingers. She barely noticed, reveling only in the feel of him, the sheer brute strength of him and how gently he treated her. How he tempered his strength to fit her smaller body.

And they did fit. Really well.

She loved the warmth of him against her and could even feel the large bulge of his cock pressing against his uniform pants. His hips moved in a sensuous pulse against her legs, her stomach, the tops of her thighs. He was massive and hard.

She wanted him.

And that's when he pulled back, breaking the kiss.

He held her gaze, both of them breathing harshly in the dappled moonlight. His body pressed close to hers so she could feel the heat of him, the need echoing loudly in her own body.

"I don't need a crystal to know that we more than Hum, Gina. We glow."

She didn't really understand his statement, but at that point, she didn't care. All she wanted was another kiss like that last one and he obliged. Only his next kiss was even deeper, even hotter than the first. This time he knew exactly what to do to make her moan.

He unlaced their fingers and pressed her open palm over his chest so she could feel his racing heart. The rapid beat echoed her own, their excitement building together as he kissed her deeply.

His tongue traced hot, wet patterns against hers, commanding, demanding, turning her on. She liked his domination, his absolute expectation of being obeyed as he asked silently for all she had to give.

Her fingers itched to touch his skin. She sank one hand into his soft golden hair, tugging the short ends to draw him closer. She stroked her other palm over his chest, looking for a way inside his uniform shirt. She was unable to find it or focus much beyond what he was making her feel.

Grady's powerful arms surrounded her. One hand moved low to cup her ass, lifting her closer to the erection tenting his pants and teasing her through the layers of their clothing. She couldn't help the pulsating movements she made against him. It had been a long time since she'd felt pleasure like this. Too long since a man had made her come alive with just a kiss. In fact, she didn't think she'd ever experienced anything quite this explosive before in her entire life.

Grady Prime was one of a kind. If she ever got the chance to make love to him, she wasn't sure she would survive the encounter. Not if this kiss was anything to go by. She could very well just spontaneously combust and float away on the wind, never to be seen again. But what a way to go.

His presence was nearly overwhelming. At the same time she felt protected, even cherished. He gave as much as he took and she could tell from the gentle way he handled her, he was being very careful not to hurt her in any way. He was almost too careful, as some big men were prone to be around her. In her father's *dojo*, big guys had often made the mistake of treating her like a China doll just once before she'd taught them otherwise.

She'd relish the chance to teach Grady the same—in the bedroom, however, not the *dojo*. She didn't want to fight with him. She wanted more than anything, to feel his strength as he slid home into her needy, greedy body.

It was that shocking thought that finally penetrated the sensual fog surrounding her. Gina pulled away and Grady Prime let her go after only a moment's hesitation. He didn't let her go far. His arms remained loosely around her as he sought her gaze, concern in his.

"Should I apologize?"

The uncertainty in his tone touched her. She knew he wasn't used to having feelings and probably had little experience with the minefield of emotion involved in male-female interactions at the best of times.

This was the worst of times. She was leaving soon. She had no time to spare for an involvement like this. She shouldn't start anything with him, knowing she was leaving. It wouldn't be fair to either one of them.

"No, Grady. It's I who should be apologizing to you. I shouldn't have let it go this far. It's not right."

"It feels very right to have you in my arms, Gina. I have been with many women, but none have ever touched me as you do."

She wasn't sure she liked hearing the part about him being with many women before her, but she did like the sincerity of that last bit. Still, she was probably just a novelty to him, now that he had shiny new emotions to try out.

She backed away and he let her go, albeit reluctantly.

"You heard the Patriarch. I'm leaving the day after tomorrow," she said with finality. "My mission is a long-term one. I won't be back this way anytime soon and I doubt out paths will cross again for a long time—if ever. It wouldn't be right to start something I can't finish. I hope you understand. Otherwise..." She had to pause to collect herself.

She was *this close* to saying to hell with it and dragging him off the path into the loamy forest. She was that hot for him. That desperate. And the thought of it scared her. She was barely in control here and that was never a good thing for a woman who'd trained her entire life to be in control at all times.

"Otherwise—" She tried again. "I'd enjoy getting to know you better, Grady. You're an attractive man. In fact, you're the first man I've been this attracted to in a long time, but circumstances are against us right now. I'm sorry."

"No sorrier than I am, Gina. I know you don't realize the significance yet, but you could very well be my Resonance Mate. That's a precious thing among Alvians. Among humans, too, if my observations prove correct. We could be each other's perfect match. Are you willing to give that up before we've even discovered the truth of it?"

His words shocked her. She hadn't been thinking beyond a roll in the proverbial hay. Maybe a few. He sounded serious and almost possessive. While one part of her perversely liked it, the rest of her was jamming on the mental brakes.

She'd only just met the man. She found him attractive. That didn't mean she wanted to spend the rest of her life with him. For all she knew, he could be a rat bastard, though she didn't really think so.

Still, she'd been proven wrong about people before. Most notably the men she'd traveled with those first few weeks in the wilderness who'd turned out to be no better than animals.

"I have no choice, Grady." She tried to stand firm. "I'm leaving soon." The hurt in his eyes made her cut him some slack. "In human relationships it's usual to take time to get to know a person before declaring that you want them to be your permanent mate."

"I didn't say we were mates, just that we could be. We Hum. Everyone but you heard the evidence of that at dinner. If I'd had a tuned crystal handy a few minutes ago I'd bet anything we could have passed the other tests as well, but now..." He looked so forlorn she wanted to hug him.

"How about this? If, after my mission is completed, you want to try this again, I'll submit to your tests. All you have to do is send a message through Sinclair Prime. He'll be sure to get it to me, if I'm back among the Brotherhood by that time."

"Compromise?" Grady Prime looked at her with those startling blue eyes. He was getting better at hiding his emotions behind that stoic façade, but she could sense turmoil within him.

"It's all I can give you." She wished it could be otherwise. Unfortunately they both had duties to attend to.

Grady watched her for a long moment then surprised her by pulling her close against his body in a lightning move that left her gasping. His gaze bore into her as he looked down into her eyes. His jaw was clamped so tight, a muscle ticked in agitation.

"You can give me one other thing, Gina."

"What's that?" Her whispery voice sounded weak to her own ears.

"Tomorrow. You can give me some of your time tomorrow so that we can get to know each other better before you have to leave. I know we both have duties and no doubt you also have preparations to make, but you must have to eat at some point. Share those meals—and whatever time you have to spare—with me."

It was clear he wanted her company almost desperately and that was heady stuff to a woman who hadn't been courted in far too long. If she was being honest with herself, she would admit she also wanted to spend more time with Grady Prime. He intrigued her. Giving in to temptation, she nodded.

"I think I can do that."

The smile that stretched his lips and lit his eyes stole her breath as well. His head descended and once more she was lost in his kiss.

It was a very long time before they came up for air and her head was swimming, her eyes refused to completely focus and her knees were weak when he moved slightly back. His arms supported her for which she was grateful. She didn't think she could stand on her own at the moment.

"You're the most intriguing woman I've ever met, Gina."

"You're not so ordinary yourself, Grady Prime." She smiled at him, loving the way his casual strength made her feel feminine. It had been too long since a man had made her feel this way.

Chapter Four

The next morning, Grady Prime was waiting for her when she stepped outside the guest quarters she'd been assigned. He'd left her at the door last night with lingering kisses that had left her head spinning long after he'd gone.

She'd lain in bed, butterflies in her tummy and a dopey smile on her face for almost an hour, reliving the way he'd made her feel. Never had she experienced such a feeling outside the steamy dreams she'd had a few weeks before. She'd known after that last dream that one of the men on her path would be Alvian. She'd also thought he'd have emotions—strange as that had seemed at the time—and sure enough, here he was.

Grady Prime was *prime* all right. A prime example of Alvian manhood. One of the best of the best of their soldier stock. Big, brawny, sleekly muscled and masterful in the best sense of the word. He'd rocked her world with a few kisses.

And heaven help her, she wanted more.

She couldn't hold back the eager grin that lit her face when she found him waiting for her. She walked right up to him, a bounce in her step as she leaned up and gave him a peck on the cheek.

The little kiss caught him off guard, she could tell, but he was quick to respond. His strong arms came around her, drawing her close as he gave her a much deeper kiss that involved his sexy mouth, lips and tongue. When he pulled back, long minutes later, the forest beyond his shoulder tilted wildly in her vision. He was that potent.

"Good morning," she said breathlessly as his eyes lit with amusement.

"The best possible morning, to be sure." He let her go by small degrees until she was standing on her own wobbly legs. "Do you have time to join me for breakfast?"

She turned and took his arm as they began walking toward the mess.

"Indeed I do. But I wonder what the rest of my brethren will make of us sitting together?"

The thought had occurred to her late in the night as she lay awake replaying their moonlit kisses. Would her fellows in the *Zxerah* Brotherhood approve of her relationship—such as it was—with Grady Prime? Would the Patriarch approve? And if they didn't, what should she do? She wanted this stolen time with him before she left on her mission the next morning. She wanted to feel this feeling for just a little while longer.

"I can handle it if you can. And I'll be right by your side, Gina. Let them look all they want. Without emotion, they will never understand what draws us together. If we feel anything for them, it should be pity." Grady squeezed her fingers reassuringly.

"Do you really pity those who can't feel?" His response would tell her just how far he'd come from the emotionless Prime he'd been most of his life.

He sighed heavily as his steps slowed. "I pity myself for having spent so many years not feeling as I do now. I pity all beings who question but can never understand the answer, even when it's staring them in the face."

She gave his arm a final squeeze before letting go and opening the door to the communal mess. "You're a good man, Grady Prime."

He followed her inside and together they went to gather their meal.

"You make me a better man, Gina. Being around you inspires me to be better than I was yesterday. You're a good influence."

His words, spoken low so that only she could hear, made her feel warm inside. They spent the next few minutes gathering food from the cafeteria-style setup. Armed with full trays, they sought a place to sit at one of the long tables arranged in rows around the room. This early in the morning, only a few were occupied by early risers or those coming off night duty.

"After breakfast I must work on my investigation. I will probably be free to eat lunch around noon. Will you join me? Or can you spend some time with me later today?"

She loved the way he couldn't quite hide his eagerness. He was so new to emotion, he had a kind of eager puppy quality to him. At the same time, she realized he was somewhat fragile. Lack of understanding could cause him to misinterpret and bruise his sensitive feelings. She had to remember that and be careful of him. Hurting this beautiful soul was the last thing in the world she wanted to do.

"I'll meet you here for lunch," she agreed, marveling at the grin that passed over his face. "And I can meet you for dinner as well. I should be through with my preparations by sundown. There isn't much left to do here. I was expecting to leave, just not this soon."

"Will you be gone long?"

She was glad to see he knew enough not to ask her where she was going. "A few weeks, if all goes well. Maybe longer. I don't really know. As long as it takes to either accomplish my goal or fail utterly."

He laughed at her graveyard humor, warming her with his easy camaraderie. She'd missed this kind of thing. Sure, the humans among the *Zxerah* were the next thing to siblings, but they'd all walked hard roads to become members of the Brotherhood. Grady Prime had been through hell too, but it seemed to affect him less. He appeared to revel in each newfound feeling and his delight in the simplest of things was contagious. It just plain felt good to be around him.

On more than one level. He made her feel feminine and almost...pretty. She hadn't been supermodel material, even in her youth. She was short and sturdy. Muscled from her pursuit of Olympic gold and her need for survival ever since, she had an athlete's body and a plain face. Neither ugly nor gorgeous, she was used to men admiring her martial arts skills, but not the kind of fascination she saw in Grady Prime's eyes. He made her feel beautiful.

"Then your mission is like mine." His words brought her back to the conversation as he scraped his plate with his fork. "It'll take as long as it takes. Though I assume the Council will reel me in at some point if I don't show results. Until then, I have some freedom."

"What will they do with you?"

It suddenly occurred to her that he was an experimental subject. In all likelihood he'd been sprung for a mission and might have to go back to being a prisoner of the medical establishment after it was over.

She didn't want that for him. It made her realize that every moment away from the city and the doctors who wanted to study him like a lab rat was precious. He might never have this kind of freedom again.

"I'm not sure really. There was a small group of test subjects in my clinical trial. I suppose it depends on how well we do as a group. If the rest show the ability to live normally in Alvian society, perhaps we will be given some modicum of freedom."

"What if they can't adjust?"

"Then I suppose we will continue to be closely monitored. Perhaps for the rest of our lives."

Gina sat back in her chair, raising her eyebrows as she pondered his words. "That's no way to live, Grady."

"I concur. Which is why I'm giving great consideration to the words of your Patriarch. If nothing changes, I have few options. If, however, other events prove the usefulness or necessity of expanding the experiment, the options for me and my group of test subjects could change drastically."

"Oh, Grady, I hope you're right. The Patriarch is the best of men, but he plays a deep game. None of us really knows for sure what his ultimate goals are. I can tell you that I believe he's on the right path to help both your people and mine live together peacefully, once certain issues are settled. I don't kid myself that it'll be easy. In fact, I think this is going to be one of the hardest things either of our races has ever attempted. I believe in my heart that it's worth it. Whatever the cost."

Grady reached across the table and took her hand. She felt the stares of the Alvians seated closest to them as they touched. She knew they were hearing some kind of Hum, and she wished for a moment she could hear it too. She only felt the electric effect of his skin on hers, his emotions bleeding through her small empathic ability. He was worried, elated, hopeful and tense, just as she was.

"I'm grateful I met you, Gina, even though we're both dedicated to other missions just now."

"I could have wished for better timing, but I'm glad we met too. You're the first Alvian I've ever met who can truly feel, and I hope you won't be the last." She kept her voice low so that only Grady Prime could hear her fervent hopes for the future.

He clutched her hand, his strong fingers applying light pressure to her knuckles and palm. "With any luck, I'm just the first of many, if not all. You give me hope for...many things, Gina. Hope for my people. Hope for yours. And hope for...us."

"Us?"

"You and me, Gina. We could be mates. Don't tell me that thought doesn't intrigue you. Even now, every Alvian in here can hear us Humming when we touch." His smile was temptation itself and meant just for her. His eyes drew her in until they were alone in the crowded room, the only air in the little bubble that surrounded them. At least that's the way it felt to her.

A commotion at the door burst the intimate atmosphere. Mara Prime had arrived for breakfast with a contingent of his personal staff, and he was heading directly for them. Gina tugged on her hand, but Grady Prime seemed reluctant to let her go as he looked over to the door, his mouth hardening into a grim line as he saw the scientist drawing closer.

Mara Prime approached, his aides fanning out behind him like a cape. He was an old man—one of the few Alvians who actually looked old to Gina's eyes. He regarded them with one eyebrow raised in mild inquiry.

Grady looked from the scientist to Gina, squeezing her hand once before letting go and turning his gaze back to Mara Prime. The elder's eyes widened fractionally as the tingling that must have signified the Hum ceased.

"An interesting development." Mara Prime nodded in greeting as he peremptorily pulled out a chair at the long table. "May we sit with you?"

There was no polite way to refuse, as Mara Prime had no doubt intended. He took a seat next to Grady, across from Gina, as his entourage ranged themselves around the table. Two young scientists flanked Gina and more sat across from her, next to Grady. She shot him a look that held both her amusement and consternation at these developments and she knew Grady understood when a ghost of a smile touched his lips, just briefly.

The rest of the meal was spent being questioned—none too subtly—by Mara Prime and his subordinates. The geneticist had been told that Ronin Prime required Breed servants to attend him wherever he went. Gina was one of Ronin Prime's *pets*, as Mara Prime had been heard to call the human *Zxerah* adoptees, since the Patriarch allowed no interference with them whatsoever.

It wasn't the most enjoyable half hour Gina had ever spent, but she did marvel at Grady's ability to answer questions without saying much at all. He confounded the scientific team in such a polite and roundabout way, they couldn't object. He had a way of drawing them off target and leading them directly where he wanted them conversationally. It was a talent she admired, a skill she had never mastered. Grady could have taught lessons on the old bait and switch. She had to give him credit.

While Grady was occupied with the scientists and their questions, Gina ate steadily. Finishing her breakfast, she was grateful to have an excuse to leave the crowded table and the probing, invasive conversation the scientists seemed to think was acceptable. In her book, it was downright rude. Then again, she wasn't Alvian. Thank goodness.

Grady was sad to see Gina leave, but he knew it was for the best. Mara Prime was digging into areas Grady would rather not discuss in public—particularly not in front of a woman he thought might be his future mate. He'd rather she learn about his weaknesses and failures— as well as his strengths—naturally, over time.

He wanted desperately to spend time with her, learning her as she learned him. But duty called. His and hers. Both of them had jobs to do and superiors to satisfy before they would be free to pursue their personal lives, be it alone or together. Grady hoped like hell it would be together.

He'd never wanted a woman so badly. He'd never been so intrigued or inspired to such passion with her slightest touch, her weakest smile. She was like a drug to which he was fast becoming addicted, and he never wanted to stop.

Mara Prime dragged out breakfast as much as possible but eventually even the cagey old scientist had to let Grady Prime go about his duties for the day. Grady was glad to take up where he had left off with his investigation. He talked to more of the winged soldiers about their former leader and was learning things that would help his mission.

Or so he hoped. He needed to narrow down the parameters for locations he would search. Right now, the field was still wide open.

Bianca D'Arc

Only through the observations of people who had known the former Prime would Grady be able to formulate an effective search plan for Sinclair Prime Past.

Grady admitted to himself, he was woefully distracted. How could he not, with the tantalizing prospect of a Resonance Mate in the offing? Gina was luscious and one of the few things that could make him forget his duty and have trouble concentrating on his mission. All he wanted to do was daydream about her and the tempting possibilities of what they could be together—if their stars were in alignment.

Lunch couldn't come too soon to suit him. He arrived at the mess hall with eager steps only to find Gina there before him. She sat alone at a table in the corner. Even as he entered the room, he saw some of her *Zxerah* colleagues stop by the table to make conversation.

"Don't sit down. Don't sit down," he chanted under his breath to no avail. A moment later with a quick, apologetic glance in his direction, Gina smiled at the two warriors as they pulled out chairs across from her. At least he could sit at her side, Grady consoled himself. He noticed she'd put a small backpack on the chair next to her, precluding anyone from sitting there when there were other chairs available around the long table. "Good girl," Grady cheered her on under his breath.

If this went on much longer, people would start to think he habitually talked to himself. That wouldn't reflect well on an experimental test subject. At the moment, however, he didn't care. All that mattered was being with her, sitting next to her, hearing her voice and basking in her light.

They dined together, but had little opportunity to really talk. Not with so many attentive ears around the table. The warriors asked her about human fighting techniques and Grady listened, keenly aware that his possible mate was a fighting champion of some stature among humankind. The idea sat oddly with him at first, but as he listened to her speak knowledgably on a wide variety of topics, including strategies suitable for someone of her size against a larger opponent, he began to glow with pride.

His mate was a warrior. He never would have expected it in a million years, but he was glad of it. She was no weak city-bred female of one of the clerical lines. The only woman to date that he'd been tempted to subject to the resonance tests had been a Jaci—a lab tech with no athletic skills that he knew of. After meeting Gina, he couldn't

62

imagine the regret he'd felt when Jaci had mated two human males.

Oh, he liked Jaci and wished her well, but he didn't regret that she wasn't his mate any longer. Not with Gina near. In fact, all others paled in comparison to the human warrior woman at his side.

Grady was able to sit back and enjoy lunch, knowing that of all the males present, only he could truly appreciate her complexities. Only a short while ago he wouldn't have understood her at all. Since his new emotions had stabilized somewhat, he knew he had something to offer her that other Alvian males could not. Just the idea of it made him feel smug—a new emotion to add to his ever expanding catalog of new experiences.

They parted after lunch with a quick promise to meet for dinner. Grady swore to himself he'd arrange it so they could dine alone. He didn't want to share her attention with a table full of males again. Not when they had so little time left together.

On a new mission, he went through his duties as quickly as possible, then spent the remainder of his afternoon setting things up for an intimate dinner for two. His fellow Alvian soldiers may not understand emotion, but they certainly understood seduction. Since the change to their people, warriors, as a general rule, had to try harder to entice the females of their species into sharing their bodies.

Warriors were seen as less evolved and therefore less desirable than other classes of Alvian society. Yet it was their curse that they needed physical satiation more than others because of the echoes of aggression left in their genetic makeup to make them effective at their jobs. They had to get creative when seeking to share pleasure with a female. As a result, the other warriors understood without being told why Grady Prime was silently demanding privacy to share a meal with a female.

He didn't have to explain to the cooks why he wanted special food items packed for travel, or why he required the best they had in the way of dishes and utensils. They also didn't ask why he wanted a bottle of the fermented fruit juice the Alvian race had come to enjoy since colonizing this planet. They simply provided the meal and accoutrements and wished him good hunting.

Everything was set when Grady Prime walked back to the mess hall. He had left early, intending to intercept Gina before she had a chance to go inside. He arrived in the nick of time, calling out to her as she was about to open the door. She spun, a smile lighting her face when she saw him. She moved toward him and he stopped dead, entranced for a moment by the feminine loveliness of her.

Her smile turned questioning as she neared, her head tilting to one side. "What?"

"You are beautiful, Gina."

A becoming blush stained her cheeks, and he could tell she was pleased with his unguarded words. He breathed a sigh of relief. This small woman could easily send him off course. She shook him up almost as much as he wanted to upset her composure—in the best possible way. So far, so good, judging by her expression.

"I have a surprise for you. Will you come with me so we can dine alone?"

Her expression softened with pleasure. She agreed, preceding him down the path. When she hesitated where the path forked, he placed his palm on the small of her back, guiding her. He kept his hand on her until they reached their destination, liking the feeling of her supple body under his fingers.

He guided her to a small clearing he'd found under the shelter of one of the largest of the redwood trees in the grove. So massive was the tree's girth and the spread of its leaves that the ground around its base was relatively bare except for a soft layer of compacted leafy debris. With the moon just rising overhead in a twilight sky, the setting was perfect for romance.

Grady had thought ahead and had a small lantern ready for when darkness fell completely, but since the moon was nearly full and shining through an opening in the leafy canopy, he didn't think they'd have to use it except perhaps when they made their way back to the encampment...eventually.

He'd taken a thick blanket from his quarters and spread it in the open area, then topped it with a snowy white tablecloth. The glasses, dishes and utensils he'd borrowed from the cooks were set out on top and the meal was waiting. It had been kept warm in self-heating containers the cooking staff had packed for him, ready to serve.

Grady had even gathered a few blossoms from the surrounding forest and placed them in a glass of water at the center of the tablecloth. He knew females appreciated flowers, and he also liked the scent.

Gina turned to him as they reached the clearing, and she saw what he'd arranged. There were tears in her eyes he found hard to interpret, and his heart stilled.

"You don't like it?"

"No, I love it." She bit her lip to still whatever emotion she was feeling while Grady's emotions rode a wave of high and low. He didn't understand. Was she happy or sad?

"Something is wrong?"

"No." She turned to him, placing a hand on his forearm, squeezing once as she looked up at him. "This is the nicest thing anyone's done for me in a very long time. I could almost believe I'm back in the old world, on a picnic. You thought of everything. Flowers, dinner and is that wine?"

"It is." He began to feel better about her reaction, though the tears in her eyes worried him. "Do you like wine?"

"I do. Even living with the *Zxerah*, I don't get to have it often. Only on very special occasions."

"This is a special occasion, Gina."

"Our first and last date." She looked so sad. He had to kiss her. Just once. Just a light brushing of lips to take her mind off whatever he'd done to make her sad.

Grady leaned forward, taking her in his arms at the same moment he claimed her mouth with his. She was as sweet as he remembered, as warm, as delicious in every way. The salt of her tears brought a pang of regret to his heart. He didn't want to think of how little time they had together before they had to part. He pushed that thought aside in the glory of holding her, the feel of her feminine curves that were made to fit so perfectly against his body.

She gasped when he pulled her closer and he took advantage, licking inside her mouth like he wanted to lick her lower down. Soon that wasn't enough. He ran his hands over her lithe body, wishing the fabric that separated them away. Eventually the distraction of her clothing brought him to his senses.

He lifted away from the kiss by gradual degrees, his head spinning in the most amazing way.

"Dinner first," Grady said when he could speak. The smile she gave him tempted him to forget dinner altogether, but good sense won out. For the time being.

He led her to the edge of the blanket, charmed when she kicked off her shoes. He followed suit and assisted her to sit, though in truth she needed no help at all. He didn't want to completely let go of her and the lovely tone they produced when they touched. It vibrated through him, making him feel alive as nothing else. Even the new emotions coursing through him and making his life so very precious these last few months was nothing compared to the sound of their Hum.

"You shouldn't have gone to so much trouble." Her quiet words brought back his wandering attention. "This is really lovely. I haven't been on a picnic in years, and never in such a romantic setting."

"I'm glad you like it." He reached for the wine as he sank to his knees opposite her, across the center of the improvised table setting. Removing the already loosened cork, he poured two glasses of the light-colored vintage.

Dinner progressed from there. They ate slowly, savoring the excellent food, the exceptional company and the beautiful night. Gina enchanted him with her conversation. At first they talked of simple things, recent events and their thoughts about the *Zxerah*. Eventually, they strayed to more emotional topics. Gina told him about her family and her sorrow at losing them. Then she asked him about the experiment and what prompted him to take part. She went further, asking him what he thought would come next and Grady felt a sense of ease, sharing his hopes and fears with this warm, intelligent woman. Her compassion was genuine and easily seen on her beautiful face. She also had some good insights into things that had plagued him.

"It was difficult to accommodate the aggression at first. Warriors are trained to control it, of course. Even that training failed when I felt real anger for the first time," Grady admitted. He'd never discussed this with anyone—not even the techs who had witnessed his near meltdown.

"What did you do?"

"When I started fantasizing about smearing one of the scientist's faces against a wall, I took myself to the gym for some unscheduled training. I pummeled a training droid, all the while imagining it was that scientist." He had to laugh at the memory now. "I actually broke the droid." Gina gasped, then laughed along with him. "I knocked its head clean off. The gym tech said they'd never seen anything like it before."

"We have a few of those things at our home base. They're built solid. I can't believe you did that!"

"Neither could I. The gym tech explained it away, saying the droid must've had a flaw in manufacture, but the lab techs walked wide around me for the next few days. They'd heard the story and had of course been monitoring my levels. I wore sensors at all times in the early days of the experiment. It was actually an adrenaline surge that gave me that momentary strength. The techs were dumbfounded by it at first. Apparently the level was off their charts."

"Oh, I've heard about that kind of thing in humans. In moments of utter rage or dire need, an adrenaline surge can give someone a moment of super strength. It's not common, but in the old world, it did happen."

"Well, it hasn't happened in Alvians—at least not at that level—in generations. They tried to get me to repeat it, but I never could. Frankly, I didn't want to feel that kind of raging anger ever again. I was close to murdering that man. It's not something I'm proud of or want to repeat."

"That says a lot for you, Grady." She raised her glass and drank, watching him over the rim of the stemmed wine glass. "And the fact that you controlled your anger and channeled it into something that wouldn't hurt anyone. Well," her eyes sparkled with merriment, "except for the droid."

She made him feel better about the black moment in his recent past. He even joined in her laughter, charmed by the way she saw the good in what could have been a very dangerous—not to mention deadly—situation.

"You are good for me, Gina. I never thought I would meet a woman like you. Or that such a woman would want to spend time with me. You do, don't you? You'll forgive me if I'm not good at interpreting your preferences. Emotions are new and often confusing to me."

"Don't worry, Grady. I wouldn't be here tonight if I didn't want to spend time with you. If I had more time before my mission, I'd spend it all with you." She put one soft hand on his face, cupping his cheek, and the Hum enveloped his senses in an almost drugging tingle. "I only regret we have so little of it."

He turned his head, kissing the soft palm of her hand with slow deliberateness, holding her gaze. His pulse leapt when her eyes widened and her pupils dilated with pleasure.

"We have tonight. That is something."

"It's not enough."

He moved closer, putting one arm around her shoulders and drawing her near.

"I begin to realize that eternity would never be enough with you, Gina."

A smile tilted her lips. "You say the sweetest things."

He closed the gap between them, kissing her sweetly this time, slow and steady, heady and drugging. He placed his other arm at her waist as her hands slid around his neck, her fingers digging into the short hair at the nape of his neck. It was both ticklish and divine. Never had a woman caressed him in such a way.

He eased her downward, onto the blanket, supporting his weight above her so as not to crush her delicate, delectable body. She made room for him between her legs, spreading them as if to invite him between. He wasted no time taking the offer, placing his hardened cock against the place it most wanted to go. Layers of cloth separated them, but the heat they generated together was undeniable.

Grady felt his temperature spike. He'd been warned about such a reaction by the techs. While it was normal for Alvian physiology to have raised body temperatures during copulation, it seemed that among those in the test group who had indulged in closely monitored sexual activity for the scientists' benefit, the temperature spikes were more intense.

"Gina," he panted, breaking the kiss to look deep into her eyes. "We have only tonight. For this one night, will you be mine?"

She seemed to think about it for a heart-stopping moment, during which he suffered the pangs of uncertainty and a fear of rejection he'd never felt before. She rewarded him with a smile that melted his bones and made his cock even harder, if such a thing were possible.

Gina realized Grady was giving her the choice. He wasn't seducing her into anything. No, if she made love with him, it would be with full consent, knowing what she was doing before he swept her off her feet. She respected him for it, but in one way, she'd rather have had the need for a conscious choice taken out of her hands.

Still, this was best. She knew how new he was to emotions. She knew he needed reassurance that he was reading her correctly. And damn it all, she wanted this. She wanted him. Tomorrow she was going on a mission that could end badly. For tonight, she wanted to cling to these feelings only Grady elicited.

He was something out of her experience—a man who stirred her senses, challenged her mind and who seemed genuinely dazzled by her, though she was by no means a dazzling sort of person. He made her feel that way. Just being around him, seeing that special light in his eyes when he looked at her made her feel special in a way no man—human or Alvian—ever had before.

For this one night she wanted to bask in that wondrous feeling. And if they had to part tomorrow, she wanted to know what it felt like to be with him tonight.

"Yes," she whispered, loving the joy that lit his eyes, the expression of wonder that graced his handsome face. She felt like she'd given him the world. She felt treasured. Cherished even. And it felt good.

She suspected he'd make her feel even better before long, and she couldn't wait to find out. Decision made, she lifted up for his kiss, meeting him halfway with an equal aggression, an equal ardor. She wanted him, and she wasn't going to let anything stand in their way.

Her hands pulled at his clothes and her own, meeting his fingers bent on the same task. Between the two of them, they got the most important parts of their clothing out of the way.

She nearly screamed when he bent to lick her breasts. He tongued one nipple, then the other, even using his teeth in a gentle, provocative bite that set her senses reeling. Nobody had ever handled her so masterfully, owned her so completely.

Not to be left out, she swept her hands over his hard body. He was built like a Greek god, sculpted out of flesh and bone in the most perfect way imaginable. He was big and muscled, but not overly so. He had the lithe physique of a natural fighter, honed by years of study and practice. His abdomen had that ripped texture that she loved, his biceps bulging as he used his arms to keep the majority of his weight off her.

But she wanted it all. Nibbling on his shoulder, she used her teeth, her hands, her entire body to tempt him. His groan of pleasure made her grin, knowing she was getting to him.

"I can't wait." His voice was harsh at her ear, his body hard between her legs as he covered her, pushing her into the ground with his bulk. She loved it. He was powerful and rugged, the way a man should be, and his huge frame shuddered with anticipation...of her.

He was shaking—just slightly—for her. It was a silent, stark statement of his need and it touched her more deeply than all the words he could have said. He needed her. And she craved him in return.

"Don't wait. Do it, Grady. Hard and fast." The whispered words were barely out of her mouth before he pushed inside, forceful and deep, just as she wanted.

He thrust, pumping into her with strong movements, sending the fire of passion through every nerve ending she possessed. Each thrust made her gasp and he held her gaze throughout. She could see in his eyes the overwhelming fury of his desire, paired with the concern, regret and joy along with even more complex emotions.

It was the emotion in his gaze that touched her heart. She looked into his eyes as he took possession of her body and her responses. She could see his struggle for control down to the flicker of an eyelash. When his eyes narrowed as he neared his crisis point, her own body followed suit. She was perfectly attuned to his every move, his every silent command. He owned her body and her passion.

Short digs made her think he would never be apart from her again.

"I can't hold it. It's never been—" he panted, his gaze going in and out of focus as he tried to withhold his climax.

"Ssh. I know. Same for me." She cupped his cheek as he pounded home once again, his massive body dwarfing hers, simultaneously pushing her up and deeper into the loamy ground beneath the blanket. "It's never been this good. Make me fly, Grady."

The last was said on a gasping cry as her climax overtook her, almost too fast to keep up with. She'd told the truth. She'd never come so hard or so quickly for any other men. Not that there'd been a lot to compare him with, but a few. And they all lacked in comparison to this hurried, desperate coupling under a canopy of leaves, stars and dappled moonlight. No other experience could equal this. She had a feeling nothing ever would.

They came together twice more in the night, dozing in between, naked under the stars. It was a breezy night. Grady cuddled her and eventually used the tablecloth to cover her like a blanket, while the actual blanket kept them warm and dry beneath.

Grady was a considerate lover. He made certain she was ready for him before sliding home and pumping for what seemed hours, making her come over and over before finding his own pleasure in her body. He encouraged her to be creative and she rode him during one of their more memorable climaxes, bouncing hard against his thighs, shouting her delight to the moon.

They lay together deep in the night and slept in each other's arms. When the sunlight roused them, Grady took her again, loving her slow and long, drawing out the pleasure, to hold against the future when they would be parted.

As they dressed and packed up, Gina felt sad. She'd only just found this wonderful man and within hours, she'd be leaving, perhaps never to see him again.

"What's wrong?" Grady Prime was observant, she'd give him that. For all that he was new to having and interpreting emotions, he was getting very good at it.

"Just thinking about things I can't change." She tried to put a brave face on it, but apparently failed when he drew closer, pulling her into a loose embrace. His eyes, when she met them, were filled with determination.

"I will find you again, Gina. I will come for you, no matter where you are or what you are doing. You're mine." His possessive words shocked her. "I'll give you some time to get used to the idea, but remember this—I have never failed to track down a target and you just rose to the top of my list."

"I'm not your enemy, Grady." She made a small attempt at humor though her heart was in turmoil.

His lips brushed lightly over hers, and she struggled to focus.

"Never that, little one. But I will be your mate. Mark my words and do not forget me while you pursue your duty. As soon as I am free to do so and you have had time to come to terms with my claim, I'll come for you, Gina. Even the Patriarch cannot stand in the way of true mates. It is our oldest and most sacred law."

"You believe so strongly that I'm your mate? How can you know this soon?"

"My race has done it this way for centuries. A Hum, a Kiss, an Embrace. That's all we need to recognize our perfect mate. I believe in my heart that you're it for me, Gina." He released her fully, though his gaze stayed locked with hers. "We will do the tests so you can see the proof, when I return. For now, think of me as you go about your mission. I'll most certainly be thinking of you."

Chapter Five

There was no one in her life that Gina respected more than the *Zxerah* Patriarch. He'd taken her in and given her a home when all she'd ever known had been destroyed. He and his followers had protected her when she could no longer protect herself. She owed him. But more than that, she loved him like the family she'd lost. He was part father, part protective brother at times, and he made her feel secure. It was unfortunate that he could never return the sentiment.

He was Alvian and therefore emotionless. Even the *Zxerah* had embraced the genetic alterations that had changed the rest of the Alvian population from almost ferally aggressive to completely unemotional in a matter of a few generations. The *Zxerah* had rushed to embrace the genetic changes that they now realized were detrimental to the further existence and evolution of the Alvian race. Now the *Zxerah* embraced a new strategy. They worked behind the scenes—as they always had in Alvian society—for change. Big change.

And Gina was going to be instrumental in the first steps of that change. Or so she had been informed by the Patriarch. He'd come to her weeks ago with a mission she was loath to reject. In fact, she relished the idea of being among the first to set the wheels in motion that could save both their races—Alvian and human alike.

"Your skills and your temperament are perfect for this mission, Gina. And Eve says too, it must be you, though I would have chosen you for your skill even without her input." The Patriarch had given her a smile, though it lacked true emotion. He'd once explained he felt echoes of emotion that sometimes plagued him—most often longing for something he couldn't understand.

Eve was another adopted human member of the clan who had a

strong gift of prophecy, and it was her gift that often guided the Patriarch in his seemingly quixotic moves. Gina had just a touch of foresight herself, and she'd felt the rightness of his request that she take on this mission. Though she might very well be going into a lion's den, she knew she was the right person for the job. Why? She couldn't say exactly. But this was as it should be.

"I understand, Patriarch." She had bowed her head, but hadn't broken eye contact—a show of utmost respect.

"You must make contact with these people and put them in touch with the others. It is vital they discover each other's existence and learn to work together in whatever small ways they can as soon as possible. Things are moving fast. We must all be ready when the time comes."

"Yes, Patriarch. I'll do my best."

"You will succeed, daughter."

Gina had stilled. He'd never called her that before. It was a sign of respect reserved for those students granted the highest rankings in the *Zxerah* way. Gina had come to the *Zxerah* as an adult, already highly trained in traditional human martial arts. The way of the *Zxerah* was even more intense. She'd learned a great deal in the years since her adoption into the clan, but none of the human adoptees had ever been granted the title of daughter or son of the clan. It was a high honor and totally unexpected.

Tears had gathered in her eyes. She had refused to let them fall. The Patriarch had noticed anyway and a kind smile graced his face.

"You deserve the honor, Gina. You are the best of the human students in our clan. And it is good to see evidence that this honor touches your emotions, though I cannot fully comprehend such things. It gives me...hope...if the ancient ones allow me to take such a word to describe the echoes I feel when I look into your eyes. I pray all our clan will one day be able to feel as you and your human brethren do."

"I hope so too, Patriarch. We human *Zxerah* will keep the flame of hope alive for you until you can join us in feeling its warmth."

He had grasped her hands and she felt the tingle of his power. He wasn't an old man, but he was one of the holiest, strongest, most powerful and at peace beings she'd ever known. He had vision. Not the kind granted to some psychic humans. It was a powerful, non-psychic kind of vision. He knew what he wanted and believed in his convictions strongly enough to act on them in a way that would change not only his life or his clansmen's lives, but the lives of all Alvians and humans on earth. He was a visionary with no psychic gifts. Only the power of his own beliefs.

It was enough.

It had to be.

Gina set out on her mission later that morning. She had said farewell to Grady Prime as they left the small clearing that had been their own private Eden for the night. He was utterly devastating, but she had a mission to perform that was more important than anything else. No matter how much she might wish otherwise.

She felt his eyes on her as she left the compound accompanied by the two winged soldiers the Patriarch and Sinclair Prime had chosen for this mission. The team of winged brethren was tasked with flying her across the many miles she had to traverse. They would take turns carrying her short distances, then they would rest a few moments and tackle the next leg of the journey.

Hanlon was a strawberry blond who would be cute if he ever smiled and Shaugness had dark blond hair and a constantly dour expression. This was the first time, to her knowledge, that the winged brethren had been asked to work closely with one of the human adoptees. She knew they were curious about her—as curious as they could be, seeing that they had little emotion to call their own—but they didn't ask any questions other than to inquire how she was holding up every once in a while.

To be honest, she loved flying. It was an amazing feeling to be as free as a bird and see things from above as the hawks and eagles must perceive them. It made her long for wings of her own. Of course that was impossible.

She tried not to think about Grady. Being carried like a satchel across vast expanses of woodland without the ability to talk easily to her companions while in the air made for a lot of time alone with her thoughts. She wondered where he was and what he was doing. She wondered when she would see him again—if ever. And mostly, she wondered if a relationship with a warrior Prime was even possible for someone like her. They both had limitations. She was a secret inductee in a secret society. He was a closely monitored experimental test subject. How in the world could a relationship between them work? And did he really want a relationship, or was he being a romantic fool, carried away by the moment and the new emotions bombarding his system?

She grew depressed thinking that in all likelihood he'd find some other woman before they ever saw each other again. A hunk like him wouldn't go unclaimed for long. Not if the Alvian females got wind of how truly gifted he was in the sack. She'd never had better. Heck, she'd never even *dreamed* of anything better than Grady Prime, between her legs, pumping them both into ecstasy. She shivered, just remembering the climaxes he'd given her. They were that good.

And likely never to be repeated. After a while, she decided to chalk it up to a great memory and try to get on with her mission. She had a complicated road to walk over the next weeks and thoughts of Grady, and what might never be between them, could only cause her problems. She had to focus. Things were bound to get dangerous in the next few days, and she had to be on her best game.

She only let herself think of Grady deep in the night, when she was preparing for sleep. She said a little prayer for him, hoping he was safe and hoping he'd meant what he said about finding her one day. It would be nice to see him again, she decided. Even if he'd moved on. But if he hadn't...

She was making herself crazy with thoughts of him. She had to coax herself to sleep each night when she and the winged brethren made camp.

After a few days of near constant travel, they had arrived near their destination. They'd flown through mountain passes that allowed them to keep their altitude as low as possible. It was still heady. The air had been thin and the temperatures cold, but the high tech fabric of her uniform had been designed by Alvian materials engineers to withstand worse. The Patriarch himself had overseen her supply and had given her the best clothing and equipment, though her most valuable assets were her martial arts skills and her mind.

The same mind that plagued her with thoughts of Grady when she least expected them. She'd replayed their night together in her memory many times as the soldiers flew her through the sky.

She couldn't go on this way—distracted by memories of a man

who frankly scared her now that she had time to think about it. She had important work to do. She had to at least try to scour him from her mind and concentrate on the work at hand.

Hanlon set her down after the final leg they would travel together and gave her the smallest lift of one side of his mouth. She was right. He was charming when he smiled.

"We are instructed to go no farther with you. You will walk from here."

"I know," she said, smiling back and earning a quizzical look from the handsome angel. That's how she thought of them. Angels. Though she tried hard not to call them that to their faces. But what else could they be? Tall, gorgeous, fair-haired and muscular with *wings*, for cripes' sake. Those were angels in her book all right. "Thank you for taking me this far. I really enjoyed flying with you and Shaugness. It is an experience I will never forget."

"It was our duty." He didn't seem to understand the concept of gratitude, but he was so cute, she couldn't resist teasing him.

Gina stood on tiptoe and placed a kiss on his cheek that brought even more puzzlement to his eyes. She giggled. It felt good. She hadn't had a lot to laugh about in recent years.

"Duty or not, flying is amazing. You are a very lucky man, and I thank you for sharing that with me. Have a safe journey back and please thank Shaugness for me too."

"You're welcome," he said belatedly. They'd left Shaugness at the last stopping point where he'd made a small camp. Hanlon would fly back to meet him. They would rest a day or two, then begin the arduous journey back.

He left her without further ado, and Gina got down to the business at hand. She had a trek through the wilderness ahead of her and more than likely a confrontation of epic proportions when she reached her destination. She checked the compass on her wrist chronometer and oriented herself with the landscape. It looked very different from the ground, but she knew where she was.

She set out hiking and hoped she'd reach her destination within a few hours.

It was actually only three hours later when Gina recognized the first of the monitors that had been set around the perimeter of the old base. Her target was the old NORAD installation in the mountains of what had once been Colorado. The Patriarch and the seers believed there was a group of humans holed up inside the high security facility and it was her job to make contact.

The human inhabitants weren't going to make her job easy.

She'd managed to go minutes at a time without thinking about her encounter with Grady Prime, which was an improvement. The silent forest weighed on her. She loved the outdoors, but the solitude sometimes led to too much introspection. This was one of those times when she wasn't comfortable being left alone with only her thoughts for company. Grady Prime's kisses were still fresh in her mind.

The very idea that an Alvian could possess emotions was foreign to her. Foreign and intriguing, God help her. Grady Prime was attractive in every way. She knew he was of the highest rank in one of the top soldier lines, but she'd never seen him fight. Gina surmised that he would be a gifted opponent in the sparring ring from the way he moved and used his body. She'd been around martial artists her entire life and found it a good way to judge men. The way they acted and reacted in the *dojo* often reflected the way they lived their lives.

She would never get a chance to learn that about him, and regretted it. The timing was all off. Neither of them was free to pursue the magic between them. And, oh, what magic it had been. For a little while, Grady Prime had made her forget everything. That he was Alvian didn't matter. The world around them had ceased to exist and only the two of them mattered.

His lips on hers, his warm body pressing against hers, his passion, his emotion. It was all she needed and all she wanted.

There was more to her life now than that. More obligations. More duties. She couldn't afford the distraction—and he was one hell of a distraction—of this complicated thing called a relationship.

They both had secrets to keep and people watching them. Gina couldn't come out into the open in Alvian society. Not while the rest of the *Zxerah* remained hidden. For one thing, she was human and therefore perceived as inferior—fit only for imprisonment and study. She would never be accepted into the Alvian-dominated world, even for Grady Prime's sake. He couldn't keep a pet human. It just wasn't done.

For another, Grady Prime's life was monitored on a much closer level than other Alvians. He'd volunteered for a genetic study and that meant his life was no longer his own. He was at the beck and call of the High Council and the scientific community. He would never be permitted to be with her.

Resolved, Gina strode through the forest, aware of the tripwires and other devices monitoring her progress toward the hidden cave.

Gina made it to the entrance to the old tunnel system that led to the underground facility. It was dark—inside and out. Night had fallen and there was only a sliver of moon. Its illumination didn't reach inside the old tunnel complex. Gina walked into the darkness, sensing the others there...waiting. Clearly this was an ambush, but there was no other way. She controlled her breathing, ready for anything.

A fist came at her, out of the dark.

Gina ducked and spun, coming up fighting as her opponent engaged. She was fighting blind. She'd trained to do this many times in her youth, and many more since then in her time with the *Zxerah*. Her psychic gifts also allowed her to sense displacement in the air. That skill usually helped her stay well ahead of the blows headed her way. Her opponent either had to be as telekinetically gifted as she or else he was using night vision goggles or something similar. There was no hesitation in his strikes or his blocks. He was one hell of a fighter, whoever he was.

Gina marveled at his skill even as she spun into a flying roundhouse kick aimed at his head.

"Hold!"

It was the single command given in the proper tone of voice that would stop Gina dead in her tracks, as she'd been trained since childhood to do in her father's *dojo*. She landed and stood ready, waiting, prepared for anything that might come at her out of the darkness.

"Lord help me, but I'd know that flying roundhouse anywhere." The man's voice stirred a distant memory. "Is there a Hanson under that ninja suit?"

"Show yourself." Gina whispered, careful to keep her voice husky and low.

A flame flared in the darkness and a torch was thrown down in front of her. Gina wasn't fool enough to follow the torch's progress. Instead, she protected her night vision as best she could, seeking the shadowy man who stood some distance in front of her in the darkness.

The man strode forward into the small pool of light created by the torch. His face was only a little older than she remembered, his eyes even harder than they'd been when he'd trained with her father. She knew this man. He'd been one of the elite the government had sent to study with her father—one of the few men who had caught her eye when she was just a teenager, striving to compete for Olympic gold.

He'd been a defender of the innocent in those days. Some kind of top secret operative she hadn't been supposed to meet, but had run across from time to time as he came and went from her father's studio. On one memorable occasion, she'd been part of an advanced class he'd participated in. He was a good fighter. Honorable and fair. It was good to see his skills hadn't diminished over the years.

But was he the same man of honor her father had trained? Many years had passed. He looked roughly the same, thanks to the aliens changing their DNA to slow everyone's aging. She needed to know what kind of man he was on the inside.

There was really only one way to find out.

Gina took off her mask and held his eyes as she bowed. The shock written plain on his face was almost comical. The joy that followed made her feel warm inside.

"My God, little Gina Hanson. I thought you must be long dead."

"A touch of foresight saved my life."

"And the rest of your family?"

"I don't know." She dropped her hands to her sides. "I was traveling when the bombardment started. I never made it home, and I don't know what happened to them."

"Then how—" He cut himself off, remembering their circumstances. This girl had always had a way of ruining his concentration, though when he'd known her, she'd been only a charming teenager, well protected by her family and totally off limits. "Forgive me." He stepped back and gave the signal to his men.

Lights flared and the chamber came to life. He watched Gina blink in the sudden light and take in her surroundings. She was just as petite as he remembered, though there was no doubt she was fully grown. She had the curvaceous figure of a woman and the sleek muscles of a fighter under her close-fitting black garb. The fabric was of alien origin he saw immediately. He had to tread lightly. For all he knew, she was an Alvian spy. He had more than just his own life to think about.

"I'd love to reminisce about old times, but that will have to wait." He hated the wary look that entered her lovely dark eyes, but he had to think of his people before his own desires. "How did you find the tunnels and why are you here?"

"I got the schematics of this place from one of its smaller partner sites. There's an old NORAD installation in California. I've lived there for the past few years, under the protection of a secret sect of Alvians called the *Zxerah*. They're sort of like old world ninjas. They answer only to the Alvian High Council and sometimes not even them. The Patriarch of the *Zxerah* has known about this network of installations for a long time."

"Then why haven't they come for us before? And why send you? Are you the scout for a larger invasion force?"

"The *Zxerah* have no interest in capturing humans. They took me in, and I've lived and trained with them as a member of their clan since just after the cataclysm. They have quite a number of human adoptees in the clan. One of them is a gifted visionary, and she works directly for the Patriarch. She foresaw it was the right time to act, to put all the enclaves of humans in touch with one another. I'm the one she said had to be sent. And now I understand why...it's because of you, Jim. We knew each other in the old world."

"I knew your father and your oldest brother. You were just a shadow in the *dojo*—a pretty face that looked good wearing a gold medal at the Olympics. I didn't really *know* you." Her face crumpled at his harsh words, but he had to take her measure. "I'm willing to listen, Gina."

"That's all we ask."

"We?"

"You have allies you can't even imagine, Jim. The resistance is building and every day more Alvians see the light. They've begun experimenting on themselves—returning emotion to selected volunteers among their population. Do you ever wonder why the only humans who survived had some kind of extra-sensory ability?"

Her change of subject caught him unawares. "Of course I've wondered. Do you know the answer?"

Gina stepped closer to him, putting herself into his personal sphere. "We all have some of their DNA. The Alvians sent an expeditionary group here centuries before the rest of them arrived. Those early explorers never made it back to Alvia. Instead, they settled here and mingled with the locals. We're the result. Didn't you ever wonder why the Alvians shared so much in common with our mythology about elves? As near as I can guess, the explorers mostly settled in Northern Europe and the DNA spread to every corner of the globe from there."

"No shit?" That certainly would explain a lot.

"Apparently when Alvian and human DNA mix, the result is something altogether new to both races. Telepathy, foresight, telekinesis, healing, you name it, we've got it. They've been running experiments. One of their top female researchers even had a child by a human. He's more powerful than any of us psychically. From all accounts, the kid's like the second coming of Merlin or something."

"He's half alien. Where do his loyalties lie?"

"He has full human emotions and was raised by his human family. Where do you think?"

Jim liked the way Gina challenged him. Holy shit. Little Gina Hanson had survived. Not only was she alive and kicking with Olympic Gold Medal accuracy, she was all grown up and a knockout in more ways than one. He had a hard time concentrating on what she was saying, distracted by her ultra-feminine form under that space-age black suit that hugged every hot curve.

"It's almost dinner time. Let's discuss this over a meal. What do you say?"

"I wouldn't turn down food. Thanks for the invitation." Gina smiled and it nearly took his breath away. He had to concentrate on business. Gina Hanson was just a kid. Or...she had been a kid when he'd known her all those years ago. With the way the Alvians had monkeyed with everyone's DNA, nobody aged anymore—or at least not much.

The gap between them didn't seem so vast anymore. After all, it was the mileage sometimes, not the years, and every human survivor had been through hell and back in the years since the cataclysm.

He made a few discrete hand signals to his top lieutenants and ushered Gina into the first ring. He wouldn't let her any deeper into the complex until he was sure of her, but this would do for now. There was a room they'd turned into a conference room that could be used, and a secure bunk where he could house her for the night, if necessary. And he thought it would be necessary. No way was he letting Gina Hanson out of here now. She was a puzzle he wanted to solve—with her Alvian clothing and claims of friendship with some secret ninja sect. Either she was completely batty or she was the messenger his friend Tory had claimed would come.

Nobody put much store in Tory's visions. The poor woman had been driven insane when her baby had died, but she was still the strongest foreseer in his group. He heard her words, though he took them with a grain of salt. Half the time she rambled. The other half...well, he'd learned a thing or two from those rare moments of clarity.

There weren't many women in his group, but he demanded they be treated with respect. Even crazy Tory. They fed her, gave her a place to stay and work to occupy her hands. Her mind was another thing entirely. Jim had heard there were mind healers, but he'd never met one. If he ever came across one though, he'd do anything to get some help for Tory. Nobody deserved torture like she went through on a daily basis, constantly reliving the death of her beloved baby.

Luckily Tory wasn't among the group that brought food from below for the impromptu feast. Jim signaled his command group to stay. They all should hear what Gina had to say so they could discuss it later. Plus, each of his men had different talents. Pierre, for instance, was gifted at telling lies from truth, while Max had a touch of empathy that often came in handy.

Gina seemed comfortable among his men, though most women nowadays had reason to fear any group of strange males. Women were scarce and though he hated to admit it, a lot of men had turned into animals.

He knew Gina could defend herself. Maybe not against a crowd, but certainly against a few rogues. For that reason, perhaps, she didn't walk with the fear Jim saw all too often in women these days.

She dropped her small pack on the table and pushed it toward him as she sat.

"Feel free to look through it. I've got some rations, water, a map and spare socks in there."

Jim motioned to one of his men who flicked the satchel open with

Bianca D'Arc

his mind. If it was booby-trapped nobody needed to lose a finger or hand. The bag floated into the air and was upended over the table. Out dropped the items she'd claimed would be there. Nothing more was revealed when Larry showed off his fine-tuned telekinetic skill, turning the bag inside out with his mind. He dropped it on Jim's signal and Gina picked it up, using a pull of her own telekinesis to draw the bag and objects to her side of the table. Apparently she didn't have—or didn't want to expose—the same deftness Larry had shown.

"That was pretty cool," she said, nodding at Larry. Gina turned the bag right side out the old-fashioned way and stuffed her possessions back with her hands.

Larry smiled at her, tipping the brim of his hat as Jim watched uncomfortably. The bastard was flirting with her and it irked the hell out of him.

"Back to business." Jim shot a glare at Larry.

"Aren't you going to search me?" The comically innocent blink of her big brown eyes set Jim's teeth on edge. He had to hand it to her—she hadn't lost that infamous mischievous Hanson sense of humor.

"I'd volunteer for that dangerous duty, sir," Larry said immediately as Pierre and Max cursed him jokingly.

"Thanks." Jim shook his head, not amused. "That won't be necessary at the moment. Gina," he warned her, "behave."

She bristled, but the smile lingered. Still, she'd effectively broken the ice. The plates were passed around and food deposited in the center of the table as others brought it to the conference room's door. They peered in, trying to get a look at the newcomer. This meeting was for command staff only and nobody else was invited to stay. They'd hear about it soon enough, once he'd had a chance to question Gina.

A commotion at the door drew all their attention and Jim cursed under his breath to see Tory there, her hair a mess, her eyes hollow. She was in one of her crazy moods. He hated seeing her this way. He tried to intercept her but Tory only had eyes for Gina.

"I saw you," she accused in a broken whisper.

Gina stood, moving closer to the distraught woman. Her gentle words surprised them all. "I saw you too. Come here, Victoria."

Gina held out her arms and the other woman rushed into them. Gina shushed her as she would a child when Tory's body trembled and her arms wrapped around Gina, clinging for comfort. Gina put her

84

hands over Tory's head and murmured soothing sounds. Even Jim could feel there was something more going on. Tory quieted quicker than she ever did when she was in one of these wild moods, and Jim could reach no other conclusion than it was another of Gina's talents at work.

"You're a mind healer too?" He heard the note of awe in his own voice. Mind healers were rare. He'd never met one.

Gina met his eyes over Tory's trembling head. "Only a touch. I'm a jack-of-all-trades psychically. Master of none. But I can help calm her until we can get her to someone who really can help. My brother Bryan was the truly gifted one in the family." She kept her tone gentle and calm, stroking Tory's wild hair into some semblance of order until the woman quieted.

When Tory pulled back, she was more lucid than Jim had ever seen her.

"I saw you in a vision. You're going to bring the angel to us."

And there she went, Jim thought with a grimace. Talking about angels again. A quick look at Gina's face didn't show the disdain he figured she'd feel at such a wild claim. Instead, she smiled kindly.

"I will, Victoria. If your leader here is willing to listen." She cocked her head at him, sending a smile that warmed him straight down to his toes. Tory, too, was looking at him, a graceful blush staining her cheeks. She would be a pretty woman, he suddenly realized, if she could ever get over the horrors of her past.

"You need to listen to her," Tory said as she let go of Gina and walked toward the door—toward Jim. Her eyes were earnest and thankfully sane. "She's going to bring great changes to us all. They'll be good changes—or at least—the chance for good. We'll need to take a stand soon. She'll help." Tory looked back and smiled at Gina once more. "And the angels."

Jim didn't know what to make of Tory's ramblings. He didn't believe in angels. Tory seemed to be obsessed with them lately. And Gina didn't seem to think Tory's words were all that farfetched. Maybe it was worth thinking about. Perhaps the angel was a metaphor for something else. Sometimes visions played out that way.

Tory left, much calmer than she'd arrived and everyone sat. Gina looked a little worse for the interlude. Jim knew healers often gave their own energy to help others. Mind healing was rumored to be even more draining.

"Are you okay, Gina?"

She looked down at her plate, then nodded. "I'll be fine. The food will help." She began to eat steadily, and Jim let her be. She'd need strength for the questioning ahead.

"*What do you think, guys?*" Jim sent the private telepathic message to his command staff. One by one, they gave their opinions of the woman and the situation while she ate quietly.

"*She's hot. And she has skills,*" Pierre said. Jim had noticed the appreciative way the French Canadian watched Gina move. "*So far, she hasn't spoken a single untruth. Her aura is pure and as powerful as any I've seen. Beautiful really.*"

"*Her emotions read true too. Her response to Tory nearly broke my heart. And Tory's response to her healing was amazing to feel. The girl is truly gifted, though I tend to believe her when she says she's not a specialist in mind healing. She felt genuine regret at not being able to do more,*" Max, the empath of the group, reported. "*And I think she's attracted to you, boss. She gets nervous every time you look at her. It's feminine nerves, not the nervousness of a liar.*"

"*Her telekinetic push was sloppy. That of a novice,*" Larry reported. "*She does have some power in that direction. I think she was using it when she fought you. Probably in conjunction with her martial arts skill. Some can use it to sense proximity and that kind of thing. Takes a lot of focus to learn to use telekinesis that way, but it can be done.*"

"*All right. Stay sharp guys,*" Jim warned his top men. "*I knew her when she was a kid, but not well. I trained with her father and brothers for a year. They were master martial artists, and she learned everything they could teach her. Don't let her size or gender fool you. She was going easy on us in the cavern. She could take any one of us down if we underestimate her.*"

"*I thought I recognized her,*" Max said. "*She was on the U.S. Olympic team, wasn't she? Won a gold medal and had her picture on the cereal boxes there for a while.*"

"*Yep. Little Gina Hanson, black belt extraordinaire. She won the medal for* tae kwon do. *Her dad taught all kinds of mixed martial arts in his dojo. Don't expect her to play by the rules if you get in a fight.*"

When she'd cleaned her plate and sat back, she did look better. Jim watched her closely, as did his men.

"Are you guys through talking about me?" She dared them all with the saucy challenge and the others grinned while Jim merely raised one eyebrow in her direction.

"Yeah, I think we're through for now. Are you telepathic at all?"

"*A little.*" She broadcast the thought to everyone in the room. "Like I said, I have a lot of small talents, but no real specialty. I get a vision every once in a while. They're not usually very strong. I can move things with my mind, but not very accurately. Not like Larry over there."

"How'd you know his name?" Jim asked with suspicion.

Chapter Six

"Your name is really Larry?" The surprise on her face was easy to see when Larry nodded in response to her question. "Jeez. I was calling you three Moe, Larry and Curly in my mind since you didn't bother with introductions." She laughed at her own joke, and the men joined in to varying degrees.

"My three stooges are Max, Larry and Pierre," Jim clarified, pointing to each as he introduced them. "Back to you—what else can you do?"

Her attention shifted away from the men and back to Jim. "I can talk telepathically over short distances." She sighed, looking at her hands. "I guess the thing I'm best at is healing, but even there, I'm not great. Nothing like my dad or brothers. They were truly gifted."

"How about we start at the beginning. We all probably saw news reports of you with a gold medal around your neck. Where were you when the crystal bombs started to fall and what did you do after that?"

"Man," she pushed her chair back and got comfortable. "You really want to delve into ancient history, huh? Okay. Well, let's see. I was in California, doing a publicity tour for the presidential children's athletics drive when the bombardment started. I called my dad and managed to talk to him for a few minutes before all hell broke loose. I'd had a dream a few hours before it started while I was sleeping in my hotel room. I don't really remember the specifics of the dream. I woke knowing I had to get to higher ground. I got in the rental car—I didn't even check out—and ran for the hills. I warned my family back East using my mobile phone, but I was only able to tell them that something was coming and to take cover. I didn't know what was coming. I'd never felt anything so strongly as the urge to run. I told them I loved them." Her voice caught. "And that I'd be in touch again when we were all safe." She looked at her hands through the retelling. Every man in the room could feel her sorrow—empathic or not. "The crystals took out the satellites and cell towers and the earthquakes and tsunamis did the rest. I never talked to my family again. I made it up into the hills just in time."

She was quiet a moment, and Jim let her have the time to regroup. They all had painful memories of that time. He didn't want to intentionally cause her pain by reopening those wounds, but he needed to know.

"I kept driving as long as I could. I found a gas station or two along the way to refuel as I got deeper and deeper into the mountains. I just knew I had to keep going. Eventually I had to take cover, and my rental car was demolished by a huge crystal shard. I went on foot then, trying to stay clear of the path of destruction. I wandered for days—maybe weeks—before coming upon other humans. We walked together for a little while. Then some of the men turned ugly. I was the only woman in the group. I knocked the snot out of two of them and took off on my own. That happened a few times. I lost track of time. I was drinking out of streams and eating berries and leaves. My strength was pretty low when I saw my first Alvian."

"Did you fight the alien?" Jim asked, wondering how that confrontation had gone. Gina didn't look tough on the outside, but he knew she had skills few human men could match.

"Not at first. He watched me like a bug. Like he'd never seen anything like me before. It pissed me off, but I was so weak. He spoke a little English, which I thought was weird, but was glad for at that moment. He gave me water and something to eat, then when he called his companions out of cover and tried to have them take me into custody, I went ballistic on them."

"How many?" Larry asked.

"There were five of them. It was the weirdest thing. After their initial group response, the leader called some commands to them in their language and they came at me one by one, like they were testing my limits. Each one tried a different tactic—a different style of fighting. I felt like I was back in my dad's *dojo*, taking some kind of elaborate test. And these guys could fight. They were as good as my dad or better."

Jim knew that was really saying something. "What happened? Did

89

they finally wear you down and capture you?"

"Oh, they wore me down all right. I was weak to begin with. By the end of it I wasn't captured so much as adopted. The leader was the *Zxerah* Patriarch. The fighters were his students. These guys weren't interested in capturing humans. They'd gone out into the wilderness with the express purpose of finding some and seeing what we were like. It was pure fate they ran into me first. And I do mean fate. These guys are like highly skilled Tibetan monks. That's the closest analogy I can come up with. Even that doesn't fit completely. The *Zxerah* are a secret clan of Alvians that have existed for centuries in complete anonymity. The only Alvians that know they exist for sure are the Alvian High Council and those they allow to have contact with the Patriarch and his people. The *Zxerah* spend their entire lives training and teaching fighting skills to other warriors. When they go out among the Alvian army, they're introduced simply as advanced teachers. Nobody knows where they come from or where they go, and the Council keeps it that way."

"What does the Council get in return for keeping their secret?" Jim asked.

"The best assassins money can't buy," she answered bluntly. "*Zxerah* never miss."

"*Merde*," Pierre cursed, clearly shocked by the idea. "A secret Alvian hit squad? And you're friends with them?"

"More than friends," she admitted. "I'm a member of the clan. They adopted me and a few other humans they protect. Even the Council doesn't know the *Zxerah* have been interacting with humans almost from their first day on this planet."

"Why would they do that? I mean, what makes them different from the rest of their kind who want to put us in pens?" Jim didn't know if he believed her. A quick check with his team told him she wasn't lying.

"The *Zxerah* value innovation," she said. "They've come to believe that psychic abilities are the manifestation of the next logical evolution of both our species. The Patriarch also believes that by breeding emotion out of his people, they've made a giant mistake. He studies these things—population growth and sustainability—and he thinks that unless the process is altered, his race is doomed."

That idea sank in for a moment while Jim thought about the

implications. This could be big—if the Patriarch was someone they could work with.

"You've lived with these *Zxerah* since then? You've spent decades with them, right? Can you tell me why nobody ages anymore?"

"Oh, yeah. That was a surprise even to the Patriarch," Gina said. "He discovered well after the fact that one of the lead Alvian scientists discovered lost Alvian DNA in certain humans she was studying. It turns out all human survivors have some amount of Alvian DNA and it was a simple matter for their geneticists to design a treatment that would turn on the Alvian aging gene that was dormant in us all. The scientists figured it would give them more time to study us, so they disseminated the treatment planet-wide. It was an airborne thing that eventually infected us all. That's why our aging slowed. We age like Alvians now, and they live several hundred years."

"If that don't beat all," Max murmured.

"Your Patriarch sent you here for something." Jim brought the conversation back on track. "What did you hope to accomplish?"

"I've been sent out from time to time over the past decades. Always in secret and always to advance the Patriarch's own secret agenda. Most often, I've gone out to rescue human women who were being mistreated by their males. I've also been used to find other human martial artists and bring them into the *Zxerah* fold. Seems more than a few remember my face from the Olympics and the ad campaigns that came after. We have a small cadre of human fighters that had some training in martial arts before the cataclysm and have since been taught *Zxerah* fighting styles. We train hard every day. We're as good as the Alvian *Zxerah* and in some notable instances, even better. When the Patriarch realized the difference that made humans better at the ancient *Zxerah* arts than his own people, he decided on his current course of action."

"What was the difference? And what's his course of action?"

"The difference is heart." Her gaze held his as she made her revelation. "Emotion makes the difference. Too much emotion is not good in a fighter, but the Patriarch believes that too little emotion is just as detrimental to his brethren. His current course of action is to do everything he can to return emotion to his people. Like I said before, some Alvian scientists are already experimenting with such things. It's the Patriarch's plan to help those experiments along as best he can from the shadows. More than that, he's vowed to help protect humanity because he sees no future for his own people without humans too. He believes a blending of our races is what will save them both—eventually."

"Then why come here? We're one small enclave, and we don't get too involved in what goes on outside our complex."

"Your group is one of many, Jim. There are other strongholds, like this one, scattered around the world. A large number of them are on the North American continent. The Patriarch sent me to try to put you in touch with the others. I'm hoping yours will be the first to reach out to another encampment of humans—if you're willing to take the chance. Eventually, all the different groups of humans could be organized into a real resistance working in concert with each other, if and when necessary."

Jim sat back, regarding her steadily. "That's a mighty tall order, sweetheart. Many of our folk don't want anything to do with the outside world. A lot of them barely made it here and this place represents safety. Opening it up to others puts them at risk, and I'd hazard to say many of them won't want to take that risk."

Gina sighed deeply as she seemed to consider his words. "I see your difficulty. There's got to be some way to bring you together—at least into communication with each other—without jeopardizing everyone's safety."

"We can't decide something this big in a matter of hours. Maybe not even in a couple of days." Jim stood and his men followed suit. "I hope you planned on staying a while. We have some guest quarters nearby where you can sleep. There'll be a guard. Sorry for that, but by your own admission, you've been consorting with Alvians. To us they're still the enemy."

"I understand." Gina stood and followed the men out the door and down the hall. Max, Larry and Pierre said their farewells and stayed in the hallway, but Jim followed her right into the guest quarters.

"So what now?"

Gina turned to face Jim—a man she had secretly admired when she was a teenager. Heck, if she were being honest with herself, she would admit to the huge crush she'd had on him. He'd been a hottie then and things had only improved with time. He was tall, muscular and lean in the way martial artists often were, only he carried himself with more assurance than any man she'd ever known outside her own family.

Jim had that indefinable something that made him nearly irresistible. She stacked him up in her mind against her dad and brothers and knew he could have held his own with the men she admired most—both intellectually and physically. He'd been a talented fighter when she'd first seen him in the gym training with her dad. After only a few months of her father's instruction, he was a force to be reckoned with.

She'd watched him from afar, even though she'd known better. Her dad was the specialist the CIA had sent certain people to when they needed extra training. Only the most gifted athletes and operatives were sent and more failed at the rigorous training program her father subjected them to than passed. Jim was one of the latter. He'd not only passed the months of training, but he'd earned *Sensei* Hanson's respect.

The object of her thoughts closed the door firmly behind them and leaned back against it. His expression was guarded. She thought she sensed regret mixed with something indefinable that almost felt like attraction as he watched her from half-closed eyes.

"Now you'd better strip."

"I beg your pardon?"

Jim sighed and pushed himself away from his leaning position against the door.

"You heard me. I'm taking your clothes and your bag for safekeeping. There's a jumpsuit in the bathroom for you to wear."

"You're kidding right?"

"I'm afraid not, Gina." His deep voice growled across her skin, raising goose bumps. "Take off your clothes."

"Taking your security measures a little far aren't you?"

His sensuous lips firmed into an unrelenting line. "Never far enough, sweetheart. I've learned the hard way that I can never be too careful when it comes to my people's safety."

She recognized the determination in his jaw and the bitter truth of memory in his eyes. He wouldn't relent on this point, and she realized she should have expected something like this.

"Oh, all right. Turn around."

"Can't do it. If you're hiding anything on your person, I need to see it. And if you're hiding anything *in* your person, I'm going to do my best to find it."

She gasped. "This is a body cavity search? You've got to be kidding." She felt shaky when she realized what such a search would entail.

Jim moved toward a small bathroom on one side of the guest quarters. He opened a small medicine chest and took out a couple of things—among the most daunting was a jar of something that looked like petroleum jelly.

"Afraid not. Look, I had medical training back in the day. I know what I'm doing and I promise not to hurt you, but this has to be done. I won't allow you to smuggle anything that could be dangerous to the safety of my people any farther into this facility than you already have."

"I'm not smuggling anything!"

"I've trusted you this far on instinct alone, but I have to be certain. Now strip. I won't say it again."

The edge of steel in his voice made her shiver, but it wasn't all in fear. No, something started to stir in the pit of her stomach at his dominant tone.

"Isn't there any other way?" She shifted her weight from foot to foot, agitated at the idea of what he was asking.

"If you don't agree voluntarily, I'll call in the troops and after what I suspect will be a painful fight, we'll restrain you and do it by force. You can't be allowed to leave now that you know about us. You'll be a prisoner."

"Some choice." Gina held his eyes as she began to unfasten her top with rough motions. She was angry and not shy about showing it. He looked relieved, but his expression also held a hint of anticipation she found hard to ignore.

"Throw everything onto the chair by the door." He nodded toward it as her top came undone, but his eyes followed her movements closely.

The dark, alien fabric shrugged off her shoulders, and she threw it over the chair with deadly accuracy. She removed her pants next and his gaze flicked over her skin like flame, making her hot in an inexplicable way. The pants dropped to her ankles, and she kicked them upward toward the chair. Her soft shoes and socks followed, leaving her in her underwear. There she hesitated.

"Everything, Gina."

She felt a flush steal up her cheeks, lighting her face bright red, she was certain, as she debated her next move. Before Grady, Gina hadn't been intimate with a man in more years than she could count on one hand. Her few liaisons hadn't ever involved this kind of thing. She couldn't recall ever being totally naked in front of a man who wasn't also bare-assed. It was an uncomfortable feeling, and now Jim—this man she'd lusted after as a teen—was ordering her to not only get naked, but allow him to...to...stick his fingers in places she'd never had anybody's fingers.

Why did that thought turn her on? Especially since her stolen night with Grady. She must be depraved for the idea of this invasion to be even remotely exciting. But she couldn't help the little gasp that caught in her throat when Jim walked closer to her.

"I won't hurt you, Gina, but I have to be sure. Turn around and keep your hands where I can see them." His voice was pitched low, coaxing and demanding all at the same time.

Gina did as he asked, feeling her body quake with fear, excitement and...was that yearning? She gasped out loud this time when Jim's warm fingers undid the clasp on her bra. He pushed the straps down her arms and moved closer, his tall body warm against her shivering back as he pushed the garment all the way down her arms and off. He threw it behind them to the chair before stepping back.

Gina knew he could see her breasts, tall as he was, looking over her shoulder, but he moved away, restoring the illusion of privacy. She breathed easier until his hands returned to her body, this time skimming her panties down over her hips, dragging them slowly to the floor.

"Up," he commanded, leaving himself vulnerable to a kick as he crouched behind her legs. He trusted her not to take advantage and try to hurt him. It was a significant gesture that made it somewhat easier to do as he said. She lifted one foot, then the other as he flung the panties to the growing pile on the chair.

Jim took her hand and led her into the small bathroom. She felt his eyes on her. She was too mortified by the situation and her body's response to this compelling man to meet his gaze.

He positioned her in front of the countertop and used a cotton swab and a pointed light to look into her ears first. That done, he did the same for her nose and then instructed her to open her mouth. She did, finally meeting his eyes, unable to ignore his handsome face close to hers as he poked around inside her mouth with a small mirror and the light. Apparently satisfied, Jim laid the instruments down on the counter, then ran his fingers into her hair, stroking all over her scalp and down her neck.

"What are you doing?" she asked breathlessly.

"I'm feeling for any synthetic patches on your epidermis. You look clean, but touch is a better way to tell for sure."

"This is insane." A shiver raced down her spine as his warm hands followed the same path. He touched every inch of her back and sides, his palms skating over her arms and even under them. Then he returned to her shoulders and began his journey down her front.

Gina had to look away when he cupped her breasts. Her nipples hardened in his palms and he paused, giving them a tweak that made her jump.

"Just wanted to see if you were paying attention." His grin made her want to smack him.

"You're not supposed to enjoy this," she ground out, accusing.

"Who says?" Jim countered, his big hands still cradling her breasts, kneading them now with gentle motions that caused her stomach to flip.

She sputtered for a smart reply but came up short. "B-b-because!"

Jim laughed, finally releasing her breasts only to continue his examination of her body, stroking each leg as he knelt before her. Again there was that trust he gave, putting himself in the vulnerable position that would leave him open to attack if she chose to launch one. The gesture calmed her as much as his roving hands stirred her.

When he moved closer as his fingers worked their way up the insides of her thighs, she was hard pressed not to moan. It should have felt wrong or awkward. This wasn't about mutual pleasure, as her night with Grady had been. This was something else entirely, but it sure felt like the real thing. Having Jim's hands on her felt like the most natural thing in the world. The thought scared her.

Who was she? What was she becoming? Gina didn't even recognize herself anymore. Had Grady's lovemaking flipped some hidden *on* switch inside her and now she was ripe for any man? She wasn't sure, but she didn't think so. She hadn't had this reaction to any of Jim's men. But all Jim had to do was touch her—even in the most clinical way, and this touch was far from clinical—and she melted. She didn't understand herself at all.

"Open for me, Gina." His words whispered across the bare skin of her belly, warming her, exciting her. "Spread your legs."

As much as she wanted to keep her legs locked together to hide the wetness now coating her most intimate place, she had to comply. She closed her eyes and bit her lower lip as she stepped out with one leg, giving him access. Jim took immediate advantage, sliding his hands up into the warm juncture of her thighs.

"I see we won't need to use the lube for this part," he growled, still at eye level with her pussy. "I thought you didn't want to enjoy this."

"I don't," she gasped as he combed his fingers through the neat patch of curls she kept meticulously trimmed. He spread the outer lips and ran one finger down her grooves, sliding in the slick wetness of her arousal.

"You have a funny way of showing it, Gina." His breath puffed across her spread folds, making her quiver. The warm, masculine chuckle that followed rumbled through her body like an earthquake of sensation. At that moment, he struck, sliding one thick finger into her channel.

Gina realized suddenly what a terrible idea it had been to close her eyes. Locked in sensation without the distraction of vision, she could feel every last rasp of his calloused skin against her sensitive tissues as he pushed all the way inside.

Then he began to move.

Gina opened her eyes, but it was worse to see his rapt expression as he watched his finger sink into her. There was color on his high cheekbones, showing he wasn't completely unaffected by what he was doing. That gave her some satisfaction. She wasn't the only one being brought to her knees here tonight.

"Do you do this to everyone who comes knocking on your door?" Her voice was a breathless whisper.

"Not me personally, no. Usually we let Pierre do the honors since he's a doctor."

"Then why? Why you?"

"Because that French bastard was flirting with you." He

punctuated his unguarded words with a particularly fierce curl of his fingertip as he reached right up inside and hit her G spot. She cried out as he rubbed it again and looked into her eyes. "You like that, baby?"

The grin he gave her melted her bones. She could only nod as he stroked inside again. She was so excited, it wasn't even funny. Only her teeth biting into her lower lip kept her from crying out when he started a concentrated rhythm, his dark eyes watching her face intently.

"Come for me, Gina. Do it now," he ordered her, leaning forward as she mounted the final rung of the ladder on her way to oblivion. The touch of his tongue on her clit sent her over, spiraling upward as he rode her through the explosion.

A minute later he pulled out, positioning her limp body to his satisfaction. He turned her and laid her out over the counter, bent at the waist so her ass was up in the air. He moved behind her, and her foggy brain dimly recorded his use of the lubricant in the jar before he slid one long finger into her ass.

She'd never had anything up there before and wasn't sure she liked the feeling, but it didn't really hurt. Of course, her body was in a state of bliss from the amazing orgasm he'd just given her.

To her horror, the finger in her ass made the fire in her blood rise again. It wasn't possible. Was it?

Before she really had a chance to find out, he pulled out and washed his hands in the small sink. Gina barely had the strength to stand. After a moment to catch her breath, she straightened by slow degrees.

Jim turned away, pulling the promised jumpsuit off the peg on the back of the door and handing it to her.

"Get dressed."

Gina considered the jumpsuit. "You want me to go commando?"

That got a smile out of him. "We don't have spare undies for you at the moment. Your stuff will be examined and returned once the techs have a look at it."

It was only as she tugged on the jumpsuit that she realized Jim wouldn't be leaving here totally unaffected by what he'd done to her. Gina's gaze fell to his waist and the huge bulge below his belt. The man was hard and had a huge cock if that long, thick ridge was anything to go by.

"I—" he began, hesitating as she tugged the zipper on the suit all the way up. Covered now, she faced him, trying hard to suppress the flush in her cheeks.

"What?"

"I'm sorry, Gina. I was too trusting once before with disastrous results. It's better to be sure."

"Do you believe me now?" She was surprised he'd unbent enough to apologize. She appreciated the very real concern she sensed from him. Her empathic skills were low, but she picked up more from Jim than she had from anyone in a long time. Anyone except Grady—but she promised herself she wouldn't think of him. Especially now, after coming so easily and so hard for a man she hadn't seen in years. She didn't know what being able to read Jim's emotions meant yet, but she was intrigued.

"I wouldn't go that far." The twinkle in his eyes warmed her though his words spoke of caution. "But it's a beginning. I'm satisfied you didn't smuggle anything in here on your person. At least nothing I can find. The techs will go through your gear and that'll bring you one step closer to earning my trust. For now, let's take it one day at a time."

"Fair enough. One thing—when you take the maps out of my bag, you might want to handle those yourself, or keep them among your top men."

"Why?" His eyes narrowed. "I thought they were just maps."

"They are. Maps to get me here and one very special map the Patriarch sent along for you. It shows the coordinates and locations of the other sites we know of where humans are hiding out, plus some we suspect based on other data. That's very valuable information, Jim. It's meant for you alone. It would be a catastrophe if it somehow fell into Alvian hands."

"It came from Alvians." His posture was challenging. The man who'd brought her to such heights of pleasure only moments before was all business now.

"It came from the *Zxerah* Patriarch. He's very particular about what he tells the High Council and what he keeps to himself. This information is held closely among the brotherhood. The rest of the Alvian race has no idea these sites even exist."

"Show me." He walked out of the small bathroom to where her belongings were lying in a heap on the chair. He dug through and pulled out her pack, laying it on the bed where he could observe her every movement.

Gina was careful to keep her hands in plain sight as she opened the bag and took out the maps. She spread them on the bed, pushing the bag aside to make room.

"This one helped me get here from the coast. I can't tell you exactly where I originated. The location of the *Zxerah* base is known to only a handful of non-*Zxerah* on this planet."

Jim's jaw firmed. He didn't go to the trouble of pointing out that trust went both ways. For her part, she was beginning to trust Jim but the secret location of the base wasn't her secret to share.

"And this..." she carefully peeled away a layer of the laminated map to reveal another, thinner layer of map beneath. "This one is for you." She laid out the map and pointed to a few features. "This is where we are now. There are a few known locations where our scouts have actually seen humans living in large numbers. The mountains of what used to be New York have a very large population. There are also sites in most of the surviving mountain ranges throughout the United States and Canada. The closest suspected site to you is the one in the Canadian Rockies. We don't have confirmed reports of habitation yet. We do believe there is a strong possibility humans have moved in based on increased power consumption and other data."

"You can read their power consumption?"

"Only marginally. The *Zxerah* site was part of a network of prototype artificial intelligence-controlled computers. The core was damaged almost beyond repair during the crystal bombardment but they managed to reestablish a few of the dormant computer links to the other sites. A very slight increase in power consumption was noted from this facility," she indicated the one in the Canadian Rockies again on the map, "in the last year or so. That, combined with some other data I'm not at liberty to divulge has led the Patriarch to believe people have moved in."

"Do you even know what the other data is?"

"Not all of it, but I've pieced together some from little things I've heard. Rumors of missing test subjects, escaped prisoners, *et cetera*. I think there's a better than good chance they're hiding out there."

"And you want us to get in touch with them?"

"I believe with all my heart that doing just that is humanity's best hope for the future."

"All right." Jim folded the maps and tucked them both into his pocket, then grabbed the bag off the bed and the rest of her things from the chair. "We'll go through this stuff as quickly as possible. There will be someone outside in the hall if you need anything. Otherwise, I'd ask that you don't leave this room until we come get you tomorrow morning."

"Sure thing." She sat, her arms folded as she watched him go. "I'll be a good little prisoner and won't make waves. For now."

He turned to stare her down. "The guard is for your own good, and the good of my people. Give us some time to get to know you, Gina."

"Oh, I think you just got to know me pretty darn well, Jim." She felt heat rush to her cheeks as the words popped out of her mouth. Too late to call them back. She had to brazen the awkward moment out.

"I'm sorry to have put you through that but I'm not sorry I gave you an orgasm, sweetheart." He winked, and she had to stifle a gasp at the heat that entered his gaze. "In fact, I already plan on doing it again, when you're in a better position to agree willingly to letting me fuck your brains out."

The raw words hit her like velvet punches to her midsection, leaving heat in their wake and an almost painful arousal. No man had ever been so bold with her. She was shocked to discover she liked his blunt talk.

"Surely you have a woman here—or two—to see to your needs. You're in charge, aren't you?"

"I protect my people," he bit out, his eyes going hard. "I don't take advantage of them. Ever. Especially the weakest of them. The women here are either part of existing families or have been traumatized. Like Tory. We protect them. We help them. We don't take advantage of them. We're not barbarians."

The very real anger in his tone brought her up short. She'd grown too used to the way most human males had coped with the shortage of females since the cataclysm. Many were downright savages. Most shared whatever women they could find, "protecting" them as best they could in small groups. Gina hadn't given much thought to how a large group like the one living here would make do, but she remembered Jim as a man of honor.

At least, he had been when she'd known him briefly in her youth. From the look in his eyes and the tone of his voice, the honor remained. Gina wondered what else of his previous existence had stayed with him and what parts had changed. She wanted to know what made him tick.

"If that's the case, then you have my respect."

"It is the case." Challenge was written in every line of his tense body. Then he began to relax. "You'll learn that for yourself once you meet the rest of my people."

Gina thought it was telling how he claimed caretaker status over the group. He probably didn't even realize his word choice implied so much. He said it so matter-of-factly that she knew he felt a strong sense of responsibility for the people under his care.

"Then you think there's a chance I'll make it past all your inspections and actually get to meet the rest of your group? I have to tell you, the only reason I came here was to meet you, Jim, and pass on what I know."

"There's no going back, Gina. Once you learned of our existence— and especially with the knowledge you have—I can't let you go back to your Alvian masters."

"They're not my masters, Jim. The Patriarch is my *sensei*, my leader. I follow him of my own free will."

"So you say." Jim held her gaze. "We'll take this slow for now, but know this: I want you, Gina, and I intend to have you. You're not off limits like you were when you were a kid."

His commanding voice sent a spear of heat through her belly as his words sank home.

"So you were looking at me when I was a teenager? I think I'm flattered." She tried to keep her tone light. There was more truth in her words than she dared let on.

"Oh, I noticed you sashaying around the *dojo*, little girl." A sexy grin lifted one side of his mouth as he stepped right up to her, invading her personal space. "I noticed you then, but kept my distance. This time nothing stands in the way. Not your age. Not your father or brothers. Not my honor."

"You're still a man of honor." Her words whispered across the scant space separating them as his head lowered toward hers.

"How can you tell?" His voice was pitched low, his lips dragging across hers as his arms came around her body.

"I just know."

Her words were swallowed by the sweep of his tongue over her lips. He kissed her then, delving deep. It was a kiss of possession, of learning and heat. She didn't want it to end. He'd already been more intimate with her than a mere acquaintance, but they'd yet to share a kiss.

As first kisses went, this one was damned near perfect. Jim seemed to know just where to touch, just how much pressure to apply, just what to do with his talented tongue to make her bones melt. She flowed into him as his arms tightened around her, craving his nearness, his strength, his warmth. She'd never felt anything like it, never dreamed such complete possession could be so freeing, so exhilarating, so much like flying.

Her head was still spinning when he pulled back, letting her go by slow degrees. Her blood pounded through her veins, her breath labored, and she watched him with dazzled eyes to see what he'd do next.

But Jim stepped away, setting her free. It was the dead last thing she expected and the one thing that restored her faith in him as a man. He wouldn't take advantage of her dazed senses. He wouldn't push her into anything on such short reacquaintance. He'd give her space and the time she needed. He wasn't the barbarian she'd nearly accused him of being.

"You have more faith in me than I do, Gina," he said, putting his hand on the doorknob. "Keep this locked, and don't go out until I come get you tomorrow."

As the door closed behind him, Gina realized two very important things. First, her life had just become very complicated. And second, she finally knew who the second man in her dreams had been.

Chapter Seven

Little Gina Hanson. Jim couldn't get her out of his mind as he continued down the hall toward his core group of men who led and protected the complex. He knew they were waiting for him.

The past few astounding minutes distracted him. He couldn't stop thinking about her. About the past and the present. About the way her skin felt and how she'd responded to him.

Gina Hanson was gorgeous. He'd always known she was beautiful, with an athlete's body that wouldn't quit, but she was clever too—an almost irresistible combination for a man like him who valued brains as well as beauty.

She'd been too young for him in the old world, and he wouldn't have disrespected her father by messing around with his daughter. Messing around was all it could have been then. Jim had been devoted to his work as a CIA operative. There'd been no time for relationships or family. Jim had always figured if he survived long enough to retire, he'd start thinking about the white picket fence, family and dog that went along with it then.

All that had changed when the Earth was attacked. In a matter of days his priorities had shifted from protecting his homeland to just trying to stay alive. He'd thought long and hard about where to go once the bombardment had stopped. Slowly, he'd made his way on foot— occasionally on horseback, when he could find a mount that wasn't too traumatized. It had taken him months.

In that time he'd gathered around him a core group of people. He hadn't planned it that way, it just happened. The single horse he had originally found multiplied into a small herd with people and their few possessions atop each one.

One day, Jim had turned around and taken a good look at his posse and realized they resembled one of the Old West wagon trains, without the wagons. The majority of his people were men, but there were a few families and single women in the group. They were a large enough group that nobody hassled them on their way West.

When they got to the Rocky Mountains Jim led them to the site he had visited a few times in his official capacity. He knew a few of the codes and hoped that would be enough to get them all inside where they could be safe from the aliens who had started to colonize the Earth and capture human survivors. Although he hadn't seen the aliens himself, everyone they met along the trail warned them of what was coming and what they'd heard. The human grapevine was alive and well. Even without television, radio, cell phones or any other kind of electronic communication, humanity was still in contact with one another.

Telepaths warned about the aliens, broadcasting their fear and their knowledge as far as they could. Those without telepathy learned from those who could receive the messages and word spread.

When they had arrived at the caves, they found the place in bad shape—at least on the surface. They had been able to pick their way through the debris clogging the entrance to the cave system Jim knew was there. Beyond the first level they'd found the facility mostly intact. They had also found more human survivors—military personnel and some of their families who had been stationed deep within Cheyenne Mountain.

Once Jim had rattled off his credentials to the few who were left inside the mountain, they were welcomed. Among Jim's group, there were those who had skills the people already living inside could use. It had made for a much easier joining of the two groups. Leadership had been in question for a time, but Jim never craved the position. He'd been content to let the military run the show, happy to help and act as a lieutenant from time to time. Eventually leadership had fallen once again to Jim.

Years had passed and everyone in the facility still looked to Jim as their leader. He was comfortable in that role—or had been until a fight in the dark had brought a living, breathing memory of the past into his life.

Gina Hanson was going to be a problem. Oh, he didn't truly think she meant any harm to his people, but he'd been wrong before and he had learned the hard way to take all necessary precautions. In his gut he felt the changes already beginning. The changes she brought with her that would alter every human life under his protection and possibly every life—human or Alvian—on the entire planet.

The thought was staggering. Yet, if anyone could accomplish such a lofty goal, Jim would bet good money on one of the Hanson clan. Her father had been a force of nature. Her brothers had been good, honorable, formidable men. If they were anything to go by, little Gina could be just the woman to change the world.

Grady Prime was given full run of the compound with only occasional intrusions on his work for checkups on his health and psyche as part of his participation in the ongoing experiment. He'd spent a couple of days letting the winged soldiers get to know him, sharing quiet meals in the mess hall and talking with those who were off duty. Many of the men remembered him from joint exercises the squadron had run with his own men in years past.

That prior knowledge worked both for and against his investigation. Some of the men—particularly the youngest of the group—seemed to be intimidated by his rank and were less forthcoming with their words. The older and more outgoing of the men spent more time talking about military maneuvers and seeking Grady Prime's tactical knowledge than speaking about their former leader.

Grady listened to it all and assumed whatever role the particular individual seemed to need. He played tactics teacher when necessary and found gratification on a level he'd never before experienced as he taught the younger men. Emotions made the act of sharing his hard-earned knowledge all that much more satisfying. He felt genuine affection for some of the youngsters and great respect for many of the men who had superior intellect and skills.

And he loved to watch them fly.

There was a sentry post clearly visible in the lower limbs of one of the massive trees he could see from his bedroom window. Every morning, his first sight was of the winged sentries overlooking the compound and the surrounding forest. Sometimes he'd catch them flying up or down from the post during shift changes, and the sight never ceased to amaze him.

All in all, the emotional storms of the initial few weeks of the experiment were dying down. But the yearning in his heart and soul since his night with Gina hadn't abated. If anything, it grew with each passing minute. He tried to calm himself with words of caution and internal promises that as soon as possible he'd track her down, but it didn't really work.

At night, lying alone in his bed, he burned. He yearned. He cursed the fact that he hadn't had a suitable crystal nearby to perform the tests of resonance that night. He needed to know one way or the other. He needed to touch her and hear the Hum, Kiss her and see the crystal glow. Most of all, he needed to Embrace her and learn if she really was the answer to his prayers, the light to his darkness, the possible savior of his sanity. He believed she was, but his analytical Alvian mind needed to see the proof of the crystal. Only then would his inner beast settle down, secure in the knowledge that he had a true mate.

Grady Prime understood how easy it would be to lose all perspective in the pursuit of a mate. Thoughts of her occupied him every other moment with no respite. He wondered if the condition would worsen or be relieved if he Embraced her with a suitable crystal nearby, only to discover she was not the woman for him.

He had to prepare himself for that disappointing possibility. His optimistic heart wouldn't let him dwell on the idea for too long. No, his heart whispered that she was his and the small creature that was hope spoke whispers of joy and excitement every time he thought of making the crystal glow so bright, all would know they were true Resonance Mates.

First he had to find Sinclair Prime Past and then he had to find her again. If the *Zxerah* Patriarch had any pity in his soul, he would not hide her when the time came. If necessary, Grady Prime would bring his demand to the Council to let him perform the ancient test on the woman who could—should—be his. It was their oldest law. Resonance Mates should never be parted under any circumstances.

If there was a possibility Gina was his, Grady Prime thought he had a good chance of persuading the Council to make the *Zxerah* produce her for the final test. After all, they would owe him once he took care of their Prime Past problem one way or another. And he believed he could talk Mara 12 around to *enhancing* her study by adding a good old-fashioned mate search to the equation. He thought he knew just how to phrase it to get her to go along.

But the mission had to come first. How he would deal with

Sinclair Prime Past, Grady didn't yet know. He had ideas about how to convince the Council that Prime Past would no longer be a problem to them. Nothing was certain yet, but he didn't like the idea of assassination. He'd never been an assassin even before he had emotions, and he couldn't stomach the idea of it now. He couldn't kill Prime Past in cold blood and any fair fight between them would be evenly matched. Grady hoped it wouldn't come to that. If Prime Past was at all reasonable, Grady would be willing to strike a deal with the rogue *Zxerah*—a deal his superiors need never know about.

It all depended on what Prime Past was up to and how sane he was.

"Prime Past especially liked this forest, you say?" Grady Prime returned to his questioning of one of the young Fallons. Fallon 41, if he remembered correctly. The young man had bright blue eyes, golden hair and brown wings with patterns of gold and red in striking shades. He was one of the more talkative and had been a keen observer of his former leader, having been assigned as one of his personal attendants for one cycle.

"Prime Past told me many times that he preferred colder weather. He also loved tall trees. Pine trees, especially. And snow. I can't stand the stuff myself, but he loved it. High wilderness with snowy pines."

"He didn't take well to warm weather? Were you ever assigned to work in the tropics?"

"I traveled with him and the squad to a small island to the south once, near the equator. I liked it, but the heat was tough on all of us. Our feathers make us very warm, you see. Prime Past couldn't wait to leave. He hated it. That's when he first relayed his liking of snow and pine forests, and he restated it several times over the year I served as his assistant."

"I assume you've all had the standard field survival training," Grady Prime said offhandedly. "Do *Zxerah* do extra training that would account for extended periods of survival in the wild?"

The youngster nodded, and the pieces started to fall into place for Grady Prime. "We do long-term survival training in different climates throughout the year. That's part of the reason we went to that tropical island. We survived on coconuts and other indigenous plants for nearly a month and were graded on things like muscle mass, strength measurements and weight loss when we got back. Anyone who scores low on such a test has to repeat the exercise until they can survive without significant deterioration in their physical abilities for a sufficient length of time."

Grady Prime was impressed by the strict regimen. He had to keep reminding himself that these winged men were not only soldiers, they were *Zxerah*. They had superior abilities because they could fly. They also had superior training and discipline because they were members of that fabled sect.

He thanked the young soldier after a few more minutes of discussion and headed for the mess hall. It was nearly night, and he had a few more interviews to conduct that evening and the following day. The puzzle was coming clearer, but he was still missing a few vital pieces.

The Patriarch sent for one of the winged brethren. The soldier who answered his summons moments later was one of their fastest flyers. A young man, he had great stamina and a calm personality that would serve him well on this special mission. He was also of sufficient rank to neither threaten nor insult the prey he would stalk.

The Patriarch gave him the coordinates, a map the Patriarch had prepared on the long flight back from the Southern Engineering Facility, and a plan of attack for the search he would conduct. The young soldier left shortly thereafter, hot on the trail of his newest quest.

Chapter Eight

Bill Sinclair felt a tingle in the shafts of his feathers that meant another of his kind was near. They hadn't understood why, but of the battalion of men created with wings, all had the ability to sense when another of their kind was close by.

Now that Bill had spent time living among humans and their special abilities, he almost thought it might be a manifestation of some kind of rudimentary psychic ability, but he was no expert. Still, there was no doubt that if he was aware of the other winged warrior, that same warrior was most certainly aware of Bill's presence.

He'd dreaded this moment.

There was no way to hide and if he ran, the other warrior would see him and know that Bill—former Sinclair Prime—wasn't dead. Either way, he was in trouble. He'd been found out. And all this time, he'd worried about the humans figuring out what he was. He should have worried more about his former brethren.

There was nothing for it but to confront the danger head on. Bill would not be shot in the back or captured fleeing.

Bill launched himself into the air, rising above the tree line with powerful strokes of his wings. He knew his brother waited for him up there, in the air that was their domain alone. There were so few of them. He knew every single one of the men who used to fly at his command. They were his brothers, his friends, his sons. He missed them more than he ever would have imagined before gaining emotions, though he doubted any of them would ever understand the depth of his loss when he'd had to cut himself off from them and all he had ever known.

He'd forged a new life for himself among the humans. He was

needed here. He helped keep them safe. He was useful. That's all he could ask for in life—what life was left to him now that he faced the daily specter of insanity. But he wouldn't trade the freedom and revelations of the past few months for the world. He lived a full, rich life. He knew what it was to feel—really feel. Nothing could compare with that and even if he ended in madness, it had all been worth it.

He rose above the uppermost branches and did his best to hover on wings that were meant to glide. He looked around as he circled, trying to spot his brother of the skies. The other winged warrior wasn't far away.

Bill signaled to the man he recognized as one of the young Dougals. He was a fast flyer and possessed a steady temperament. All in all, Bill could have done worse. If anyone had to find him, Dougal 17 was a good choice. The young man was smart enough to listen and might still be impressed enough with his former rank to be susceptible to persuasion.

The best of all possible worlds would be if Bill could convince the younger soldier to turn around and forget he'd ever seen him. Although he knew that outcome wasn't very likely, it was within the realm of possibility. More likely was the prospect of convincing Dougal 17 to temper his report to his superiors. Bill might be able to get him to alter the record of his exact location if he could get Dougal 17 to believe he would be protecting innocents by doing so. The winged brethren never harmed innocents. It was part of their creed.

Flying closer, the two winged men circled as they descended through the canopy of trees. They'd have to land if they wanted to have any meaningful conversation. Bill took it as a good sign that Dougal 17 was willing to talk.

They landed and faced each other. Bill felt the pull on his heart, seeing one of his brethren for the first time since his emotions had become fully active. He missed his men. Missed them to the point of heartache.

"You're looking well, Dougal 17."

"As are you, Prime Past. I was sent to look for you."

"Just to look for me? Not to eliminate me?"

"Those were not my orders, sir. I came only on a reconnaissance mission. The Patriarch himself gave me the order."

"How is Ronin Prime? Still hatching his plans, I suppose."

Dougal tilted his head, clearly not understanding the intonation in his voice. "The Patriarch looked well when I last saw him. He is a sturdy being for a wingless one."

Did he detect the barest hint of pride in the young warrior's voice?

"What is your message then, Dougal 17?"

"The Patriarch sends his compliments and wishes you well. He also cautions that you can expect company soon."

"Company is not welcome here, Dougal 17." Bill felt anger welling up in his soul. "I will leave before I put innocent humans in more danger. You may report back my location, but I will not be here if it will lead to a threat to those under my protection. In fact, I would prefer that you do not report my exact location. There are those nearby who have good reason to conceal their presence from all Alvians, and I respect them too much to put them deliberately in danger."

"My orders are to report back directly to the Patriarch. No one else. He suggested you might feel this way if I was fortunate enough to locate you. He bade me give you his promise that your human companions will be protected. He also wanted me to tell you that the time is fast approaching when they will no longer be able to hide. The foreseers in the clan have foretold of a time not far off when humans from all over this continent will band together. The Patriarch believes that you will play a significant role in this occurrence. It's why he tasked me with finding you."

Bill was conflicted. On the one hand he lived for danger, conflict and confrontation. On the other, he knew concealment was the best option not only for himself but for those he lived with now. Yet the *Zxerah* Patriarch had sent specific information gleaned from the human clairvoyants adopted into the Brotherhood. Living among humans and watching over the O'Hara ranch had taught him the real value of such premonitions.

"I don't like the sound of this but I thank you for passing on his words. The fact remains, no Alvians are welcome here. Please remind the Patriarch of that fact."

"I will." The young soldier moved back, then hesitated. "We were lost when you left, sir. The new Prime has done well but it took some time for him to gain the confidence and respect of the men. In many eyes, you are still our leader. I am pleased to have found you alive and thriving."

The innocent words touched Bill deeply. "I have missed you, my brother, more than you will ever know."

"Do you regret the experiment, sir?" The young soldier's head tilted as he considered him.

"Not for a single moment. I wish you could feel just a fraction of what I experience, Dougal. If you could, you would understand."

"I hope someday I'll be able to, sir. I must return to base. Having found you, my mission is complete. I must report back."

"I understand, son." The word rolled off Bill's tongue much the way he'd heard it used among his human friends, but he'd never used the term himself. It felt good. It felt right to acknowledge the relationship of teacher to student, father figure to son, leader to subordinate. He held out his hand, gratified when Dougal took it. The handclasp was a gesture among soldiers—among brothers in arms. He'd missed the companionship of men like him who had trained their whole life in tactics and combat. He'd especially missed the company of those who could fly. "Clear skies to you, Dougal. Please give my regards to the Patriarch, but tell him I will brook no interference in my new life. The Council believes I am dead. It is best to keep it that way."

"Now more than ever, it appears the Patriarch goes his own way. Only rarely does it match the way of the Council."

"The Patriarch has always been a wise man. I'm trusting him—and you—not to betray me, or the people who have helped me."

"For my part, I wish you no harm, Prime Past. I do not believe the Patriarch holds any ill will toward you either."

"I hope you're right, Dougal. Fair winds on your journey back."

"And to you, sir."

The soldier left with a final sign of respect. All in all, that had gone better than Bill had expected. He knew the Patriarch to be a thorough man and realized he shouldn't have been surprised to find a scout had been sent out to look for him. The only truly shocking part was that it had taken this long to be found.

Bill started through the woods, taking a circuitous route to the entrance of the underground complex where he lived with an ever growing population of humans, and one very special Alvian woman. Jaci was on the run every bit as much as he was, but she had her mates to keep her safe and share her life. She was a very lucky woman indeed.

Gina spent a restless night behind the locked door. Jim made her feel things she never expected and didn't really know how to deal with. She was confused about her body's response to Jim after the tempestuous night she'd spent with Grady. Was she becoming a slut? Had years of abstinence in the *Zxerah* compound resulted in some kind of weird sexual craving that was finally forcing its way out? Even her habitual meditation didn't help much. By the time she actually fell asleep it was nearly morning. When the door finally opened, she blinked awake with abnormally groggy eyes.

"Get up, sunshine." Jim was disgustingly cheerful in the morning. That had to count against him.

"Good morning to you too." She pushed her hair out of her eyes and blinked a few times, hoping to clear the sandman from her vision.

"Here." Fabric flew across the few feet separating them to land with a whoosh on the foot of the bed. "You clothes checked out. Get dressed. We have a big day ahead of us."

Reluctantly, she edged out from under the thin blanket. She still wore the baggy jumpsuit he'd given her the day before. It was scratchy against her skin, but it was better than nothing to sleep in. It was good to have her own clothes back. The Alvian-engineered fabric was soft and resilient, and much quieter. When she moved in those clothes, there was not even the whisper of cloth brushing against cloth. She hadn't really realized how loud that sound seemed until she'd moved around a bit in the heavy cotton of the jumpsuit.

Woodenly, she took her black clothing into her arms and headed for the small bathroom. Jim let her go with no comment, merely resting against the door to the room, watching her with an amused curl to his lips as she shut the door.

She used the toilet, washed her face and tried to clean her teeth as best she could, then dressed gratefully in her own clothes. When she emerged from the bathroom, Jim was still leaning back against the door, waiting patiently.

"Are you always this grumpy in the morning?" The teasing note in his voice warmed her, even though she knew it would be safer to stay on a less emotional footing with him.

She'd had a lot of time to think about the situation the night before when she couldn't sleep. Jim was a figure out of her past and that alone made her want to trust him, but he'd proven beyond the shadow of a doubt that their past wasn't enough for him to return the favor. That so-called search had disturbed her on many levels.

First, she'd felt betrayed. Jim had known her in the old world. He'd known her family—her father and brothers. That should have counted for something, but instead he treated her worse than a stranger. He'd treated her with suspicion and hostility, and even a bit of animosity.

Second, she wondered if he'd only been using her. If his claims were true and he didn't partake of the females he *protected* within his community—if protection was indeed all that was offered and given— then the body cavity search that had devolved into a quasi-sexual encounter might've been something real between them, something legitimate. But, on the other hand, if it was just the big bad male asserting his dominance over the little female, she should have punched him in the nose. In fact, she was still considering it.

"You'd be grumpy too if you had to sleep in that itchy fabric." She'd left the much-despised jumpsuit in the bathroom. Her Alvian-made clothing was much better. It didn't stain easily, it made no sound and it didn't smell, even after a hard workout. The fabric had been engineered specially by the *Zxerah* over many generations, to aid them in their work.

Jim's lips widened into a grin and she fought hard against the butterflies flitting around in her stomach. The man hadn't lost any of his appeal over the years that separated her teenage crush on the young operative studying martial arts with her father and the hardened, world-weary man he was today. She was attracted to him whether she liked it or not.

"If you're ready, I've got breakfast waiting in the conference room. We have a lot to discuss." He levered himself up from his leaning position against the door and motioned for her to precede him, but as she drew closer and put her hand on the doorknob, he reached out, closing one hand over her arm. "I'm sorry about last night, Gina." His voice was pitched low, the intimate rumble vibrating through her. "I didn't mean for things to get out of hand. I won't apologize for what happened between us, but I will apologize for not being able to trust you. Things happened here in the past. Things that were my fault for being too trusting. I hope you can understand and forgive me."

She looked up at him, trying not to let the appeal in his eyes get to her on an emotional level. It was a losing battle. He was already under her skin, but she had to fight against it. Her *Zxerah* training didn't erase emotion but taught her the value of controlling it. No emotion, the *Zxerah* had learned, was a detriment to a warrior, but too much was equally—if not more—incapacitating. A balance was required. In all things.

But Jim had already shot her equilibrium to hell.

"I think I understand. So does this mean you trust me now?"

He stepped closer, his subtle scent surrounding her, his warmth tempting. His eyes smoldered down at her as one of his brawny arms snaked around her middle and drew her right up against him.

"I'm getting there. Gina..." Her name was a whispered caress as his head dipped.

This kiss he claimed was one of mastery, of possession, but it was also the sweetest foray of exploration and tenderness she'd ever experienced. He seduced her with his lips, his tongue, his heat. She succumbed readily. No matter the chastising talk she'd had with herself deep in the night. This was not to be fought against. This was a force of nature. *He* was a force of nature. Inevitable and unwavering.

Only one other man had brought out such a response in her. She felt a pang of uneasiness as Jim lifted his head, ending their kiss. In that moment, the image of Grady's handsome Alvian face appeared in her mind. He'd kissed her just this way, with the same tenderness, respect and ardor. He'd touched something hidden down deep inside where she hadn't known it even existed. Jim touched off those same feelings and he unintentionally reminded her of Grady and all they'd shared.

"What?" Jim breathed the question as he searched her gaze.

Gina turned away. She couldn't face this now. She couldn't deal with these confusing, conflicting thoughts. How could she let Jim kiss her but think about Grady? And how could she think about Grady and still be attracted to Jim?

"We should go," she said into the silence. She knew Jim was looking at her with questions in his eyes, but they were questions she couldn't answer. Not now. Perhaps not ever.

She had no answers for him. Or for herself.

The conference room was full of people when she entered with Jim a few minutes later. The three men from the night before with there, eating breakfast with others she hadn't yet met. All were male, but some of the newcomers didn't have that same soldier swagger as Jim and his top lieutenants. They looked more like accountants. Rugged accountants, sure, but still with that scrawny, geeky look that only developed when you spent the majority of your life in an office behind a desk.

Jim led her to the small buffet that had been laid out on a side table. He passed her a plate and she filled it, surprised by the bounty of eggs, bacon and good fresh bread.

"You do all right for yourselves down here, don't you?" She directed her question to Jim, but it was one of the newcomers who answered.

"This facility is very self-sufficient. We were able to adapt several areas to house livestock including chickens, hogs and even some cattle. The hydroponics areas only needed seeding, which we did in the first few days of settling our families here." The man held out his hand for her to shake, using the other to adjust his glasses on the bridge of his nose. "I'm Wallace Dexter. I was the lead scientist in this facility before the crystal bombardment started. You can call me Wally."

"Gina Hanson," she replied politely, shuffling her plate into one hand so she could shake with the other.

"I know." The scientist grinned at her. "I watched you win gold at the Antwerp games. You were terrific." His enthusiasm reminded her of the old days when people—fans really—had often stopped her on the street or in restaurants to say hello and ask for autographs or pictures. She'd never taken their adulation for granted but had always made time to talk with each and every one.

"Thank you, Wally. Antwerp was really the high point of my career, but that was a long time ago."

"Yeah," Pierre agreed, gallantly taking her plate and escorting her to a seat at the table. "She's even better now. You should have seen her take on the boss last night. Gave him a real run for his money."

Wally took a seat next to her, still smiling, while Jim sat quietly on her other side. Pierre went to his seat across the wide table after sending a teasing wink in her direction.

"I believe it," Wally said, still enthusiastic. "Jim's good, but very few could ever match what I saw in Antwerp."

"Young Dex is almost as good as she was back then," Jim offered, making Wally beam. Only then did Gina notice the young man sitting on Wally's other side. They looked a lot alike.

"This is my son, Wallace Junior," Wally introduced the younger man.

Where Wally was built like an accountant—or the scientist he actually was—his son was something altogether different. Wide shoulders and sleek muscles filled out his frame, and he had the eyes of a wolf—cunning and dangerous. He was a warrior. A young warrior, but someone to be reckoned with, she was sure.

"They call him Dex, short for our last name," Wally continued, oblivious to the sizing up going on in both directions. "Because you can't have two Wallys now, can you?" He laughed and Gina responded politely, smiling at the older Dexter.

"My dad's told me about your bouts. I even saw some old DVDs he has of the Antwerp games. You were damned good, Ms. Hanson." The young man was polite but not gushing the way his father had. He was more serious than his scientist dad. More serious and watchful. Very little got by this young man, Gina thought, and she respected him for his vigilance. The world was so different now. Without the protected environment of the underground facility, she doubted Wally Senior could have lasted this long.

She thanked Dex for the compliment and turned her attention to eating breakfast. The men were all halfway through, and she didn't want to hold them up. Whatever required this many people to discuss had to be pretty important. Her curiosity was piqued, but she would bide her time until they got around to the reason they had all gathered together. She let the conversation flow around her, participating when she was asked a question and offering comments here and there.

Wally explained the history of the base while she ate. He was a gregarious sort of person who liked to talk and probably rarely met strangers. She didn't mind at all. In fact, his openness was refreshing and also very helpful since Jim, like most warriors, was reticent. He wouldn't talk much about himself, she knew, so Wally was a good source of information.

As breakfast wound down and the table began to clear of plates and utensils, they were replaced with large rolls of yellowed paper. They looked like rolls of schematics or some kind of engineering drawings, but she couldn't tell much more until they were unrolled.

Her curiosity was an annoying itch she hoped would be scratched soon.

When Jim cleared off his plate and turned to her, she was about ready to scream. She wanted to know what was in those rolls and patience had never been her strong suit.

"Now." Jim resumed his seat. "As to the reason we've all gathered here." He looked directly at her. "We've known about the other NORAD locations for some time. As you just learned, a lot of the personnel who had been stationed here, stayed here, bringing their families to live in safety. As a result, most of the knowledge about the systems and capabilities of this facility has been retained. For instance, your map confirmed old maps we already had indicating the locations of sister facilities—both hidden and known. What we didn't know was which ones survived the cataclysm and which ones might house human survivors."

"We've been working on clearing the tunnels for a long time," Wally put in.

"Tunnels?" Gina asked, intrigued.

Jim signaled for the rolled drawings, opening them up when they slid across the table to him. Gina took a minute to try and figure out what she was looking at.

"This is a drawing of one of the lower levels of this installation. This is what we call the transit level." Wally sounded excited as he shared his knowledge. "In the old days, there were a couple of tunnels leading from here, through the mountains to the north, south and west. None of the tunnel engineers survived, but the commanding officer, General Yeager, told me about them. They were made to house maglev pods that were used occasionally to shuttle the higher-ups from facility to facility covertly. There's one tunnel in particular that I think leads to the Canadian installation. We've explored most of the tunnels for some distance past the blast doors and that one is the clearest."

"Are you saying there's some kind of subway that will lead you right to the Canadian site?" Gina was amazed by the thought, but then, NORAD had been a very well funded government program designed to protect the North American continent from things like intercontinental ballistic missiles. It shouldn't have surprised her that they could build something like this. And it could come in darn handy, if it still worked.

"Better than a subway." Wally sat forward in his chair. "It's maglev—magnetic levitation. The system uses electricity to create a magnetic field. The car, or pod, doesn't actually touch the rails. It floats above. There's no friction, so the speeds it can reach are dramatic. In the old days, when the system was being maintained on a regular basis, the hundreds of miles between here and the Canadian facility could be traveled in a matter of hours."

"That's remarkable," Gina was both pleased and amazed by the idea that the system might still be usable in some fashion. "Does this maglev thing still work?"

"I've had it powered up a number of times, and it's functional to the point we've been able to explore. I would advise caution however, beyond the scouted area. There may be obstructions on or near the rails that we don't know about. You could still use it, at reduced speeds, as long as you watch ahead for obstructions. There are lights in the tunnel and lights on the pods, so even if the tunnel lights no longer work in sections, the pod lighting is independent and will still allow you to see for some distance."

She turned to look at Jim. "He makes it sound like we're going somewhere."

"That's because we are." Jim grinned at her, and her tummy did a little flip. "We talked it over last night and decided we should try to make contact with our neighbors to the north. If anybody's living there, we should see if they want to open up communications. At the very least, we could share information."

Gina felt hope take hold and expand in her chest. This was going to work. They were going to take a chance on making contact. It was the first step in the plan the Patriarch had laid out for her. She might yet succeed in her mission and humanity might have a fighting chance after all.

"We've explored up to this point and the tracks are sound." Wally flipped through the large drawings until he reached a section of tunnel that looked a lot like all the other sections of tunnel that preceded it to her untrained eye. "That should give you a good few hundred miles or so of fast coasting. After that, you'll have to take it slower."

Jim took hold of the pile of drawings and flipped to the beginning. "Each section of track, as I understand it, is powered separately. We'll have to get out and flip a switch every once in a while, right?" He brought the scientist back to the beginning with ease, and Gina realized he'd probably done this before.

But Wally's enthusiasm was undimmed as he explained. Jim had been so diplomatic in his choice of words that he hadn't hurt anyone's feelings. Gina was pleased to see the brash young man she remembered had been tempered by time.

"Yes. There are certain points, here..." he pointed to a spot on one of the early drawings where the tunnel took a sharp turn, "...and here. You'll have to apply brakes at a predetermined point. There's actually a switch on the rail that will trigger it for you if you're on automatic, but it'd be safer if you drove manually since these rails are old and we've only been up this far once before."

"What do we do then?" Gina was curious about the system and wanted to be sure she knew as much as she could about it before they set off into the unknown.

"There are power grids that will allow you to power down the previous section of track and power up the next section. You'll have to have both powered up for a short time as you coax the pod onto the new set of rails. I think they designed it this way to conserve energy by powering a section at a time. This is a long line of track and the mountains above dictate the shape of the tunnel in some spots. It creates sharp angles that are impossible to glide around at speed. By having to stop and manually turn the vehicle, it adds time to the trip but also a factor of safety to the journey. Of course, the generals and other bigwigs who used this system in the past had aides with them who did the grunt work. In this case, you'll have to do it yourselves. I suggest one gets out and sees to the power grid while the other maneuvers the pod."

The scientist babbled on about technical specifications and exactly how to work the apparatus, but one thing was clear to Gina as she listened with one ear. She was going with Jim. Alone. Nobody else would be accompanying them on this excursion. She didn't know what that meant. Did Jim want to use caution when approaching the Canadian encampment? If so, she thought it was prudent, but she also thought they could take at least one or two of his men with them.

She wasn't sure why he was making this a solo trip for just the two of them, but then, she hadn't expected to be able to make the journey in just a matter of a few days either. She'd fully expected to have to go over land—by foot, if necessary—evading Alvian patrols all the way. This maglev tunnel would save an incredible amount of time and if it really worked, it might open up yet another secret road of communication and even transportation between the human encampments. This could be a real breakthrough for human freedom.

When Wally finally wound down, the questions started in earnest. Each of Jim's lieutenants had questions relating to the safety of the tunnel and what to do in case of problems. Jim also talked about how to best approach any strangers he and Gina might encounter along the way and at the other end of the line. He particularly asked about other entrances to the tunnel system, which Gina thought was a really good question. Who knew what might be in those tunnels? It was a good idea to know how and where they could get out if they had to.

"There are access tubes leading to the surface in several places along the tunnel's path," Wally explained, indicating various points on several different drawings. "After the blast doors, which we keep closed for safety reasons but will be opening and manning while you're gone, there are no access points for about fifty miles. Then they begin to appear closer together. Mostly, that section of tunnel is in the literal middle of nowhere. The terrain is too rugged for even the hardiest of mountain men to live in, so chances that anyone's found their way into the tunnels is remote at best. If you find the way blocked ahead of where we scouted, you can always climb out of the pod and hike to the nearest access tube. There should be a ladder leading upward and the way should be clearly marked. At least, all the tubes we've encountered in the length we've been able to search were well designated and in good condition."

Gina liked the sound of that. She'd never been fond of enclosed spaces and wasn't looking forward to spending so much time underground. She wasn't claustrophobic, but the thought of being underground in unexplored sections of tunnel that had somehow survived the earthquakes and upheaval of the cataclysm gave her the creeps. It was good to know there were ways out should they run into problems.

The questions eased finally, after about an hour, but the biggest question of all loomed big in her mind. Finally, she just had to ask.

"This is all great, but when do you plan on us going?"

Jim looked at her, and she had a hard time reading his expression. "The sooner the better. How about we set out this afternoon?"

"All right." Well, he certainly didn't let any grass grow under his feet, did he? Gina was taken aback by the speed with which he was acting, but she knew it was for the best. The human race was already behind the eight ball. The sooner they came together to fight for their freedom, the sooner they would be free.

She thought it was appropriate that the struggle for freedom start in North America. The place that had once been the home of the greatest human democracy ever to grace the planet. It would start here, in the center of the old United States, hopefully in partnership with the Canadians. But they were all humans now, not Americans or Canadians. Just humans, fighting not for a country, but for freedom itself. Hopefully it would start here and spread to every corner of the globe.

From here, smaller pockets of human resistance in what had been Europe, South America, Africa, Australia and the Asian continent would be united in the fight against Alvian domination. The *Zxerah* kept tabs on human activity all over the world, ready to coordinate and aid where possible when the time was right. Any day now, the time would finally be right.

Chapter Nine

Gina noted the path Jim led her on after returning her pack. Someone had filled it with provisions for their trip. He hadn't been kidding when he said he wanted to leave immediately. No sooner had the meeting in the conference room broken up than they were on their way down a series of elevators into the depths of the facility.

She noticed she wasn't invited to see any more of the base than she'd already seen near the top and what she could glimpse on her way down. She wasn't being given the run of the place, but she didn't mind. She'd build on the kernel of trust from their shared past while she traveled with Jim to Canada—and hopefully back. By the time they returned, he would know beyond a shadow of a doubt that she was on the level. By that time he might have begun the even bigger leap of faith to trust the Patriarch, but she wouldn't push it. It was enough that she'd be getting this group of people in touch with the others.

If there were, indeed, any to find living in the Canadian facility. She thought there were. The best intel they had said it was more than likely a group of humans had taken up residence, but nothing was one hundred percent certain. That was why she had to go and check things out herself.

Under normal circumstances, they would have sent a human scouting party to verify the theory before they did anything else but events were happening quickly now. The Patriarch had sped up his plans for a reason known only to him, but her trust in him was absolute. He'd never harmed her or any human. He'd never led her wrong. He'd done nothing but help her since the moment she'd passed his test of combat, and the *Zxerah* had been true friends to humanity ever since.

It would take time to convince Jim and his people, but it would happen. In the end the truth always prevailed.

The elevator dropped rapidly, taking them to another level. They got out, and Gina followed behind Jim, flanked by Wally and his son, Dex. Jim's three stooges brought up the rear as they made their way to another elevator that took them down further into the reinforced concrete citadel.

Each level was clearly marked though the paint had faded with time. Gina saw some evidence that they'd made an attempt to keep the place in good repair. A small maintenance drone whizzed by on the side of the corridor at one point as they walked along. There was definitely some high tech equipment in the place and the added bonus of scientists who probably knew how it worked to keep it that way.

"Did you and your family ride out the crystal bombardment here?" Gina asked Wally as the other men discussed schedule alterations during Jim's absence.

"The first round hit while I was on duty. After the satellites went down, the commanding officer let us get our families and bring them here. He was a good man, General Yeager." Wally's voice throbbed with emotion, and his eyes filled with moisture that he refused to let fall. In that moment, Gina saw the toughness behind the man that had allowed him to persevere, and she knew where his son got his grit.

"Did you go out and get them? I mean, by that time, transportation was pretty iffy, right?"

"I took one of the SUVs. I went with some of the others who had family living in the same neighborhood. We went in the dark of night, during one of the clear times when the bombardment engines were on the other side of the planet. We went in, grabbed as many possessions as we could, whatever vehicles and tools we could salvage and anything else that looked useful and caravanned back. There were few people left in my old neighborhood, but I took the lady next door and a few others with me. General Yeager, God bless him, didn't turn them away. He made room for everyone and led us all in those first few days of utter confusion. We were doing well until the aliens started appearing. He sent out some of the soldiers to do reconnaissance, but most of them never came back. The few that did told us how the aliens were capturing people and taking them away. That's when he drew everyone inside and locked down the facility."

"Didn't the Alvians search this far? The entrance on top is pretty visible despite the damage from the bombardment, and it's been years. They had to have seen it."

"Oh, they did," Wally's mouth tightened into a grim line. "We had to abandon the first few levels and hide below. We hunkered down and made it look like the place was empty. After descending deep into the ground, they seemed to give up when they hit the lowest level of blast doors, just as the general hoped. He said they probably figured it wasn't worth the effort of blasting the doors and bringing the entire mountain down on their own heads since it looked like the inhabitants of this base had abandoned it long ago."

"Smart man, your general," she agreed.

Alvians were tenacious but strict followers of logic. Their cold adherence to risk-benefit analyses had led to their current problems— including the mess their geneticists had created and the unforgivable choice to proceed with crystal seeding of a planet when there was some evidence of an advanced culture already living there.

"General Yeager was the absolute best. There's not a day that goes by when I don't pray for him."

"Then he's still alive?"

"I don't really know. He went out on a mission and never came back. He's either dead or captured. Otherwise he would have come back. He cared for our wellbeing more than his own life. He was a great man."

Gina made a mental note to ask the Patriarch to search the Alvian databases for news of this General Yeager if possible. If he was a captive, the *Zxerah* might be able to get custody of him and put his experience and his warrior's heart to good use in the fight for human freedom. Every honorable man they could find was one more who would aid their cause. This one had the added benefit of proven leadership abilities if he was still the man Wally remembered with such respect and admiration.

Finally they arrived at the transit level and got off the last elevator. They had to take a few flights of stairs down further, but it wasn't far. During their journey through the complex, Jim's lieutenants had worked out a duty roster and Jim had given them some last minute instructions while she talked with Wally. The scientist had integrity. She could tell by his words and actions that he was concerned for his fellow man. He still had the eager mind of the scientist he'd been in the old world and the love and pride he had for his son was obvious to anyone who bothered to look.

Gina had a sense of satisfaction that here, at least, humans were living and thriving in family units...as it was meant to be. Too many humans had been ripped from their homes and families. Here was a small group that managed to stay together and help each other. It reminded Gina in a very tangible way of what they were fighting for. It was a good reminder.

Wally gave them some last minute instructions on how to operate the small pod. It wasn't a train, per se, but rather a sort of bubble on rails. The nose was pointed, probably for aerodynamics, and it was relatively small. There were two seats up front for a pilot and co-pilot like an airplane, and an area in the rear of the small pod meant for passengers. There were spare seats and tables made to lock in place in a utility area off to one side, and Gina was reminded that top brass had used this method of travel. They'd probably left the driving to the grunts while they worked or held meetings in back. But Gina and Jim took only two extra seats—in case anybody from the Canadian facility wanted to make the return trip with them—and a few items of gear that had been packed by someone beforehand.

There was a tent, some camping equipment and more food. A quick glance at the piles of stuff that had been tied down in back told her that much. Jim motioned her into the pod and took a moment to say goodbye to his men. Wally and Dex were at the end of the chamber, Wally standing at a console, flipping switches, his brawny son muscling open a blast door that worked on some kind of hydraulic crank.

She settled into the co-pilot's chair and waited. Jim hadn't said much to her since they left the conference room, but she figured they'd have plenty of time to talk on the trip. His standoffishness didn't offend her. In fact, she would rather have a little distance between them than the uncomfortable closeness of the night before.

Gina wasn't one to fall into intimate situations with men. Her days running in the wilderness had made her leery of most human men, except for the ones tested and accepted into the *Zxerah* Brotherhood of course. But those fellow warriors were more like brothers. She hadn't been sexually attracted to any of them, but then, she had always been rather picky about who she dated and who she became intimate with. Since the cataclysm had changed the very fabric of her existence, she hadn't really gotten involved with any man, much less two.

And now in the space of a few days she'd been approached by two attractive males who both managed to devastate her with the slightest touch and made her yearn for more. Circumstance had taken her away from the mysterious Alvian Prime and thrown her into Jim's arms. Jim was larger than life. He was the man she remembered, but now he was even more. He'd filled out and grown hard, his life's experiences forging the young blade he'd been into the finest of tempered steel.

He'd brought her more pleasure than she could ever remember experiencing—except with Grady Prime. It had been so long since a man had given her that kind of pleasure, she'd almost feared she'd never find a man she was attracted to in that way. Now there were two of them and though Grady Prime wasn't in her life now, he was still in her mind. Jim, though, was much closer and much more frightening.

She would be alone with him for days on this journey and she had no idea what his expectations were. For that matter, she didn't know what she expected either. Would she throw herself into his arms at the first opportunity? Or would she be too afraid to take the leap of faith that would lead her straight into his bedroll?

Even she didn't know the answer to that.

Thankfully, she was distracted from her whirling thoughts by the crackle of an intercom that she could faintly hear echoing outside in the rest of the chamber. She was safely ensconced in the co-pilot's chair as Jim sealed the hatch on the side of the vehicle after taking leave of his men. He settled into the pilot's chair at her side, brushing her arm with his muscular thigh as he maneuvered into the small seat.

"Everybody clear the track area and stand back on the platform," Wally's voice crackled over the loudspeaker.

Gina watched as Dex jumped clear of the track to stand next to his father by the control console. All the others were standing farther back on the low platform from which they'd boarded the pod. The platform wasn't strictly necessary to board, Wally had explained, but the actual stations had them installed to make getting on and off easier.

"I'm powering up the rails in three...two...one." Wally flipped the switch, and the lights in the tunnel station dimmed for just a second or two as the rails hummed to life. The pod lifted and swayed slightly before stabilizing, and Wally gave them a thumbs-up. "And we have levitation. Have a good trip, folks!" He waved them on with a huge grin as Jim hit the accelerator.

The pod started slowly out of the station, gliding above the electrified rails. The magnetic field generated by the electric current allowed the pod to hover in a frictionless adherence. Gina didn't know how it all worked, but once they got going, the ride was smooth with only a little sway side to side as they followed the gentle curve of the rails and gradually picked up speed. They left the station and the people behind and were soon out into the old tunnel, lit here and there by a string of widely spaced light bulbs.

Jim concentrated on getting the pod going at first, but then switched it over to automatic drive. Wally had assured them the path was clear of obstructions for at least the first two stops. Scouts had been in the tunnels as recently as a few days ago, so there was little to worry about.

Gina felt Jim's eyes on her as he shifted in the pilot's chair to watch her. She wanted to resist the pull of his gaze but was powerless against his allure.

"Now what?" She turned to face him, deciding offense was a much better strategy than defense.

"Now we get where we're going. And we get to know each other better." He reached out and tucked an errant strand of hair behind her ear. She nearly shivered at his gentle touch but did her best to hide the reaction. This man set her senses on fire, and she wasn't used to it at all.

"I really liked your family," Jim startled her by saying. His eyes spoke of regret and sympathy. "I was cocky as a young agent. I thought I had it all over ninety-nine percent of the rest of the world. Your father showed me how wrong I was. He took me down a peg or ten, then rebuilt me into something better. He taught me humility and the value of so many things I'd taken for granted before. He was a good man, and the best teacher I ever had."

The softly voiced words touched her heart. "I miss him."

"I know," Jim answered simply. She hadn't meant to show her vulnerability, but it had been so long since she'd been able to talk about her father with someone who'd actually known him. "I never knew my father," Jim went on. "He died in the war before I was born.

129

He was a special ops soldier, and it was because of him that I went into the service in the first place. Then the Company approached me and by that point I believed I was invincible. They sent me to your dad, and he taught me the truth. I looked up to him. He was the father I never had for the year I studied with him. I think of him all the time and wonder what he would have done in my current situation. His teachings still guide me."

Tears gathered in her eyes. "He would have been proud of what you've accomplished here, Jim. I know he really liked you. So did my brothers."

"They were good guys, Gina. It was because of them that I ignored you. You were too young, but I couldn't help but watch you. Your brother Paolo caught me looking once—just once—and he didn't even have to say anything. He had that stone face of disapproval down pat. One look and I knew he didn't like me watching you. After that, I made sure to keep my eyes to myself. At least when he was around."

She grinned, remembering her eldest brother. "He sure could glare, couldn't he?" A little laugh slipped out of her mouth. "Peter and I used to call it his death glare."

"Peter was like lightning in a bottle. He had the fastest punches, blocks and kicks of anyone I ever sparred against. The only one I thought ever had a chance of beating his speed was you, Gina, when I watched you in the Olympics."

"You were there?"

Jim nodded. "I was working a case in Prague, but I made time and bought scalper tickets at ridiculous prices to get in to most of your matches in Antwerp. You were poetry in motion. A credit to your family and one of the most elegant and commanding duelists I'd ever seen. You inspired a lot of kids to take up martial arts. I thought you were a great spokesperson for what was becoming a dying art."

Gina was touched that he'd come to see her during the most important sporting competition of her life. Since those long ago days she'd fought more desperate battles, of course. The fights in the Olympic ring had been sparring only. Nobody really wanted to kill the other fighter. There were rules and a referee. Since the cataclysm, she'd learned how to really fight. Life or death, no holds barred, no referees and no second chances. She'd become harder. Faster. Tougher.

"I sometimes wish..."

"What?" His gentle tone coaxed her to speak.

"I wish I could go back to those simple days when a fight was for fun, not for survival."

Jim sighed long and hard, turning back to scan the rails zipping by in front and underneath them.

"We all wish that, Gina. The trick is to not get caught up in dreams of what was. It's good to remember, but unhealthy to dwell. We have to move forward, not back, not stay in place."

"So that's why you agreed to this journey? I was a little surprised you moved so quickly on the information I brought you."

Jim looked at her, a smile in his eyes. "You're not the only one who knows a precog. Tory isn't completely sane with her talk of angels, but she's been right about too many of her oddball predictions for me to ignore her. She's been telling me for weeks, in her veiled way, that I was going to take a trip somewhere cold. Canada is north, therefore cold in Tory-speak. I figure this is the trip fate has in mind. It's a bonus that I get to go with you—a ghost out of my past whom I thought long dead."

"I'm not a ghost, Jim." She didn't like his wistful tone. He made it sound like she was haunting him—in a bad way.

"Yes you are, Gina. You were the girl I could never have. For all of Paolo's death glares and all the respect I had for your dad and family, I still couldn't help myself. I watched you when they couldn't see. Even after I stopped training with your dad, I followed your career. I took time off from a vital national security case to go watch you win Olympic gold. I watched you from afar." He didn't seem pleased with the memories. "And now you're not so far away anymore, and everything's changed."

"You don't have to sound so happy about it," she muttered. If this was some kind of declaration, he was really screwing it up.

"I'm saying this badly." He turned in his seat to face her fully. "Gina, I can't help my nature. I can't help the need I feel to watch over you and make certain you're safe. I know intellectually that you can take care of yourself, but the caveman in me wants to lock you up and make sure nothing ever harms you again."

Okay, this sounded better. Her temper began to subside as he bared his innermost thoughts.

"When this trip is over, I want you to come live with us in Colorado. Your family is gone, but I'm here and I want to take care of you, Gina. I need to take care of you."

Well. She didn't know what to think about that. Did he mean like a sister? Or something more? She couldn't tell from the earnest look on his face, and he didn't even try to touch her. Did he want to be her lover or just her friend?

She thought she could handle the former, but being only a friend would drive her batty after the pleasure he'd shown her. She sensed that had been only the tip of the iceberg of what could be between them—*if* he wanted her. And that was a big if from the way he was looking at her.

He didn't look like a man declaring undying love. Then again, he didn't even look like a man who wanted to get into her pants. He sat there looking more like a friend and that depressed the hell out of her.

"We'll see."

"Gina..." He almost growled at her, and she knew he didn't like her answer.

"Look, Jim. You have a duty to your people. I have a duty to mine. The *Zxerah* are my family now. The Patriarch looks after us. He sent me here and after this mission is complete, I have to report back to him. In all likelihood he's already plotting where to send me next."

"Is he your lover?"

The accusatory tone surprised her. Maybe he was thinking in more intimate terms after all. He sure *sounded* jealous, but she wasn't able to read him that well. Still, she had to laugh at the idea of her and the Patriarch as a couple.

"He's good looking enough, I suppose, but if you ever meet him, you'll understand why that idea is ludicrous. The Patriarch is even scarier than my dad was. He's the best martial artist I've ever met, and he's the nearest thing to a holy man—like those old Tibetan monks, or the Dalai Lama, or something—that you'll ever meet. He's a force of nature. And completely out of my league. Besides, he's Alvian. He has no feelings, though I've seen him struggling to understand."

"You're close to him," Jim accused.

"He's a good friend and an insightful leader. I'd follow him to the ends of the Earth and so would any member of his clan. He inspires that kind of loyalty."

"Sounds like a cult leader," Jim scoffed.

"Not on your life," Gina was quick to defend. "Every member of the Brotherhood is there because they want to be. We chose life with the *Zxerah*, and there's definitely no mind control or drugs involved. We don't have to worship the Alvians or even agree with everything they say. We're free among them, and they protect us from their fellows."

"So what's in it for them? Why did they take you in? They could have just left you to rot or be captured by the goon squads."

"It's not the *Zxerah* way to let other beings suffer."

"And yet they're assassins."

"Some are, yes. And I'll admit that's the main value the Council sees in keeping the Brotherhood around. But even when they are sent to kill, they do it swiftly and silently. There is no honor in making a being suffer unnecessarily."

"Are you an assassin, Gina?"

The look in Jim's eyes was bleaker than she expected. The thought that he'd believe she could be so cold made her realize he didn't really know her at all. Not the woman she'd become or the values she still held close to her heart.

"None of the human *Zxerah* have ever been asked to kill. We won't do it. For that matter, only a very few of the Brotherhood—those who are already part of the Alvian military machine—have ever been sent on such missions. As a general rule, the Council doesn't rub out every thorn in their side with a bullet. They have a lot of political muscle they can bring to bear on those who dare oppose them."

"You stick up for them. Gina, I don't understand how you can feel safe with them. They're aliens."

She had to find a way to make him understand. Too much was riding on gaining his—and eventually all humans'—understanding of Alvians and how they could all live together.

"Soldiers are different from most Alvians, and *Zxerah* are a cut above that. It has to do with their genetic lines. Soldiers were left with the echoes of aggression that was completely obliterated from the rest of the population. They can *almost* feel. It makes them question and think more deeply than the worker bees in the city. They want to *understand*. I think it's because they're kept separate from the rest of the population. All that time for introspection and study. Many of the soldiers are well read and highly educated. They're the thinkers of

Alvian society, regardless of what the scientists believe."

"You know a lot about them." Jim's tone was neither accusing nor warm but she figured at least he was listening.

"I've been with them a long time. I was the first human to encounter the Patriarch and his men, not long after the Alvians landed. I was the first to be invited to their compound, but certainly not the last. Human martial artists often join the Brotherhood, but no human is turned away from the clan. The clan protects the weak and helpless, the workers and the nurturers, so the Brotherhood can perform its tasks."

"Who decides what tasks they perform?"

"The Patriarch."

"And who pulls his strings?"

Chapter Ten

Gina was uncomfortably aware of what Jim was driving at, but she had to speak the truth.

"The High Council is the only entity aware of the Patriarch's existence. They give him and his men orders directly." She saw Jim's jaw tighten and his gaze harden.

"But—" she added quickly, "—the Patriarch has always been a power unto himself. He plays a deeper game than even the Council realizes. He has his own agenda, and I believe he plays them as much as they try to play him. The time is coming when the *Zxerah* will come out of hiding. They've kept the rumors about the ancient Brotherhood alive in the populace, enlarging their role to mythic proportions among regular Alvians. When the *Zxerah* show up on Earth after generations of secrecy, the rest of the Alvian population will sit up and take notice."

Jim was silent a long time, watching the railway ahead. She could almost feel his thoughts flashing through his mind.

"It's an ingenious idea if this Patriarch of yours is interested in creating a monarchy or a dictatorship. He'll hold a lot of power if and when he pulls off his coup."

"It won't be like that," Gina said quietly. "If you knew him like I know him, you'd understand. He guides. He protects. He never dictates, and he doesn't seek power for power's sake. He knows the Alvian people are driving themselves toward extinction, and he has some comprehension of the horrors his race has visited on humanity. Soldiers feel more than any other Alvian line. He has echoes of emotion—not much—but enough to tell him something's terribly wrong with the status quo."

The pod started decelerating, and Gina realized they'd been

talking for close to an hour. Wally had told them it would take some
time for the pod to come to a complete stop as it slowly lowered toward
the rails as the magnetic field became weaker toward the turning point.
The first leg of the journey was the shortest according to the maps.
Once they got the pod onto the next set of rails, there would be a few
hours before they had to stop again.

"I'll be honest, Gina, I don't understand how you can be so close
with Alvians, no matter what kind they are."

"We have time." She watched the rails in front of them,
illuminated by an overhead string of bulbs that created a flashing
effect as they passed. "I want you to understand them, Jim. I want you
to realize why I think they're vital to our survival as a race—as a joined
race."

"I've heard rumors of a human woman who married an Alvian, but
I still don't understand how it's possible. They said that guy had
emotions. I've never met an Alvian yet who did."

"You're talking about the Chief Engineer and his mate. Funny, I
was just talking to someone who knew them both rather well before I
came here—a warrior named Grady Prime." She felt warm thinking of
the serious man who'd learned how to cope with new emotions. "He
said Davin—that's their Chief Engineer's name—had always had
emotions. He was what they call a throwback. He was born with
emotions and was considered a bad experiment genetically, but he was
so talented with their crystals, they let him live, though they would
never let him reproduce. Then he found Callie, a human girl. Grady
Prime said they were true Resonance Mates, which is something rare
and special among Alvians."

"What's a Resonance Mate?"

"You probably have realized by now that the Alvians planned the
crystal bombardment from space to change the resonance of our planet
so they could survive here. They resonate on a higher level than us. We
can't hear it, but their voices, their brains, their bodies, their very cells,
operate on slightly different frequencies than we do. That vibration is
something they need to survive. They chose our planet because we had
a lot of what they call *untuned* quartz crystal deposits. The
bombardment was the fastest, dirtiest way they had to sort of wake up
our crystal deposits and get them resonating to their frequency. People
like Davin take the raw crystal and tune it so it can be used for
everything from powering their cities to communicating over long

distances. Almost all their technology is based on crystals. That's why Davin has so much power and was able to defy the Council and take a human mate."

"I heard they tried to kill him not too long ago."

"You heard right. Rogue members of the Council activated a *Zxerah* assassin. They wanted him to take out Davin, but the man they sent had recently retired so he could take part in a genetic study. He was the first to be treated with a gene-altering agent that changed his DNA on a molecular level. He gained emotions. When it came time to pull the trigger, Sinclair Prime—the assassin who'd been sent to kill Davin—couldn't do it. He missed on purpose and has not been seen since."

"So that's what happened." Jim watched the rails carefully as the pod continued to slow. His thoughts were racing though, if the look on his face was any indication. "We only hear disjointed reports of what goes on with the Alvians. It's something I'd like to remedy, but we have to be careful to keep a low profile."

"Good tactic, but if we're successful, perhaps new avenues of information will be open to you."

"There is that." One side of his mouth lifted in a slight grin as he looked over at her. "So tell me more about their experiments with emotion."

"The man I told you about before—Grady Prime—he was part of the next group to be given the treatment. He has feelings, and he was…"

"What?"

"He was different from any other Alvian I've ever met. He has feelings, Jim, and he isn't nearly as cold or indifferent as they always are. He was actually nice."

"Just nice?"

Was that jealousy in his tone? She couldn't be sure.

"More than nice, if you want to know the truth. He was warm and gentle and considerate. He had a quick mind and when he touched my hand, he had this look of wonder on his face. He said we—" She broke off as she realized she was saying too much. She still didn't understand her feelings for Grady and it was hopeless anyway, given her mission, but he held a place in her heart, nonetheless.

"You what?"

She'd gone too far, she realized, to stop there. With a sinking feeling in her stomach, she swallowed and answered.

"He said we Hummed. It's one of their ancient tests for Resonance Mating. I didn't hear it, but human hearing is less sensitive than Alvian. All the other Alvians at the table heard it, and they remarked on it."

"So you're his mate?"

Oh, she definitely heard the growl of disapproval in his tone that time, but she wasn't exactly sure what it meant. Was he staking some kind of claim or was he only objecting to the idea of her being with an Alvian in a general sort of way?

"No. It's only the first of the tests, they tell me. It just means that we have the potential to be mates, not that we really are. Besides, he's on a mission and so am I. I'll probably never see him again."

"Why do you sound sad about that?"

"Damn it, Jim!" She rounded on him. "You can stop right there if you're going to go all judgmental on me. I liked Grady Prime. He was nice to me. He treated me with respect, and he was the first man in decades that sparked my interest. There's no shame in that." He'd sparked a whole lot more than just her interest, but she figured it wouldn't be too smart to tell Jim *that*.

"He's an alien, Gina. You deserve better."

She couldn't believe his nerve.

"He's a good man, Jim. Don't judge him. You've never met him. And there isn't exactly a parade of men knocking on my door. Frankly, with my past experiences of human men and the barbarians most of them have become, I might be better off with an Alvian. At least I know they won't act like starving savages."

Jim became quiet, his eyes penetrating her very psyche as he held her gaze.

"Who hurt you, Gina?" His words were whisper soft in the darkness of the pod interior, inviting her to share confidences, to tell him of her most harrowing experiences—the events that haunted her dreams at night.

"It was a long time ago."

"Apparently not long enough if it still bothers you. If it's given you a distrust of your fellow man."

"You know what men have become, Jim. You know how they hunt women. I've done my share of fighting *my fellow man.*" She nearly spat the words. "I'm safer with the *Zxerah.* At least I know the males in the clan won't attack me in my sleep and try to rape me."

"Fuck." The strength of his curse brought her up short. "I'm sorry, baby. No woman should have to live in fear of rape. It's one of the first and most important rules of society—of the society we've built in the old NORAD bunker. Violence against women is not tolerated. Anyone attacks anyone else, they're either locked up or out on their asses in the snow. I won't allow that kind of behavior in my house."

"Not all men are like you, Jim."

He was silent a long time.

"You don't know how sorry I am for that."

The pod coasted to a stop shortly thereafter and they set to work silently, side by side, coaxing the vehicle onto the next set of rails. The turn was sharp—almost ninety degrees—and Gina got a feeling for why they'd designed the system this way considering the sharp turns that could not be taken at speed. She made note of the well marked escape tubes leading up to the surface but wasn't comforted by the fact that when she looked upward into one of the tubes, she couldn't see the sky. They were deep underground, and the realization of that fact gave her the willies.

Jim, sensitive as he was, picked up on it of course.

"Don't like it down here, do you?" He pushed the pod onto the track spur in preparation for putting it onto its new course. Gina was at the console and had powered down the previous section of track and was ready to power up the new section as soon as Jim was clear.

"Can't say I like tunnels much," she allowed. "And we're down pretty deep. I don't think I've ever been this far below the surface before."

"It's not bad once you get used to it. It's quiet and still, and a nice constant temperature." Jim shook his arms as he moved clear of the pod. "Cold, but constant. As long as you have heat, you can do pretty well down here. Purified water isn't usually a problem, and we've learned to cultivate mushrooms as well as the hydroponically grown produce. We even managed to get some livestock to live below for at least part of the time. We let them out into protected pastures a few at a time, but we can't risk a herd being seen. The sheep are best at living at altitude but the other animals have fared reasonably well as long as we keep a sharp eye on them."

"It's amazing what you've built, Jim. You deserve a lot of credit."

"Not me." He stood next to her as they powered up the next section of track. "The folks who were already there figured out most of it. There were a lot of scientists in that installation, and some of the things they came up with to survive were ingenious. By the time I got there, General Yeager had already set up a thriving community."

"Wally was telling me about him. He sounds like a great man."

"That he was. I had nothing but respect for the general, and I miss him every day."

"You and Wally both. Your general must have been an impressive man to stir such loyalty. Of course, an outsider looking in might say he sounds like some sort of cult leader." She looked up at him as the hum of electricity filled the chamber and the pod began to levitate once more. Bumpers held it in place for now, but they'd be withdrawn once they boarded the craft.

"*Touché, mademoiselle.*"

She liked that Jim was quick enough to realize she was echoing his earlier words about the Patriarch. She nodded her head in acknowledgment and would have left the console, but Jim took her hand, spinning her around to face him.

He stood much too close, and her hand was imprisoned against his chest. She could feel the pulsing beat of his heart against her palm as her mouth went dry at his nearness.

"I'm reserving judgment on your Alvian friends, Gina. I won't lie to you about that. I don't understand it and maybe I never will, but I'm willing to try."

"That's all I can ask." Now why did her voice sound so breathy and hot? She really had to have more control around him than this. It was embarrassing.

Jim shifted closer, his free arm going around her waist and drawing her into his warmth. His head drifted down, his lips angling along hers until he was kissing her for all he was worth.

He didn't coax. He didn't ask. He just took her on the ride of her life. She was with him though, and she didn't object. Not at all. She'd been wondering where she stood with him all day and this was a definite answer. The most delicious answer possible.

His tongue dueled with hers, eliciting a response that lit a fire in her womb. She couldn't hold out against him. He was too tempting, too commanding, and he knew just what to do to make her moan. A sound tore from her throat and it seemed to bring him back to his senses, drawing him back. But he didn't go far.

"I've been wanting to do that all day." His forehead rested against hers, their breathing matched in raggedness and tempo. Both had been affected by the tumultuous kiss, she was glad to see. She'd hate to be alone in her uncontrollable response to this man and his stirring passion.

"You could have fooled me," she muttered, glad when he backed away. He searched her gaze with questions in his eyes.

"What do you mean by that?"

"I'm getting mixed signals from you, Jim." She valued honesty and wanted it from him. "You tell me you want to protect me, you want me to live with your people in Colorado, but what do you want from *me*?"

He ran a hand through his hair and looked away. "Hell if I know." He turned back to her and she could see the confusion in his expression, feel it coming off him in waves...along with the undeniable attraction and heat. "I want you near, Gina. I have all these protective feelings for you, but they go deeper than normal. I want to watch over you. I want *you*."

"But you don't want to want me, is that it?" The thought hurt more than it should have.

"Right now? Honestly, I don't know. I don't understand your relationship with the aliens, but when I touch you it doesn't seem to matter. Nothing matters but you in my arms. But when I have a clear head, I worry about it—about you—about the aliens and what they mean to you. I want to mean more to you than they do, but I fear I've already lost too much ground. You've been with them a long time and from all appearances they've been good to you, but you've got to know it's been hell for me and my people out here with the rest of them. Pure hell. And I'm not so sure I'll ever be able to forgive...or forget."

Silence held for a long moment while she thought about his words.

"I appreciate your honesty, Jim. Let's just give it time, okay?"

"I'm not sure I can give you that, Gina." He stepped close once more, his gaze pulling her in, his expression daring her to step into his arms, into his world. "I want you too much."

"Dammit, Jim." She shook her head, marveling at the way he could turn her head with just a few words. A fire erupted in her belly and though her mind told her no, her body was screaming yes, yes, yes!

"It doesn't have to be complicated," he coaxed. "I think you want me too. Don't you, Gina?"

"You are the most infuriating man."

"I think you like infuriating men. Particularly me. So how about it? Can we boil this down to the most basic things for the moment? You, me, desire and pleasure?"

"And let all the other stuff wait? It won't go away, you know."

"I know. It preys on my mind. But I can't walk away from you. I can't keep my distance. I stayed awake deep into the night, thinking about you. About this trip. About all the myriad possibilities. But what it all came down to was my desire—my need—for you. Am I wrong in thinking you want—and need—me too?"

"I—" She had to be honest. "I want to be with you. Right or wrong, heartache or happiness, I want more of what you showed me last night, Jim. And you should know I always had a crush on you. You might've watched me in my dad's *dojo*, but I was watching you too."

"No kidding?" A grin lit his face as heat blossomed in his eyes. He pulled her into his arms and shifted his weight from foot to foot, rocking her against his hard body. "Last night wasn't supposed to be about sex, Gina. I didn't mean to push you that far when I walked into the room with you. It was supposed to be a search, plain and simple, but the moment I touched you, all my good intentions went right out the door. I'm sorry for that."

"I'm not." She rubbed her cheek against his, breathing in his breath, reveling in his warmth as he drew her into his arms. "After I got over the shock, I liked what you did. It was exciting and probably the kinkiest thing ever to happen to me." She laughed as he started, then gazed at her with open fire. "It shocked the heck out of me, but I liked the feeling. And I want to feel that again."

"You ain't seen nothing yet, baby."

His hands went to the fastenings that held her top together, parting them expertly until she was bared to his gaze and his hands. He kissed her again, taking her lips with savage fury as his hands molded the roundness of her breasts. As his thumbs rubbed over the excited peaks, she gasped into his mouth. He broke away to trail his lips downward, capturing one tortured peak in the wetness and urgency of his mouth, rolling the other between thumb and forefinger, plucking gently. She cried out as his other hand delved beneath her waistband, seeking and finding the hot spot between her legs that cried out for his touch.

He wasted little time, sliding one long finger through the slick wetness of her arousal and pushing deep. She cried out as he began to rub that spot he'd discovered the night before. The tiny point deep inside that brought her so high, so fast.

She shuddered as he pushed her higher, his teeth raking over her skin gently, arousingly.

"Come for me, baby. Give it to me."

She shuddered and shook in his arms as her sheath convulsed around his finger, a sound of indeterminate pleasure ripped from her throat.

"That's it. You're so hot, baby. You set me on fire." He stroked her through the last of the shudders, stroking the flame to make her rise once again. It was so fast. She didn't remember it ever happening this fast or this hot.

She leaned back against the rail that surrounded the console as he stripped off her pants, pushing his own down past his straining erection. He was built on the large side, as she'd guessed. As she'd hoped. His thighs were a work of art, muscle and sinew straining as he moved back to her, taking his place between her legs.

"I don't have anything to protect you, Gina, but I'm safe from disease. How's your cycle?"

"I'm on birth control. The *Zxerah* are careful about reproduction and I'm clean too, so it's okay."

"God, you don't know how good it is to hear that. Damn, baby, I wasn't thinking straight or I would've been prepared. I'll take better care of you from now on, I promise."

She stroked his sexy, stubbly cheek with one hand. "You take care of me just fine, Jim. Now *take care* of me some more." She sent him her sexiest smile, her libido racing far ahead of its normal pace. This man brought out the siren in her, and she wanted him. She needed him. Now. "Come into me, Jim. I want to feel you inside me. I want it so bad."

"Your wish..." he stepped up to her, pushing the large head of his cock between her slick thighs, "...is my command." They both watched him push in, gaining entrance as she strained to take him. He was thick and long. She shimmied against him, seating herself on the railing, trusting him to hold her upper body so she wouldn't fall off onto the electrified tracks. The danger only added to her excitement.

"Deeper, Jim," she urged in a low voice. She was nearly incoherent with sensation as he slid home, hard and deep within her. "That's it!" A cry wrenched from her depths, ripping out into the silence of the tunnel, echoing back to her.

"Damn, baby, you feel good around me. You're tight and wet and hot. You were made for me." He began to thrust, holding her shoulders tight, keeping her in place for his powerful thrusts. She gave control to him, trusting in his strength, his power.

His cock felt good against the sensitive walls of her sheath. The sensation stole her breath and made her want to moan in pleasure as he increased his pace. Her hands clenched his thickly muscled shoulders. His shirt was on, but she'd managed to undo a few of the buttons. She worked on the rest now. She had to feel his skin, see his abdomen rippling as he drove into her.

She achieved her goal only moments before the biggest wave yet hit her, sending her over into mindless pleasure as he pounded into her. She screamed then, and he followed not far behind her, jetting into her in hot waves of wet heat, sending another spiral of pleasure deep into her core.

Gina clutched his ribs, leaning heavily against his chest as he held her through the last of the spasms, the last echoes of incredible rapture. She'd never come so hard in her life. She'd never thought it was even possible.

No words could describe the whirlwind that had just taken her on the wildest ride of her life. She wasn't even capable of speech at the moment and Jim didn't seem inclined to break the silence either, for which she was grateful. He held her to him, rubbing her shoulders almost absently as he placed sporadic soft kisses on her hair and shoulder.

At length, he pulled out, lifting her off the railing and placing her gently on her feet. She wobbled and he steadied her, sparing her a smile of pure male satisfaction. She wondered what it did for his ego to know he'd fucked her dizzy.

"That was..." He seemed to search for words as he found her clothes and handed them back to her. "Baby, you blew me away."

"Not yet." She felt the desire to tease him. "But we can try that next if you like."

He growled as he stalked closer, pulling her in for a quick hug and a nipping kiss. "You're a vixen, Gina."

"And you're a stud. But I'm sure you knew that already."

"Seriously?" he asked as he fastened his pants and she did the same. "I haven't been with a woman in a long time. I wasn't kidding when I said I protect the women in our community. Most are already involved with another man or are too old or too young to get involved with. It's been a long time since I had the pleasure of spending time with an unattached female who wasn't under my protection, and I don't ever recall it being as explosive as we just were."

"Me neither." She had to be honest, though, her night with Grady had been explosive and exciting—just in a different way.

She continued dressing until she was presentable again and found him watching her with a strange, soft expression on his face.

"So are we good? I didn't hurt you, right?"

"No, you didn't hurt me." She smiled at him, stepping into his arms to place a gentle kiss on his jaw. "And we're definitely good."

"You're okay with this? I mean, you're okay with the sex?"

"The sex was way more than just okay, Jim." She blushed even as she teased him. "And I'm definitely okay with it. In fact, I'd like to do it again, whenever you're up to it."

"We'll have things to settle when we get to the end of this road, Gina. Even the hottest sex I've ever had won't make me take chances with people's lives."

"I never expected anything different," she assured him. "Let's take this one step at a time, Jim. We'll get to know each other and maybe by the end of this trip you'll be able to come to terms with things as they stand with the Alvians and me. All I ask is that you think about it. And the sex isn't meant to coerce you. That's strictly between you and me and has nothing to do with anyone or anything else. Agreed?"

"Agreed."

They walked together up the small ramp and into the pod. She was seated and the pod was accelerating before she remembered what he'd said and she couldn't help but tease him.

"So, the hottest sex you've ever had, eh? I think I like the sound of that."

Chapter Eleven

They got underway again, the pod speeding up as Jim tried to wrap his head around what had just happened. He'd lost control. Completely and utterly. He'd taken her like a savage, pushed up on a railing, leaning over certain death.

He should have been more careful with her. He should have at least waited for a safer place to screw her into the wall.

Jim was disgusted with himself.

Gina Hanson had always been a special girl, and he'd treated her worse than a low-rent prostitute. He'd been a barbarian.

Yet she smiled at him.

Every time he turned toward her as he checked over the equipment and settings, she gave him one of those sexy little grins that made his knees weak. She'd been a hellcat while he was fucking her, hotter than he ever would have suspected. She'd blown his mind, and he was already hard again just thinking about it.

Down boy.

The next time, he'd find a safer spot to have her. There was no going back now. Once he'd been inside her, he knew he wasn't strong enough to resist the delicious temptation of her body anymore. He'd take her as often as she'd let him over the next few days while they traveled north. What would happen after that? He had no idea.

The future worried him, but not enough to deny himself the intense pleasure of making love to Gina Hanson. He'd wanted her for a long time and had even mourned her supposed death. During the upheaval of the cataclysm and after, Jim had dwelled for a long time on all he'd lost. He'd thought about the people he hadn't been able to protect from something larger than politics, larger than international terrorism, larger than the planet itself. He and all the others who'd dedicated their lives to keeping the rest of the population safe hadn't stood a chance against the crystal bombardment.

His helplessness in the face of that had caused deep depression. The utter devastation that followed brought grief the likes of which he hoped never to feel again. But it was the thought of all those people special to him that had been lost that had almost tipped him over the edge into insanity.

Jim had spent days—or maybe it had been weeks—thinking about the people who'd died. He'd found a church—one of the few structures still standing in the small mid-western town he'd sheltered in—and prayed for the first time in years for the souls of those killed in the cataclysm.

He'd remembered little Gina Hanson and her family. *Sensei* Hanson had been a father figure with incredible skill and the ability—the gift—of being able to pass it on. He'd been a teacher of martial arts, but also of life. Jim had learned much from the man both in class and from his example and the way he interacted with his children.

Jim had prayed for all the Hansons. He'd admired the *sensei*, but he was friends with Paolo, Peter, Bryan and Christopher Hanson, Gina's brothers.

Now that he knew Gina had survived, there was a chance at least some of the other Hansons had too. The fact that they had psychic abilities in the family increased the likelihood that they'd been able to adapt to the changed world. Gina had gotten word to them to take cover, so more than likely they'd taken steps to protect themselves even before the bombardment started.

But they'd lived on the East Coast. Millions had died up and down every coastline in the world as the oceans stormed ashore. The big coastal cities had been decimated. Jim hoped the Hanson family homestead had been far enough inland to avoid the tsunami damage that had wiped out the cities, but he hadn't heard anything from further east than Indiana in years. If anyone survived on what was left of the coast, he didn't know about it.

Of course, human communication was severely limited. Telepathy only worked over short distances for most people. A few stronger telepaths could reach people farther away, but there weren't many of them. Messengers passing over land the old-fashioned way were hampered by aliens who would chase and capture any humans they saw. So movement on the surface was limited and covert. No Pony Express could get messages from one place to another like in the Old West. No, nowadays, messages had to pass clandestinely and as slow as molasses while messengers avoided patrols and hid out as best they could.

"Penny for your thoughts," Gina ventured, gazing at him from under her lashes. She was truly the most innocently sexy woman he'd ever known.

"They're probably not worth even that much." He put the controls on automatic now that they were coasting at speed and turned to face her. Leaning forward, he touched her face, unable to help himself. The feel of her skin under his hands was addictive.

Her smile lit his insides, firing up a reawakened libido that didn't need the extra pressure. He shifted in his seat as he drew back.

"Did you notice the seats swivel?" A devilish gleam had entered her eyes.

She reached forward, sliding her hand under his legs to a small lever he hadn't noticed before. A second later his chair turned to face hers, his legs sliding along the slick, molded plastic surface to keep pace with it. The result was him facing her, his legs spread and her hand still dangerously close. He sat up a little straighter when her palm shifted to his thigh, creeping slowly upward.

"Now how could I have missed that?" His voice got noticeably deeper as her hand settled over his cock through the fabric of his pants.

"It's okay. I checked everything out while you were making your farewells. These seats also recline. And the ones in back fit together into a nice-sized bed of sorts. Maybe we can make use of that...later."

"Nothing would please me more," he agreed, licking his lips when her other hand went to the buttons at his waist. She undid the closure and his cock sprang out. "Yeah, baby. That feels good."

She slid to her knees in the small space between the two front seats, her luscious mouth coming closer to where he most wanted it.

"I bet I can make it feel even better."

"I know you can, vixen." He winked at her when she smiled coyly up at him. All the while, her little fingers stroked over his hardened flesh, applying just the right pressure, but he wanted more. He wanted it all. "Put it in your mouth, baby. Let me watch you lick it."

"Ah, I see it's my turn to grant your wish…master."

She did a fair imitation of the genie on that old TV show, he thought. She was every bit as sexy and even more desirable, and most importantly, she was here—the woman he'd dreamed of for years whom he thought at first unattainable and later, lost forever. She was here, taking him in her enveloping mouth, licking him for all she was worth, her gaze meeting his with genuine warmth and the sexiest expression he'd ever seen.

She moved right up onto him, her head nestled in the bend of his lap, her mouth opening wide as she took him right to the back of her throat. She gagged a little and he immediately eased back, but her hands on his hips urged him forward once more as she got the hang of how much she could take. She wasn't used to this kind of thing. That much was clear.

The idea that he was getting something she didn't normally give made him feel special. He didn't know what he was to her, but at the moment he didn't really care. All he could focus on was the feel of his cock sliding against her tongue, the feel of suction around the head while her delicate fingers played with his balls. He'd never seen anything even remotely as enticing as watching gorgeous Gina Hanson sucking his dick.

He wanted to see more of it in the future. And he wanted inside of her.

But he was too close to losing it, and when she touched him just…so…

He came in a rush, pleased when she swallowed, licking her lips like the siren she was.

She pet him until he could breathe somewhat normally again and then sat back in her chair, still facing him, smiling like a cat who'd just dined on the canary. He felt like he should go down on his knees and thank her for the incredible orgasm, but the sultry look on her face distracted him.

"How long did Wally say we had on this section of rail?"

"About six hours, give or take. It's clear sailing to the end of this section, then we have to slow down and watch our path for obstructions."

"Hmm." She glanced back at the two seats they'd stowed in the rear of the small pod. "Don't you think we should take advantage of the clear road while we can?"

"Damn, baby." Jim shook his head. "Come to think of it, I do owe you one and this is probably the last stretch of safe road we'll have on this trip." Her grin widened as he stood in the gently swaying vehicle. "You want to show me how to put these seats together into a bed?"

"Oh, yeah." She practically purred as she stood and moved toward the stowed seats.

He intercepted her with an arm around her waist, pulling her into him for a long, hard kiss. The way she melted in his arms was gratifying to say the least. When he let her up for air, they were both breathing hard and his dick was starting to revive. The way she gazed up at him helped the process along considerably.

"Gina, I have to thank you." He wanted to get the words out, no matter how stupid they sounded. "You're a giving, generous woman and I count myself a lucky man to have this time with you."

He was glad he'd spoken when her smile widened and her eyes filled with wonder.

"I feel the same about you, Jim. It's like recapturing a tiny part of my past to be with you. It's something I'll never forget."

He shouldn't have been surprised to know they were on the same wavelength, but it still touched something deep inside himself he'd thought long dead. He cared about all the people under his protection, but Gina Hanson was burrowing even deeper into his soul, coming dangerously close to his heart. He'd have to guard against it, but he knew it would be all too easy to fall deeply, madly, hopelessly in love with this woman.

Hell, she'd already owned a little piece of his heart when she was a girl. Now that she was a woman, and in his bed, all bets were well and truly off. He would have to tread lightly and keep reminding himself this was only temporary. As soon as their journey together was over, so would their affair. He had a duty to his people. She had a duty to her adopted tribe of aliens. Even if Ronin was on the level, Jim doubted Gina would choose to give up her work for the aliens to come live with Jim and his group, and they needed him too much for Jim to leave. They'd turned to him for leadership, and he'd made too many promises to leave them in the lurch. Likely, Gina had too.

He didn't have to like it. That was the way it just had to be. Unless something changed drastically, they'd be parting sooner rather than later.

Pushing the gloomy thoughts aside, he went to help her set up the bed where he planned to spend the next few hours learning every inch of her body. If this was the only time they'd really have together, he was just scoundrel enough to take full advantage. He had to make memories enough to last well into the future.

Their sexual marathon was interrupted only by short bouts of sleep. By the time the pod decelerated to a stop at the second platform, they'd fucked each other nearly into oblivion. They worked together to move the pod onto the new set of tracks, then put the inside of the pod to rights, airing it out and cleaning it up as best they could.

They decided to leave the bed in place. The journey would be much slower now and they weren't even halfway there. One would keep watch while the other slept, so they could keep rolling and make the most of their time. Moving was also safer than trying to stop somewhere and camp out. A moving target was less likely to be hit by whatever might be out there waiting.

Jim got them going with just a very little pulse of acceleration. They had to go slow now and watch every yard of track for possible obstructions.

"I can see this is going to take a while." Jim kept his attention on the path in front of them but spared a quick glance for her. "Why don't you go in back and get some shut eye? I can keep watch here and then we'll switch off later."

"Sounds like a plan," Gina allowed. She was worn out from all the unaccustomed activity of the past few hours. It had been delicious, but also deliciously tiring. She could use a few minutes of sleep to help recharge her internal batteries. "Wake me if you need me."

"Baby, it feels like I always need you."

The devilish smile made her tummy clench almost as much as her heart did at his words. But he meant them in a purely sexual way. What she wouldn't give to have a man like Jim need more than just sex from her. It was a dream she'd thought long lost when the world changed, but Jim was making her yearn for things she couldn't have.

She went to sleep with a heavy heart, trying her best to put thoughts of the future that could never be to rest. But thoughts of Jim followed her, even into her dreams.

"Where are we?" Her jaw cracked as she yawned. The gently swaying sensation of motion had ceased.

"We just hit the end of the line on this track. I was going to wake you in a minute to help me move us onto the new set of rails, but I wanted to finish up my notes for Wally. I promised him we'd make some observations of the sections of rail they hadn't yet seen."

"I can help with that, if you like." She pushed up off the makeshift bed and stretched. She felt Jim's eyes on her and liked the way his attention made her feel—feminine and attractive. It had been a long time since a man she was also attracted to looked at her that way.

"Yeah, I figured we'd take turns taking notes as well as driving."

"Sounds good to me." She headed for the pod door. "Shall we?"

She was down the ramp and on the small station platform when she felt the unmistakable heat of him come up behind her. He crowded her against the powered-down console, letting her feel the hard ridge of his arousal against the soft flesh of her ass through their combined layers of clothing.

Just like that, her libido raged. This man could get her going faster than anyone ever had. All he had to do was touch her and she went up in flames.

"Do you think it's safe?"

"Honey, when I get you in my arms it's never safe." His mouth nuzzled the side of her throat, sending shivers of awareness down her spine. "But if you're asking if the tunnel is safe, I think so. I haven't seen any evidence that anyone else has been down here since the cataclysm. I think it'd be okay to take a little break here and indulge ourselves. Now take off your clothes and chuck them into the pod. I want to hoist your little ass up on this console and fuck you into next week."

"Only if you get naked too." She wanted to see him in the worst way but there was precious little room to maneuver in the pod. She'd been able to see him bits at a time, but not all at once. It was something she craved.

"What's this?" He turned her in his arms to smile down at her. "You're making demands now?"

"Yeah." She stroked his chest with her fingers, loving the feel of him under her hands. "I figured I should get my way once in a while

153

here and right now, I want to see you naked too."

He seemed to consider her request for a moment before stepping back. "All right. Together."

And with grins on both their faces, they began to strip for each other. Gina's mouth watered as each piece of Jim's clothing was pitched into the open pod door. Hers followed close after.

Jim was all lean muscle and sexy rippling abs, just as she'd thought. His body was perfect symmetry of the male form. His eyes—always so serious at other times—smoldered at her. She'd bet only his past lovers had ever seen that look on his face and it thrilled her to know that she was part of a select group. Only a woman could bring about such a drastic change in this man who had lived the life of a protector, a guardian who could seldom let down his guard for the sake of his people. That she had the power to make him drop his façade in favor of pure passion was a heady thought.

Of course, he did the same thing to her. She, who had prided herself on her control of almost any situation, was powerless in the face of his fire. All he had to do was look at her and her composure shattered—her body became his for the taking.

They came together in a rush, meeting each other halfway on the platform. It was about the size of a good old-fashioned king-sized bed, probably designed for a few people to stand comfortably while waiting for the pod to be redirected onto its new path. Jim and she put the open space to an altogether different use as they twined together, mouths seeking, lips blending.

Jim walked her backward toward the wide console. A large master switch had to be thrown in order to power up the old electronics. So far, neither of them had tried to light up to the console—at least not with electricity. No, they had voltage of a different kind running through their systems as Jim hoisted her upward, so her bare bottom rested on the edge of the console.

Luckily, there was a small, flat desktop workspace right before the buttons and levers started their march up the surface of the console. She could feel them against her skin when she inadvertently leaned too far back. Jim shifted her closer and the distracting sensation disappeared to be replaced by a much more alluring one—the feel of Jim's hairy chest against her breasts, teasing her nipples as he kissed her breathless.

154

Within minutes she could no longer stand being separated from him. She reached down and pulled at his hips, silently communicating what she wanted most. Him, inside her.

Jim complied with a low growl as he pushed into her in one long, stretching slide. He felt glorious. And even after all the times they'd come together in the past hours, she still couldn't get over the rightness of this feeling, the wonder of it all. It felt like she was made for him and after this was all over, she'd be ruined for any other man. She knew it, and accepted it. There was no other way for them. No hope for a future together. He had his duty, and she had hers. Both were too important to their people, their planet, to put aside.

Jim rocked her with bone-shattering intensity, saying so much without any words at all. He looked deep into her eyes as he thrust deep into her body, the expression on his rugged face speaking of the power of his attraction, the force of his desperation, the very real desire that sparked so uncontrollably between them. She knew her face probably mirrored the same feelings.

His touch also fired her empathic sense. For some reason she was able to read Jim better than most people she'd just met. Sure, she'd known him before but only from afar. The stark truth of their relationship—such as it was—was that they were reacquainted strangers with a shared memory of the past but little intimate knowledge of each other. God willing, they'd have time to really get to know each other on this journey. They'd already started, sharing long hours talking about their past, their hopes for the present and their dreams for the future. She hungered for that knowledge. She wanted to know him—really know him—and to understand what made him tick.

She sensed an answering need in him. He yearned for something from her as he searched her eyes. She couldn't put it into words but she felt the emotion coming from him in waves as he rocked them both toward the pinnacle they'd visited together before. The pleasure was addictive. Given a few more rounds of this, she'd readily agree to anything he proposed. He'd made her his slave.

That was saying a lot for a woman who prided herself on her independence and ability to handle almost anything life threw at her. He was a strong man who didn't throw his strength around. He led by making people want to follow him, not by fear or intimidation. She'd seen that back at his base. He was so strong, so powerful, so steadfast, the men who followed his lead did so out of deference to the force of his personality, the strength of his convictions and the fairness in his heart.

She'd follow his lead for all those reasons, but also because her body had gained an intrinsic understanding of his dominance over the past hours. It was instinctive in humans, as in many animals, to stand back and allow the alpha male to lead. Gina was quickly learning how easy it would be to give over all control to an alpha male like Jim.

"You're killing me, baby, with that look on your face."

His words penetrated directly into her mind. It was the first time he had initiated telepathic communication during an intimate moment. The rumble of his thoughts through her mind brought an even deeper level of intensity to what they were doing.

"What look is that?" She strained against him as he drove deeper, higher.

"It has heartbreak written all over it, Gina."

Gina blinked, knowing instantly she'd been too unguarded. She, who'd been taught since early childhood to never telegraph her next move or allow her thoughts to show on her face, had crossed that line with him. Only with him. Jim Brown was the only man to ever make her forget her training—to make her forget herself.

The plateau of pleasure they'd reached stretched on as he looked into her eyes. She was shocked by how easily she'd forgotten everything she'd been taught. It was time to regroup, but first, it was time to make him come.

Turnabout was fair play, and her new goal was to make him as crazy as he'd made her. Wresting control from him would be difficult and had an added flavor of danger, but ultimately she thought it could be a lot of fun.

"I love the sound of your thoughts in my head." She sent her thoughts into his mind, lowering her eyelashes so she regarded him through pleasure-soaked slits. *"Almost as much as I love the feel of you in my pussy."*

Jim growled at her changed tone and moved more decisively within her.

"I can feel your excitement, you know. This close, my empathic senses are nearly drowning in your need for completion, your need to come."

"Two can play this game, baby." The growl in his tone made her

shiver all the way down to her toes. *"Your body is like warm velvet fisting around me, slick and hot. I know you can feel how much I want to shoot into you. Almost as much as you want to shimmy in climax around me. Don't you, honey?"*

She sent him a wicked smile. *"You must be a mindreader."*

"Not quite, but I do recognize when a woman wants to come. Do it now, baby. Come on me, and I'll come in you."

His words were accompanied by yet another increase in pace and a slight shifting that brought him into her on a slightly different angle. That slight change was enough to send her to the moon. She cried out both vocally and telepathically as she orgasmed hard in his arms. The peak was so high, she was only dimly aware of him following right behind her, spurting in warm waves that prolonged her pleasure.

They were both sweaty and breathing hard as they came down from the highest peak they'd yet achieved together—and that was saying something. Gina had never had a better lover. He'd shown her things about her own body that she never would have imagined just a few days ago. She could read his satisfaction with what they did together—a sort of masculine pride and something that felt almost like a claim of ownership, or perhaps a desire to command and dominate.

Rather than objecting, the taste of his thoughts and emotions made her yearn for something that could never be. The two of them together was just a temporary thing. Both of them knew it was highly unlikely it could ever be more. They were resigned to it. Or so she believed. But it was clear from what she could read of his emotions that he wished for more.

Just like she did.

Chapter Twelve

Gina took watch on the next leg of their journey while Jim slept. She watched the rails carefully, taking notes for Wally in short bursts. Her handwriting suffered because she wasn't looking down most of the time as she wrote, but she figured Wally would just have to deal with it. There was too much at stake. One moment of inattention could cause them to crash into something obstructing their path. And although the maps looked as if the rail system extended all the way to the Canadian base, no one had been able to explore this far yet, so no one was really one hundred percent sure.

This section of track was a little different than the straight lines they'd encountered on the previous sections. This one curved slightly in a westerly direction, but the curve wasn't steep. It was just enough to make watching the track ahead interesting. Gina was glad of the need to pay strict attention to her task. It kept her from thinking too deeply about the new relationship between herself and Jim.

She would try her best to protect her heart, but at this point she knew she wouldn't escape completely unscathed when their interlude was over. She'd carry a piece of him in her heart forever. He was a considerate and adventurous lover. And her small empathic gift told her he felt much the same.

It was an emotional disaster waiting to happen, about which they could do nothing. Their course had been set long before either of them had embarked on this journey. This journey alone was the only time they could count on. More than likely, it would be the only opportunity they ever had. The only course of action that made any sense was to make the most of it while she could.

Hell, she had more of a chance of seeing Grady Prime again than she did of making a relationship with Jim work. Why the Alvian warrior should come to mind now, when she'd done her best to stop thinking about him, she didn't know. Their one encounter had changed her fundamentally. It had opened her up to new possibilities and probably even made this time with Jim possible.

Before she'd met Grady Prime, Gina had been much more protective of her heart, but Grady had blown all that away. He'd stormed her senses and freed her soul, unknowingly readying her for what came next. Too bad she didn't see a happy ending in her future with either man. No, Grady had opened her to the possibilities of emotional entanglement without any promise, or even hope, of a happily ever after.

It was depressing really, but by the same token, she wouldn't trade her time spent with Jim for anything in the world.

They traveled in relative safety for another day or so, switching off every few hours to change drivers. At every station along the way they took the opportunity to walk around, stretch their legs and make love. Jim was nearly insatiable. She wanted his kisses, his gentle touches, the small movements that said she was special to him. And she wanted his cock.

He was a talented and inventive lover. He made love to her like he wanted to fit everything into the few days they had together. Like he had just this one chance to show her everything she meant to him.

It wasn't that far from the truth and the thought of it—of never being with him again—was unbearable. So she tried not to think about it and focused on the here and now and the amazing things he made her feel.

They christened every platform along their path as they made their way slowly toward Canada and the possibility of another human colony waiting for them there. The trip became less about their goal and more about their relationship, but Gina didn't mind in the least. It had been years since she'd concentrated on herself and this enforced intimacy was special.

She was free to indulge her senses for this short period, knowing that at the end of their journey, duty awaited them both. She lost track of time as they traveled but she figured that was a good thing. The lack of day or night in the tunnels gave her a false sense of timelessness— an illusion that they could be together forever—as long as they remained in the tunnels.

But every journey must eventually come to an end.

As the pod rounded a long, sweeping curve, Gina slowed the vehicle. It looked like something blocked the way in the distance, and she didn't want to take a chance. The big pod took time to decelerate.

The slowing motion awakened Jim. Rubbing the sleep out of his eyes, he joined her in the front of the cabin.

"Problem?"

"Possibly." She pointed into the distance where they could just make out something blocking the rails.

"We packed some shovels in case of rubble. Could be that's all it is. If we're lucky."

"But the rails are still powered up. How do we clear the tracks if they're electrified?"

"There should be a kill switch every once in awhile along the tunnel wall. Don't you remember Wally mentioning it? Look." He pointed out the window at a small box on the tunnel wall as they glided past slowly. "There's one. I'll hop out once we come to a stop and jog back here."

"Sounds like a plan." She didn't want to admit she'd been distracted during some of Wally's briefing. Her head had been filled with questions about the journey ahead and the man she'd be sharing it with.

They cruised to a stop and as promised, Jim jumped out and headed for the emergency kill switch. A few minutes later, the pod dropped slowly to the ground, no longer hovering on the electromagnetic field generated by the electrified track.

Gina jumped down from the hatch, a shovel in one hand and a broom in the other. Jim met her, stealing a kiss as he reached for the shovel.

"It looks safe, but keep your eyes peeled." His words came telepathically into her mind. She was glad of the warning since all her experience and training seemed to fly right out the window whenever Jim distracted her with one of those devastating kisses. *"I'll shovel the debris out of the way while you stand watch, then we'll switch and you can sweep off the rails while I stand guard."*

"Do you think we're getting close?"

"I'd bet we were almost there, but it's hard to judge distances down here. According to the schematics, we should be on the last set of tracks

leading to the facility. Frankly I'm amazed we haven't run into obstructions before this. With all the upheaval of the cataclysm, these tunnels have remained mostly intact."

"Well, they were built by the military. Chances are, the old Army Corps of Engineers had a hand in the design. Those guys built things to last."

"Good point." Jim shoveled the larger rocks away from the tracks. "I think someone put these here deliberately."

"What makes you say that?"

"See the way these rocks lay? They form almost a straight line across the tracks. That's not natural. Someone put these here to stop any vehicles that came this way. This could be an ambush."

Gina let her telekinetic senses stretch out in the way she perfected over many years of study. She could sense movement—even the tiniest twitch of an opponent's muscles. This skill was her early warning system, her personal radar, and it had made her an invaluable part of many missions for the *Zxerah*.

"No movement yet besides you and me," she reported to Jim.

He stopped shoveling for a moment to look at her. "So Larry was right. You really can use your gifts to detect movement."

"It's the only really good skill I have." She shrugged her shoulders. She'd never been comfortable with having such a paltry ability compared with the rest of her family. "I'm sorry I didn't tell you before."

"That's okay, sweetheart. We all deserve to keep a secret or two."

She didn't like the sound of that but was prevented from commenting by movement in the tunnel ahead.

"Heads up. My spidey-senses are tingling."

He was instantly alert, she could tell by the tension in his shoulders, but he kept working as if unaware of the approaching danger. Gina shifted her weight subtly into a ready stance. The broom in her hands became a weapon, a bo staff that could be used to fend off an attack.

"What can you tell me?"

"They're approaching cautiously, and there's more than one. Two. Men, I think, judging by the displacement of air."

"Jeez, baby, you can sense air displacement? That's some sharp skill you have."

For just a moment, Gina basked in his praise. Her father and brothers had always been complementary and kind about her gifts, but back then she hadn't been this skilled. She'd always felt second best in the psychic department because the rest of her family was incredibly talented in demonstrable ways. Her meager skills had been weak compared to theirs and mostly untrained. To have Jim's admiration meant more than she could say.

"They're getting closer, and they're good at stealth. There are definitely two of them. Men. Big men. About your size, I'd say. And..." she reached for the information floating in the air currents, *"...they're armed. Long sticks. Could be rifles, could be brooms. I can't tell you more than the size and shape."*

"That's more than enough. We'll let them dictate how this encounter starts out, but if they mean us harm, you and I will finish it."

She liked the way he included her in his plans. Jim never underestimated her. He had never asked her to take a back seat while he did all the work. She liked having his respect as an equal partner. Hell, she just plain liked *him*. Perhaps even loved him.

She was in big trouble when the notion of loving him didn't even faze her. She understood it then, in that moment, with possible enemies stalking them. She was in love with Jim.

A tall man stepped out into the middle of the track a few yards from their position. He held a rifle at the ready.

Jim stopped shoveling and turned to face the newcomer, keeping his hands in sight, leaning on the shovel handle casually.

"Who are you and what are you doing here?" the man wanted to know.

"I'm Jim. This is Gina. We just came up in the pod from the Colorado facility to see if anybody lived here. I assume I'm talking to someone who lives in the old NORAD site?"

The man shifted his weight, and Gina read caution in his every move. His companion remained hidden in the shadows near the tunnel wall.

"The tracks are clear and functional all the way to Colorado?" The man sounded surprised to Gina. He was more curious than dangerous at the moment, if she was reading him correctly.

"Yes, though we had to take it slow past the first few sets of tracks since none of our scouts had been able to go much further. We're an exploration party, if you will."

"Well, you found us. So how about you tell us what you want?"

"That's pretty easy. You're human. We're human. We both have secure facilities where I assume you've got more people living. We want to make an alliance. To share information. If the foreseers are right, the time is coming when we'll need allies."

"You've got a foreseer?" The man's gaze turned to Gina speculatively.

She smiled. "Not me. But yes, there's at least one among Jim's people."

The man quirked a brow at her phrasing.

"Are you sure about this?" Jim asked in the privacy of her mind.

"Honesty is always the best policy. Better they find out now so they can't accuse me of hiding anything later."

"All right." Jim sounded reconciled to her bold move. *"I've got your back, baby."*

She could've kissed him right then, for his support. God, she loved this man.

"Jim's people," the stranger repeated. "But not your people? Why's that? And what are you wearing?"

Gina stepped closer to the man, her palms open in an unthreatening pose. "Noticed my duds, huh? Very good. I'm an emissary from a secret sect of Alvians called the *Zxerah*. The Patriarch of my clan doesn't want humanity to fail. He wants to facilitate us getting in touch with each other so we'll be stronger when things come to a head. My clan has a few seers in it too, and the *Zxerah* Patriarch listens to them closely."

"So he can figure out how best to hoodwink the humans?" the man challenged.

"So he can figure out a way for us all to live together in peace," she countered.

"Burt, can you hear me?" The stranger spoke seemingly into the air, confusing Gina for a moment until a computerized voice answered in the affirmative. "Could you patch this through to Bill? We need his input."

"Right away, Michael," the computer answered. Only then did Gina notice a small speaker placed high on the ceiling of the tunnel.

She hadn't seen those before. Apparently they were much closer to the Canadian facility than she'd thought.

"I'm here, Mike. What do you need?" A new voice came over the speaker. It was a beautiful voice...with that distinctive Alvian trill, though it was well hidden. Still, Gina heard it. She'd lived with Alvians a long time, after all. She knew them well.

"Tell him what you just told me," Mike directed her. The rifle in his arms was in a relaxed position, but it was still there.

"Greetings, brother," Gina said hesitantly.

"What are you doing?" Jim asked, shifting toward her protectively.

"Trust me. That voice is Alvian, and there's only one explanation I can think of."

"Am I speaking with Prime Past?" Gina continued. She noticed Mike's rifle move up to cover her once more, and the man in the shadows tensed.

"Who are you?" the disembodied voice came over the speaker, suspicion in his tone.

"Gina Hanson, adopted daughter of the *Zxerah* clan. Ronin Prime sent me."

"Keep her there, Mike. I'll be down shortly."

"Well, that got a response," Jim groused in her mind. *"Mind telling me what's going on?"*

"I told you the Alvians were experimenting on returning emotions. The man who just spoke is most likely the first of those experiments. The seers said one of the Brotherhood would encounter him at some point and that he'd be an ally in our ultimate quest, but I didn't think I'd be the one to find him. This is really good, Jim. I promise."

"Give us lights, Burt," Mike ordered and lights flared in the tunnel, showing them for the first time just how close they were to the end of the line. Just a few yards ahead the track ended in an open chamber much like the one they'd departed from. She saw the second man, also armed with a rifle, standing near the chamber entrance. "I'm Mike, and this is my cousin, Dave."

The second man nodded at her. "You're the girl from the Olympics, aren't you? Some kind of ultimate fighter?"

Gina smiled. "I won gold for *tae kwon do*, but I've learned a few other things since then."

"And got mixed up with the aliens apparently." David's tone invited her to say more.

"I literally ran into one of them during my flight from the coast. He took me in and protected me—even from the rest of his race. The *Zxerah* Patriarch has adopted many humans into his clan."

"So how do you know our friend Bill?" Mike asked.

"If he's who I think he is, I trained with him and his men once or twice. He's part of the Brotherhood."

"Not anymore." There was real force of emotion behind the words as a tall, blond man entered the chamber and came forward to face her. "You're looking well, Gina."

"You too, Prime."

"I'm not Prime any longer. Call me Bill."

She dipped her head in agreement even as her lips curled upward. "Bill. It suits you. I'm glad to find you."

"Dougal 17 didn't tell you I was here? I ran into him in the skies a few days ago."

"I've been out of touch with the Brotherhood for more than a week. I didn't know you'd be here."

"So why did you come?"

"My mission started in Colorado, making contact with Jim and his people. My goal was to inform him of the other confirmed and suspected locations throughout North America where we think humans are gathering and living in sites like this."

"To what end?"

"To put them in touch with each other. Humans have few reliable ways of communicating nowadays. But these old military sites may hold the key not only for communication, but cooperation among the various groups of humans living together and hiding out for safety."

"Why?" Mike asked. "Why would we need to band together? As long as we stay hidden, the Alvians pretty much leave us alone."

"If you know any seers, you should have a good long talk with them," she advised. "More than one visionary tells of a time when everything's going to come to a head. The outcome for humans will be much better if we can speak with one voice. If we can show the Alvians that we know how to survive and rebuild our society, even in secret.

That's something their social engineers will respect, even while they can't understand the emotion that drives us. But they will."

"They will what? Understand emotion?" Dave asked, moving a few steps closer.

Gina nodded. "Sinclair Prime—or Bill, as you know him—was the first of what we hope will be many. Already another group of test subjects has been treated with the same gene-altering agent with good results. Little by little, the Alvian race is embracing a change for the better. A drastic change that will restore emotion to many, if not all of them, in the fullness of time."

"You've got to be kidding." Mike sounded amazed.

"I'm not. That's the goal of the *Zxerah* Patriarch."

"And he hasn't got you all brainwashed or something? How can you be sure he's not rounding us up? Getting everyone in one place to make it easier for them to capture us all at once?" Mike insisted.

"I have enough empathy to feel even his weak echoes of emotion. The *Zxerah* are warriors. As such, they have more emotion than other Alvians. He's told me the truth. I know it."

"Will you let me touch your mind?" Dave asked suddenly. "We need to be sure."

"You're a mind healer?" Something inside her softened as she remembered her family and the rare gift some of them had.

"You've known one before?" A raised eyebrow indicated his curiosity as Dave moved closer to her.

"My brother." She swallowed hard against the emotional memory her brother brought. "I'll allow it, if it will help convince you."

Dave smiled at her. He was a very handsome man, and he had kind eyes. She didn't get to think much more about him because at that moment he touched her face, his mind seeking hers. She could feel Jim moving close behind her, but he let the situation unfold. He was the perfect partner for her. He allowed her to be who she was but was always there to back her up if necessary.

Dave stepped back, leaving her with a glowing feeling as his power left her. She remembered the feeling from when her brother touched her mind and it made her nostalgic.

"She's telling the truth as she knows it," he told his friends. "Her mind hasn't been tampered with."

"All right." Mike lifted his weapon upward, pointing it at the ceiling. "Let's take this upstairs where it's more comfortable. Burt, please secure the area and continue to monitor for intruders."

"Yes, Mike," the computer voice said over the speaker.

"Do you have a computer like that in Colorado?" Gina asked Jim as they followed Mike out of the tunnel and into the larger chamber.

"Not that I know of. But a lot of systems were damaged in the earthquakes. I bet Wally would know. I'll have to ask him when we get back."

"So you think there's a good chance we'll live to tell the tale?" She couldn't resist teasing him.

They followed Mike as Dave and Bill brought up the rear in a guard position.

"I'd say our chances are improving all the time. But what in the world are these people doing sharing their hideout with an Alvian?"

"He's on the run, just as much as they are—possibly even more so. He was given an assignment by the Council and not only failed in his mission, but precipitated the Chief Engineer's ability to effectively hold the Council hostage to whatever he wanted. They didn't like that one bit, and the man ultimately responsible for that fiasco got away. They've been hunting him ever since. I'm just glad we found him first."

They all piled into a large elevator which started to climb. Gina lost track of how many levels they rose but was glad when the elevator came to a stop and they all got out. Rather than climb higher, the men led her and Jim to a small, utilitarian room. It looked like a conference room of sorts, though at one time it had probably been somebody's office.

Their hosts indicated they should sit, and Gina took the seat next to Jim. His presence helped calm her nerves. She was surprised by just how nervous she felt now that contact had been made. Her mission was on track, and she wanted to keep it that way.

"Why don't you tell us more about this secret sect of yours?" Mike invited once they'd all been seated.

"The *Zxerah* Brotherhood is hard to describe. They're part ninja, part Tibetan monk and all focused on individual study and enlightenment. A small cadre serves in the Alvian military as a sort of ghost squad. The rest of us live in secret, serving as their support system and spending our time studying and doing reconnaissance for the Patriarch. I first met him not long after the cataclysm. Fate put him in my path, I'm sure. I mean, what are the odds that the first human this man finds is an Olympic gold medal-winning martial artist?"

"Did they try to capture you?" David asked.

"Sort of. Their form of capture would have been more like protective custody, but I didn't know that at the time. I fought. The Patriarch had his men back off and tested my skills one on one. Each pushed my boundaries a little further. Ultimately my strength gave out but not before they'd learned a heck of a lot about human unarmed fighting techniques which were amazingly a lot like their own."

"I can confirm this. I had reports from the men who fought her," Bill spoke unexpectedly from his seat near the door. "Her acceptance into the clan was controversial at first. Once we saw her skills and realized how her psychic abilities enhanced her physical attributes, Ronin confided to me that he thought it was the right thing to do to adopt her into the clan and learn from her and the others he adopted after."

"Ronin is this Patriarch she mentioned?" Mike asked.

"The same," Bill confirmed. "Ronin Prime is the Patriarch of the *Zxerah* Brotherhood. I once counted him as a friend. I believe at heart, he is a good man, but he plays a deep game. Not even I know what his ultimate goal is."

"There is no Ronin genetic line that I'm aware of." A new, feminine voice sounded from the doorway.

"Sweetheart, I thought we asked you to stay put." Mike was clearly exasperated by the Alvian woman's appearance, but he pulled her into the room and sat her between himself and his cousin. The affection both men felt for her was obvious to Gina at this close distance.

"Who the hell is she?" Jim's voice in her mind had a hard edge of suspicion. *"This place is crawling with aliens."*

"Relax, Jim," she cautioned. *"I didn't know about her but look at the way those cousins treat her. And look at the way she treats them. She's in love with them."*

"You're a romantic fool," he chastised, but there was no real scorn in his voice. Rather, he seemed to be watching them carefully.

"The Ronin genetic line is top secret," Bill carried on the conversation. "Mara Prime oversees them directly along with a few other select genetic lines that are unique to the *Zxerah*."

"*Zxerah?*" The woman sounded truly shocked. "They're real? And you were one of them, Bill? How come you never told us?"

"*She seems really hurt,*" Jim observed silently.

"*She is. She has feelings.*" Gina was as surprised by the observation as Jim was.

"That discussion is for later." Bill shut down that avenue of questioning. "For now, we must decide what to make of our guests." He effectively turned the attention back to Gina and Jim.

"Just how many aliens are you hiding down here?" Jim's voice held a challenging note.

"Only these two," Mike promised with a grin. "I know this looks like we're consorting with the enemy, but once you get to know them you'll understand they're different."

"They both have feelings." Gina let her statement hang in the air for a minute. "I know Bill volunteered for a genetic experiment, but what happened to you? Are you a throwback?" She looked directly at the other woman.

The elegant blonde shrugged. "I was the lab tech assigned to prepare the dosages for the next run of the experiment. I got sloppy in the lab, made a mistake and here I am."

"Damn," Jim swore without heat. "This Patriarch's plans really may have some validity after all. I never thought to meet an Alvian who could understand emotion and now I find two of you in one day."

"*Ah ha!*" Gina joked with him privately. "*So now you're starting to believe me.*"

Jim shot her a considering look. "*I'm keeping an open mind.*"

"So what do you have in mind by way of cooperation between our two installations?" Michael brought the conversation back on point.

"Communication to begin with." Jim took charge. "Information exchange. Reconnaissance of what goes on outside in our respective areas. We have very limited information about what goes on in the rest of the world. I think that works to our detriment. Knowledge is power and all that. In return, we have some of the original scientists who worked in and designed these facilities living among us. If you need information on how to repair or work some of your systems, we might be able to help you. Hell, we might even be able to trade. Our hydroponics farm unit turns out more than we can use sometimes. I hate to see food go to waste and if we can keep the tunnels open, we can use them to transport goods back and forth."

"I like the idea, but I'd want to see your facility and meet your people before we agree to anything." David was cautious, but it was good to see he was interested.

"That can be arranged. We have extra seats in the pod if anyone wants to travel back with us, but I noticed on our way up that you had a couple of pods yourself." Gina hadn't noticed any pods, but then Jim was a lot taller than she was and could see more of the area while her view had been blocked by the big men all around her.

"Bill is our head farmer." Dave gestured toward the Alvian man. "He's gotten the hydroponics section started and now that we have more people, he has some help, but we've only been living down here a few months."

"Really? The Colorado facility has been in continuous habitation since the cataclysm. Like I said, a lot of the original staff hid out there and brought their families in when it became clear there was no going back to the old world. I arrived later, having made my way over land to get there."

"You knew about the facility before the bombardment?" Mike asked shrewdly.

"I was CIA. I'd been in spec ops and had done some work for NORAD. I'd been to the Cheyenne Mountain facility a few times and knew the codes. It was the most likely place I could think of to regroup after I heard what the Alvian goon squads were doing."

"Good thinking," Dave agreed. He took the woman's hand and brought it to his thigh, a clear and unconscious sign of affection. "We only found this place a couple of months ago when Jaci needed a place to hide out, but it was in really good condition. The base computer had been powered down in preparation for a new crew's arrival according to BURTIN."

"Is that the computer you were talking to before?" Gina had never heard of such a thing, but she'd seen it with her own eyes, like something out of an old science fiction book.

"Yeah, this whole place is monitored and maintained by an artificial intelligence prototype. BURTIN stands for Basic Underground Resident Type 1 Intelligence Net, but we just call him Burt. He monitors everything and lets us know if anyone or anything stumbles upon us. That's how we knew you were in the tunnels, though nobody's ever arrived that way before." Mike scratched his face, which was showing the beginnings of a beard. "Now that word's got out here and there about Bill, we get a lot of people tromping through the woods looking for us. Burt helps us find them before they hurt themselves or alert the sporadic patrols to something fishy going on down here. We mostly take them in, though a few bad seeds have been sent on their way with a warning not to return. Bill's real helpful in that department too."

The cousins shared a laugh, and Bill just looked uncomfortable.

"Must be good to have a shadow warrior around." Gina was upset on Bill's behalf. It wasn't right for them to use him that way. Not if he'd truly given up his assassin's ways. "I assume they come because you've been out flying? You should know that the Council has heard the rumors spreading among the human populace about an angel. They sent Grady Prime to investigate, and he was given full access to your former squadron."

Bill stood violently, overturning his chair as emotion swamped him. Gina could feel the almost overwhelming confusion, despair, anger and regret mixed up in his conflicted soul. She stood and went to him, holding out her hand where he could see it before she touched him. One didn't sneak up on a former *Zxerah* assassin.

"I'm sorry." She touched him, offering what little mind healing power she could to help settle his emotions. "I didn't say that to upset you."

A hand settled on her shoulder. It was David. "Stop before you deplete yourself. Mind healing isn't your true calling, is it?"

She let go, giving up her place to David. The man took Bill's arm, and even Gina could feel the instant peace he was able to transfer to the confused Alvian male.

"No. I'm not much of a mind healer. Not like others in my family. Not like you."

Gina felt her strength ebb and she swayed on her feet but Jim was there to catch her, holding her back to his chest as they stood together. He gave her strength, and she realized both Alvians were looking at her strangely.

"You Hum," the woman said softly, a smile spreading over her face. "Are you true mates?"

"I don't know what that means," Jim answered carefully.

"But you do." Mike's tone was accusing as he looked at Gina. "You know what it means to Hum for an Alvian."

"I've heard the term," she admitted. "Grady Prime told me I Hummed with him, but of course I can't hear it. If it really exists."

"Oh, it exists all right. You Hum with both Grady Prime and Jim? This could get interesting." The grin the other woman gave her was mischievous. "Both are warriors and leaders. I wonder if they'll try to dominate you—and if you'll let them?"

Gina was confounded by the woman's knowing grin. "Look, I'll probably never see Grady again."

"Did you have sex with him?"

Gina gasped at the woman's rude question, and Jim's arms tightened around her.

"What's this about Humming?"

"It's an Alvian thing," Mike explained almost offhandedly. "When mates touch, their bodies resonate on a cellular level, creating a Hum. It's a sound audible in a range beyond our hearing, but the Alvians can pick it up. According to our two resident aliens, you Hum with Gina."

"So then we're mates?" Jim didn't sound too happy about that, and it was Gina's turn to be upset.

"It's not that easy. The Hum just means you have the potential to be mates. The other tests are the Kiss and the Embrace. Do those with a tuned crystal nearby and watch the fireworks. If you're true mates, each of those will generate a more intense response from the crystal, confirming your resonance. If you can make the crystal glow like a star, you're Resonance Mates, like we are with Jaci." Mike tugged a crystal out of his pocket and placed it on the table, then pulled Jaci into his arms, laying a kiss on her that could melt rubber.

The crystal glowed.

"Well, I'll be damned. I never saw a crystal do that before." Jim let Gina go as he bent to get a good look at the shining shard of quartz.

Mike let Jaci go, and the crystal dimmed until it no longer glowed. "Why don't you two try it?"

Jim didn't even give Gina a chance to object. He just tugged her around and laid one on her. She couldn't see the crystal and didn't care, frankly, what it showed. She was too wrapped up in Jim's kiss.

But the room was definitely brighter and when he let her go, the crystal slowly dimmed as they drew apart.

"So we're mates?" Jim asked again.

"Close, but to be really sure, you need to Embrace her. Take the crystal. Try it later, and you'll see. If the crystal glows even brighter, you're definitely Resonance Mates and according to ancient Alvian law, mates can never be separated for any reason. It's a good ace to keep up your sleeve, if you're so inclined." Mike tipped his nonexistent hat to them both.

"Thanks." Jim pocketed the crystal. "I'll give this back after we've tried it out."

"I guess you'll only need one room for the night, eh?" Mike teased them, and Gina felt a blush rise up her cheeks.

They all sat again, and Jim took the conversation back a bit. "So what's this stuff about angels and flying?"

Chapter Thirteen

Arch looks shot between everyone in the room except Jim. He was definitely being kept in the dark about something. Jim had taken Tory's talk of angels as ravings, or at best, as a metaphor for something else. But now these people were talking about them too—and none of them sounded like they were on the edge of insanity. Maybe there really was something to Tory's visions. If so, he'd damn well find out.

Bill gave Gina a narrow-eyed look. "How much have you told him about the *Zxerah*?"

"Quite a bit, but not that. It is your secret to share or not, as you see fit. I assume your companions already know?" Gina glanced around the room at the others. Jim didn't like being left in the dark, but he'd play it cool for now. It sounded like he was about to learn something.

Bill gave a most un-Alvian sigh. The guy freaked Jim out a little. He just wasn't used to seeing Alvians displaying human emotions.

"I've got wings."

"Come again?" Jim didn't know what he'd expected, but this stark declaration shocked him.

"Wings. I can fly. Like your mythological angels. If the Council has heard rumors, I guess I haven't been as circumspect as I thought when flying out over the forests."

"Hell, it's not your fault, Bill. There are mountain men and hidden villages all over this area," Mike said in what sounded like an old argument. "Humans around here have gotten good at hiding their presence from aerial view. The Alvian patrols usually come by aircraft, so they keep an eye to the sky. I'd have been surprised if nobody saw you."

"With our culture's religious beliefs, we figured it couldn't hurt anything if a couple of humans saw you flying around. If anything," Dave stressed, "we thought it might give people hope. An angel is a powerful symbol in most human religions."

"I am nobody's deity."

The true anger and frustration Jim heard in the Alvian's musical voice gave him pause. He had to keep reminding himself that this guy was different from the other Alvians he'd seen—very different if he really did have wings—but that was something Jim would really have to see to believe. And so would a lot of people he knew. Jim made a decision.

"I think you should come back to Colorado with us, Bill. Just for a visit. And I'll guarantee your safety. But there's one foreseer in particular who needs to see you—if you're willing. She's been talking about angels for as long as I've known her and when she first saw Gina here, she swore up and down that Gina would be the one to bring the angels to us. Nobody knew what she meant and we all figured she was half-insane from the loss of her family, but if you really do have wings, I think you're the answer to the puzzle. It would be a kindness if you'd let her see you—even if she's the only one you show. Tory is special, and she needs hope. I think you can give it to her."

Jim noticed David's eyes narrowing in thought as he'd started to talk about Tory. "We're getting ahead of ourselves a bit, but if Bill goes back with you, I'll go too. It sounds like your seer could use my help."

Jim felt a weight lift off his shoulders. "I've protected her as best I can but what she really needs is a mind healer, and we don't have one. I'd be much obliged if you'd take a look at her and see what you can do."

David nodded. "Let's table this discussion for the time being. It's late, and I'm sure you're tired from your long journey. Bill, do you want to show them to the guest quarters? Fair warning, you'll be locked in and Burt will be monitoring you, but he won't report back to us unless you try to sneak out."

"Sounds reasonable," Jim allowed. "We're the strangers here. We'll abide by your rules."

"All right then." David stood, and the others followed his lead. "Bill will show you around a bit on your way to your quarters, and we'll arrange for some food to be brought down to you. We'll reconvene in the morning, once we've all had a chance to think this over."

Jim was glad of the way David took the lead, though he sounded more like a chairman of the board than a general commanding his troops. Whatever his past life had been, he'd come out on top. He had a wife, a solid place to live and what promised to be a thriving community here. He was luckier than most.

The others said good night and left Gina and Jim with Bill. He led them up a flight of stairs and down a hallway to a large open area that looked a lot like the hydroponics section of the Colorado installation. This one wasn't completely filled, however. It had the look of something just starting up. There were a few people working at the far end of the large expanse, and Jim was pleased to note they all looked human.

Bill started muttering when he saw them and shook his head. "Please stay here for a moment, I need to get the crew back on track or we won't have much of a harvest."

Jim expected him to walk the long distance between where they were and the crew's position at the far end of a cavern the size of a football field, but he was wrong. Instead, shockingly, Bill shrugged off his jacket and huge golden wings expanded on either side of his torso. The man lifted off the ground with a few beats of those magnificent feathered wings and crossed the vast distance of the cavern in just a few seconds.

"Holy shit."

Gina laughed at his reaction.

"You knew, didn't you?" He turned to face her as Bill landed and started talking with the group of people at the far end of the cavern.

Gina's expression was grave. "I knew. I've known his kind for a long time. They are part of my clan."

"How many?" Jim's thoughts sped ahead to the implications of having large numbers of winged beings roaming around the Earth. "How many more like him are out there?"

"I don't know the exact numbers, but at least a battalion was created. They're genetic experiments. They had another alien race's DNA spliced into their own chromosomes in order to give them wings."

"Another alien race? Do we have to fear another invasion somewhere down the line?"

"I don't think so. From what I've heard, the Avarel stopped visiting

Alvia Prime and all the Alvian colonies—except perhaps the *Zxerah* enclave—a very long time ago. I have a feeling they might already have visited Earth in the distant past. Otherwise why do most religious traditions talk about men with wings? By all accounts, the Avarel were a peaceful people. They exchanged knowledge with the *Zxerah*, and it was they who first warned that selective breeding to eliminate aggression in the Alvian populace could lead to disaster. When the Alvian government refused to listen, the Avarel broke diplomatic ties and were never seen again."

The Patriarch approached Grady Prime at the hidden base of the winged brethren. The encounter seemed to be purely accidental, but Grady had his suspicions. The *Zxerah* leader seldom let coincidences rule his life. No, this was a man who made his own fate and decided the fate of many others on a routine basis.

"How goes your search, Grady?" the Patriarch asked. Grady Prime thought it significant that the Patriarch often fell into the speech patterns of the humans, leaving off the rank designation of other Alvians with whom he spoke.

Now that he had emotions and a better understanding of humanity, Grady Prime often thought the use of full names to be stiff and formal—much like the majority of his race and their habits. Formality seemed to go hand in hand with Alvian culture and it chafed Grady Prime's new perceptions at times.

He wasn't quite ready to let go of his past. He still thought of himself as Grady Prime. Perhaps one day things would change for him, but that day had not yet come.

"I have learned much about the former Sinclair Prime and have formulated a theory as to where he would have gone."

"Truly? What is your theory, if I may ask?"

"From all accounts, he is a lover of woodlands and temperate zones. I surmise that if he was able to depart the southern continent, the forests in the northern section of this continent would be much to his liking. Of course, there are some areas on the southern continent that would be just as agreeable, but they are even more remote and harder to get to. His last mission was in the southern continent, so it would be logical to start my search there."

"Logical, yes. But what does your gut instinct tell you?"

Grady's answer came quickly and unequivocally. "He's not there."

The Patriarch seemed surprised...and pleased? "Have you always had such strong instincts? Or is this a new development since taking the experimental treatment?"

That was a question Grady Prime hadn't expected from this man, even though he'd been asking himself similar things for many weeks. He was intrigued enough to engage on a more detailed level with the Patriarch than he had ever revealed to the techs.

"I always had inexplicable instincts, but they have sharpened and evolved since the treatment. I have no real reason to explain my certainty that Sinclair Prime Past is no longer on the southern continent, but it is a certainty in my mind."

"Fascinating. And enlightening. I thank you for your candor, my friend, and in return I will tell you this. Seek him in the high places. Seek him near your friends of old. Seek him among the natives, fulfilling his lifelong role as warrior and protector."

"Then you know where he is?"

The Patriarch paused, watching him with those uncanny eyes. A slight nod was all the confirmation he gave, but it was enough.

"When you find him, you will also find your heart."

"What?" The words shocked him, their meaning ambiguous, yet striking to the heart of him—the place that yearned for understanding, for acceptance, for love.

"So I was told by the strongest of the foreseers in my clan. I know not what it means, but thought you deserved to know what had been said. I wish you clear skies and fair weather on your journey. If I am not mistaken it will take you far both physically and spiritually."

"I thought our race no longer believed in the spirit." Grady Prime couldn't help challenging the Patriarch's strange words.

"Perhaps not, but the *Zxerah* have never given up all that we were and all that we can become. The humans in my clan have taught me much and renewed my faith in the teachings of our ancestors. By the First Crystal and all that came after, my spirit—blindfolded and gagged by my own lack of emotion—still wants to break free. I have made it my mission in life to help it do so for myself and for all other Alvians."

"That is a dangerous task, and one I'm not sure we're ready for."

"Ready or not, it is a step we must take. To stay as we are is to die—to kill all that we are and could be. And humanity cannot wait any longer for us to realize the error of our ways. Killing ourselves is one thing, but we can no longer destroy them with impunity. We've made a mess of this world. It is our duty to all sentient beings—to all life in the universe—to the spirit itself—to fix it."

Grady Prime was humbled by the Patriarch's words and his goals. Such matters were things he had thought of in the abstract but never dared believe he could change on his own. That the *Zxerah* Patriarch contemplated life on such a grand scale should not have been surprising but the idea that he could, and would, act to change the very nature of all Alvian existence on this planet was daunting to say the least. Grady Prime wasn't sure it was even possible, but the more he thought about it the more he realized he had to help in whatever small way he could.

"I admire your goals, Patriarch. I don't know what a simple soldier like me can do to aid them, but aid you I will, should you need my assistance."

The Patriarch seemed surprised by Grady Prime's declaration of support but also pleased in his calm, Alvian way.

"Thank you, Grady. I will remember your words and hope you will as well. There are many obstacles and tests in your path. I don't need the gift of prophecy to be able to see that. I wish you well on your journey. Be strong of heart and have faith in the rightness of your quest. And know that by the time you leave here, your craft will have been made completely untraceable."

"By anyone but the *Zxerah*, I presume," Grady challenged with a friendly grin.

The Patriarch gave him a wicked smile and left without further words, disappearing in a moment as was the way of the *Zxerah*. His words of what his people had foreseen stayed with Grady Prime however, haunting him deep into the night and all the next day as he planned the next part of his mission.

Grady Prime knew exactly where he was going. He'd been there before when he tracked a runaway Alvian lab tech named Jaci 192. He'd found her frolicking in a pool with her two human Resonance Mates, laughing and displaying emotion he couldn't understand at the time.

He thought he knew better now and wanted an experience like

that for himself. He wanted a woman who could care for him as Jaci cared for her two mates, Michael and David.

Grady Prime didn't know why he was so sure he'd find Prime Past hiding out with the natives in that old bunker he'd found, but the more he thought about it, the more he knew he needed to check it out.

Sinclair Prime saw him off when he decided to go and they parted as warriors...and as friends.

"Tell him I miss his counsel," Sinclair Prime said when Grady was about ready to close the hatch.

"You're that sure I'll find him?"

"I know your skill. If he's to be found, you'll do it. Besides, I know you're on the right track."

Immediately he grew suspicious. "You sent scouts ahead, didn't you? That's how the Patriarch knew to nudge me in the right direction."

"You'll learn the Patriarch seldom leaves anything to chance, my friend." Sinclair Prime shook his hand in the way of warriors. Grady Prime returned the sign of respect. "Your mission is important to us all. Fare well on your journey. Clear skies and gentle winds, brother."

Grady Prime was touched by his words and the appellation. Still, he felt some chagrin to realize his mission had been completed already by one of the winged scouts. No doubt they'd already tagged and perhaps spoken with Prime Past. The other warrior would know Grady Prime was coming, and he'd be prepared. They'd just made his quest either impossible or all too easy. He didn't like the idea of either alternative, but the seer's words that replayed constantly in his mind kept him on his path. He'd go, if for no other reason than to meet his destiny, whatever that may be.

Grady Prime landed his craft in a copse of trees just shy of the entrance to the subterranean complex he'd found before. He hid the ship under a layer of fallen pine boughs and leaves, camouflaging it from casual discovery before he set out on foot.

The trek was as he remembered, with the bite of refreshingly chill mountain air on his face. He loved this country. The terrain was challenging enough to keep him entertained, and the weather was cool and mild at this time of year. The scenery was breathtaking.

He topped a ridge and looked around, in awe of the wonder of nature. Even Alvia Prime hadn't been able to match this new planet for the sheer vastness of its open spaces and the majesty of its vistas. Then again, Alvia Prime had many more people living on its surface before it was destroyed. Now all those souls were scattered across the galaxy, trying to colonize a handful of worlds that were capable of supporting their unique needs.

When he felt the first of the sensors, Grady Prime made the conscious decision not to hide his approach. Coming in openly was a risk, but a calculated one. Prime Past already knew someone was on the way due to the Patriarch's interference so the element of surprise was gone. Grady Prime also had a history with the people he'd last seen living in the belowground complex. If they were still there—and he thought it likely they were—he'd gain more by approaching openly than by trying to sneak up on them.

Decision made, Grady Prime sought out the sensors. He deliberately tripped the heat and motion detectors, then smiled and waved to the miniscule cameras. If anyone was monitoring the system, they had to know by now that he was on his way to pay a call.

He liked the challenge of finding all the well-camouflaged sensors and cameras. The game was afoot as the human detective Sherlock Holmes would say. He'd enjoyed reading the adventures of the mythical sleuth when Mick O'Hara loaned him the books. Now that he had emotions, he found true joy in testing his tracking skills, and in the game itself. If his grin for the cameras was a little wider than a normal Alvian's, well, that couldn't be helped. He was having fun. Fun! It was a new and thrilling concept.

Grady Prime got about ten yards from the hidden cave entrance before the greeting party made itself known.

"You have a hell of a nerve showing up here again, Grady." Michael, one of the human mates of Jaci 192, stepped out from behind a boulder, a weapon pointed at Grady Prime's heart.

"I gave you enough warning. I wasn't trying to sneak in. Thanks for coming to meet me."

"This isn't a welcoming party. This is a get off our land and don't come back meeting." Jaci's other mate, David, moved in from the side, flanking him. Grady Prime held his hands up, palms outward in a show of peace.

"I need to talk to someone I think may be living with you."

"Son of a bitch." It was David that spoke, lowering his weapon slightly. "You can feel."

Grady remembered this man had healing talent and some empathy. He was no doubt sensing Grady's feelings of exhilaration, trepidation and sheer joy in the hunt.

"As your mate recommended, I took the treatment. Officially, I'm retired from active duty. Unofficially, I've been sent to find a former Prime I believe may be hiding out with you."

"Don't you mean you were sent to kill me?" A new voice spoke as the man in question strode boldly from the cave entrance.

Grady Prime was shocked to see how Prime Past had gone native. He dressed, walked and even sounded like a human. Even his pale blond looks no longer set him apart as Alvian. Long hair masked his pointed ears and his pale skin had started to tan with exposure to this planet's yellow sun.

"I was," Grady agreed easily, earning new vigilance from the two humans who raised their weapons once more. "But like you, I've got a mind of my own now. I came to talk to you, Sinclair Prime Past."

"Call me Bill."

Grady Prime shouldn't have been surprised, he supposed, that the Council's best assassin had reinvented himself. He was well trained to blend in to whatever came his way. He'd outdone himself in this case. Grady Prime wasn't sure he would have recognized him had he run across him in the open.

"Bill." He tested the name on his tongue and found it strong. "The Patriarch hinted I might find you here."

Bill held his hands out to his side and shrugged. "Found me you have. Speak your piece, Grady."

"The Council wants you dead." Grady Prime's voice was harsh in the light of day. "But you already knew that. They sent me to kill you, but I've had much time to think and to talk with your brethren, especially Ronin Prime. What I seek is your knowledge, not your death."

"If that's the case, then be welcome. I'll talk with you, but I won't put my friends in danger. I want your word that nothing about our location or this facility will make its way into your report."

"You have it." Grady Prime relaxed a little, letting his weariness show. "At this point, I'm not even sure I'm going back. I find it hard to live among them now. Even harder than it was before."

Bill walked over and put a hand on Grady Prime's shoulder, surprising everyone with the compassion in his gesture. "I understand, brother. Let's talk and we'll see what strategy we can devise. You may yet be able to do much good from within Alvian society."

A short conference between Dave, Mike and Bill ensued, during which it was decided that Grady would be given access to the facility on a limited basis. As they walked to the cave entrance, Grady felt the animosity coming off the human men. He'd have to make an effort to show them he wasn't the same man who'd hunted them down and captured them so many years ago.

"I hope your Jaci is well," he began hesitantly. The human men gave him dirty looks, but Bill seemed surprised.

"You know about her?"

"I've been here once before, when they sent me after her," he admitted to his fellow soldier. He was very conscious of the humans listening as they all walked. "I found the three of them in a hot spring some way into the mountain. They Hummed so sweetly, it made my heart stutter. That was what decided me to take the treatment. I have to thank you for that, David and Michael. I also have to apologize for capturing you those many years ago, though you have my admiration for your evasive skills. I remember that mission more than any other. You were worthy opponents and earned my respect."

"You still caught us," Michael said in disgust. "We must not have been that good."

"Oh, I assure you," Grady chanced a smile, "you would have gotten away had it not been for the snow. I had the advantage in such weather."

"But you came after us on foot. You didn't have a ship to protect you. We figured the odds were even," David spoke at Grady's side.

"Our higher body temperature allows us to move more quickly in cold weather, with less protective gear. Surely you've noticed Bill only wears a thin coat in the cold?"

"I thought that was so he could—" Michael broke off and looked at Bill apologetically.

"It's all right. Since he's been working with my men and the Patriarch to find me, I think he knows I can fly. Don't you?" Bill shot him a knowing look.

"I do," Grady admitted. "And you have my admiration for that ability."

Bill only shrugged off the compliment as they entered the tunnel that would ultimately lead to the underground facility. Grady had been here before, but he'd never been as far inside as they were going to take him now. He was eager to see what the humans had built—both the facility that had been wrought before the crystal bombardment and what the current occupants had done with it.

The tunnels were as he remembered them, twining around the mountain as if following ore deposits. In all likelihood the outer section of this facility had probably started as a mine and only later turned into the underground city that Grady assumed he would find below.

He wasn't disappointed. When they rounded the final curve, well past the grotto where his search had ended before, Grady saw a massive steel door standing open. Through the doorway he could see a very large manmade corridor that terminated in another steel blast door.

As they walked along the corridor into the facility proper, Bill walked beside him making conversation.

"Tell me of my men. Are they well?" As Grady had suspected, the ties of a commander to his men were never lost. Even in exile, Bill's concern for his people was strong.

"The new Prime asked me to tell you that he misses your counsel. He seemed to think your decision to take the treatment was a good one, but I suspect he wasn't ready to take command—at least intellectually—when you failed to return. He would have followed your leadership for the rest of his life, happily. He was very devoted to you, as were most of the men I spoke with. That's a credit to you as a commander. You inspired loyalty and even love among a group of men who had little to give."

"All that will change if Ronin has his way. I believe he is working on a way to get all of them the same gene-altering therapy that I had. Especially after meeting you, and seeing that you haven't gone completely mad." Bill chuckled at his own dry humor. "He'll be pestering Mara Prime to move up the schedule. Mark my words."

"I don't doubt you're right. Ronin seems like a man of strong convictions and intense will."

"He is one of the strongest people I know. Among Alvians, he is the most dedicated to his beliefs, the surest of his purpose and the bravest I have met. Since exiling myself among the humans though, I have found much to admire among them. The things they have gone through to survive in the world we made for them would break your heart if you let them."

"You've revised your opinion of humans then?"

"I have. They have a strength and resilience our people have lost. They survived against all odds and continue to thrive both in captivity and on the run. They are resourceful, intelligent and cunning, as I'm sure you know."

Grady nodded in agreement. "I have often found myself respecting those I have hunted and captured, including the two men there." He indicated David and Michael with a jerk of his chin. "They were among my most challenging missions. I regret their animosity toward me, but I do understand it. No one in their right mind could actually like—or forgive—the person who stole their freedom. And back when I did it, I didn't even realize the full impact of my actions. How do you live with the regret, Bill?"

"It's not easy." A chilling desolation entered the former assassin's eyes.

Grady wasn't proud of the things he'd done to humans in his past as a warrior Prime, but he'd never killed in cold blood. He'd never been used as an assassin. At the time it wouldn't have mattered, but now that he could feel, he was grateful for the oversight. Grady could only imagine the guilt Bill felt. Killing in self defense or defense of others could be considered acceptable but killing in cold blood was something Grady didn't know if he could have lived with.

They entered through the second blast door, and Grady both felt and heard the reverberations of both heavy steel doors being closed and locked behind him. If things were going to turn ugly, now would be the time.

But his hosts didn't turn on him. Instead, they led him through a central area from which he could see multiple buildings of various sizes and indications of human habitation. In fact, he could see more than a few people going about their business around the vast space, walking from building to building, carting things in small hand-powered vehicles from levels below and generally doing things to keep the facility running.

"This is quite an installation." Grady admired the orderly way the people moved around. He even noted a few infants with their mothers and older children at play behind one of the larger buildings.

"It grows almost daily." Bill indicated a group of people being taught how to work some of the automated instruments. "We've had to institute a schedule of classes so newcomers can learn how everything works down here. We're nowhere near capacity, but it feels like a crowd. In the beginning it was just me, Michael, David and Jaci living down here. Then the others started to arrive. First, we took in people sent to us by our allies then later people started looking for us themselves as rumors spread."

Grady would bet anything that the allies Bill had mentioned were the O'Haras. Their ranch wasn't too far away as the Avarel could fly, and Grady had long suspected they worked covertly to assist what humans they could. He didn't begrudge them that. It was only natural they would try to help their fellow man. They were good people he had come to respect.

As they crossed the open area, Grady became aware of another group of people. He recognized Jaci 192, who stood facing him. She was talking with two others, a male and a female. Just then the female turned, and he caught sight of the gentle curve of her cheek.

Could it be?

"Oh my God." Gina's voice was a whisper of sound. "Grady."

She took off as Jim watched. She jogged toward a strange Alvian male who stood a few yards distant with Bill, Mike and Dave. She jumped into his arms, joy clear in her expression.

Her response seemed all out of proportion with what anyone could have expected. The alien man's too. At first he seemed shocked, but he recovered quickly, folding her in his arms, kissing her for all he was worth. There was real emotion showing in every tender caress of his hands over her hair, her shoulders, her back. They were lovers reunited, and no one watching them could be unaffected.

But Jim stood frozen, taken completely by surprise. Jim felt Gina's response to the alien like a sucker punch to his gut. He'd been blindsided by the hushed joy in her voice, the slight tremble as she recognized her old lover. Jim knew that was what he was. Even in those cold blue alien eyes, he could see the love shining down on her.

It was pure, and it was deep.

Jim felt it like a burning saber to his soul.

"Who'd a thunk it?" Jaci used one of those odd colloquialisms she'd been learning from her mates. "They Hum."

"Who is he?" Jim needed confirmation, though in his heart he already knew.

Jaci turned to him, a smile in her eyes and innocent happiness on her pretty face. "Why that's Grady Prime. I think he's finally taken the treatment if the look on his face is anything to go by."

"You mean the emotion-restoring drug?" Jim didn't like the sound of this at all—or the look of his woman in the alien's arms. But then, he had no real claim on Gina. He'd been careful to let her know he wouldn't leave his people. Not even for her. They were a couple for this trip only and now it seemed their time together had come to an abrupt and premature end.

"I prepared the doses for him and a new test group before I left. In fact, that's when I accidentally dosed myself. It was the best mistake I ever made." Her smile turned nostalgic as she looked at her two mates. "Grady found us here later, after I'd made a run for it with Michael and David."

"He found you?"

She nodded, turning her happy expression on him. "He did, but he let us go when he heard our Hum and saw evidence of our resonance. It's the oldest of Alvian laws—Resonance Mates may not be separated for any reason. He used that to justify letting us live here in peace. He didn't report us to the Council. As far as anyone knows, I was his one and only failure at tracking and I thank him every day for allowing the false ruination of his perfect record."

Jim had some idea what that might have cost the man in pride—especially an Alvian warrior who had emotions. No soldier liked to have a blemish on his record and letting Jaci go would have been a big mark against him. Maybe there was more to the man than just another pretty Alvian face, but Jim was reserving judgment.

"Well, would you look at that." Michael joined them, standing beside his mate Jaci. David took up a position on her other side, as all three turned to watch Gina and the Alvian warrior, necking like they were teenagers in a carpark. "I reckon they've met before."

"They Hum brightly." Jaci sighed wistfully, a smile playing about her lips.

"Really?" David dug around in his pocket, finally retrieving a small, glowing crystal. "Do you think they're causing this?" He gave the crystal to his woman.

A tear gathered in her eye. "They are. They Kiss, the crystal glows, the Hum increases. Now if they take it a step further, we'll know..." Her voice trailed off as the couple did indeed take things a little further. Gina jumped up, wrapping her legs around the alien, aligning their bodies, for an even deeper embrace though they were both fully clothed.

There was an impatience in their movements Jim understood all too well. Clearly they'd both forgotten, or didn't care, that they had an audience of people watching them with varying degrees of indulgence, interest and in the case of Jim, jealousy. He admitted it. He was jealous as hell of that stranger and the way Gina was climbing all over him. They might've known each other before, but until a few minutes ago Gina had been his girl. He wasn't ready to let her go just yet.

If he were being honest with himself, he'd admit he wasn't sure he'd ever be ready to let her go.

But that was beside the point. His plans—whatever they were—had just been shredded by the appearance of the Alvian warrior.

"That's clinched it, I think," Michael picked the crystal out of Jaci's hand. It was glowing yellow like a miniature sun.

"They're mates!" Jaci grabbed both Michael and David by the arm, pulling them close for a quick squeeze. Each man bent to kiss her briefly, adding to the crystal's illumination slightly from Jim's vantage point. He didn't understand everything, but he knew when he needed to bow out gracefully.

Only thing was, he didn't want to bow out at all. In fact, he felt like going over there and punching that big Alvian badass in the nose, then breaking an arm or maybe a leg for good measure.

Jim seethed while the couple embraced, apparently lost to the world. They were that wrapped up in each other.

"Tough break, Jim." Mike took a position beside him as Jaci headed toward the main building, grinning like a fool. Dave stood on Jim's other side, arms crossed as if the two cousins thought they could stop Jim if he took it into his mind to go break up the two lovebirds.

"Of course, this could also be the start of a nice little family." Dave turned toward Jim with a raised eyebrow. "Men today don't often get to keep a woman all to themselves. In fact, you'll be lucky if you only have to share with one or two other guys. Much as I hate Grady, he's a strong man and he'll be a good protector for Gina—not just physically, but also from other Alvians."

"Gina can take care of herself." Jim had to bite back the fury that suffused his mind and try to think logically. He hated to admit it, but Dave did have a point where the Alvians were concerned. Any person in this day and age would do well to have one of the aliens on their side.

"I'm sure she can," Dave said in a voice that sent soothing vibrations down Jim's spine. Damn it all if the nosy mind healer wasn't trying to use his gift to calm him down. And double damn it that he needed calming in the first place. Still, the force of Dave's gift brought some much-needed clarity to Jim's troubled mind. "But you should consider what it would mean to have Grady Prime as your third. He was one of the most powerful Alvian soldiers before he got emotion. We saw firsthand how not only his fellow soldiers, but most Alvians, deferred to the guy. I can't think that's changed no matter how much he has. And believe me, he's changed."

"You got that right," Mike put in. "That bastard used to be cold as ice. As much as I despised him, I had to respect him for his skills and the way his people revered him. He could be a useful ally."

"Fuck." Dave laughed ruefully and shared an ironic look with his cousin. "I suppose we'll have to make peace with the bastard now."

"Looks like it." Mike grinned, but it wasn't a pleasant expression as he looked at the newest Alvian in their midst. "I sure as hell didn't expect to be welcoming so many damned aliens here when we moved in."

"Me neither, cuz, but I'll never regret mating Jaci. Bill saved her life, so we owe him. But Grady?" Dave scratched his head as he watched the alien warrior with narrowed eyes. "Hell, we'll just have to see what happens. We should probably call the O'Haras. Maybe Caleb has some advice for us."

"Who's Caleb?" Jim seized on anything for respite from seeing Gina in some stranger's arms. Thankfully, they broke the embrace and started talking, walking away as they went, clearly in their own little world.

"Caleb O'Hara is the one they call the Oracle."

"No shit? I've heard of him. I even have a copy of the book of his prophecies somewhere. One of the newcomers brought it in with him and gave it to me. I passed it to my lieutenants to read."

"You should read it yourself," Mike advised.

"I took a look, but it's kind of vague."

"He had to be vague in case it fell into Alvian hands," Dave said. "Believe us, you should study that book. In the meantime, we have an in with the man himself we should make use of. He's a *guest* of the Alvians at the moment, but his nephew 'paths messages from him to his family. They're friends of ours."

"Nice to have such powerful friends." Jim followed the cousins as they headed toward the communications center. His mind was still in chaos, but he felt better to have at least some task to occupy him. He wanted to hear what the infamous Oracle might have to say, if anything, about this totally fucked up situation.

Chapter Fourteen

"I told you I'd come for you," Grady teased as he held Gina's hand. They strolled aimlessly around the main cavern. "I didn't mean it quite this way, I'll admit, but perhaps fate had other plans for us."

"You believe in fate?"

"Even before I could feel, I always knew there were things that happened for a reason. Fate plays a large role in most soldiers' lives."

"Then—" Gina didn't know quite how to tell him. She had to be honest. She had to tell Grady about Jim, but she didn't want to hurt his feelings. They were so new and fragile she hated to wound him.

"What is it? You know you can tell me anything, Gina." He turned, clutching both of her hands in his, holding them against his chest. She could feel the strong beating of his heart, and she sent up a silent prayer that she wasn't about to break it beyond repair. Of course, maybe she was thinking a bit too highly of herself, but then, Grady seemed so devoted... She didn't know what to think anymore.

"I believe in honesty."

He looked at her strangely, tilting his head to one side. "I believe I've heard you humans say honesty is the best policy."

"Yes, I believe it is. That's why I have to tell you about my trip here. I didn't travel alone, Grady. I came with the leader of another group of human survivors. His name is Jim, and I knew him in the old world. He was a student of my father's. I even had a crush on him back then, though I was just a girl and he was too old for me."

Grady's eyes grew troubled, his stance more rigid as he pulled slightly back from her. "You went to meet him after you left me?"

"No! It wasn't like that at all. I didn't even know he was still alive. For that matter, he didn't know I was either. I was as shocked as he was when my mission for the Patriarch led me straight to him and his people."

"But I sense there's more." Grady's expression held a world of hurt and Gina felt the echoes of his growing despair. She'd give anything to spare him those feelings. She had to make it right. Somehow, she had to make him see that she hadn't set out to betray him.

"Jim and I grew close on the journey here. Jaci and Bill said we Hum and the cousins gave us a crystal. Jim and I...we make it glow. I know that means something really special to your people, but we're both human. We both have responsibilities and duties to people and places far apart. Jim and I made no commitments to each other. I can't, in good conscience, make a commitment to anyone at this point in my life. I owe the Patriarch my allegiance and my loyalty. I'm his to command. I can't promise anyone—you *or* Jim—anything beyond today. My future is uncertain and not mine to choose."

Grady dropped her hands and moved a few steps away, clearly processing her words. He seemed to be struggling with what she'd just told him, making her feel guilty. She hated the feeling.

"I want to do the tests with you." Grady whirled on her, causing her to take a step backward with his vehemence. "Now." He shook his head, his voice strong. "As soon as possible."

"Okay." He must have sensed her hesitance because he stepped up close to her and reclaimed her hands in an almost desperate grip.

"I believe in my heart—in my soul—that you are my mate, Gina. I want to see the proof before we go any further. I want the world to see that you are my true Resonance Mate."

Her body vibrated in an echo of his desperation. She felt the urgency in his tone and his grip. She could do this for him. It was a simple enough request.

"All right. Jaci can witness. Or Bill. Both can hear the Hum."

"But all can see the crystal glow." Grady's eyes snapped with fire, his lips curling into the smallest of grins, daring her.

"I don't know—" Gina didn't really care to be put on display, but she feared nothing less would satisfy him in such a dangerous mood.

"You're mine." The growl in his voice surprised her, as did the possession in every line of his body.

"You'd best stop manhandling my friend, Grady Prime, or friend or not, I will kick your ass."

Bill's voice broke like an icy wave over Gina's senses. She dragged her gaze from Grady's to find the other Alvian warrior just a few feet away, watching them. Grady looked over at him too, but didn't move for a long moment, staking his claim clearly for the other warrior's benefit.

Then, little by little, he let her go. Gina stepped back, but not far. She wouldn't allow her actions to shame him in any way.

"We will perform the resonance tests right away," Grady announced. "You can be a witness."

"No need. You already have passed all three tests. Congratulations. You are true mates," Bill shocked them both by saying.

"When? How?" Gina asked, unable to say anything more coherent.

"Just now. Jaci took out a tuned crystal when you two said hello. Everybody saw it glowing but you. You were, shall we say, *otherwise engaged.*" Bill chuckled at them and Gina started to realize just how lost to the world she'd been after spotting Grady.

"You are certain?" Grady seemed to want further proof.

"Yes, my friend. I am absolutely certain. And seeing this miracle— in addition to that granted Jaci and her mates—gives me renewed hope for the future."

All of a sudden, Gina realized that Jim must have seen everything. Her heart sank like a stone.

"This is welcome news." Grady took the hand Bill offered in congratulations. Only then did Gina realize Jim and their hosts had left the area while she'd been oblivious in Grady's arms. She worried over what that might mean—what Jim might have seen and how he might have reacted.

Jaci came over to them and offered her congratulations. Gina decided to let things unfold as they willed for the moment. She'd deal with Jim at the earliest opportunity, but for now she wanted to bask just a little longer in Grady's presence. She didn't know what the future would hold, but something inside her wanted to be near Grady for as long as possible.

No doubt, she had a lot to think about, but for the moment, she latched onto Grady's arm and let it all ride.

This installation's communications center looked even more advanced than the one in Jim's facility in Colorado. Jim was suitably impressed with the artificial intelligence computer that ran most of the systems in the underground complex and told the cousins so. They took his words in stride, but Jim could tell they were pleased as they unveiled the newest console in the chamber.

At its heart was a clear, shining, quartz crystal. Its surface sparkled in the dim light of the chamber, throwing sparks of light around the room like an old-fashioned disco ball.

"We've made a few modifications with Bill and Jaci's help." Mike sat at the console, flipping switches and powering up the system.

It didn't take long at all. The crystal glowed from within when power started flowing through it, but not as much as Jim expected. Certainly not even as much as he'd seen when that newly arrived Alvian bastard had kissed Gina. That glow had been brighter and the crystal much smaller. Jim didn't know what that meant just yet, but he planned to find out.

Mike placed a call that was answered a minute later by a cheerful, female voice.

"Hi, Mike, it's Jane. How are you all doing out there?"

"We're just fine, Mrs. O'Hara. How's the family? Good, I hope."

Damned if this didn't sound like a good old-fashioned telephone call. For just a minute, Jim felt nostalgic for the old world and the millions of easy conversations he'd had with friends and family. When the aliens took out the satellites and most of the ground-based infrastructure, telephones had become impossible tech for humans to maintain.

Jim listened as Mike exchanged pleasantries with the woman on the other end of the line for a few minutes longer, finally asking to speak with someone named Mick.

"Mick O'Hara is one hell of a telepath. He's the one who's in direct communication with their boy, Harry. He's the relay from the city and from Caleb," David explained. He stood beside Jim, a few feet behind the console and Mike.

A few moments later, a male voice came over the line. "Harry said you'd be calling sooner rather than later. How's it going over there?"

Mike explained the situation, giving Mick O'Hara more detail than

Jim would have expected, but then, he didn't really know these people or their resources. But the more he saw, the more he decided to cultivate a relationship with these people and their facility. They could definitely learn things from each other.

"So what have you got for me, Mick?" Jim was glad when Mike finally got down to business.

"Caleb had a good chuckle over your situation. We all know how much you two despise Grady Prime, but I have to tell you, you're going to have to put that all behind you if you want to move forward. He's a changed man and with him will come even greater changes. Managing them is going to be the key. You two are poised to do that, along with the girl and her contacts. Caleb can't see much about them yet, only vague images and what he thinks are metaphors."

"Metaphors?" Mike shot a look back at his cousin, clearly curious.

"He's seeing angels, Mike. Near as he can figure, that's got to stand for something else."

Dave laughed out loud and stepped forward to the console, taking the mic. "You know as well as I do, doc, that sometimes a cigar is just a cigar."

The other end of the line was silent for a moment. "You trying to tell me there are dudes with wings on this planet, Dave? Have you been smoking the drapes?"

Both cousins laughed at that.

"No, Mick. I'm telling you, I've seen it. Dudes with wings. They're real."

"Alvian?"

"A genetic hybrid. Alvian and some other alien race that really did have wings. They were one of the aliens' famous experiments."

"And you know this...how?"

"Sorry, Mick. That's not my secret to divulge at the moment. For now, just take my word for it, okay?"

"Son of a bitch." Mick sounded both perplexed and intrigued. "Well if that don't beat all."

"Does Caleb have any words of advice for Grady's competition?"

"Competition?"

"For Gina's affections," Dave qualified. "She traveled here with a human guy—a former spook from Colorado named Jim. I get the

195

impression there might be a threesome in the making."

"Hang on, I'll ask."

Silence reigned for a minute while Mick placed a telepathic call to his brother via his nephew. It was a complicated relay, but it worked. And more importantly, it was untraceable.

"All right." Mick came back a moment later. "What's this about the Olympics? Caleb is seeing Olympic rings."

"That's Gina. Gina Hanson. Remember her? She won gold for martial arts."

"No kidding? I remember her. She was a cute girl and very talented. Came from a line of martial arts teachers and champions, didn't she?"

"Sure did. She's been living with the aliens since just after the cataclysm, but her group is different, she claims. A secret sect like ninjas or something. Turns out, Bill was one of them. He confirmed everything she told us."

"Wow." Mick sounded both skeptical and worried. "Caleb saw some of this, but he had a hard time interpreting it. I'm going to need some time to talk to him. Can I give you a call back later?"

"Sure. Burt's always here to answer. He'll let us know you're on the line. Thanks, Mick."

Dave signed off with a few more words of farewell and sat back.

"Nothing to do now but wait. Come on." Dave stood and motioned for Jim to follow him out. "I'll show you the gym. Maybe you can work off some of your anger before you confront the happy couple."

As it turned out, Jim spent a few hours training in the state of the art gym area that was similar to the one at his home base. Mike and Dave left him there with some of the other inhabitants of their facility who had been martial arts enthusiasts in the old world. Among them, Jim found a few sparring partners and eventually ended up teaching a few moves to the guys and making friends.

By the time he headed back to his assigned room for a shower and change of clothes from his pack, he was feeling a little better. The physical exercise had allowed him to work through some of his anger, but his heart was still sore from the emotional beating it had taken earlier that day.

Gina wasn't in the room they'd been given, but her pack was. He didn't know what to make of that, so he just shrugged his shoulders and went about his business. It was almost dinnertime, so he headed for the big cafeteria where most of the people living in the facility gathered for meals. He almost dreaded what he'd find there.

Sure enough, Gina was there, sitting next to the big Alvian warrior at a large table with Mike, Dave, Jaci and Bill. Jim squared his shoulders and picked up a tray and utensils, filling a plate from the buffet line. When he turned back around to look at Gina, she was staring back at him, an uncertain expression on her face.

"I saved you a seat," came her tentative voice in his mind. She wasn't a strong telepath, but this close, her voice was clear as a bell. He was surprised she'd initiate such intimate contact seeing as how she was sitting with her alien lover.

"Are you sure that's wise?"

"Jim..." she trailed off, a pained look crossing her face. *"Yes. I want you to meet Grady."*

"Again, I have to ask, are you sure that's wise? He's your lover, isn't he?" Jim started a slow amble toward the large table and the empty chair next to Gina.

"He was. We met only a couple of days before I was sent to make contact with you. We only had a day or two together, but..."

"He moves fast for an alien." Jim hated the jealousy he felt biting into him.

"It wasn't like that. We Hum. That really means something to the Alvians. He was kind to me. If you must know, I've been with you longer than I was with him, but I feel attached to him...like I do with you."

Jim didn't like the sound of that. He stood next to Gina, looking down at her while the others at the table became aware of his presence. Tension was thick in the air as the men noticed him. Mike and Dave undoubtedly knew what was going on and Jaci actually cringed when she met his eyes. When his gaze fell on his competitor though, it seemed as if the big Alvian warrior had no idea who he was or what he'd been to Gina.

That was going to change.

But Jim was polite enough not to punch him out at the dinner table. Jim pulled out the empty chair and took possession of the seat on Gina's left while eyeing the strange warrior who sat on her right.

"Grady, this is Jim. He was a student of my father's in the old world, and we traveled here together." Gina's quiet voice reached only to the men she was introducing.

Jim felt a jolt of triumph when understanding dawned in the blue alien eyes as Grady looked from Jim to Gina and back again. Now the man knew who he was and that he'd have some hefty competition if he wanted Gina all to himself.

Grady held out a hand, startling Jim by initiating the human custom of a handshake. Apparently this guy had been observing humans enough to emulate the greeting. Even more impressive was the friendly gesture when he knew darn well they were competitors for Gina's affections.

Jim shook Grady's hand briefly as he sat, but said nothing. The man's grip was impressively strong, but Jim got the impression that he was holding back his full strength. There was no show of bravado, just a simple greeting.

Jim let the conversation flow around him as he ate his meal. After some initial stiffness, the others at the table renewed their talk about life in their facility and the newcomers who had been joining them recently.

He found it interesting that they'd only been there a comparatively short time. Just a few months, really, and already they had a thriving community. To be sure, they were working out a lot of the kinks in their workflow and living patterns, but they were on the right track. Jim and his people by comparison, had already been on a proven schedule set up by the U.S. military and those who had staffed Cheyenne Mountain before his time.

Jim realized a lot of the new arrivals to this facility had been drawn there by talk of an angel flying in the skies near and above. After seeing Bill's wings in action, Jim could well understand the attraction. Not only did Bill have most human religions and mythologies speaking well of people with feathery wings, he also had a natural command presence that you couldn't help but feel when he was around.

He'd been a Prime among his people, in charge of a battalion of warriors just like himself. No doubt he'd been the best of the best, even among Primes. He was used to command and even though he deferred to his human friends and didn't seem to want to lead, people still looked to him for guidance, instruction and leadership.

Luckily for them, Bill seemed tired and confused. He looked like a lot of the refugees Jim had seen pouring into his own home. Bill had issues. There was no doubt about that. But he was growing stronger— just as Jim's people had grown stronger as they healed in a safe place with plenty of food to eat.

He wondered what would happen when Bill finally recovered from his trauma. Would he take up the mantle so many of these human survivors seemed to want to put around his shoulders? And if so, would he be a good leader of men or a tyrant?

Jim didn't necessarily want to be around to find out. Bill—with those amazing wings of his—could easily use the influence of being an *angel* to hoodwink a lot of people. By virtue of that alone, he was a dangerous man. Even more worrisome were the skills and knowledge Bill had as a former Alvian Prime warrior. He knew how to lead. It came as naturally as breathing to him. He knew how to fight and he knew the Alvian system and forces better than almost anyone. Would he want revenge on the people that had thrown him out? Would he feel any loyalty at all to the humans who had taken him in?

Jim really wanted to know the answer to those questions before he got his own people more involved, but there was little likelihood he would have those answers in time. He'd have to make a judgment call, but he couldn't do it alone. Jim had to maneuver a way for Bill to meet his people so they could judge for themselves. At the very least, Jim wanted his inner circle to meet Bill. All were sound judges of men who probably wouldn't be swayed by those angelic wings.

When Bill started talking about his hydroponics experiments, Jim finally joined the conversation, offering for the experts in his facility to consult with Bill on the best way to proceed. That would be the easiest way to get his people to meet Bill. The Alvian was cagey, neither accepting nor declining the offer. Jim could handle that. He understood that the folks in this installation had to be just as careful as he was. He respected that and was also impressed that Bill appeared to be as concerned about the safety of the people in this facility as Jim was about his own people. It was a mark in Bill's favor.

From there, the talk flowed into other areas. Mike and Dave eventually brought up the subject of Gina's celebrity and her skills as a martial artist. Jim watched Grady carefully, unsurprised to see that Gina's reputation among humans was news to the Alvian warrior. Gina was a modest woman. She didn't go around boasting about her skills or her former glory.

Bianca D'Arc

"I remember seeing your gold medal bout on television," Mike said to Gina. "You had a slammin' roundhouse kick back in the day."

"She still does." Jim joined in the conversation when Gina said nothing. "She nearly knocked my block off the night we met."

"How did you two meet again after all those years?" Jaci asked innocently.

"She snuck into the cave entryway, but we had seen her long before on the sensors and from scout reports. We were there to meet her, but I had no idea it was Gina under the ninja suit. We doused the lights, and I confronted her."

"You *attacked*, you mean," Gina put in with a laugh.

"Hey, give me a break, I didn't know it was you. I didn't even realize you were a girl in that get up."

"And you don't attack women?" Jaci asked, interested. "I've read about something called chivalry in the human texts. Is that why? Women don't fight?"

"Oh, women fight," Gina was quick to answer. "Though I'll admit, in our culture's past, women were expected to stay home, sew, clean, cook, et cetera. Only a few ever were warriors back during the times when it took real muscle to fight. We are much smaller, on average, than human males."

"But you were a fighter?" Jaci leaned forward, apparently intrigued by the concept. "You train with the *Zxerah* if Bill is to be believed."

"In the days just before the cataclysm, our people had advanced to the point where wars—if we had them—were conducted by machines. Jet fighters, tanks and guns could be operated by almost anyone. While it's true that the majority of our military forces were male, there was an increasing number of females ready, willing and able to defend our countries. As far as martial arts go, the ancient fighting forms were studied for many reasons—physical fitness, mental discipline, competition—but not necessarily for large-scale warfare."

"I was sent to study at the Hanson *dojo* with Gina's father because I was an intelligence agent," Jim put in. "I was a member of the U.S. military, where I learned basic hand-to-hand fighting. When I finished my tour of duty, I was recruited by the Central Intelligence Agency and given advanced training in several different areas."

"Like what?" Jaci asked.

200

"Languages, computers, covert operations, acting, special munitions, explosives. All kinds of things that would come in handy on top secret undercover missions." Jim leaned back in his chair, pushing his tray slightly away, finished eating. "Training with Gina's dad was actually one of the more enjoyable training details I was ever sent on. After I finished the two-month class the Company had paid for, I asked *Sensei* Hanson if I could stay on as a student, paying my own way. I really liked the man and respected him. Gina's brothers became good friends of mine. I miss them all, dearly."

"Then it must have been some comfort to discover Gina was alive." Jaci's voice held sympathy, which still struck him as odd, seeing as how it came from an undeniably Alvian face.

"I admit, I was suspicious at first. Don't get me wrong, I was glad to see that any of the Hansons had survived, but Gina was wearing Alvian clothes and she arrived on my doorstep out of the blue. Her gear was Alvian, and she claimed to be on a mission from some secret sect I'd never heard of. It all still seems a little impossible."

"If there's one thing I've learned," Dave said, taking Jaci's hand with a fond smile, "nothing's impossible."

Jim looked from Dave to Jaci to Mike. They were a threesome, odd as it seemed.

"Gina, I would like for you to spar with me tomorrow in the gym. Will you?" Bill spoke in his low, commanding voice, jarring Jim from his speculation.

"I would be honored," Gina answered with a small smile for the alien. "I've missed our training bouts."

"I want to show some of our newcomers that even someone of your size can have an impact with proper training. We have more women and children coming in every day, and I would feel better if they knew at least the rudiments of self-defense." Bill hesitated before going on. "I teach fighting techniques to a few of the men, but I think some of them are afraid of me." Incredibly, the alien man's cheeks flushed with embarrassment.

"And no doubt others are in awe of your wings," Gina agreed readily, glossing over the moment. She seemed on friendly terms with the big winged warrior.

"I still don't understand it," Bill agreed, "but it seems to be the case. No matter how many times I explain to them that I am nobody's angel, the wings somehow make them think otherwise."

Gina laughed, and the pretty sound distracted Jim for a minute. "Don't worry," she said through her chuckles, "I know better. I'll be happy to show anyone who cares to watch how even the mighty angel can fall, given the right counter move."

A big smile spread over Bill's face. "That would be most welcome, Gina. Thank you."

"I think you may have more of an audience than you expect, Gina," Mike put in from across the table. "A lot of people remember you. It's not every day a person gets to watch an Olympic Gold Medalist in action."

"And not every day we're confronted with someone who can remind us so strongly of the world we once knew." Dave's sobering words struck all the humans at the table.

"Bill," Gina ventured into the silence. "I wanted to tell you how glad I am to see you this way. I'd hoped, when I heard what happened to you, that you would be able to handle true feelings. You always struck me as one of the more sensitive Alvians. I hoped that would help you after your DNA changed, and I'm glad to see you healthy and whole."

Bill seemed genuinely surprised by her earnest words. He gazed at her with a touchingly vulnerable expression. "Thank you, Gina." His soft words seemed choked as Gina smiled back at the alien warrior.

"I think everyone's here now," Mike broke into the moment, standing from his chair. "If you don't mind, I'll introduce you," he said to Jim, Gina and Grady. "We've found after dinner is a good time to hold town meetings and discuss things. I know a lot of folks have been interested in your arrival, and I think more than a few have already recognized Gina." He winked at her and Jim looked around the large cafeteria, noting how full it was. There were more people in this installation then he'd realized.

Jim watched as Mike fetched a wireless microphone and switched it on. They seemed to have a lot of undamaged equipment—some of it more advanced than the stuff in his facility.

"Good evening, my friends," Mike said as the room quieted. He stood, facing the group, and Jim realized why the cousins had chosen the table near the door. They were able to see the entire room from their vantage point, and everyone could see them.

Mike introduced Jim first, as the leader of one of the other old NORAD installations, which caused a stir among the people. Mike gave them the facts, which Jim silently applauded. He dealt with his own people in much the same way. Democracy ruled the day in his facility and he was glad to see it had survived here as well. Mike was understandably cautious, telling his people there would be ample time to discuss the possibility of opening communications and trade with the Colorado facility. Jim took the room's cautious but optimistic response as a good sign.

Then came the time for general announcements. Mike read off reminders about events and safety issues, including a warning about a big cat that had been seen hunting near the facility. Jim knew a lot of exotic zoo animals had survived the cataclysm to breed with native species and the results were often deadly predators it was best to avoid.

Mike then introduced Grady as a visitor who had a history with the three *de facto* leaders—Mike, Dave and Jaci. Mike made no secret about the fact that Grady had emotions and had been a soldier until recently.

"I know some of you have seen him before. He was, in fact, the man who finally captured myself and my cousin Dave. We hated his guts for a good long while," Mike admitted ruefully as the crowd laughed. "But now he's different. Hell, even when he didn't understand us, he was a fair-minded man. We've never had reason to tell anybody else this, but back when we first found this underground installation and it was just me, Dave and Jaci here, Grady was assigned to track us down. Jaci's people wanted her back in the worst possible way." Murmurs of sympathy came from all around. "Grady actually found us." A few gasps sounded as Mike shook his head and grinned in memory. "Naked as J-birds, playing in the hot spring. He could have had us all right then, but he let us go."

"Why'd he do that?" a woman in the back called out.

"It's complicated, but the aliens have this phenomenon called Resonance Mating. When two mates touch skin to skin, there's an audible Hum the aliens can hear. It's out of the range of human hearing, but machines can pick it up and we know for a fact the sound is produced whenever either of us touch Jaci. We're her Resonance Mates. According to ancient Alvian law, Resonance Mates can never be parted for any reason. Grady can hear the sound. He knew what it meant. Because of it, he let us go. He's known where we lived all this time and has never told his superiors about this facility. Much as I hate to admit it, he's a friend. Dave and I have put the past behind us to welcome him here. I hope you'll all give him a chance."

"He's got feelings, like Jaci?" another woman asked nearby.

Mike nodded. "He's part of an alien experiment. They're tinkering with their own DNA, experimenting on a few volunteers to give them emotions." Loud murmurs this time from the crowd. "We confirmed this with the Oracle and he said to take it as a good sign, which I'm inclined to agree with. I know firsthand what having emotions can do to the Alvians. They begin to understand what they've done to us and our planet. They become more human, more compassionate and understanding. First Bill, then Jaci and now Grady. All three have turned into friends of humanity with deep regret for what their race has done. Can you imagine what would happen if more of them took this treatment?"

Mike let the murmurs rise to open discussion and noise filled the hall. After a few minutes, he handed the mic to his cousin and Dave stood while Mike sat back down at the table.

"Friends," Dave spoke as the crowd noise slowly wound down in volume. "Friends, there's one other newcomer you should know about." Everyone was finally quiet as Dave continued. "Some of you may have already recognized her and I'm glad to confirm the gossip, that yes, indeed, Olympic Gold Medalist, Gina Hanson is among us." Whispers sounded as Gina turned in her seat to wave. She was a consummate professional when it came to making public appearances, though she hadn't done one in years. "Tomorrow afternoon, she's agreed to give a little exhibition of her martial arts skill in the gym. I hope you'll all attend. In the meantime, I hope you'll make our guests welcome and Mike and I will be around to answer questions if you have any. Have a good night, everybody."

Jim stood when everybody else did. It looked like dinner was officially over. Everybody started clearing their own tables and busing their trays back toward the kitchen area.

"We set up shifts once we got enough people." Mike fell into step beside Jim as he walked with the crowd toward the dumping area. "We're on a rotation. Everyone takes turns cooking and cleaning every few weeks."

"We do something similar," Jim agreed. "But there are some folks who actually prefer kitchen work so we let a few of them—two older ladies in particular—run the show. Claudette and Sylvia used to run the busiest diner in town. Luckily somebody had the good sense to rescue them in the first days after the bombardment started. Since they took charge of the kitchen, we eat a lot better."

"I bet." Mike dropped his tray on the conveyor, and Jim followed suit. He turned to see the three Alvians right behind him and Gina bringing up the rear. "So what now?" Jim asked Mike, who hovered at his side.

"A couple of weeks ago, Dave instituted social time after dinner. All those who want to, gather outside in the main area and Burt plays music that some kind soul programmed into his memory long before the cataclysm. We talk, play games, even dance. Dave, Jaci and I try to make ourselves available every night for at least a little while. I think it would be a good idea for you and Gina to sit with us for a bit. I'm sure people have questions about your facility and your people."

Jim agreed and followed Mike outside. The lights had been lowered to a twilight setting and people were already setting up folding chairs and tables that had been stored along one wall.

"Is that beer?" Jim almost didn't believe his eyes when he saw a refrigeration unit being opened. Sure enough, there was more than one small keg inside and a few of the men were already pouring out mugs of a frothy golden beverage.

"Mrs. O'Hara shared her brewing secrets with us, and Bill's had good success growing hops. Those kegs represent our very first home brew as a matter of fact. It's darn good, if you ask me, but I think we'll get better the more we brew. It's not quite up to the O'Hara standard just yet, but it works." Mike headed over toward the keg, and Jim followed eagerly. "We ration it. One cup a night. We want to make it last until our next batch is ready, and we definitely don't want to encourage alcoholism by allowing some to get carried away."

"Good idea. We haven't had any alcohol since the General's private stash ran out decades ago." Jim was eager to try the home brew. He'd liked the occasional beer back in the old world but had never been much of a drinker.

Mike worked through the line and brought back two glasses—one for Jim and one for himself. He then motioned Jim over to the table where Dave and Gina were already talking with a few others.

Grady was at Gina's side, and Dave had Jaci next to him. Mike took the seat on Jaci's free side and Jim chose to stand at the side of the table, watching.

A young boy came up to Jim and asked him about Colorado. Jim spent an enjoyable few minutes talking to the boy but was aware of Grady's scrutiny as he did so. Sure enough, when Jim looked over, Grady was watching him.

Two could play that game.

He turned to the boy, already hatching plans to keep tabs on the Alvian warrior. But the boy was joined by his mother and father, who kept Jim talking about the outside world. By the time Jim was able to look back at Grady, he was gone. The seat at Gina's side was filled by a woman who seemed to be hanging on Gina's every word.

"I wanted to thank you."

The deep, musical, Alvian voice surprised Jim. Son of a bitch. Grady had snuck up on him.

"What for?" Jim didn't know how to play this little scene yet.

"For keeping watch over Gina. I worried about her while she was away on her mission, but had no way to contact her and a mission of my own to fulfill." Grady seemed serious enough but Jim still wasn't sure if there wasn't some ulterior motive. "Thank you for making sure she came to no harm."

"No thanks are necessary. Gina's a talented woman. She took care of herself."

"She is that." Grady's attention seemed to be snagged as he looked at the woman in question. His gaze softened and a tender expression touched his otherwise hard features. "She is a very special woman."

"You'll get no argument from me." Jim felt jealousy, but also a kind of understanding for the other man. Grady probably believed himself in love with Gina. Jim was familiar with the idea. He recognized the emotion on the alien's face for what it was and couldn't fault the man for it.

"I love her."

The bald statement was tinged with wonder, as if the alien was just discovering the truth of his words. Jim had to fight against his compassionate nature and remember Grady was talking about Gina— the woman Jim had just spent a passionate journey with and had deep feelings for himself.

"We completed the tests for resonance and she is my true mate, as I anticipated. I knew the moment I saw her that she was special."

"Hell." Jim drained his glass of beer and placed the empty on the table. "For your information, I knew her when she was just a kid. A gorgeous, talented, spunky teenager, studying in her father's *dojo*. She was off limits to me then, but she sure as hell isn't now." Jim felt his anger translating into clenched fists and tight muscles. If it weren't for the crowd, he'd gladly take out his confusion on the Alvian warrior, but he held himself in check. "If she loves you back, you're a lucky man, Grady. But know this. I won't make it easy on you. I saw her first."

Grady regarded him steadily for a long moment before speaking in a low, serious tone. "I envy the fact that you've known her longer and I value the challenge you've issued, but it could be for naught."

"How so?"

Grady looked pointedly at Jaci and the two men flanking her. "If she will have you, I won't object to sharing her love. I know there are few human females. I never expected to find even one who could resonate with me, but having seen three true Resonance Matings, I knew it was likely I would be one of several men, should I be lucky to find a mate."

Jim had to admit, he'd thought about the idea, but he still had a hard time separating the young girl he'd known from the woman. He thought of her as she had been with her family and he knew her father and brothers would have had strong objections to her getting involved with Jim in any way. Forget any kind of ménage relationship. The Hansons would have killed any man who even suggested it for their little princess.

"Look, buddy." Jim tried to master his confusion and unrest. "I don't know you, but I do know Gina. She'll make her own decisions. Let's let her be our guide."

Grady looked at him strangely for a moment. "You are indeed wise," he finally said, making Jim a little uncomfortable. He hadn't expected the man's respectful tone. So far, this Grady guy wasn't acting in any way Jim could have predicted. "Gina will decide. It is for us to live with her decisions. I'm glad we had this talk."

Funny thing was, Grady didn't look glad. He looked as if he'd lost his best friend or something. The Alvian warrior left him then, walking away into the darkened part of the massive main cavern.

Jim stewed when Gina got up and went after him, but he was stopped from making an ass of himself when Jaci came over to him.

"Grady Prime is a good man," she said without preamble.

"I'd expect you to say that, if you don't mind my candor."

Jaci laughed and the sound was musical and enchanting. "Back when I was a lab tech, I was a little in awe of him. Most lower ranked Alvians are, even though they don't fully understand the emotion." She moved closer to him, and her voice dropped. "Grady Prime is a considerate, skilled lover. I was only with him once in the course of my duties, but he's the only man besides my mates who has ever shown me true pleasure."

Jim wasn't sure he wanted to know that. It was a little too much information for his peace of mind.

"I'm just saying," she went on, "that Grady Prime will be good to your lady. He may even give you some competition in that area. Of course, the benefactor of such a competition will be Gina. I could almost envy her if I wasn't so happy with my own mates."

Jim didn't know what to say when she paused dreamily, but assumed some response was required. "I'm very happy for you," he finally managed, but she hardly noticed.

Jaci put a hand on his arm. "I think you could be just as happy, Jim, but it will require you to bend a little. Having been mated to two human males for some time, I'm beginning to understand their nature a bit. I know Grady Prime and I know he will never tell you what I am about to reveal, but I feel you must know it to understand the seriousness of the situation."

Jim didn't know what to make of her words and almost feared some new revelation of a sexual nature. For all he knew, Alvian guys had two cocks or something equally as weird. He just hoped whatever Jaci was about to tell him was something he could handle.

"Ancient Alvians—before emotion was bred out of our people— were highly aggressive. More so than even your human ancestors. Alvian males, warriors in particular, lived short, harsh lives spent fighting and searching for their Resonance Mates. If they didn't find their mate, they were fated to a horrible end. They would often end their own lives in battle before facing that final challenge of madness."

"What are you saying?"

Jaci's face went pale and her eyes solemn as she turned to him. "Without their mates to complete them, Alvian males go insane. Grady Prime is a man of honor and pride. If Gina rejects him in favor of you, Grady Prime will not put up a fight. He'll take her at her word and leave." A tear fell unheeded down her pale cheek. "You'll never see him again. In all likelihood, no one will ever see him again. Grady Prime will end his own life before the madness claims him because he knows it's the only way to protect his mate. If he went mad, knowing she was in the world, he could do her harm while he was out of his mind. He'd take his own life before he'd let that happen. If Gina rejects him, she will be sentencing him to that terrible end."

Jim was shocked. He'd had no idea. The very concept was appalling. Certainly a broken heart wasn't something anyone wanted to experience, but actually going insane as a result was too much. These Alvians never did anything halfway, he thought. Claim your mate or go nuts. No middle ground.

Of course, it also meant that if Gina chose Jim over Grady, Jim would have to knowingly let the man go off to die. Jim didn't think he could live with that on his conscience. Not even knowing the bastard was an alien.

Grady Prime was real to him now. Jim had seen a little of his vulnerability and couldn't fault the way he treated Gina. The others seemed to respect him, but Jim wanted a chance to discover the real man. He wanted to get him in the sparring ring. The way a man fought told Jim a lot about a guy. Knowing what he knew now, Jim would take the time to learn more about this Grady character.

It was an untenable situation all the way around, but nothing had to be decided in the next few minutes. They had time. Not much, but some. It would have to be enough.

"So, just to be sure I've got this right, if Gina rejects him, Grady will go nuts?"

Jaci looked away, toward her mates, nodding. "If he is like our ancestors, then yes."

"What about—" Jim didn't want to say it out loud, but the possibility was there, staring him in the face. "What about if we formed a threesome? Would he be able to deal with it then? Or does this resonance stuff require full, one-on-one commitment?"

"Judging by Chief Engineer Davin's mating, a threesome would work fine, if all three of you were willing to share. It works beautifully for my mates and me. I've heard that Davin and his mates are happy and well balanced, even though from all accounts, Davin was much closer to insanity than Grady Prime appears to be."

Jim had a lot to think about. He was confused and didn't know how to resolve any of these issues, but time would tell. Hopefully. He didn't have a lot of time to waste, but surely he deserved a few days away from his responsibilities to think through his future. He didn't think his people would begrudge him that. And besides, he was making contacts and working out details for opening communication between his installation and this one. If all went well, he could do that and figure out the rest of his life at the same time.

"Thank you, Jaci. I'm glad you took the time to tell me these things." He lifted her hand and placed a kiss on the back, politely. She smiled at him with understanding in her eyes.

"I wasn't sure if I should speak, but I think it was the right thing to do. There have been too many misunderstandings between our peoples already. This is the time for clear communication—especially with something as important as this."

"You were right to tell me, Jaci. I'll think about what you've said and appreciate your concern."

He left her then, heading for his quarters. He definitely did have a lot to think about.

Chapter Fifteen

"Grady, wait up." Gina's voice carried in the dark recesses of the giant, manmade cave.

The main area was a massive cavern hollowed out by machines long ago. Pillars of rock had been left every twenty yards or so as support columns, rounded at the top and bottom, arching into the roof and floor, giving the chamber a cathedral-like feel.

Gina followed Grady Prime into the far recesses of the cleared area, past the buildings that fit within the massive cavern, to an area that sloped gently downward toward an underground lake. Water gathered in the massive area, purified by its trip through the rock above into an ice-cold, totally contained and safe water supply.

Grady paused when Gina called after him, but didn't turn. She caught up with him, walking around his tall body to face him. His features were in shadow, but her eyes had adjusted to the dark. She could tell he was upset. His eyes glittered down at her in the darkness.

"Please tell me what's wrong. Did Jim say something?" She put a hand on his forearm, seeking answers.

"This is not Jim's fault." Grady sighed and looked at her, relaxing a bit. She took it as a good sign. "We agreed that you would decide which of us you wanted in your life."

Taken aback, she straightened, looking at him in surprise.

"Well, you've got that part right at least."

Grady stepped close, facing her toe to toe as one hand rose to cup her waist and the other her cheek.

"Forgive me for not handling this well. I, of course, understand why one of your own race would be preferable to me but please, say I at least have some chance of winning your heart."

Right then, her heart melted. She moved into his arms as they closed around her.

"Of course you do, Grady." She rested her head against his chest, searching for words that would ease his turmoil. "Jim shouldn't have said anything to you. I honestly don't know what I'm going to do about the future, but I want to find a way to allow all three of us to be happy."

"A threesome? Is that what you want? With Jim?"

She hadn't really thought in those terms but after seeing Jaci with her two mates, the idea did seem to have some merit. Still, the obstacles in their way were big. Perhaps insurmountable.

"Honestly, I don't know." She pulled back, trying to see through the darkness to meet his eyes. "Jim has responsibilities to the people he leads. I have responsibilities to the Patriarch and the clan. You—" She hated to think what he had to look forward to when he got back to the Alvian scientists who were experimenting on him. "You have a high profile role in regular Alvian society aside from the experiment you're taking part in. Even if you weren't a test subject, it would be hard for us to be together, but I have to hope there's a way."

"There is always a way. That is one of the many things I've learned from observing humans for so long." Grady smiled in the gloom. "I don't know how yet, but I want to be with you, Gina. I...love you. You are in my heart, and you always will be. I must be with you." His voice went from sure to tentative. "If you will allow it."

"I want that too, Grady." Her words were whispered against his stubbly cheek as she reached up on tiptoe to place gentle kisses on his jaw. "I love you too."

"I know we have problems, but I have to believe fate would not be so unkind as to let me find you, only to take you away. You are my perfect mate, my resonance partner. I can be happy with no other but you, Gina."

Now that she was in his arms, his words flowed more freely, as if a dam had broken inside him. He clutched her waist, pulling her against his hard body. She could feel his hardness through the layers of their clothing, and she wanted nothing more than to feel him claim her in the most elemental way.

"Let's go to your room," she suggested. "I need you, Grady. I want you to make love to me. Now."

She'd barely finished speaking when Grady swept her off her feet. She wasn't sure where he was taking her, but she didn't care. All she wanted was to be with him—making love with him—as soon as possible. She nibbled his neck, his ear, his firm jaw as he strode swiftly through the cavern and into one of the buildings. A door opened and closed and then he placed her on a soft bed, following her down onto it.

"I've dreamed of this," he whispered as he leaned over her. He kissed her, claiming her mouth with a thoroughness that left her gasping.

When he let her up for air, she smiled. "I thought about you too, during my travels. I missed you, Grady."

"Your words are music to my ears." He rewarded her with a series of nibbling kisses that eventually trailed their way down her neck to her collarbone and lower. He nudged her clothing out of the way, unfastening tabs and baring her as he went along.

Before long, she was naked beneath him and she was tugging on his clothing eagerly. One of them was overdressed.

When she had him bare, she spent time rubbing against his heated skin. Alvian body temperature was a little higher than a human's. She loved the feel of his warmth against her, teasing her, comforting her, but she wanted more.

Wrestling him into a roll, she straightened atop him, straddling him, her hands on his muscled chest. She smiled down into his questioning eyes, petting him and purring like a kitten. She loved the feel of him under her.

"Let me touch you, Grady. We've never really had time to explore each other. I want that. I want to learn your body's secrets. What makes you gasp. What makes you moan. What makes you come." She interspersed each sentence with a teasing lick of her tongue over his flesh. Bending over him, she teased him, loving the way his temperature rose and his breathing increased. She was having an effect on him. That was good because he was affecting her as well.

Already she could feel dampness gathering at her core. It would ease his way when she was ready to claim him. She liked the feeling of power he gave her. She knew he could easily reverse their roles, but he was giving her this time, this exquisite moment, to learn about him as she wanted. She loved him for that...and for so much else.

What she felt in her heart for Grady was deep and true love. She didn't know what that would do to their futures, but she had to take the risk. She had to act on the love pouring out of her heart for him. He was so alone. He needed...so much. She wanted to give him everything, be everything he needed, to stay with him forever.

But circumstances were against them. They both knew it and yet were powerless against the love that drove them both toward each other.

She teased his hard body, loving the way he was letting her have control. He was so much bigger than she was, in close quarters like this, he had all the physical advantage. If he'd wanted to fight her for dominance, he would surely have won. But he wasn't fighting. He was letting her do as she liked and oh, boy, did she *like* his hard body.

"You are beautiful." Her words whispered against his sternum as she kissed her way down his chest.

She felt his chuckle. "Men are not beautiful."

"You are." She took a moment to meet his gaze. "On the inside. You have a beauty of spirit. A sense of honor and a gallantry about you that women dream of. And on the outside...you're just plain hot."

He seemed uncomfortable, squirming a little from side to side. "My body temperature is higher than a human's—"

She cut him off with a finger over his firm lips. "That's not what I meant. I love that higher temperature, by the way. You keep me warm." She smiled and licked her lips. "I meant *hot* as in, totally buff, handsome and gorgeous. Your body is *hot*—wickedly attractive to the opposite sex. Women drool over your physique, and men are jealous of the feminine attention you get."

A perplexed frown creased his forehead. "Really?"

She kissed the frown away. "Really." She sat up, moving downward, straddling his thighs. "And I get jealous every time a woman looks at you, but I know you're all mine. And then I gloat inwardly. They'll never know how truly magnificent you are."

"Yours, eh? I like the sound of that." He reached up and stroked her hair away from her face with one hand as she lowered her head again and began kissing her way from his chest to his abdomen.

"All mine. So don't even think of spreading your love around," she teased.

"I'm a one woman man, Gina." The teasing had gone out of his voice. "You're the only woman I want or need."

Gina paused, her hands on his hips, his cock hard and needy only inches away from her head.

"I love that, Grady. I don't know how this will work. How it will end for any of us. But I love that you want me as much as I want you. I love you, Grady. I want you to know that and never doubt."

If she were a betting woman, she would bet she rocked his world then, sliding her tongue downward, around his hard cock. She took him inside, bathing his sensitive ridges with swirling licks and light suction that increased as his response did. From the way his thigh muscles strained against her hands and the groans he couldn't hold back, she knew he liked what she was doing.

That was good because she'd never considered herself any kind of expert when it came to giving head. The opportunities in her past had been few and far between. Truth be told, she'd never felt so strongly about any of her past partners that she wanted their pleasure first and foremost above her own. With Grady, that all had changed. Jim too, she had to admit. What was it about these two men—so different, yet so alike in the way they made her feel?

When she cupped his balls in one hand, Grady stiffened and reached down to hold on to her shoulders. He moved fast, shifting his hands under her arms and lifting, drawing her away from his cock and back up his body.

"Now why'd you do that? I was just getting into it."

Grady laughed aloud at her teasing. "So was I. A little too much if you must know. I want to be inside you when I come, Gina. I want you to come with me."

"Oh." Her body revved up at his words. "Okay. I can do that." She grinned at him, reaching between them with one hand, positioning him. All she had to do was raise her hips and then lower...

"Let me go, Grady. Let me do this. *I* want to make love to *you* this time."

"You always make love to me, Gina." He drew her head down for a quick kiss that he met halfway, his abdominal muscles rippling in a way that made her mouth water. "Every time."

But he let her have her way, releasing his grip on her arms and allowing her to do as she willed. She enveloped him, bit by bit, dragging out the pleasure of their initial joining, loving the way he filled her. He was long and strong, hard and hot. He filled her so completely she wanted this to last.

Passion rose and she was helpless in the fierce tide that swept over her, dictating her actions. She began to ride him, her thighs working alongside his as she met his upward thrusts with downward pulses of her hips. It started slow, and quickly rose to a fever pitch to the point where she was crying out at every thrust. He fit her perfectly, hitting the secret place inside her that set her off like a skyrocket.

Just when she thought she couldn't take any more and stay sane, she felt him gathering beneath her. Having all that raw, male power between her thighs was something she could easily become addicted to. The only thing that could make it better was if Jim could share in this moment somehow. Even as she made love to Grady, she missed Jim, illogical as it seemed.

Grady tensed, pulsing up into her as she met his thrust eagerly. She was so close, she knew she'd come the moment he did. And then she didn't have to wait anymore. Grady came with a roar of her name, and she screamed as she climaxed long and hard.

She felt his heat inside her, and it set off another spasm of pleasure. She collapsed over him after long moments, placing drowsy kisses along his chest.

"I love you, Grady," she said just before sleep claimed her.

"I love you too, my mate."

Jim woke up on the wrong side of the bed. Any side was the wrong side when Gina wasn't in the bed at all. She hadn't come to their room last night, though her pack was still in one corner. He had her stuff, but not her.

Of course, he knew damned well where she'd spent the night. With that bastard Grady.

Jim tried not to let it get to him, but damn it, it hurt. Without even a word, she'd gone to the alien bastard. She'd forgotten Jim easily, it seemed, but he knew he'd never forget her.

Gina Hanson had haunted his memory for years—and that was when he thought she was lost forever. Now, having had her, knowing she was alive, it would be impossible for Jim. It would drive him nuts if he let it.

Maybe he and Grady had something in common there.

Jim swiped at his itchy jaw as he dragged himself out of bed and headed toward the small bathroom. He showered and shaved by rote, enjoying the slightly updated facilities in this complex. In comparison to his home, this was a much newer facility with more modern—for the old world—conveniences.

Much as he hated to admit it, he thought he understood how Grady might feel if he was forced to live without Gina. Jim felt the same way. Maybe Jim wouldn't go clinically insane without her, but knowing she was with Grady would definitely make him a little crazy.

The aliens were different. Maybe there was some truth to the idea that they really couldn't handle emotions. The pain of heartbreak might just turn the guy psycho. Jim wouldn't be really surprised if it did. Grady was an alien after all. He'd lived most of his life without emotion and now, suddenly, had to deal with things humans spent a lifetime trying to figure out.

No one ever went crazy from happiness, but heartache and depression were hard for even well balanced people to handle.

There was a solution—loath as he was to admit it. He'd seen the way the cousins both enjoyed the company of their shared mate. Jaci seemed happy and well balanced between her two men, but then, Jaci was an alien. She might have emotions now, but she hadn't been raised with them, with the expectation of one husband to share the rest of her life.

Of course, humans didn't age anymore. Not like they used to. Jim had heard they could live for a couple hundred years, so maybe they weren't fully human anymore. Maybe there was an opportunity to reshape the world in which they lived. To make it what they wanted instead of what they were used to. Maybe a three-person relationship might actually work.

It would depend on Gina.

Jim would never force her into something she didn't want. Hell if he knew how he'd handle being in a three-way relationship with her and that damned Grady, but if the alternative was not having her in his life at all, he'd learn how to deal with it. Somehow.

That is, if she wanted him. Could be she only wanted the alien. Jim didn't know what he'd do if that were the case.

That dismaying thought in mind, Jim left his quarters and headed for breakfast. Besides the personal turmoil, he still had work to do here. He was here on behalf of his people in Colorado, and he couldn't forget it. The connections he made here could prove useful in the future, and he had to do his best to scout out the possibilities and make assessments of both the people and the facility while he was here.

Jim shared a companionable breakfast with some of the people who lived and worked in the facility. After breakfast, Mike and Dave signaled him through BURTIN's paging system. Mick O'Hara had called and wanted to speak to him. The call was already in progress as Jim entered the communications room.

"...and the home crystal will replenish the Earth and reawaken those waiting in the coldest places, wielded by one who is of both worlds."

"What do you think it means?" Mike asked over the line.

"Caleb is seeing people trapped in ice. Not just any people. Tall, blond, beautiful people."

"Alvians." Dave's voice was full of accusation. Jim noted they'd set up a speakerphone so they could all talk and be heard over the communication array. It was a nice mix of alien and human tech that seemed to work, though Jim had never seen such technology blended before. He was amazed it worked at all and knew Wally would have a field day with something like this.

"Yeah, he thinks so. He also thinks our son, Harry, is the one who is of both worlds. The big question is, where are these frozen Alvians hiding out?"

"We haven't seen anything like that around here." Mike looked to his cousin, who nodded in agreement. "But we'll let you know if we find any Alvian popsicles."

"Ask your newcomers. Something like this—if anyone's stumbled across it already—would be ripe for gossip. We need to find these frozen guys. Caleb says it's imperative."

"We could send out some search parties. At the very least," Dave looked pensive, "we could search the depths of our cave structure. We've been here for months, but we still haven't managed to reconnoiter every tunnel. This place is vast and there's a network of intricate natural caves and tunnels beyond the boundaries of the installation proper."

"That's a good idea. Do that," Mick directed. "Once you have your own domain mapped out, we'll consider where to look next. There's a lot of frozen tundra north of us. I'd hate to send anyone out into that, but there are mountain men who live there already. If we could contact some of them and ask if they've seen anything..."

"That's a good idea," Dave answered, then straightened. "Mick, Jim is here, if you want to deliver Caleb's advice."

Jim and Mick exchanged greetings. "Caleb and I had a lot to talk over last night. If there really are dudes with wings flying around, as my good friends assure me there are, then you need to know they'll be both real and symbolic help in spreading news among the different enclaves of humans around the continent. They are working for their own agenda, Caleb says, but in this case, their cause runs parallel with ours. They can be trusted to have only our best interests at heart in the coming confrontation."

"Is it going to be all out war then?" Jim steeled his spine. He didn't want war, but if there was no other way, he'd lead his people through it as best he could.

"More like an underground movement. A bloodless coup would be the best result, but if things go wrong, they could go terribly wrong. Caleb sees all the possible futures in this case because a lot hinges on decisions made by those who lead. You among them. If you work together, the likelihood of success is greater than if you go it alone."

"I've already decided to recommend ongoing communication with this facility to my people. I think we could help each other a lot. If Mike and Dave agree, we can start slow, but I hope to keep the tunnels open and possibly send small groups back and forth to work with each other."

Mike and Dave were nodding. Dave spoke for both of them. "We want to visit your place first, but we're leaning in the same direction. Isolation is no way for humans to live—or succeed."

"Good," Mick spoke through the crystal. "That's the first step. Now for the rest. Jim, you may not like this next part, but there's an alien in your future. A big guy who loves your girl." Jim could tell Mick was trying to soften the blow with humor, but it didn't really help. "I've known Grady Prime for a long time. He's a good guy, but in addition, Caleb foresees that he'll be helpful in the coming confrontations. He's one of their most respected Primes. He can argue for our side very effectively with his people, and his words will sway a lot of regular Alvians. We need him on our side—sane and whole. That means you either need to cede the field to him, or learn to share."

The gym was packed. In fact, the bleachers had been pulled out from the wall on one side and were filled with people watching the central matted area where one small human woman held center stage.

When Jim arrived, Gina was warming up, running through progressively more advanced *kata*. He joined her, standing a few feet away, running through the same *katas* he'd learned from her father years ago, in parallel with her, much to the audience's delight. He could feel their interest, their admiration and their fascination. Good. He wanted them to realize that others could replicate what Gina could do. It might give them the desire to try it themselves.

It felt good to be working side by side with her. Her skills—which had been world class to begin with—had only improved with time. Jim enjoyed the challenge of keeping up with her in routines he had first learned from her father. It brought back old memories in a good way.

When she completed a final, very complex *kata*, she bowed to him, a tentative smile on her face. He hadn't said anything to her since her desertion in favor of Grady the night before, and he assumed she had to be wondering where they stood with each other. This wasn't the time or place to get into it, but he left her with a wink and a grin that seemed to put her at ease. He wasn't sure where they would go from here, but the more he thought about it, the more he realized he wanted—no, needed—her in his life. They'd figure out the details later.

As Jim left the main area, Bill was already setting up to challenge Gina. They stood facing each other across the mats and Jim turned to watch, eager to see how the winged warrior would do against Gina's skill.

Bill wore loose clothing, his wings out of sight and apparently off limits during this bout. Jim was glad. Those phenomenal wings would most likely give the big alien a huge advantage over any normal human being. Even one as skilled as Gina Hanson.

Gina took over the role of teacher, explaining the rules of the bout to the people in the stands. She did it with style, humor and grace, easily winning them to her side. When they were ready, she faced Bill with an eager light in her eyes.

The match began with a flurry of lightning-fast strikes. Jim held his breath at how rapidly the alien warrior moved in on Gina's much smaller frame. But she met him, move for move, blocking and parrying, evading and counterstriking with blindingly fast movements. Jim remembered how she had moved in the past. This was unlike anything she had been before.

A gifted student at the top of her rank then, she was now, without a doubt, a grandmaster. Every move was breathtakingly beautiful to watch and deadly accurate.

To say she ran circles around Bill would be overstating it—but not by much. Bill was talented and skilled as well, but Gina outclassed him. After the initial contacts, he was unable to get in even one glancing blow.

The *coup de grace* came when Gina sidled in beneath Bill's reach and laid him out flat on the ground. A collective gasp went up from the audience, followed by raucous cheering as she helped Bill to his feet. The alien warrior was gracious in defeat, bowing to his opponent as Gina bowed in return.

"You have only gained in skill since last we sparred, Gina." Jim heard Bill's compliment as he and Gina walked off the mats.

"I think you went easy on me, Bill, but thanks."

Bill winked at her as he left her at Jim's side.

"Nice work out there," Jim said, hoping to bridge the gap between them.

"Thanks. Same to you. I'm surprised you remembered all those *katas*. Seems like I learned them a lifetime ago." She snagged a glass of water from a nearby table, drinking daintily.

"It was a lifetime ago. But sometimes the discipline your father taught me was all that kept me going."

"I know what you mean." A tense moment passed between them. Jim looked around, noting the crowd was beginning to disperse and the large matted area was filling up with people. Bill led a group in one corner. They were learning a *kata* Jim had never seen before. Jim looked farther and saw Grady Prime standing along one wall, his gaze steady and proprietary on Gina. Jim's anger flared, but he tamped it down. He had to be cool.

"Look, about last night..." Gina was uncharacteristically hesitant. "I'm sorry I didn't leave word. I didn't want you to worry about where I was."

"Oh, I knew where you were."

Gina had the grace to blush. She perused her toes for a moment before meeting his gaze. "I didn't plan for it to work out that way. Things just got...out of hand. Before I knew it, I was with Grady. I'm sorry."

Jim sighed, striving for calm. "Can we discuss this someplace else?" He looked pointedly at the people filing past on their way out the door and those who remained, all eyeing Gina with interest.

"You're right." Gina shook her head. "We'll talk after we're done here okay?"

"Sounds about right."

Gina looked relieved. "Then how about sparring with me? We never got to see who would've won that night I showed up on your doorstep."

Jim smiled, on surer ground as he followed her back onto the mats. They took positions opposite each other and it was game on.

If Jim had any idea of going easy on Gina because she was a girl, it was gone within the first few moments when she scored more than one point off him with quick jabs and a kick to his middle. She pulled her punches, as he did, only hitting with minimal force. Still, they moved like lightning and garnered attention from those around.

Jim had perfected situational awareness in his years with the CIA and it had only improved since. Even as he spun into an attempt at a leg sweep, he caught sight of Grady moving closer, his expression like thunder as he watched them. Others gathered round, varying degrees of interest and respect on their faces as they watched Jim and Gina spar.

Gina jumped clear over his leg sweep, into a dive roll and up to deliver a counterstrike that he just barely evaded. They were both back on their feet, facing each other milliseconds later, and the game continued.

Grady drew closer.

"Your boyfriend looks like he wants to knock my block off," Jim observed to Gina privately.

Her reaction was not what he expected. She gasped and looked away to find Grady just as Jim launched an attack sequence. Too late, he realized she wasn't evading as he'd anticipated. She was going to get clobbered, but it was too late to pull back. He was already in motion and unable to redirect, though he tried like hell to alter his own trajectory.

A displacement of air was all the warning he got as another body blocked him. A bigger, more solid, masculine body protected Gina, who stood motionless behind the newcomer. It was Grady. He had put himself between Gina and Jim, taking the blow for her, blocking but still receiving quite a hit even as Jim tried to pull back.

It all happened in less than a second.

Jim's momentum, arrested by Grady's intervention, took him off to the side. He landed hard, rolling away, regaining his feet seconds later, breathing hard. His heart was in his throat.

"God, Gina!" Jim moved toward her but Grady stepped between them menacingly.

Jim assessed the competition, looked Grady up and down. "Thanks for intervening, but I had it under control."

"It didn't appear that way to me." Grady folded his arms, implacable.

"She took me off guard. I didn't expect her to stop dead." Jim sounded defensive even to his own ears, and he didn't like it one bit.

"So now it's her fault? If this is the way you treat women, I'm surprised any follow you."

Now *that* was a challenge if he'd ever heard one. The sneer that accompanied the blond giant's words cinched it.

"First of all—" Jim poked Grady in the shoulder with one pointing finger, "—nobody *follows* me. I'm not a tyrant. I may lead my people, but it was by their choice and I never make unilateral decisions if there's time to consult. Second—" he jabbed Grady again. "—I did *not* blame Gina. I merely stated that I made a mistake. I didn't expect her to lose concentration like that. The old Gina never would. It was my fault for baiting her telepathically."

"Of course it's your fault."

Grady sounded really angry as he stepped forward, advancing threateningly on Jim. But Jim wasn't backing down. He'd love to get a piece of Grady Prime. A good ass kicking is just what he needed—whether it was his own or Grady's ass that would ultimately get kicked, he wasn't sure, but either way, he was spoiling for a fight.

"I just said that, didn't I?" Jim shouted.

"Guys." Gina tried to intercede but she couldn't get between them.

They kept her off to the side while they stared each other down, in each other's faces. "Please don't do this."

Jim was aware of the gym around them going quiet. Only Bill had the guts to come up to them, putting one arm around Gina's shoulders.

"They need to get this settled." Bill guided Gina away. "Just don't kill each other," Bill threw back at them as Grady backed off and Jim went to stand in opposition across a section of cleared mats.

Spectators vanished, making room by climbing into the bleachers, out of harm's way. This wasn't going to be an exhibition bout. No, this was going to be the real deal.

Within certain bounds. Jim bowed, never taking his gaze from Grady's. This was a formal challenge, and both men knew it. If there was ever going to be peace between them, they had to settle this. They had to know who was stronger, who was faster and who could or should take the lead in their odd, forced partnership.

Grady opened, stepping up to Jim and allowing his first blow to be easily blocked. It allowed him to grab Jim's arm in a hold, but Jim had the same leverage and realized it was because Grady wanted to test his strength. Jim learned Grady had a punishing grip from the brief hold before they broke apart.

Jim launched a lightning-fast volley that Grady just managed to evade. The Alvian fighting style was different than what he was used to, but Jim had mastered many different forms of martial arts in his years of study and practice. He adapted. And he discovered he was just slightly faster than Grady, though the alien was stronger.

They circled and it was Grady who made the next foray, landing a series of blows to Jim's midsection. Jim countered, using his legs and speed to advantage, tripping Grady up and throwing him down on the mats with a resounding thud. Jim hoped he'd stunned the big man, but no such luck. Grady popped back up ready for more and the game was on again.

This went on for some time while they tested each other's weaknesses and strengths. Jim learned a great deal from their fight and earned just as many bruises as he dealt. Little by little strategy overtook anger and fatigue slowed response time. Grady landed a lucky final blow that knocked Jim flat on his ass but Jim managed to drag Grady down with him and neither man got up right away.

Gina ran over, falling to her knees between their prone bodies. She put one hand on each of their chests, as if to push them down, keeping them on the matted floor.

"This stops now." Jim could hear the tears in her voice and hated that he'd had any part in making her cry. He grabbed her hand in both of his, stroking her fingers tenderly.

"I'm sorry, babe. I didn't mean to distract you. I would rather die than ever hurt you."

She turned to him and he saw the emotional pain in her gaze, as well as the understanding. "I know that, Jim. It wasn't your fault." She leaned over and kissed his cheek, forgiveness in her every move. His heart began to beat again, sure of her acceptance. "And you," she turned to Grady, taking Jim's heart with her. "Thank you for trying to protect me. It wasn't really necessary, but I do appreciate it."

Grady sat up, and Jim followed suit.

"Alvians have no female soldiers. Women are to be protected, never hurt." Grady sent a glare in Jim's direction. "While I admire your skills, Gina, it will take some time to get used to the idea that my mate can protect herself. I'll try, but I will never stand by and watch you get hurt when I can prevent it. Don't ask me to."

Gina sobbed and threw herself into Grady's arms, hugging him close. Jim let her hand go, admitting momentary defeat.

Grady didn't like the sensations coursing through his veins. He'd experienced anger before, but never this kind of all-consuming rage. Was this the first sign of approaching madness?

His heart stilled.

He wouldn't put Gina in danger. If he was going mad, he'd leave before he exposed her to his illness.

Grady drew back from her. He needed to think this through. While his heart ached to hold her close and keep her next to him for all time, he had to do what was best for her. But first he had to get to the bottom of what had just happened.

He stood, and she followed. Jim also stood, and Grady met his eyes over Gina's shoulder. He would use all the skills he'd learned as a commander of soldiers to assess the problem and devise a solution. This could not be allowed to happen again.

"You admitted to distracting Gina. How?"

Jim shook his head, chagrined. "Telepathy." He met Grady's gaze solemnly, accepting blame. Grady respected that. "I said something to her, but I didn't expect it to break her concentration."

"What exactly did you say?" Grady stepped around Gina, though she tried to remain between them, and stared the other man down. Jim didn't back off, but then he wouldn't be worthy of a warrioress like Gina if he had.

"I told her you looked like you wanted to knock my block off." A challenging smile curved one side of Jim's mouth.

Grady regarded him for a moment, analyzing the situation.

"I did," he finally admitted with an answering hint of humor. "I find I am jealous of the past you share with Gina. I've only known her a short time. I feel at a disadvantage because of it when compared to your history." Grady didn't mention the agony he felt every time Jim and Gina touched. Their Hum went straight through him, making him ache with pain, knowing they belonged together—without the alien interloper, even if he was also a true mate to Gina.

Unpredictably, Jim's antagonism level decreased. He stepped back, his posture changing from one of challenge to one of understanding.

"I can't blame you for that. I'm sure I'd feel the same if our roles were reversed."

"Would you?" Grady watched him carefully for any sign of deception, but could find none. "I do not understand why it makes me want to beat you senseless. I have never felt such urges before and I worry..." He broke off before he could reveal his deepest, darkest fear—the fear that he would go mad—but Jim's eyes cleared with understanding. Somehow, he knew.

Grady turned away, finding Gina there, waiting for him. Her soft smile and gentle touch soothed him as she reached up to stroke his cheek.

"It's all right, Grady. Jealousy is something all humans struggle with."

He wanted to stay right there and revel in her compassion but the ugly truth came between them.

"Gina, I'm not human."

He left before she could say anything, seeking solitude in which to think over these upsetting events. He strode from the gym building and headed for the darkened end of the huge, main cavern, toward the lake.

Small eddies of current lapped at the sandy shoreline, indicating the lake was fed by some underground water source, but he couldn't see it. Grady sank down onto the cold sand, stretching one leg out in front of him, raising the other knee on which to lean his crossed arms. He had much to think about.

"That could've gone better." Gina muttered as she watched Grady walk away. Something in the set of his shoulders was so forlorn, she wanted to go after him, but knew he wouldn't welcome her interference right now. He was learning to cope with emotion. She knew he needed some time alone to think things through when they came to a boil.

There was no doubt, the turmoil of the past minutes had been hard for all of them to handle. Gina hated seeing Jim and Grady at odds, knowing she was the reason for their strife. She hated being in the middle, stuck between them, a point of contention.

"I'm sorry I distracted you. I could've really hurt you." Jim's voice was gentle as she turned to face him.

"Forget it. Accidents happen. I shouldn't have been so easy to distract. My dad would have my head for such a stupid mistake." She offered him a small smile, which he returned.

"Nice try, but it was my fault. Things are...unsettled between you and Grady right now. I shouldn't have mentioned him during our bout. It was petty and potentially dangerous."

"So why did you?" She looked up at him challengingly.

Jim met her gaze though he seemed uncomfortable. "I don't know. I guess I've got some jealousy issues of my own."

Chapter Sixteen

A man tended the garden. Everyone else was probably preparing for or eating dinner at this point in the early evening, but Jim couldn't be around people. Not yet. The lone gardener had given him a curious look when he first entered, but went about his tasks, leaving Jim to his thoughts.

It didn't do much good. Jim's thoughts were racing a mile a minute and for the first time in a long time, he didn't know what to do. He'd made an ass out of himself in the gym. He owed Grady an apology for that, at least, but couldn't bring himself to seek out the damned alien and make things right. Jim despised himself for the pettiness of his emotions. He hated the way love screwed with his control. He didn't want it, but he had no choice. He was in love with Gina and he'd do anything to keep her.

After about an hour, the gardener finished his work and headed toward Jim. He didn't want to talk to anyone, but he was the trespasser here. The gardens were some of the most sensitive areas of the installation since any sabotage here could ruin the food supply. He understood vigilance and knew he should be going, but he also valued the peace of the open space filled with green, growing things.

"I guess our little operation can't really compare with what I hear you've got going down south," the man observed as he sidled up to a position a few yards from Jim's bench. Both men faced outward, perusing the rows and rows of vegetation.

Jim appreciated the man's oblique approach. He seemed a nice enough sort, and Jim didn't mind talking about the gardens in his home facility with someone who was truly interested.

"We've had the hydroponics sections up and running since just after the cataclysm. We also have a few of the scientists who designed the whole thing in residence. They've been able to work wonders."

"I bet. We're learning as we go here. Bill and I found some old written manuals and BURTIN helped us locate information in his memory banks, but neither of us were farmers before. The O'Haras have given us some pointers, but they aren't real familiar with this kind of farming either."

"I bet." Jim looked around, finally settling his gaze on the man. He looked fully human, yet his words indicated a familiarity with the Alvian hybrid. "You work with Bill?"

"Son of a bitch saved my life," came the surprising answer, given with a smile. "I wanted to hate him at first. I escaped from the city and was on the run when he found me—delirious with pneumonia and burning alive in my lean-to. I was so sick, I let my campfire get out of control and nearly paid with my life. Bill found me and brought me to the O'Haras. He and Doc Mick nursed me back to health."

"When did you figure out he was an alien?"

"Not for some time." The man sent him a sideways look. "I was sick as a dog for the first few weeks. When it came time to consider moving on, the O'Haras suggested Bill and I move along together. We both had mountaineering skills and were both on the run. It was a good idea, even though I had to get used to the idea that my companion was a goddamned alien. Then Jaci came along, and we both realized we had to protect her. That's why we decided to come to this cave complex, though neither of us knew the full extent of the facility until we actually got here. We thought it was an old mine. Then Mike and Dave showed up, and we had the beginnings of a little community. A few weeks later other people began to arrive, and we've been taking in strays ever since."

"You've got a thriving community now from what I can see."

"Yeah, I reckon we do. But I've got to tell you, without our alien friends it would be a lot more primitive. Jaci is a wiz with technical stuff and has figured ways to use the crystals the O'Haras smuggle up to us from Davin. She's mostly responsible for restoring full power to this entire facility. Then the cousins set Bill up as the Farmer in the Dell, and he took to it though he'd never even seen a seed before in his life. He and I run the hydroponics area together for the most part now. It's too big for just him alone and we've got work crews to help us out as it gets bigger. The gardens are good for him. They bring him peace,

229

which to my mind, he richly deserves."

"What makes you say that?"

The man shifted and settled back against the table he'd been leaning against, seeking a more comfortable position.

"He was the Council's top assassin, and the geniuses over there decided to use him for their very first guinea pig. He's lucky he's not completely insane. You train a man to kill people all his life, then give him emotions. They were playing with fire, though they didn't even realize it. He could've become a complete psycho. Or he could be wracked with guilt over the lives he's taken. Lucky for us—not so much for him—it's the latter. That man has a lot of demons that haunt him. More than anything, he deserves our compassion and sympathy, or we're no better than those who made him what he was."

Jim could tell this man felt strongly about his words, and Jim even understood why. He'd heard about the inhuman experiments the Alvians routinely perpetrated. He wasn't too surprised to find out they'd done the same thing to their own people.

"You were a prisoner?"

The man nodded. "As far as I know, I'm the only one to ever escape that city and it cost me dearly. I've got a baby daughter I've never seen."

"I'm sorry. My name is Jim, by the way." Jim extended a hand in friendship, which was taken.

"I'm Sam." They shook hands, and Sam moved back to his leaning position some feet away. "It's not all bad though. We're free here, and I know my daughter is as safe as she can be in Davin's engineering facility. He's another alien who's got a heart. He took Ruth and my daughter in and they live in relative comfort while learning about the aliens' crystals. It's both a blessing and a curse. They were moved there because of Ruth's special gift for working with crystal, but for the same reason, Davin can't let her go like he did Mike and Dave. Officially, they're dead. Davin was able to arrange an accident for them so they'd be free to live here with their mate, Jaci. But Ruth's gift is something special. As a result, the Council has taken a special interest in her. It would be hard for Davin to devise a way to smuggle her out and impossible for me to go there. I killed an Alvian solder to escape and have taken out a few since." Cold sorrow entered the man's eyes as he looked out at his garden. "I'm a wanted man as far as the Alvians go. For now, I have to stay under the radar."

"I hear that. Some of my people are in a similar situation, having taken out Alvian patrols and the like."

"It's not easy living with a price on your head, but it does make you realize what's important. My advice to you, whether you want it or not, is to grab onto your gal with both hands and don't let go." Jim looked up at him as Sam smiled. "Oh, I heard a bit about what's going on with you, Gina and Grady. If she's willing—and if you think he'll be good to her—then you should probably consider making it a threesome. Better to be with her. Take it from someone who misses his woman every day."

Some time later, after leaving the garden, Jim found Grady sitting in the cold sand at the edge of the lake. Little glints of quartz lit the area with a soft glow that came from the sand, the walls, even the ceiling far above.

"Mind if I join you?" Jim didn't wait for an answer as he sat a few feet away, facing the gently rippling lake.

Grady didn't even look up. Jim found some flat rocks easy at hand that were just perfect for skipping and took a shot. The first one skipped three times before sinking below the surface in the dim light. The second bounced off the surface four times. He'd been good at this in his youth. It was good to see those old skills gained in idle summers at the lake house with his parents hadn't been lost over the many years since.

"You know, there is a solution to our mutual problem. It's not one I can say I ever would have entertained before—and I'm not sure Gina will go for it—but we could try it as a threesome."

There. The proverbial olive branch had been extended. Jim wasn't sure if it was the right thing to do, but he didn't see any other choice that would satisfy them all. After his talk with Sam, the least he could do would be to entertain the idea. If the other two potential partners in this little drama were amenable, he'd give it his best shot.

"You mean like Jaci and her mates?" Grady turned to him, acknowledging him for the first time. "From what I have seen, Mike and Dave were best friends even before they met Jaci. You and I have no prior connection. We do not know each other. We have little in common and are not even of the same race. Do you think we could really share Gina's love?"

"Well, when you put it like that, it does seem difficult...but not impossible. Perhaps we should try to see if we could be friends at least. There's too much tragedy in this world already. I don't want to be responsible for yours, if Gina chooses me. On the other hand, I can see this is difficult for her and I want to at least explore any idea that would make it easier. This is all about her happiness as far as I'm concerned."

"A valid and important point." Grady nodded, clearly thinking through what Jim had said. "Gina's happiness is paramount."

"We agree on that at least."

"True." Grady sported a rueful grin, but his eyes held darkness as he gazed out at the rippling lake. "So much is new to me. Emotion, interaction, true friendship...love. I don't understand a lot of what I'm feeling at times. I know that makes it difficult for you to understand me, and it doesn't help that I am one of the soldiers responsible for capturing so many humans. I don't think I'll ever be able to forgive myself for that, and I don't expect you will either."

Jim decided to let that statement sit for a while. He was touched by the man's candor and his regret. Jim didn't think Grady was sophisticated enough yet to be able to fake the deep emotion Jim sensed from him. Guilt ran deep in Grady Prime's soul. The feeling was overwhelming. Nearly crippling. It would take time for him to come to terms with that kind of regret.

"So you're a soldier. And a leader. That's what Prime means, right?"

Grady seemed surprised at the change in topic, but went with it. "Prime is the designation given to the top of each hereditary line. I am the top Grady on this planet. All other Gradys are my subordinates. The Grady line is the top of the regular soldier lines. There are special ops branches, of course. Sinclairs head up the covert operators and Pfins lead the waterborne forces, but the majority of the regular army reports to me."

"So you're like a general. Or maybe a commander in chief." Jim thought out loud. "I was a special operator, which I assume means the same thing in both our systems. I started my military career in the army, then sought special training to become what we used to call a Green Beret. That was our army's special forces, but each division of our military had their own brand of special operator. After I got out of the military, I was recruited by the Central Intelligence Agency. That was my country's covert operations group that would work in secret, in other countries."

"I am familiar with the concept. I've read a lot about the governmental and military structures that existed before my people came here. Justin O'Hara explained quite a bit of it to me as well. I believe he was also a Green Beret at one time."

Jim thought that was interesting. He recognized the name. He'd known a new recruit named Justin when he was on his way out, right before he'd been hired by the CIA. He hadn't made the connection until now.

"I think I knew him, but not well. Someday, maybe we'll have a chance to catch up, but my duty to my people in Colorado means I'll have to leave here soon. At least for a while. I owe them that much. If Gina and I do get together on a permanent basis, I'll move heaven and Earth to be with her wherever she wants to be, but I have to square things in Colorado first. I can't leave them high and dry."

Grady looked at him with respect. "A good leader does not leave without putting his best man in charge. I made sure the army would be in good hands before I agreed to participate in Mara 12's experiment."

"So you're retired?"

"I thought I was. But the Council recalled me for one special mission." Grady sighed heavily and threw a rock out into the lake. It didn't bounce. It made a huge splash about fifty yards away. Jim was impressed. Grady had a good arm. "If they truly understood what the experiment did to me, they never would have sent me on this fool's errand."

"They sent you to kill Bill, right?"

Grady scowled. "I am no assassin. That is what special operators are for. I agreed to track him but I never said I would kill him, even though I knew that's what they wanted. I accepted the mission because I wanted to find him for my own reasons. I knew he'd had the treatment. I wanted to see for myself how it had turned out for him."

"I can understand that." The fact that Grady was no longer blindly following orders given by the Alvian High Council said a lot. "So now that you've found him, what have you learned?"

233

"I am left with more questions than answers, but I'm glad to see him stable and coming to terms with his new life."

"How are you going to square this with the Council? I assume you're not going to kill him."

"No. I never thought to try—unless it was an act of mercy. If I found him deranged or posing a threat to others, I would have put him down out of respect for the friendship we once had. The man I knew would not have wanted to live that way."

"But he's sane, so everything's cool. What now?"

"I don't honestly know. The only thing I know for certain is that the secrecy of this base—and yours—must be maintained. I will not betray the humans living here no matter how this turns out."

Jim felt a wave of relief for a worry he hadn't known he carried. "Thank you," he said with quiet respect.

"It's the least I can do."

"Are you two okay?" Gina's voice came to Jim telepathically. She was nearby.

"Yeah, we're okay. This Grady guy is an interesting character. Why don't you come over?"

She hesitated. *"I'll be there in about five minutes."*

"Gina will be here soon," Jim said to Grady.

"Did she communicate telepathically with you?" Grady's eyes looked both stormy and wistful.

"Yeah. We both have psychic talents. That bother you?"

"Yes." Grady was truthful almost to a fault. "That and other things will make any joint relationship difficult."

"Like what other things?"

"My jealousy, for one. It is new to me and very powerful. Even now I am jealous that you can speak to her privately, without me knowing, unless one of you lets me in on the secret."

"We could agree not to use telepathy around you. It's not like we have to, and I can see how secret communications could be divisive. As for jealousy, you're not the only one who has to deal with it."

"You too?" Grady looked over at him, seeming surprised.

"I wouldn't be human if I didn't feel some discomfort with the idea of sharing. As you said, we don't have a history like Mike and Dave do. We're relative strangers. But I think we could be friends given time.

Rome wasn't built in a day."

"Rome?"

"It was an ancient city on another continent." Gina joined them on the sand, sitting between them and jumping right into their conversation. "The Romans ruled most of the Western world at one time before their civilization fell. So why are we talking about Rome?"

"We weren't," Grady said, seeming lost himself as he tried to backtrack. "Jim used a phrase I did not understand, and I asked for clarification."

"Ah." She nodded sagely, looking from one to the other with a gentle smile. "Rome wasn't built in a day. That's a very popular saying. It means things will improve with time. What, in this case, were you speaking of?"

"The possibility of friendship between Grady and me," Jim supplied. "We were just saying that we don't know much about each other, but we're willing to learn."

"That's a good start." Gina seemed really pleased. "So why the turnaround? I thought you two were on the outs."

"It's because of you, Gina." Grady Prime was so earnest Jim almost rolled his eyes, but Gina seemed genuinely touched by his words. Grady took advantage, moving closer to her, cupping her cheek in his hand. "I am in love with you, Gina. If you could only hear the Hum of our resonance, you would understand. I would die for this. For you."

"Grady." Her voice trailed off as she moved into his arms and they shared a passionate kiss, oblivious to their surroundings.

Jim was about to get up and leave when he remembered Sam's words. He could see how much Grady loved her and that she wasn't indifferent to him either. How could he fault her for responding to such an impassioned declaration?

But Jim loved her just as much, if not more than Grady did. Could he really stand by and let the alien walk off with his prize?

He had three options. Walk away. Fight for her. Or the toughest of all—work to make all three of them happy, if such a thing was possible. He looked to the example set by Jaci and the cousins, and the other threesomes he'd heard about. If they could make it work, perhaps he could too. It was worth a try. Anything was better than doing without her or making everyone miserable.

Making a decision, Jim scooted forward on the sand, reaching out to touch Gina's waist. It startled Grady enough to break the kiss and stare over her shoulder at Jim. A silent moment of understanding passed between them before Grady looked back at Gina's upturned face.

"Do you want this, my love? Do you want both of us?"

"What?" Gina moved away, confusion on her lovely features. "Is that what you guys were talking about? You want to try this as a three-way?"

"Want? Honestly, no." Jim was man enough to admit. "But we can't always have what we want, and I think this is what we need to do. It's the only way I can see for all three of us to be happy."

Gina didn't know what to think. The idea of having both of them was tantalizing, though she'd only just started thinking about it since meeting Jaci and the cousins. From what she could see of their relationship, it worked for them. Could such an arrangement work for her and these men? She had no idea, but if they were game, she was willing to try.

More than willing, if truth be told. Each man turned her on in his own special way. Together, they would be devastating, she was sure. But was she brave enough to try? There was only one way to find out.

Turning to Jim, she leaned into him, kissing him deeply. When Grady's arms came around her waist from the other side, she suppressed a shiver of lust. Having two men at once should have shocked her. Instead, the naughty idea tantalized, making her want to try all sorts of things with them.

Jim broke the kiss and stared down at her. "Are you sure?"

There were still doubts, but they were eclipsed by the kindling flame in her womb as Grady's hands stroked between her thighs. "I want to try."

The cloth barring Grady's touch was too much. She wanted to feel his fingers against her skin, just as she wanted to feel Jim's. At the same time.

Just the thought of it made her hot.

Jim's hands went to her shoulders, pulling her in for another deep kiss. His kiss spoke of possession, of desire, while Grady's hands worked on her trousers. He tugged them off completely, along with her panties and shoes, placing the pants on the sand beneath her bare butt. Gina was almost too far gone to notice, but the special care he took for her comfort was appreciated.

Grady manipulated her lower body until she was half-lying on the sand. He spread her legs, coming down between them. His tongue preceded his fingers as he parted her folds and licked her clit, making her squirm in Jim's arms. Jim supported her shoulders, his fingers working the buttons on her top until her bare breasts spilled into his hands.

Jim moved, kneeling beside her, shifting her to lie in his lap while he bent over her breasts. Between his mouth on her upper half and Grady's between her thighs, she was in heaven. She'd fantasized about this sort of thing once or twice, but fantasies could never equal the reality of having two hungry males totally focused on her.

Two men she loved.

The thought brought her up short. She did love them. Each in their own way, but neither less than the other. She'd been half in love with Jim since she was a kid, and he'd only endeared himself to her more since meeting again. He was a demanding lover who pushed her to new heights every time they came together.

Grady, by contrast, was a considerate lover whose gentle handling told her without words how precious he thought her. He made her feel like a queen, and his lovemaking gave her a feeling of ultimate ecstasy she'd never known before him. He was magic.

Gina had always had a love of literature and making love to Grady was like making love to one of Tolkein's elves. He had the pointy ears, the melodic voice, more strength than most human men and the coloring. He was also so careful of her—except when he was in the thrall of his own climax. Then all bets were off and the animal inside him came out to play.

She loved that moment when he was out of control. Even then, she knew he would never use his superior strength against her. He'd die before he ever hurt her. She trusted him beyond doubt, beyond anything. She felt the same way about him.

Which is why the idea of having to choose between Grady and Jim had been so painful. She prayed this little interlude worked for all three of them. It was certainly working for her!

She wasn't able to think anymore when Grady's talented tongue began a fluttering dance around her clit. Jim's lips tightened around her aroused nipple, laving and sucking, making her want to scream.

But they were in a public place. Sure, the lakefront was deserted at this time of night, but anyone could come upon them. They were out in the open, hidden only by the gloom of the cavern and the distance of this remote lake from the rest of the facility.

Gina had never been a sexual exhibitionist, but these two men made her want to try all sorts of things that were new to her. New and exciting. Just the idea that someone could be watching them heightened her arousal.

Wanting to be more than just the receiver of such amazing pleasure, Gina reached for Jim's belt. It was awkward, but as soon as he realized what she wanted, he sat back.

"You want my cock, baby?"

His words were pitched low in the darkness but Grady stopped, looking up. Both men were totally focused on her. She had no idea what was racing through Grady's mind, but Jim's eyes spoke of heat and desire. She knew what he wanted. She wanted it too.

"Yes," she whispered, licking her lips. She'd never felt like a siren before, but as the flames in Jim's eyes roared to a new level, she knew she'd hit the right note. He made short work of his belt and the zipper, releasing his engorged cock.

Gina smiled, rising up on her elbows. Jim helped support her shoulders, moving into a position where all she had to do was open her mouth.

She took him in, loving the thick, hot feel of him. She couldn't really maneuver in the position they'd put her in, but it didn't matter. Her men did all the hard work. Jim stroked lightly, moving his hips in a slow rhythm that set them both on fire. Grady watched for a moment before returning to tease her opening with a much more aggressive tongue.

All Gina could do was squirm.

Grady lifted away, and she moaned at the loss. Jim seemed to like the vibration against his cock, so she moaned again when Grady lifted her thighs and pushed them upward, spreading her as he touched the tip of his hard cock to her eager opening. She was completely in their hands and had never felt safer or more intensely aroused.

Her eyes closed as Grady slid into her. The sensations were

unparalleled in her experience. Her body hummed, her blood sang as both men thrust into her in long, slow sweeps.

"Look at me, baby," Jim commanded.

Her eyes popped open, looking up into Jim's heated gaze. One of his hands supported her shoulders, the other stroked her hair, positioning her head just the way he wanted. His hips began to move faster but he never gave her more than she could handle. He was demanding, pushing her boundaries, but caring of her comfort.

She looked downward but couldn't really see Grady until he leaned forward, changing position slightly to dig deeper into her core. His wide cock rubbed a spot inside her on every stroke that nearly sent her into orbit.

Gina wrapped her legs around his waist, digging her heels into his ass, asking without words for what she wanted. He stepped up the pace, just as she'd hoped, as did Jim. The pressure on that spot inside her made her climb closer and closer to the sun and oh, how she wanted to get burned.

Her throat ached from the guttural sounds forced from her on every stroke. She knew the vibrations transferred from her mouth directly to Jim's cock. He timed his thrusts to take advantage of her predictable vocalizations. They were in synch. All three of them. The thought was enough to drive her over the edge as Grady moved faster within her.

Her climax broke like a tsunami over the shore, drowning her in pleasure. A split second later, both men joined her. Jim erupted in her mouth even as he pulled back trying to spare her, but she wanted it all. She swallowed what she could of his come though some spilled out over her cheeks. Grady shot into her, his elevated alien temperature warming her from within in a way no human man could duplicate. She loved the feeling. Almost as much as she loved him. And Jim.

She loved them both. This moment out of time with both her men was absolutely perfect.

"Much as I'm enjoying this, I think we should move someplace a little less public."

Jim's voice came to her minutes later. She must've dozed off because when she opened her eyes, the cavern was quite a bit brighter than it had been before. She sat up, clutching the edges of her shirt together.

"What time is it?" She scrambled for her pants, searching the area for prying eyes.

Jim's hand settled on her calf, stroking gently. "It's all right. You only slept for five minutes."

"Then why is it so much lighter in here?" She looked around at the sparkling walls of the cavern, now luminescent.

"We did that," Grady spoke from a few feet away, watching her. "Our resonance powered the small flecks of crystal present in this rock."

"You're kidding." Gina stopped and really looked at the softly glowing walls.

"No. If there had been more crystal present in this cave, it would now be glowing brightly. Our harmony is captured in the crystals, enhancing their native power."

"I had no idea." Gina dressed even as she continued to take in the luminous walls.

"Few have ever seen this kind of reflective resonance in recent times." Grady stood, fastening his trousers. "But I've seen it before, in even greater quantity. The crystal here is but a trace element in the stone lattice. The effect would be much more pronounced were we near a higher concentration of crystal."

They all heard footsteps approaching at the same time. The intruders were far away, but heading in their direction. Gina wanted to be gone before anyone realized what they'd been doing.

Jim stood, shielding Gina as she buttoned her shirt while he discreetly zipped his pants. Within moments they were heading away from the lakeshore, back into the populated areas of the complex.

"Which way?" Gina asked when they reached the main cavern.

"My rooms are closest," Grady offered.

Gina saw the way Jim hesitated, but after a moment he turned and the three of them walked together toward the nearest barracks building. There were several in the enormous main cavern, but Grady's was the nearest by far.

They managed to get inside without anyone seeing them. All three of them were good at moving stealthily. Gina's heart was pounding by the time the door to Grady's quarters closed behind them.

She looked around at the room. It was quite different from the one she'd been issued. For one thing, it was larger. The bed, too, was a king size compared to the double in her room.

"This must be the luxury building. My room's a lot smaller."

Grady was taller than Jim, and she suspected he needed the larger bed. Maybe that's why he'd been assigned to this building, even though it was farther away from the main area than the other barracks. Whatever the case, it didn't matter. All that mattered was that his bed would fit all three of them.

She felt eyes on her and looked up to find both men staring at her. Grady's face was easy to read. He wanted her. Again.

Well, she was up for that. With these two at her beck and call, she thought she'd be downright insatiable.

Jim's expression was more difficult to decipher. He looked hungry, but there was a tick in his clenched jaw that made her worry. Was he really okay with this? He seemed okay. For now.

She decided then and there, it was her job to make sure he saw all the advantages of this kind of relationship. Oh, how she'd enjoy her work. She licked her lips as she straightened away from the door.

Jim took one step forward, his dominating presence making her wet.

"Strip."

The single word made her womb clench. The look in his eyes made her want to do anything he asked. Without a word, she began to undress.

Chapter Seventeen

Jim didn't understand the myriad of strange emotions running through his brain at the moment, but he did know lust. He figured he'd go with that for now. There would be time to figure out the rest later.

Right now the most urgent thing on his mind was getting inside Gina. Again and again. The caveman in him came to the fore, and it was a good thing Grady didn't challenge him. He was just in the mood to enforce his will, no matter who stood in his way.

He liked the way Gina responded to his inner barbarian and if he wasn't much mistaken, she got a little thrill out of it too. Grady only registered as a background presence, though Jim had enjoyed watching the alien fuck Gina more than he'd thought possible.

And he'd watched. Every slide inward. Every moan from her lips that had vibrated against his own cock. He'd never been hotter in his life.

He didn't know what that meant beyond making him a pervert, but if he was, then so was Gina. And he refused to believe anything negative associated with her. So maybe being a little pervy wasn't so bad after all. She'd enjoyed it. Hell, he'd enjoyed it. He assumed Grady had too, though at this point, Grady was there because it would hurt Gina to dismiss him. Jim would have been content to keep her all to himself, but not at the expense of her happiness.

He didn't want to drive the guy crazy either. The very real possibility that the giant soldier would go insane without Gina was both alarming and brought out Jim's protective nature. Sure, he was an alien, but he was a living being with emotions. Jim didn't want to be responsible for making the guy go nuts.

Any further introspection was halted by the soft sway of Gina's generous breasts as they came into view. She was dressed only in her panties, and they were very obviously damp. He knew Grady had come inside her, but the thought of it didn't turn him off at all. Quite the contrary. It was titillating to see evidence of their shared passion.

Jim walked up to her, halting her hands on her hips as she prepared to lower the thin scrap of material that covered her pussy.

"No. Let me." His breathing grew harsh as excitement rose. She met his gaze, and he could see the spark of intense desire in her expression. She liked his commands.

Jim scooped her up into his arms and moved to the bed.

"Pull back the covers." He sent his words in Grady's general direction and a moment later the covers were whisked away, leaving a broad expense of white cotton sheet exposed. Jim lowered her to the bed, in the exact middle of the big, soft platform. Her eyes held his as he moved away, his hands reaching for the edges of her panties.

In a swift move, he slid them down her legs and off, flinging them away. Her legs parted and he sat between the firm pillars of her thighs, gazing down at his conquest. Her pussy was neat, the hair kept trimmed and tantalizing. He loved the look of her, especially now, her folds swollen from hard use.

Grady wasn't a small man. Jim had enjoyed watching her take the alien's thick cock, but he would like watching her take his own even better.

"Our woman isn't hot enough." He finally spoke to Grady, though his full attention was on Gina. "Nibble on her tits, Grady. Maybe that will help."

Gina's gasp was his reward. With another person to help surprise her, this could be fun. Grady's blond head dipped as the giant complied with Jim's order. He didn't know why, but he felt the need to assert control this time. It was a dominance thing that he needed to sort out, but for now, it felt damned good and he saw how Gina enjoyed it.

"Would you look at that?" Jim said speculatively, his gaze focused on her wet folds. "She's all creamy and wet. I like that." Dipping his fingers into her warmth, he tested her readiness. He liked the way she squirmed under his hand, as if eager for more. He started a light rhythm, building her passion, watching her progress, and he and

Grady played her body like a finely tuned instrument.

He increased his possession, adding another finger while he watched Grady play with her nipples. They were hard little points in his hands and mouth, indicating her elevated arousal. When she was near the point where every touch brought a series of harmonic vibrations, he eased off, removing his fingers from her slick pussy.

"Grady, let's flip her over. I want her on hands and knees for this." Gina shot him a questioning look as Grady eased away, but Jim didn't answer. He had something a little different in mind for this encounter, and he wanted her trust.

They positioned her, and she complied beautifully. Jim smoothed his palms over the round globes of her perfect ass, adding a little tap for good measure that made her squeak. But she smiled back at him, moving her butt under his palms in approval, wanting more. Grady seemed surprised, but refrained from saying anything. Jim was glad the warrior was letting him call the shots this time.

"You take that end—," Jim pointed Grady toward her head, "—while I keep things interesting over here." Jim insinuated himself between her spread knees, bringing himself up close to her bare ass and the wet place he wanted to claim—as soon as he got his pants off. Damn. He should've thought ahead. Every moment of delay annoyed him. He wanted to be inside her now.

Unzipping and shoving his pants down to free his aching cock, he didn't waste any more time once she was within his grasp. He slid home within her folds with a minimum of fuss, resting there once he'd claimed her channel, reveling in the warm, slick feel of her around him.

Drinking in the sensations, he looked upward, over the long, sinuous line of her back, to see Grady, his hands on her breasts as he bent over her upper half. A lean to the side showed him Gina had been busy. She had Grady's pants open, and his hard cock was being treated to the heaven that was her mouth and tongue.

Jim grasped her hips and began to thrust. As he moved forward, his motion propelled her onto Grady's cock. The warrior looked up, clearly startled as Jim did it again. Jim could only grin.

"Let me do the driving this time," he said in a low voice as he continued to pump.

Grady straightened, most likely so he could watch Gina's motion on him—probably also to be certain Jim didn't push her too hard. Jim liked the way the Alvian looked out for her. Between the two of them watching over her, she'd be in good hands.

The thought was startling and had an oddly comforting feel to it. Maybe Jim was more resigned to this weird threesome than he'd thought. He knew one thing—trying to think reasonably while he was buried balls deep in Gina's hot pussy wasn't really possible. Better to concentrate on the way she felt around him and the way he wanted to drive her to the biggest climax she'd ever known.

It was a good goal.

Jim began to move more forcefully, holding her by one hip as he slammed into her hot core, the other hand caressing around front, teasing her clit. He pinched, and she whimpered around Grady's cock. Her belly clenched, and he knew she liked it.

But he wanted to prolong this a little. He eased his hand away, rubbing her ass, then swatting her playfully while she squeaked. He loved that sound.

He spanked her again, just to hear it, and felt her channel contract around him even as her body produced even more lubrication to ease his way. It wouldn't be long.

Jim timed his thrusts, driving into her powerfully, moving her whole body. She understood the rhythm, as did Grady, who leaned back so she'd be able to take as much of him as she wanted with each forceful thrust of Jim's hips.

It worked. Better than Jim had ever expected. The three of them worked together like a well-oiled machine and it was only their second encounter. Who knows what they'd be able to do given a few months to get to know each other better.

Jim reached around, tickling her clit while his hips increased their pace once more. He was close, and he wanted her to go with him. Whether Grady would join them was up to him, but what man could resist Gina's climax? Certainly not Jim, and he'd bet Grady couldn't either.

As she peaked, Jim came in a blinding rush, jetting inside her as he pushed into her and held. And held. And held.

Dimly he was aware of Grady's final groan. As he'd suspected, the alien couldn't resist an orgasmic Gina either.

The shared climax was powerful. Pushing things beyond even the magnificent orgasm they'd achieved on the lakeshore. Jim held inside her for long minutes as his balls emptied and fire crashed through his veins. Little pumps of his hips drew out the bliss as he shut his eyes and concentrated on the incredible feeling of being inside his woman.

When the final echoes died away, he withdrew, lifting Gina in his arms and laying her on her back on the bed. She was between him and the alien warrior. As it should be. They would surround her. Walk on either side of her through life. Protecting her from all who would try to harm her.

He didn't know how it would all work out yet, but that was the goal. It was a worthy one and one he'd do his best to achieve it. There were some things to work out between his duty to his people, her allegiance to the alien brotherhood and Grady's ongoing participation in the alien experiment, but God willing, they'd figure a way to keep this bliss, this nirvana, between the three of them.

Jim collapsed at her side, barely noticing when Grady tossed the covers over all three of them. He faded into a satisfied sleep with his woman at his side.

Dawn underground was more a matter of timekeeping than actual sunlight. The base's artificial intelligence simulated sunlight in most areas of the complex, including the barracks—for those on the day shift, which included guests.

The lights came up gradually but by nine o'clock in the morning, Jim couldn't ignore the glare anymore. He stretched and yawned, puzzled to find himself alone in the big bed.

"Where the heck is everybody?" he ventured telepathically, hoping Gina was in range.

A mental giggle came back in Gina's distinctive tones. *"You looked so peaceful, I didn't have the heart to wake you."*

They kept up a teasing telepathic dialog while he dressed, made his way to his quarters, showered and dressed again, this time in fresh clothes. By the time he found her lingering over coffee in the cafeteria, breakfast was almost over. He managed to snag a tray and some food before the kitchen shut down and sat with a beaming Gina until Mike found them about a half hour later.

Grady was off with Bill somewhere, and Gina had promised to teach self-defense moves to some of the women in the gym. When Mike asked Jim to spend the day with the cousins going over plans for potential cooperation between the two bases, he agreed readily.

Jim had lunch with the cousins, reaching out to Gina telepathically from time to time. She was making friends in the gym and had been invited to share lunch with some of the women. Grady was still out, but Mike and Dave told Jim that the Alvian contingent had decided to spend the day together, comparing notes on doings in the Alvian cities and installations.

It was dinner before Jim saw Gina again. Grady was sitting with her at the cousins' table as on the first night, but this time Jim didn't feel that same jealousy he'd felt before. This time, he was able to take his seat with calm satisfaction, knowing the three of them had come to at least the beginnings of an understanding. Gina greeted him with a kiss, and he could feel how happy she was to have him—and Grady—by her side.

After dinner, they joined the group in the main hall, where a few couples were dancing. Grady went after drinks while Jim took Gina on a spin around the dance floor.

"I haven't danced like this in too long," Gina said wistfully as she rested her cheek against Jim's shoulder.

"Me neither. I think we'll have to implement something like this back home, if possible. It's good for everyone to socialize at the end of the day."

The music picked up and strains of Glenn Miller's "In The Mood" came over the speakers. Gina shot him a daring look, and he spun her into a modified Lindy step. In a matter of minutes, they were putting on a show. Both of them were athletic and great dancers. By the time the song ended, they had a small circle around them and several other couples.

The classic music ended to a raucous round of applause, and Jim reeled Gina in close to his side as they made their way off the dance floor. Grady waited for them, on the edge of the crowd, a strange expression on his face. Gina's laughter died as she went to him, hugging him close.

"*What's wrong with him?*" Jim asked her telepathically. They'd promised not to use telepathy around Grady, but this conversation was for his own good. Jim felt justified.

"*He feels left out. I guess Alvians don't dance.*"

"*So teach him.*" A gentle waltz had started playing over the speakers.

"*You don't mind?*" Gina's gaze beseeched him.

Jim walked up to them. "Why don't you give it a try, Grady? Gina can show you how to waltz."

"We don't have anything like this among my people," Grady hedged, looking uncertain. "I'm not sure—"

"You'll do fine. Anyone as athletic as you are can pick up a waltz in no time. Trust me." Gina tugged on his arm, leading him toward the dance floor. She sent Jim a parting look and a private message. "*You're a sweet, sweet man, Jim.*"

"*Don't let that get around. You'll ruin my image,*" he joked back as they took the floor.

Jim watched as Gina showed Grady the basic steps and after one false start, they were off, whirling around the floor with the other dancers. Gina was right. Grady was an athlete and well coordinated. It didn't take long for him to pick up the basic idea and start improvising as he watched the other couples on the floor with them.

By the time the dance ended, Gina was wreathed in smiles and Grady looked triumphant. Such a small thing to inspire such happiness. Jim marveled at it as they came back to him. He felt happy for them both. A strange feeling, to be sure, but one he knew he could get used to. It was actually kind of cool to watch Grady learn how to be human—how to feel and react. And it was also a big responsibility to try to help him grow into the emotions that were so new to him.

In a way, Jim felt sorry for the big guy. He seemed so confused much of the time. But Grady was also a warrior—someone Jim could respect. They could probably learn a lot from each other, and Grady would be an asset when making plans for how to best utilize the resources at their disposal should it come to war with the Alvians. He had a reputation as a superior strategist.

But thoughts of war were for another time. Right now, Jim wanted to enjoy the time he had left with Gina before he had to return home. Talks with the cousins all day had helped firm up their plans. They'd be returning to Colorado in a group. He'd take the pod from his facility back and a team from here would follow in one of their own pods. The makeup of the team wasn't decided yet, but it was a good plan and they'd leave in the next couple of days.

The idle time with Gina would be over soon. Jim hadn't yet asked whether she'd be returning with him to Colorado. He was almost afraid to broach the subject because that would bring reality all too close. Grady had to be considered. He undoubtedly had a ship secreted somewhere nearby and at some point he'd have to make a choice.

He would either return to the Alvians or go AWOL. If there was some third possibility, Jim didn't know what it was, but the cousins had counseled him to wait and see. The Oracle said Grady had a role to play, and Caleb O'Hara was seldom wrong. According to his vision, things would work out—somehow. Jim just didn't know how yet.

"Penny for your thoughts." Gina smiled at him as she touched his arm.

"Sorry. I was woolgathering." He straightened from his slouch against the table and pulled her in for a quick hug. "What do you say we blow this popcorn stand?"

"What did you have in mind?" She blinked up at him, and he knew they were on the same page.

"What do you say, Grady? You in the mood?"

"Mood for what?" Grady looked confused. "I don't understand any of what you just said. What's a penny, and why would she give you one for your thoughts?"

Gina laughed, turning to Grady and taking his arm. "That's just an old saying. A penny is a coin we used to use to pay for things."

"So you were willing to pay him for his thoughts? Shouldn't such things be free between mates?" Grady frowned at Jim, and he had a hard time not laughing in the alien's face.

"They should indeed," Gina agreed readily as she started walking, taking Grady with her. Jim followed along close behind.

"Where are we going?" Jim protested when they neared the main entrance to the underground complex. There was a series of tunnels before they'd reach the outside, but this short tunnel, sealed by two huge, metal blast doors, was the entrance to the facility itself.

"I heard about a special place, just outside, in one of the side tunnels. A hot spring." She sent him a daring look that immediately fired his libido. It didn't take much to get his motor running where Gina was concerned.

"You don't say?"

"It's secluded and private with an independent water source. The ladies I spoke to swore by it for bathing...and other things."

"Really?" Jim allowed her to coax him out into the small entry tunnel.

There were guards posted at both ends of the small tunnel—one inside the facility and one just outside, in the tunnels. The man inside gave Gina a wink as he heard where they were headed. The second guard cautioned them to be back before they sealed the facility down for the night at midnight. They had a couple of hours to enjoy themselves.

The grotto was lovely. Jim peeked into the chamber before entering, noting as Gina placed a discrete marker at the entrance.

"What's that for?"

"So we won't be disturbed. The ladies came up with this little system." She winked at him.

"Ingenious," he agreed, pulling her hips to his as he leaned in for a quick kiss.

He was aware of Grady behind them, but didn't pay the alien much mind until he brushed past. Jim raised his head and followed the alien warrior into the chamber, letting Gina precede him.

Jim crouched down at the lip of the pool, dipping his fingers into the water as he looked around. A cold waterfall doused the rocky depression, which was filled from below with piping hot water. The result was a mixture of perfect temperature, the mineral content diluted with fresh water filtered through the rocks from above. The mixture cut the earthy scent of the minerals.

Jim would bet the area around the vents was bubbly warm if one wanted to soak. He also imagined the brisk waterfall would be a refreshing way to clean up. The combination in one heavenly grotto was nature's perfection.

Grady had stripped and was in the water before Jim even straightened. Gina, laughing, wasn't far behind.

Jim took his time, watching Grady and Gina swim a little, enjoying the water. When they started enjoying each other, Jim stripped and entered the pool. He gave them a few minutes while he swam around a bit, exploring the boundaries and depths of the pool. The thermal vents were toasty warm and bubbly against his feet and legs on one end, the cold water of the waterfall refreshing on the other. If an architect had planned it, nothing could be more perfect in design and function.

But then again, the Great Architect had a hand in this place's building. Jim wasn't an overtly religious man, but he believed in the Creator. Especially when he saw someplace like this. Nature's beauty always had a way of convincing him that somebody up there had a plan for things, and just that small reminder was enough to reassure him.

Finding Gina again made him feel that way too. A relationship that would have been impossible in the old world was not only possible now, but promising. With Gina working with him, they had a chance to positively affect the world for all humans. And Grady might be an integral part of it all.

There was no way he could have imagined it just a few days ago, but now things looked good for the future for the first time in decades. Instead of merely existing and eking out a living hidden from the aliens, humans had a chance to do something proactive to change the world for the better.

Jim took another look at his friends at the other end of the pool. He couldn't be absolutely certain, but it sure looked like Grady was already buried balls deep in Gina's tight pussy. That didn't take long.

It was shallower on this end and warmer away from the waterfall. Natural ledges made this part of the pool almost like a hot tub. That was something he planned to exploit with Gina at length—once Grady was done.

He hoped Gina had eaten well today. She'd need her strength if she was going to keep up with both her men.

The thought gave him pause, but only for a moment. He kind of liked the way that sounded. Being Gina's *man* would have a lot of benefits and only a few drawbacks. The sense of belonging to another person was something he'd never really expected to feel again in his life. Not since the cataclysm had changed everything.

He'd bet Grady had never experienced such a thing—not even on a superficial level, as Jim had with a few of his girlfriends during his youth. Grady had never experienced love—or any emotion—until very recently. It made Jim feel sad for the guy. He didn't even have the memories of a family's love to fall back on in rough times. Only his emotionless Alvian brethren who seemed more like machines at times than people.

Jim swam around a bit, watching as Gina clung to the big alien. He was definitely fucking her if her soft moans were anything to go by. He liked the way her breasts bobbed on the surface of the water while Grady pounded into her below. Her head was thrown back as the muscles in Grady's neck strained, his big arms supporting her. His expression was fierce, and Jim wondered for a moment if he looked the same when he was close to ecstasy with this special woman.

One of Grady's arms slipped in the bubbly water, jiggling Gina, and Jim decided it was time to give them a hand. Or two.

He approached Gina from behind, sliding up behind her in the warm, effervescent water. Grady met his gaze over her shoulder.

"Give her to me. I'll hold her." Jim held out his hands, and Grady relinquished her upper body into Jim's care, transferring his hold to her hips. She was stretched out between them in the fizzing water, trusting them to see to her safety...and her pleasure.

Jim looped his arms under her shoulders from behind, supporting her against his chest. The position left his hands free to some extent. He could reach her nipples and enjoyed the little whimpering sounds that issued from her throat when he began teasing the turgid peaks.

She was so beautiful. She took his breath away. So responsive, she made his dick stand up and take notice. He wanted inside her, and he'd have her—again and again—as soon as Grady finished. Oddly, he didn't mind the wait. The idea tantalized him instead. It appealed to his competitive nature as well. He'd do all he could to make her peak higher, her ecstasy longer than the other man.

The way he figured it, they'd all benefit from the friendly competition. Gina most of all...if they didn't wear her out first.

Gina had never felt so decadent in her life, being attended by two gorgeous men she loved. Grady pummeled her with a hint of desperation she found endearing while Jim touched off sparks of desire wherever his fingers roamed on her eager body. She hadn't realized she was such a slut, but with these two men, she was learning her limits were much more extreme than she'd believed.

Jim rolled her nipples between his fingers with just the right pressure. He was never too rough, his touch always just right. Grady, on the other hand, forgot himself at times. The poor man couldn't help it. She knew he had moments where his emotions threatened to overwhelm him. Her empathic sense guided her at those times, helping her coax him into a gentler loving.

She liked the way he needed her, though it wasn't the entire basis for their relationship. More and more, she needed him too. And Jim. She felt incomplete without them. She needed them both in her life.

Gina rewrapped her legs, one by one, around Grady's waist, seeking a better grip as he began thrusting in short, intense digs. She was almost there, and she could tell he was damned close too. They'd come together, she knew, his climax triggering her own. Her empathy wouldn't allow anything else. Besides, Grady would hold out long enough to be certain she was satisfied before he ever sought his own pleasure. It was the way he was built.

She dug her heels into his muscular buttocks, urging him on. The motion below the water became more intense than ever, splashing the fizzy mineral water over her breasts in little wavelets that only added to her building passion. She was close. Just a little further...

She cried out as she came, Grady following close on her heels, groaning her name as he jetted his hot semen into her eager sheath.

Gina floated for a moment, enjoying the aftermath, the tingling contractions of her womb as Grady left her. She lost her sense of direction as she was turned and spun to face Jim. As his face swam out of the mists of pleasure still clinging to her body, she saw him smile. It was a devilish smile that promised something very naughty indeed.

"My turn."

Two simple words and her abdomen clenched in renewed heat. How could he do this to her with just a smile and a few words? She didn't know, but she was suddenly eager for more.

When Jim pushed her down onto his straining cock, she didn't protest. In fact, she helped, riding him eagerly in the warm water. But he apparently had something a little different in mind.

Maneuvering to the shallower, hotter end of the pool, he was able to stand, the water rising to his waist. He walked with her, still anchored on his cock, toward the ledge where there were some rocks that formed a natural seat of sorts in the much shallower water. Every step jolted through her, originating where they were joined and streaking fire straight to her womb. By the final few steps, she was crying out in need at every little jiggle of her body over his. It was a divine sort of torture and something she never would have imagined could be so stimulating.

He sat on the submerged stone formation, taking her with him, arranging her knees on either side of his slim hips. The water cushioned what would have otherwise been a somewhat uncomfortable perch on hard rock, but she was beyond thought at the moment.

All she wanted was his cock, his climax...his come. She wanted it like she wanted her next breath. It was essential to her continued existence.

"Ride me, baby. Yeah, just like that."

Jim coached her, his hands on her ass under the water as she started a fast motion, riding his cock like a champion bronco buster. She met his thrusts up with her own downward motions, loving the way he filled her, the water slippery and hot around them.

It wasn't long before her climax hit. For the second time in less than an hour, she flew to the stars with one of her men following right behind. She wasn't sure, but she thought she cried out as she came, her high-pitched voice blending with Jim's sexy groans as they reached an unprecedented climax together.

"Oh, baby," Jim breathed near her ear. "You rock my world, woman."

"Ditto." She could only get out the single word, but she felt his satisfaction, both with her agreement and her breathlessness.

They swam around the pool for long minutes, enjoying the waterfall and the hotter parts of the secluded springs. Grady and Jim pleasured her again, this time together, and she didn't think she'd ever come so hard or so long as when they both made love to her at the same time.

Grady claimed her mouth while Jim fucked her from behind. She trusted them to hold her up in the shallow end of the pool, Grady's hands anchoring her shoulders well above the water as Jim's thrusts slid her forward onto Grady's cock. She loved the heat of him, the molten rush as he came in her mouth. It was so...alien. Like him. But he was also her lover in the truest sense—the man she loved. One of the men she loved. For if forced to choose between them, she would never be able to decide which one she loved more.

They were both precious and special to her. Both her mates. Now and forever.

Before they needed to return to the facility for the night, they washed up under the waterfall. Gina finished first and sauntered over to reclaim her clothing, which was strewn near the grotto's entrance. She dressed in her shirt and pants, forgoing underwear, then went to find Jim and Grady's clothes.

She had her back to the entrance and was making a show of stretching to reach for Grady and Jim's clothing when Grady charged in her direction, fear and determination flashing across his face. Jim wasn't far behind.

She didn't think. She reacted, jumping out of the way as Grady rolled on the stone floor, coming up with the long, wicked blade he'd discarded when he undressed. Within the blink of an eye, he was hand to claw with a giant mountain cat that had stalked her without her knowledge.

Sweet Mother of God, she'd almost been shredded by the vicious claws digging into Grady's pale skin. But Grady had skills. Jim joined him a moment later, coming at the cat from behind while Grady took the full brunt of the beast's claws.

Before she could even figure a way to help them, they'd both struck deep into the beast's heart with their knives. Jim caught Grady as he staggered back and the cat slumped to the ground, in its death throes.

"Grady!"

She ran to him as Jim lowered Grady to the ground, then went to make certain the cat was no longer a threat. Grady was hurt badly. He had gouges down his chest and arms and was bleeding profusely.

"Gina?" Grady's voice was weak, but he struggled to see her. "Are you okay?"

She hiccuped, tears streaming down her face. "I'm fine. Grady, you saved me. I'm just fine. But Grady, you're hurt!"

He seemed to want to say more, but his eyes rolled back in his head as he passed out, most likely from blood loss.

Gina tore the nearby clothing into strips, tying makeshift tourniquets on both his arms and one leg. She used other bits of cloth to try to staunch the flow of blood from the deep gashes on his torso. Jim helped.

"I sent a telepathic message to Dave and Mike. They're on their way. David is a strong healer. He ought to be able to help Grady."

"God." She sat back, wiping at her tears so she could see better. "I didn't even think of that."

"It's okay, baby." He met her eyes over Grady's bleeding body. "He'll be all right. Help is on the way."

"He saved me, Jim. You both did."

The enormity of what had just happened descended on her like a load of bricks. If she'd had any doubts about their devotion before, they were eradicated.

Moments later help arrived. Dave took over and Mike ushered Gina away, bundling her into Jim's arms. They stood over Grady, watching his pale face as Dave set to work.

"This looks like the cat we've been seeing on the monitors lately, but we've never seen him in the tunnels," Mike said as he examined the cat's massive carcass.

Dave held his hands over the worst of Grady's wounds, and they stopped bleeding right before her eyes. Dave was a powerful healer, indeed. But Grady had lost so much blood. Gina still worried.

"A lot of zoo animals have crossbred with native species since the cataclysm. Looks like this could be some kind of tiger/mountain lion mix. Sure is a big son of a gun." Jim responded to Mike's observation and she knew the men were talking to help get her mind off Grady's condition, but nothing on Earth could do that at this moment.

It felt like hours later, but was probably only a few minutes before Dave stood. He swayed on his feet, but his cousin steadied him. More men had arrived with rifles and lights, searching the rest of the immediate area surrounding the grotto in case the dead cat had friends nearby. Other men held a stretcher onto which they loaded Grady's unconscious body.

As they carried him out, Gina and Jim followed right behind. Jim's arm around her shoulders felt like the only thing keeping her together. She snuggled into Jim's side, as close to the litter bearing Grady as possible.

When they got to the smooth floors of the facility, the stretcher was placed on a gurney so Grady could be wheeled to the small medical facility they'd found on the old military base. Jaci met them at the door, Bill a silent presence behind her. She took over, working closely with David while she checked Grady's vitals.

"He lost so much blood." Gina worried as Jim held her in one corner of the room.

"He'll be all right." Jaci took a moment to reassure her. "Alvians can survive blood loss that would kill a human. We have the ability to regenerate fluids—blood included—at a much faster rate than you do. However, he might require some serum in the short term, if either Bill or I are compatible with his blood type."

"Could you use human blood?" Jim asked. She felt his earnestness and his true desire to help Grady. In that moment she knew that no matter what problems they faced in the future, Jim had come to terms with their three-way relationship.

Jaci looked thoughtful. "It might be possible, but it has never been done to my knowledge. It would be safer if Bill or I could contribute." She kept moving as she replied, using pieces of equipment Gina didn't recognize. "This—," Jaci held up a small instrument that looked to be of alien origin, "—will type his blood." A quick run through the blood still coating areas of Grady's body and the small instrument chimed. "Ah, Zed Alpha. I cannot donate." Jaci's gaze rose to Bill's as he entered the room fully, already rolling up his sleeve.

"I will do it." Bill sat in the chair next to the head of the bed, talking to Jaci. "I am Zed Beta Gamma. It should be compatible enough until his bodily systems take over."

Jaci smiled. "You are right, of course. Good. This will do the trick." Quick as a flash, she set up a transfusion directly from Bill's veins to Grady's. It was only a few minutes before she removed the equipment linking the men. Gina didn't think it had been long enough, but the rosy color in Grady's cheeks gave her hope.

A few seconds later, his eyes opened and she breathed a huge sigh of relief.

"Is Gina all right?" were the first words from his lips.

"I'm fine," she cried, rushing to his side and grasping his hand. "You saved me, my love. You both did."

A beatific smile curled the corners of his mouth. "I like that. My love."

"Oh, Grady," she leaned in to place kisses on his cheeks. "I love you so much!"

"As I love you."

Chapter Eighteen

Grady was up and around much faster than Gina would have believed, had she not seen it for herself. Dave's healing power had closed the worst of his wounds, but Grady's Alvian physiology took over where that had left off. He was able to leave the medical facility under his own steam the next morning. Gina and Jim had spent the night near him, sharing a hospital bed next to his. Every hour, Gina would rise to check on Grady, glad to see him progressing each time.

In the morning, the trio walked together into the cafeteria for breakfast and Gina was touched by how many people came up to give Grady and Jim a pat on the back, a word of admiration or a quiet thank you for killing a creature that had been a threat to all of them. She knew Grady was uncomfortable with the praise. He was also surprised by it. When several of the women leaned up to give him pecks on the cheek and a quick hug, he was totally nonplussed.

Gina went to him, taking his arm and smiling up at him. He had so much to learn about having feelings, but she'd help him. She loved him. She could do no less.

"So where do you want to sit?" Gina asked once they'd gathered their trays.

"I would like to talk to Bill," Grady responded. "To thank him for his assistance last night. Alvians don't often require the sharing of blood. What he did was special."

"I didn't realize." Gina heard the reverence in his tone. Jim shrugged when she looked over at him and they followed behind Grady as he made his way to the table where Bill sat alone.

"May we sit?" Grady asked formally as they stood before the table.

"You need never ask, brother."

Gina felt the wave of feeling that rushed through Grady at Bill's words.

"Are you two related?" The nonsensical question slipped out before she thought better of it.

Jim pulled out her chair as they sat around the table. Bill held her attention as he explained.

"Sharing of blood among Alvians is rare. It forms a bond."

"Sorta like blood brothers?" Jim asked. Both aliens looked at him in surprise.

"How did you know?" Grady's gaze rested uneasily on Jim.

"It's an Old West thing from the days of cowboys and Indians. If you want to adopt someone into your family, you slash your palms and shake, mixing blood. It's a symbolic thing."

Both Alvians seemed to consider Jim's words.

"It is not like that among our people," Bill said after due thought. "The sharing of blood leaves lasting markers in the recipient. We are both of the Zed blood group. Before last night, Grady was of the Alpha variety, while I was Beta Gamma. I was born Gamma, but have shared blood once before with a Beta. That transfusion left me with a marker of Beta in my body. By giving my blood to Grady, he will in future be Zed Alpha Beta Gamma, once his body acclimates."

Gina was astonished by the idea. "I don't think it works that way for humans, but I'm not a doctor."

"In the distant past, our blood groups played a part in determining our tribal affiliations. All that changed of course, once the scientists started meddling with our DNA."

"So yours was a tribal society?" Jim asked as he ate his breakfast.

"In part," Bill clarified. "Social ranking was based on both tribe and profession. Often, certain skill sets would be found predominantly within a particular tribe. Soldiers, for example, were often Sinclairs or Gradys, to use us as examples. Not always, of course. Not like it is now. But a large percentage of our relatives would probably have naturally selected to be soldiers, peacekeepers, trackers, investigators and the like. Some would have followed their own paths, into different professions. Now, of course, there is no diversity."

"I think my great-great-grandmother—if I can call her that—was part of the Governing Council representing healers," Grady said thoughtfully.

"Who?" Bill asked, his brow raised.

"Councilor Senel Grady of the last Council before the great experiment."

The name apparently had some meaning among Alvians. At least Bill looked impressed.

"I once compared my DNA scans with hers and found a startling number of corresponding base pairs. Enough to conclude that her DNA contributed significantly to mine."

"This is astounding news," Bill dropped his fork. "I wonder if it's possible to trace my parentage in such a way?"

"No doubt Jaci could tell you. She was a genetic tech."

"I will ask her. Thank you for the idea."

He looked so hopeful, Gina found herself praying there was some way Bill could find similar information about himself. These Alvians—the ones with feelings—seemed to want so much to belong, to understand where they came from, to find their roots. It was touching really.

Mike came to the table, interrupting their conversation. He looked excited—almost eager about what he had to say. He didn't sit. Rather, he stood behind the men as they turned their heads up to regard him.

"We got a message from Mick O'Hara. Caleb says it's time. We've got to move."

Gina was glad she'd finished eating because chaos erupted shortly after Mick's statement. The men jumped to their feet and scattered. All except for Jim.

"What's going on?" she asked him.

"I'm going home." The expression on his face broke her heart. He looked so uncertain, so lost. "The question is, are you coming with me?"

Now she understood. Their idle was over. It was time to get back to work.

She put her arm around his waist. "I'm going with you."

She felt his relief, but it was short lived. "For how long?"

"I don't know." She looked up into his eyes, feeling the same uncertainty reflected back at her. "As long as I can."

Grady followed Mike and the others to the command center where plans were progressing. He had a decision to make, but really, his decision was already made. He could not leave his Resonance Mate. He would go where she did, and he could guess her choice would be to go with Jim.

So Grady set to work helping others with logistics and planning for the trip ahead.

"You're coming with us right?" Jim arrived while the others were discussing what to bring, with Gina at his side. Grady found he liked the easy way Jim asked the question, as though he already knew and accepted the answer. Frankly, Grady hadn't expected such easy welcome even though they'd done their best to get along for Gina's sake.

"I will come, if you will have me."

"You're welcome in Colorado, Grady." Jim offered his hand, and Grady knew enough about the human gesture to know what it meant. They shook hands while Gina watched, hugging them both before they joined the rest of the group planning.

It was decided they would take two pods. Jim, Grady and Gina would ride in the pod from Jim's facility and Dave and Bill would take one of the pods from here. They would leave that very day, just after lunch.

"Grady, I guess you've got a craft of some kind hidden away out in the woods, right?" Mike asked, drawing attention.

Grady nodded. "It is untraceable and well hidden. It should be safe where it is unless you prefer I move it."

"Do you think it would fit through our cargo entrance? We could keep it safe for you down here."

Grady thought about it and decided if he didn't trust these people by now, he never would. They'd held his life in their hands, and they'd proven to be friends.

"I would appreciate it. And if I don't return, perhaps the craft can be helpful to you." He had to be practical. He didn't know where his road might lead. For all he knew, he might never return to this place, never need the craft because he would never return to his former people.

Mike nodded and they made plans to move the craft as soon as the meeting broke up.

Jim and Bill conferred on the kinds of seeds Jim's people might be able to use and what they could trade. Soon Bill had a group set to help him load the pod with items from his hydroponics operation—seeds and certain crops they had in abundance.

When the meeting broke up, Gina went with Dave to see about what kind of medical supplies they could use or trade while Grady left with Mike to move the craft. Jim tagged along with Mike and Grady, and Mike told them how to get to the cargo entrance before splitting off a side tunnel to be ready to open the door for them.

Grady was surprised when Jim decided to follow him out into the sunshine past the tunnel entrance. They moved as stealthily as possible, and Grady was pleased to see that Jim had great skill in the woods. He was a worthy warrior with many abilities.

When they arrived at the craft, Jim almost stumbled over it at first, making Grady chuckle.

"Damn, that's well hidden," Jim commented as Grady began to uncover the small speeder.

"This is not my first attempt at stealth, you know."

Grady enjoyed the way they laughed and worked together. This feeling of camaraderie was something he'd missed—even though he'd never felt it as acutely as he did at that very moment.

They finished uncovering the vehicle and climbed aboard. Grady took a few minutes to monitor communications and check locations of other Alvian craft in the area. Luckily, there were none near enough to pose a danger.

"I've never been in one of these before." Jim looked curious about the instrumentation panel and monitoring stations in the small craft.

"This particular model was refurbished by the *Zxerah.* The Patriarch gave me use of it before I left their encampment. Like them, it is completely untraceable. I double-checked every system myself before ever approaching this area. I didn't want to bring attention to Jaci and her mates. As it turned out, my precautions were even more necessary than I had thought."

"Thank heaven for your paranoia." Jim laughed, and Grady joined in.

"And the *Zxerah*'s. With this craft, I can monitor all other Alvian craft and communications in a wide area without them ever knowing I am here. Unless they spot me visually, this craft is completely off their screens."

"A handy trick."

"It came in very useful on the trip here. Even as I left the top secret *Zxerah* refuge, I was followed by elements of the regular military. The Council sent their watchdogs to spy on me—probably to make sure Bill would die, even if I changed my mind and did not complete the assigned mission. I couldn't let that happen. It was foolish of them to think my own men could trail me and I would not see them. I trained them, after all. Not one of them is a better tracker than me. Some are close, and it was difficult at first to shake them, but I'm confident none were able to follow me much beyond the mountains to the south. I left a false trail going east, over the plains, which is probably where they are—still looking for me."

Grady fired up the vehicle, which made very little actual noise, and maneuvered out of the trees. He took a circuitous route to the cargo door, just in case.

"For the record, I'm glad you're coming with us to Colorado."

Grady was touched by the sincerity in the other man's tone. He was getting better and better at reading the nuances in human discourse.

"Thank you for agreeing to share Gina with me. I know it could not have been an easy decision for you."

"You're right. It wasn't. But I'd rather see her well protected, and well loved, than miserable. I realized she wasn't going to be happy unless she had both of us in her life. Likewise, as our recent encounter with that damned cat proved, two of us to protect her is much better than one. I don't think either one of us could have taken out that giant cat without help, but to be honest you were damn close. You're as strong as you are big and skilled too. That counts for a lot with me—especially since, like me, you'll do everything you can to keep our woman safe. Whether she likes it or not."

"She does have an independent streak," Grady agreed, trying not to let too much of his emotion show. Jim's words meant the world to him. The respect of this man was something he valued.

"The trick will be not to let her catch on that we're protecting her. Our girl Gina thinks she can take care of herself—and she can—but I, for one, plan to help her. I suspect you will too." Jim winked as he grinned, and Grady thought he understood perfectly.

"Oh, I will. Have no doubt."

Once he was satisfied nobody was following or could see them, Grady made for the big fissure between two cliffs Mike had described. There was the faint outline of an old dirt road that had once snaked around one cliff face, only to disappear into the fissure. If you weren't looking for it, you wouldn't see it, which was ingenious. No doubt, the natural look of the road, and its state of disrepair, kept its secret safe.

Grady maneuvered the craft into the wide, natural opening that narrowed as it twisted into the very rock, forming a natural tunnel. A fissure, really, that narrowed as it rose, permitting only the barest amount of light to penetrate to the path below. Rounding several curves, Grady saw what looked like a dead end.

Even as he watched, the rock parted and a giant door opened. The bay was lit dimly from within—a long, huge entryway that ended in a massive steel door on the other end. This then was the airlock, so to speak. The preliminary entryway that safeguarded the facility. He pulled the craft to a stop within the long, wide tunnel and waited for the massive rock-fronted doors to close.

Once they did, lights came up to full strength. Grady and Jim waved from within the cockpit as they saw a camera drone zip over to check them out. It examined the vehicle from all angles before zipping back to its storage area along one of the walls somewhere. Only then did the inner doors begin to cycle open.

Grady brought the craft to a rest next to a large group of aircraft. Some were fighter jets, some propeller craft. All were old and looked like they hadn't been used in decades, which was probably an accurate guess. Farther in, he could just make out some long, cylindrical objects he guessed were missiles of some sort. The humans had a lot of firepower in this mountain. More than he'd guessed was left.

"Holy shit," Jim breathed as he saw the armament and aircraft.

"I guess there is no doubt this was once a military installation."

Grady popped the hatch, and the men piled out. Grady had a pack with him—personal supplies he'd left behind on his previous departure from the craft. He'd take it with him this time, for he knew he might never see this craft again. With an odd pang, he realized he didn't really care. His future was with Gina now—however it worked out. He had to have faith in the spirits of his ancestors that somehow it would.

They met Mike on the floor of the massive hangar.

"Some stash you've got here," Jim commented as he looked around at the assembled craft.

"Yeah, we found this a couple of weeks ago, but we don't have anyone who can fly them."

Jim's gaze zeroed in on Mike, flashing excitement in his eyes. "I do."

"Really?"

"We kept a lot of our staff since the base was operating at the time of the cataclysm. We sent out fighters, but we didn't have this many. We lost a lot until we finally realized the better part of valor in this case was hunkering down and hiding. We have pilots and their families. A lot of the guys have taught their kids what they knew. The kids have never been up for real, but we've got a top-rated flight simulator and it's one of the things the younger generation enjoys doing for fun. As a result, we have more pilots than planes."

"That's mighty interesting." Mike's casual words belied his eager expression.

They took their leave of Jaci, Mike and the rest later that day. At first, they suggested Jim's pod go first, but after some good-natured ribbing about not being able to keep their eyes on the road being newlyweds and all, Dave, Bill and Sam went first. Sam was a new addition to the group, but a welcome one. Grady valued the man's insight and was pleased to learn he was a close friend of Bill's.

Bill needed friends—human friends—if he was going to continue to thrive on his own, without a mate. Grady didn't know how he did it, but he admired the man's strength of character and will. Grady suspected he wouldn't be half as stoic if he'd had to face life without a Resonance Mate by his side.

But perhaps Bill lived on hope. Grady wasn't sure. Bill was naturally secretive, having been the top *Zxerah* assassin most of his life. He'd also had emotions longer than any other Alvian. He was better at dealing with them. They were more integrated into his personality.

The trip back was uneventful. Every time they stopped at a station, both groups would get out of their pods and walk around a bit, exploring. Dave and Sam even scouted up some of the ventilation shafts to see what they could learn of the topside terrain.

Not needed to watch the track ahead, Jim, Grady and Gina spent most of the time making love. He and Jim had come to an understanding and even began to develop a sort of unspoken communication like he'd once had with the soldiers who served with him. They were able to anticipate what the other wanted when it came to pleasuring Gina.

She shocked them a few times as well. Such as when she climbed over Grady's lap with no preliminaries and started fucking him where he sat. In fact, that entire encounter had been surprising in the extreme. Especially when Jim moved behind her and began to penetrate her ass.

Grady had never shared a woman in such a way before. He could feel the other man's movements through the thin membranes of Gina's luscious body. It was an odd sensation. One that drove his own passion higher.

"You weren't kidding about how hot he gets," Jim whispered in Gina's ear, but it was loud enough that Grady heard him. He met Jim's gaze over her shoulder, not quite sure what the amusement in his expression meant. But he was too far gone to wonder more. Gina moved on them both, causing a violent rush of passion that resulted in a hard, fast climax that sent him reeling.

Gina sat in his lap, draped over him like a living blanket in the aftermath. Jim moved off to claim a chair for himself, breathing hard after his own climax.

"I never did that before," she whispered.

"Me neither." Grady stroked her back with long, sweeping touches.

"I have," Jim announced from beside them. Grady looked over to see a grin lighting his satisfied face. "And I'll gladly do it again and again, judging by your response, Gina. I'd say you liked it."

"Liked it?" She rolled her head against Grady's chest so she could look at Jim. "I loved it! As much as I love both of you."

Epilogue

When they arrived in Colorado a crowd gathered to meet the newcomers. Word spread like wildfire through the facility—especially about the aliens in their midst. Some were angry, some curious, others frightened, but everything changed when Bill's tawny wings made an appearance.

Of all those gathered, it was a child who saw them first. A youngster who broke the ice.

"Mama, is he an angel?" a child's loud whisper sounded, silencing everyone, and Gina saw a little girl pointing at Bill and tugging on her mother's hand.

"I'm no angel." Bill knelt on the ground before the child, his wings spread out and exposed for all to see.

A man stepped forward from the group. "Are you Alvian?" A collective murmur went up from the assembled people.

"No longer. If ever I was. I am an Alvian-Avarel hybrid, bred as an experiment, then experimented on even further. Unlike most other Alvians, I have feelings and for that I'm being hunted."

"What's an Avarel?" One of the crowd wanted to know.

"They were a race of advanced explorers that visited our worlds many generations ago. I can only surmise our leaders preserved some of their DNA without their knowledge, and I'm the result. The Avarel, it is said, had wings much larger than mine in a myriad of colorations. They were depicted in ancient artwork as having skin patterns that matched the color of their wings in a rainbow of hues. Few visited our worlds, but they were welcomed. It was from observing them that our leaders first realized our ways were too aggressive. We were killing ourselves in large numbers and the geneticists stepped in to solve the problem. They began changing us on a genetic level."

Tory came forward to stand in front of him. "He's the one I saw would come. The angel. He's not Alvian. Not anymore."

"I've seen him before. He's the one they call Wild Bill. He lives high up in the mountains, but nobody knows exactly where," one of the more recent additions to their community said.

"*People of many talents will gather around a blond giant named for Hickok, who is an angel in disguise. A former enemy, he'll become the father of the resistance. Tell those who manage to escape to seek him out in the high places.*" Pierre recited the strange words. "That's from the Oracle's book of prophecies."

"Well I'll be." Larry moved a little closer. "Wild Bill Hickok... An angel in disguise. I think we have ourselves a winner."

"Sure looks that way," Pierre agreed. "Never thought I'd meet an angel."

"I'm no angel," Bill was careful to point out again. "I'm an Alvian-Avarel hybrid, with all the faults of both races."

"You're also the man of whom the Oracle wrote," Pierre said quietly, with finality.

Ronin Prime oversaw the prisoner transfer with something like satisfaction, though of course he couldn't actually feel it. He'd change that—as soon as he could—if he had his way. The wheels had been set in motion. He just had to be patient to see his long-term plans come to fruition.

The prisoner was an older human male with an almost regal bearing despite his years of confinement. Ronin Prime watched the squadron of soldiers leave him with his *Zxerah* clansmen, waiting to be sure the other Alvians were gone before he approached.

When he drew near, his *Zxerah* brethren parted ranks, leaving him face to face with the human man. The man stood proud, sizing Ronin up with cool blue eyes as any good competitor would. Ronin respected that.

"Remove his restraints," he ordered his brethren quietly, unsurprised when the human's eyes revealed nothing of his thoughts. This man—a former general—was a cool customer indeed.

The shackles were removed one by one, leaving the human standing tall and proud before Ronin, flanked by four soldiers of the

Zxerah brethren. Ronin had taken the precaution of having this transfer take place on a military installation away from the *Zxerah* stronghold, but he'd handpicked the men who would initially deal with this prisoner who could prove to be very important.

"You are General Yeager." Ronin didn't ask. He knew full well to whom he was speaking, but he wanted the general to understand that Ronin not only knew but also respected his rank and stature.

The man nodded once.

"I have heard good things about you from your people in Colorado. Before you ask—" Ronin held up one hand to forestall any outbursts, but this general was an even cooler customer than he'd credited. "All is well in Colorado. Your people thrive in their home and have not been disturbed. They have, however, been contacted by one of my operatives, and we are in communication on a somewhat regular basis now. It is because of this, I've had you transferred to my care. The men you left behind in Colorado have never forgotten you. I respect that and because of it, I believe we can be of help to each other and to our respective races."

The general eyed him suspiciously. "I'm willing to listen."

"Excellent." Ronin stepped toward the waiting craft. "Come with us then, and we will talk on the way. I have much to tell you, and we have much to discuss."

A week later, the door to an apartment in the Northern City slid open and a young man stood on the threshold. A tentative smile touched his lips.

"I knew you would come." The young man stepped aside, allowing Ronin to enter. He did so with uncharacteristic hesitance, turning to face the young man in the entryway as the door slid closed.

"I am Ronin."

"I know."

"And you must be Harry."

At that, the young man's smile returned. "Your kind generally calls me Hara, but I prefer Harry."

Ronin took his measure. "I am not precisely like other Alvians, though I suppose I still share more in common with them than with others."

"You question things, which is good, and you see possibilities for the future. That's more than most, Patriarch."

One brow rose in question at Harry's casual use of Ronin's title. "Do you know of what you speak or it is merely premonition that prompts you to use such a word?"

"There is nothing *mere* about any of my premonitions." Harry's tone turned challenging. "But to answer your question, it is a mixture of both research and foresight. I foresaw your visit here a long time ago. After that initial vision, I conducted research in Alvian databases and histories so I would know with whom I'd be dealing in the future. I learned much about your Brotherhood, but little about you as a person, Ronin Prime."

"Then we are equally in search of knowledge." Ronin moved further into the apartment and took a seat on the couch. "I know of your ancestry but have found precious little information about you, yourself. I have come here to begin the journey of knowledge, to see if we can work together to create a better future for our people."

"Which people?" Harry challenged as he sat in a chair, opposite. With a casual thought, he moved an illicit device from the other side of the room onto the low table between the couch and his chair. The show of telekinesis was no doubt deliberate—a flexing of mental muscles designed to showcase one of his many talents that made him so different from his Alvian brethren. Another thought flipped the device on. "We are now shielded against monitoring of any kind."

"Forgive me." Ronin reached into his robe and pulled out a similar device, placing it on the table and switching it on with his fingers before sitting back. "I did not get to be Patriarch of the *Zxerah* Brotherhood by trusting others not of my clan. I mean no disrespect or insult. It is my nature to be cautious."

"I'm not offended. Caution is a good thing. I knew you would come for a long time, but I never knew when or why. So please tell me, what brings you here now?"

Ronin bowed his head, gathering his thoughts before speaking. He sorted through the many things he could say, finally deciding on the simplest, yet most troubling.

"It is time."

About the Author

A life-long martial arts enthusiast, Bianca enjoys a number of hobbies and interests that keep her busy and entertained such as playing the guitar, shopping, painting, shopping, skiing, shopping, road trips, and did we say...um...shopping? A bargain hunter through and through, Bianca loves the thrill of the hunt for that excellent price on quality items, though she's hardly a fashionista. She likes nothing better than curling up by the fire with a good book, or better yet, by the computer, writing a good book.

To learn more about Bianca D'Arc, please visit www.biancadarc.com. Send an email to Bianca at BiancaDArc@gmail.com.